THE SPIRIT OF T

Rossalyn Mat

To Julie.
Hope you enjoy the Book
Love Roz xxx
xx
x

This novel is entirely a work of fiction. The names, characters and incidents portrayed in it are the work of the author's imagination. Any resemblance to actual persons, living or dead, events or localities is entirely coincidental.

CreateSpace

A Paperback Original 2013

Copyright © Rossalyn Matthews 2013

Rossalyn Matthews asserts the moral right to be identified as the author of this work.

ISBN-13:978-1477462690

ISBN-101477462694

All rights reserved. No part of this publication may be reproduced, stored in retrieval system, or transmitted, in any form or by any means, electronic, mechanical, photocopying, recording or otherwise, without the prior permission of the publishers.

Dedicated to my Guardian Angels, living and beyond.

PROLOGUE

I lit a candle and closed my eyes, breathing slowly and deeply I allowed my mind and body to relax.

Feeling my inner self shake free from my physical shell I flew freely on an astral journey.

I travelled through icy chasms of rainbow lights, I was seeking a voice that has often called my name.

A warm feeling of love filled my very soul and I bathed in the overwhelming blanket of contentment and peace.

All my stresses and tensions were left behind on the earthly plane.

The ultimate love we all seek was here and I basked in the radiance of the light that appeared ahead of me.

As I neared the misty glow it grew bigger and brighter.

A shadow stood in the centre of the light she called my name.

'Who are you?' I asked. 'What do you want with me?'

The reply came in the voice of an Angel.

'At last you have come. I have been patiently waiting for you. My name is Sarah, Sarah Miller. I have a task for you.'

Hence, I did not write the 'Spirit of the Willow'.

I have just transcribed all the details that Sarah has related to me.

The book is an alchemy of enchantment, romance

and folklore with a subtle hint of white and slightly grey Angels.

Sarah told me that towards the end of her existence on this earth she had completed a journal of her memoirs based on her life of sunshine and shadows, it was to explain the reasons why she decided to become an eccentric recluse living in a dilapidated cottage deep inside remote woodland with only the company of the wildlife.

Her life on this earth had begun as the only daughter of a frail mother and a deeply religious father. She was gifted or cursed with a psychic insight to heal the sick and sadly to see the spirits of the dear and near departed, her constant company throughout her lifetime was her so called childhood imaginary friend, her guardian Angel Tobias.

At the young age of nine her father couldn't suffer his daughter's embarrassing strange behaviour any longer and she was banished to a family in a remote part of Cornwall. Never truly understanding what she had really done wrong she was never to see her parents on this earth again.

Her life becomes much harsher as she grows up within a hard working farming family that do not really notice her odd ways.

After a devastating tryst with an evil presence she marries a man she doesn't truly love only to have a secret assignation with what was to become her true soul mate. This sets a seed that brings about tremendous changes to her odd life.

When events take a cruel twist and she suffers the most horrendous loss she steps out from reality and chooses to become a recluse.

Sarah and I are not strangers she is the haunting voice that has frequently been in contact with me since I was a small child. We share the same

Guardian Angel, crazy as it seems it is the truth, as I see it.

Just after Sarah's death her journal was lost in time and never exposed for the world to read. This has haunted her restless spirit.

But now it is re-written, you could call it a second edition.

Sarah's soul can now move on and rest in everlasting peace.

Please enjoy Sarah's words as much as I have by being in contact with this remarkable lady.

Cry with the small lonely child
Laugh with the old lady
And most of all
Believe and Trust
In Guardian Angels.
You are never really on your own, just ask for their help.

CHAPTER ONE

Turn the rusty key and unlock the treasure chest
That box of memories safely stored within our mind.

Sarah sat with her gnarled hands firmly on the arms of the rocking chair, gently moving to and fro. The rhythmic creaking of the old wooden rockers lulled her into the minds space between awake and asleep, the area where daydreams are made and lifemares revisited. She needed to remember way back into her far distant past, of this life, to confront the faded fleeting memories that had been locked deep inside her mind, fear keeping them well concealed.

Recently, she had experienced a desperate passion to delve within her inner self and convey light to her dark cache of disturbing recollections. The reason for her urgency to remember, was that her ancient brain had started to frolic, playing a game of hide and seek, the revisiting's were becoming increasingly difficult, distant and cloudy. Her poor old body, the vehicle for her soul, had long ago started the ageing decaying process.

She was anxious that before she could finish writing her life's journal, age would envelope her and she would just become a transporter of confusion and falsified imagination. The book was to be left as an inheritance of her life a legacy to those who never understood why she became a recluse and how she lived like a hermit for most of her long life.

Sarah's love and understanding of the earth and all natures creations, now gave her insight that there was a time for living, growing, reaping and dying, a season for everything and everyone. Her journey through this earthly plane was near its destination. Sarah's soul was tired but restless, she had a yearning to travel on to the realms of the spiritual word. This physical world had just taken about all that she had to give.

Her inner knowledge that peace and eternal tranquillity awaited her removed any fears she could possibly have of dying and yet as her ghostly friend Tobias would say.

'If you think your work on this earth is done and your still alive, then it isn't.'

The rocking chair ceased to move and Sarah started to return to this earth time. After each psychic journey, she experienced an overwhelming feeling of achievement, the reason being there on her lap would be the stubby pencil and pages of written hidden memories.

As she rubbed her tired eyes a rainbow of coloured lights danced around the room. Through the multi-coloured haze a spectre materialised. His long flowing hair and white robes moved slowly in the cool breeze, created by his sudden presence.

'Don't hover Tobias, you know it always makes me nervous, if you're staying, put your feet firmly on the ground where I can see you.'

Moving without a sound, Tobias silently glided to a standstill in front of Sarah.

'Have you still not finished your writing, Sarah?' he asked. 'Already I have let you stay longer on this earth than you are really entitled to.'

'You will have to be just a little more patient with me my dear friend, I only require a few more months and then I'm all yours.'

'You're on borrowed time, Sarah, death waits for no-one, not even you.'

'Have you come with any special reason, Tobias, or just to annoy me, if so, do go and perform a few miracles or disasters or whatever you spectres do in your spare time, when you're not harassing old ladies.'

Sarah was completely oblivious of all the scheming that Tobias had performed to enable her to have a little more living on this earth, allowing her the precious time needed to complete her writing.

Even though she had met him many times over the last eighty years she was totally unaware of the stranger shrouded in black lingering in the shadows, eagerly anticipating the triumphant moment when he could reach out and claim her. Nor did she perceive that when an icy shiver trailed down her spine, that it was the icy fingers of the spirit of death taunting and sampling her soul.

But Tobias could see him and only kept him at bay by using a tremendous amount of his own powerful compassionate energy. Being Sarah's guardian Angel it was his job to protect her, he had surrounded Sarah in a pink protective light, but this would only be temporary and as the light lost its potency and became weak, so would Sarah. Tobias realising that Sarah wasn't interested in his presence today gathered his robes around him and vanished, the rainbow of colours that filled the room swirled into a spiral and disappeared as promptly as they had appeared, leaving Sarah in peace.

Outside the golden warm summer sun was starting its slow descent behind the tall trees in the woodland, incapable of filtering its weak rays through the density of the grand oaks that stood like sentries guarding the countryside and casting gigantic shadows on everything beneath them. A slight breeze aroused the trees new green leaves and sent them shimmering in the evening's half-light. If you listened carefully they created the peaceful sound of whispering waves lapping slowly over fine pebbles.

The swallows returning from their long winter's rest, dipped and dived high in the sky catching unsuspecting insects that had innocently travelled upon the thermals of warm air.

Nestled beneath the trees and down amongst the undergrowth sat Jackdaw Cottage, to an unobserved eye the cottage could be mistaken for being uninhabited and derelict, but to all nature's creatures and a few brave neighbours they knew that it was far from empty.

Village people whispered about the lady who lived there. She appeared to some that had caught a glimpse of her to be a very old women who dressed in eccentric clothes and stomped about the woods talking to herself and the wildlife that followed her. No one ever stopped long outside Jackdaw Cottage, but passed by as quickly as possible, some even fearing that if they caught just the slightest glance of the crone behind the windows, that would be enough to curse them with ill luck or some dreadful misfortune.

Occasionally as a dare a young village lad would creep up the weed strewn path and hammer on the front door. Sarah would shout loudly at the boys but she would never have hurt them.

The cottage itself was made up of mainly one floor, with just a small dormer window peeping out through the untidy thatch. Streaks of black mould and green algae decorated the once pure white lime washed walls. Over the years the garden had been neglected and returned itself to a natural state, becoming a haven for wildflowers and small creatures. Old rose bushes had long since reinstated themselves into briars, sending their unruly clinging tentacles rambling over anything they could grasp, masquerading their cruel thorns with beautiful pale pink flowers. A rusty old water pump stood at the back of the cottage surrounded by uneven flagstones. Where the water had continually splashed an amazing bog garden had established, an array of bright green ferns and mosses hugged and moulded the partly hidden stones turning them into weird green sculptures.

The evening sun now low on the horizon pushed its weak rays through the cottages windows, intruding into the main living room illuminating pictures on the wall, which were haphazardly clinging by rough twine to ugly nails. The faces in the photographs even with the fading light of the sun remained motionless, captured for a split second a lifetime ago, the eyes blank and unmoving stared out into the room.

A couple dressed in their matrimonial outfits posed for the camera, the bride with a shy smile held a bouquet of faded roses, had they faded with time or had they died like the brides happiness had a short while after the picture was taken. Beside the ceremonial memento hung a tarnished gilt frame containing two oval portraits of identical faint sepia images of twin infants, their blonde curls framing their happy cherub faces. If you looked very

carefully you would be able to make out a faint scrawl,
    'Suffer little children who come unto me.'
Sarah often found herself standing in front of the twins christening photograph remembering and reliving that day as if it were yesterday. She would spend a little time paying silent homage to this captured imagery. Dear, dear Luke and Rosie, she still had their christening robes packed away in her rusty trunk safely stored at the back of the log cupboard. Sarah and the chest had been constant companions, inseparable throughout her life and now they had both found their final resting place.

The sun slipped silently below the far horizon and the wildlife in the woodland started to stretch and awake, ready to hunt for food in the safety of the night. Something large and foreboding crept through the forest. Twigs and bracken snapped beneath its weight. An owl disturbed by the unfamiliar intruder, screeched a warning message to its fellow creatures of the night. The nostrils of a small roe deer flared and her black eyes enlarged as she tried to recognise the new scent in the woodland. A sickly cracking sound echoed around the trees followed by an unnatural silence, every eye and ear of the inhabitants of the woodland strained with silent fear.

The limp lifeless body of Sarah's beloved black cat Willow was carelessly tossed into the cruel brambles that protected the cottage. His thin neck had been snapped as if it were a dry twig. A trickle of blood ran from the corner of his mouth. The delicate petals of the bramble flower gently fell onto his black velvety coat. The breath of his beautiful life senselessly extinguished.

Willows owner Sarah instantly sensed his death

and she knew exactly who would have committed such dreadful cruelty towards one of the earth's beautiful creations and purposely towards something that she loved.

Blue Lightening flashed and the thunder crashed as the hooded shadow crept stealthily away from the cottage. The roaring thunder masked the hysterical unearthly laughter that spilled from the Spirit of Deaths cruel mouth. All that remained in the forest of his presence was a pungent odour that swirled around in a grey mist, penetrating and piercing the very soul of every living creature that breathed in the putrid air that was ridden with decaying flesh. The evil essence of the spirit of death swirled and seeped beneath the once strong oak door of the cottage.

Something in the corner of the cottage stirred, it was the latest casualty of man's cruelty that Sarah had rescued and brought indoors for healing. The amber coat of the vixen glowed in the light radiated from the candles.

'Well my lovely, you have decided to live then,' said Sarah quietly.

Sarah had been kept awake two nights ago by the agonising cries of the vixen who was trapped by her front leg in a wire snare, which as she struggled in pain and fear, became tighter and tighter, eating into her soft flesh. Sarah had reached the distressed animal as quickly as her poor old body could jump into action and after walking a fair way through the woods she had discovered the poor creature lying exhausted, its terrified eyes glazed over with fear. Quickly her gentle healing hands released the thin wire from the fox's bloody broken leg, noticing the low sagging belly of the injured fox Sarah gathered that there was sure to be cubs somewhere in the area, most probably very hungry and distraught without their mother, they certainly would not survive very long on their own at night in the woods. Listening carefully to the chattering of the night life Sarah could just barely hear muted whimpering sounds, drawn to a group of new uncurled ferns she searched for signs of a disturbance or even a lair. Eventually she came across the youngsters hardly able to walk, weak with hunger and stumbling aimlessly searching for their mother who by now had lost a lot of her life's blood and had ebbed into a state of unconsciousness. Gathering up the cubs and thrusting them into the deep pockets of her cloak she made her way back to the cottage. Carrying the vixen close to her body she hoped that her warmth would keep the animal from entering into the dangerous state of shock that killed so many injured creatures. Entering the cottage Sarah tossed the squeaking and squirming youngsters into a kindling box by the fire. Hurriedly the vixen was laid on the bare pine table, which oddly enough was quite clean, it had to be scrubbed daily, as often the outside wildlife came inside and were never very particular about their table manners. Busy fingers felt the depth of the snare cut, warm water from the ever boiling kettle was poured over a crystal of rock salt, chipped from the slab on the hearth, not enough to sting the wound but enough to cleanse the cut. A jar of soothing balm made by Sarah for just this purpose was fetched from the mantlepiece, disturbing a family of wasps that lived in a crevice behind the fire.

'Be quiet,' hissed Sarah to the wasps, 'I've no time for your buzzing tonight, there's work to be done.'

In minutes the leg was splinted with straight sticks

and bound with boiled linen strips. Satisfied with her work of this night, she laid the fox to rest on a rough blanket by the fire.

Kneeling down beside her Sarah relaxed and took deep breaths to calm her busy mind. Sarah visualised a bright white healing light shining down upon the top of her head. Only when the powerful light penetrated her crown and filled her with its vigorous energy did she feel ready to let it flow out through her hands and channel the precious warmth into the still body of her casualty. And only when she felt the slight pulse beneath her fingertips return to normal, did she remove her hands and let the fox sleep peacefully.

The next problem for Sarah were the cubs in the box, they were getting restless and by now extremely hungry, she didn't feel their mother was quite strong enough to feed the youngsters, she needed to conserve what little energy she had left to heal herself. In the kitchen was a very large pine dresser with drawers and cupboards at the bottom, one of the doors was open and inside Daisy the pure white cat was feeding her two kittens, she was a kind mother and had only one ambition in her life which was to nurse kittens, not only hers, but anyone's. She had been known on many occasions to the annoyance of the other cottage felines to craftily creep up on what she would regard as abandon babies, whose mothers were out hunting and carefully remove them to her nursery in the cupboard of the dresser. And then when she was caught committing the crime she would fight with teeth and claws to keep the kidnapped kittens. So when Daisy received three amber coated cubs to join her own two youngsters, she was in cat's element. Even though they seemed a little large and unruly, quite quickly she calmed them down with the help of her long nails and a lot of growling conversation.

Sarah, quite exhausted from the adventures of the night flopped down wearily onto the old but comfortable horsehair settee, far too tired to climb the stairs to the attic bedroom. That night she dozed fitfully waking often to check on the breathing of the vixen and the whereabouts of Daisies adopted children.

Now here it was two days later, the vixen was conscious and studying her surroundings. Very shakily the fox managed to stand on her three good legs. Sarah could sense that the creature had remembered that she had cubs and was becoming very concerned to their whereabouts. Collecting the three healthy youngsters from the dresser cupboard, Sarah placed them on the blanket beside their mother. Daisy did not protest in the slightest, when the cubs were extracted, from her once peaceful nursery. She was glad to see the back of them, in her opinion they were rude, bad mannered, rough coated, greedy common hooligans. Grooming them had been impossible, feeding them had been a full time job and when they weren't eating they were playing very rough games and encouraging her children to join in. Law and order in that dresser cupboard had definitely not existed over the last few days.

The excited cubs instantly nuzzled up to their mother, she lay down to feed them contented that her family was united with her again.

So many animals had passed through the cottage over the years, most of them would return to the wild once they were fit and healthy but a few refused to go and became residents.

Many years ago the cottage had been the gamekeepers, it was well hidden by the woodland that grew densely on the edge of the estate of High Markham, the austere grey mansion was still standing high up on the hillside overlooking the village. The House was the family home of the Trevallian family and even to this day the estate's manager still made provisions for Sarah to live in the cottage until her death broke the contract. Sarah had not thought about the Trevallian family for years, she had shut them out a lifetime ago, just as she had the outside world. But now she wanted people to know everything that had happened to her and how cruelly she had been treated.

Sitting back in her rocking chair, Sarah felt a cold wet muzzle nuzzle her hand. A scruffy cross collie with one blue eye and the other one brown looked up into her own faded blue eyes.

'Hello Moses, Did you think I had forgotten about you, you're not jealous of that lady fox are you?'

Moses sat leaning his weight against Sarah's legs, she fondly stroked his grey muzzle and soft ears, his eyelids became too heavy to keep open and he flopped down across Sarah's feet so that if she moved he would soon know about it.

Sarah reached from her chair to the bookcase beside her and picking up her stubby pencil and licking the lead she felt the time was right to revisit and record a few more pages of her past.

She took long deep breaths to relax her body and rid her-self of all the busy thoughts and worries that crowded into her mind throughout the day. As she started to relax into her inner self she focused her eyes on the beautiful crystal ball that sat on the small window sill beside her. An image started to appear in the room and she was pleased that Tobias was going to join her on her visit into the past.

Tobias stood in front of Sarah. His face was rugged and tanned and held an overwhelming expression of kindness. He carried all the emotions that one could ever wish a friend to have. He was wisdom, knowledge, truth and strength. He radiated a light of love and compassion that swept its arms around you enveloping you in its warmth, giving you a feeling of love and perfect security. He was ageless and had always been with Sarah as her guardian Angel and best friend.

'Let us journey back Sarah. I am here to share your pain. Come, let us remember together.'

CHAPTER TWO

Hen wlad fy Nhadau. (The land of my Fathers).

The small child swirled and cavorted around the nursery swinging her arms and legs in gay abandon. Every so often she would glance over her shoulder to look at the book on ballet that was laid open on the bed, she would try to copy the dancer's positions. This well-worn book was the most precious of all her possessions in the whole wide world, the only book that she ever wanted to read over and over again. She would idle away many hours studying the graceful figures in their pretty flowing costumes and practise the movements. But it didn't matter how hard she tried she could not stand on her toes or be as graceful as the dancers in the pictures.

With a sudden movement, which resembled a clumsy arabesque Sarah's foot lifted too high, too quickly. Before she could control the movement she had unfortunately dislodged the nursery clock that had moments before been perched happily on the mantle shelf. Before her clumsy hands could catch the timepiece it smashed onto the marble hearth, shattering it's glass face and sending a squall of brass mechanisms spiralling over the carpet.

Slowly a burning sensation started in the pit of her stomach and travelled slowly up over her chest until it reached her cheeks that now felt like they were burning. She took a deep breath and braced herself for the onslaught that she knew would burst into her room at any moment. And sure enough it was just as though Nursey Banks had been lurking on the landing with her eye to the keyhole and her ear to the door, waiting for a disaster to happen and a reason to punish Sarah.

'That's it my lovely little bitch,' said the round, as she was tall nurse, grabbing the precious ballet book from the bed.

'You can't say I didn't give you enough warnings and chances. What do you think your father's going to say when he knows you've been dancing and prancing again and this time you've broken the precious clock.'

'Please, you don't have to tell him, you could say it was an accident,' replied the very red and bewildered child.

'I'm not lying for you young lady, it's about time you started to behave, you know your father always blames and holds me responsible when you get into trouble and I've just about had enough of you and your strange ways you're bloody mad. I've already told your Father you are no different than that grandmother of yours and look where she is now. And mark my words you'll be joining her, very, very soon.'

Sarah stood dumfounded and completely surprised, that yet again she was in such a predicament. She found it hard to comprehend to how without really being aware she managed to cause so much trouble. Now she had lost another precious item that had given her so much pleasure and filled the long hours that she spent in the attic nursery. And she would most probably have to go to the place that they sent Grandma to. Well she would not mind that because she loved her grandmother and knew that she would be happier living with her.

With her chin resting in her hands she stared out of the small window, her eyes scanned the garden and grounds of the house searching for some kind of movement to take her mind off what her father's reaction would be to her clumsiness and disobedience. He had lectured her many times about dancing and singing. He had told her a million times he considered it to be vulgar behaviour, the only exception to his strict rules being, singing hymns which they used to do every night before he read a passage from the heavenly Bible. But these days he never ever allowed her out of her room not even for prayers or hymns.

The nursery had become Sarah's life, occasionally in the past, nursey Banks would take her out to sit in the garden but only if she promised to not touch anything and if she did, not to wipe her hands on her clean smock. They would sit on the stone seat, which had ugly staring monster gargoyles at each end. Nursey would crochet with fine cotton and Sarah eyes would follow the flight of the birds, if she concentrated really hard her vivid imagination could connect her with the birds spiralling above and she could join them in their flight over the house.

She would look down upon the roof and garden and see the nurse sitting far below on the seat crocheting, she chose only to return to her body when she could see the nurse getting extremely panicky and anxious. Nurse would be tapping the face and shaking the arms of Sarah's empty shell sitting next to her on the seat, and then nurse would completely lose control and hysterically plead.

'Come along child, pull yourself together, you're having one of your turns again, now wake up.'

Sarah would wait as long as she possibly could and then eventually let her free spirit drift back down into the imprisonment of her body. Nursey would then threaten her that if she did not behave normally that it would be the last time she would be allowed to go out into the garden. The women accused Sarah of being able to control her strange blank behaviour and that the child created it on purpose to frighten her. Of course the nurse was partly correct Sarah could control her astral projection, but she did not do it to scare the nurse, she did it so she could be free from the bonds of her tightly controlled childhood. So many times nurse tried to explain to Sarah's Father that she thought it was a form of severe daydreaming that the child suffered from. Malakai Miller agreed with the nurse that the child did bring it on herself and her problem was that she didn't have enough discipline to control her wandering mind. The stoic man said he was exasperated and at a loss as to what to do with the awkward child, he had approached Miss Jenkins the ex-tutor from St. Pagans Manor to spend more time with Sarah, perhaps teaching her to speak the Welsh language. Miss Jenkins tried to explain to the arrogant man, that it was a waste of her precious time and his money to try to teach the child anything, the girl had a butterfly mind. She said that even when she had been trying to teach the girl the very basics of Maths or English that she lacked the ability to concentrate. She could never listen and would keep interrupting asking useless ridiculous questions, 'How high is the sky? What is the moon made of and where did the sun go at night.'

And then if she ignored Sarah's questions Sarah would repeat them word for word to her imaginary friend and then come out with some ridiculous answers that she said he had told her. No, she certainly did not think she could teach the child to speak welsh or anything else. Malakai Miller had been most annoyed with Miss Jenkins attitude and this had led to the young tutor most rudely leaving his employment. Since then he had found it most difficult to find anyone who was prepared to take on his daughter. All he required was to hire a reasonably intelligent person to educate Sarah to the standard that he set out for them. He could not understand what the problem was. He did not realise that word had passed rapidly around the village about him being a very difficult and mean man to work for. He did not see anything wrong with reducing their wages drastically if his employees did not arrive five minutes before hand, allowing themselves to take their coats off in their own time. Also he thought it perfectly normal to charge them for their refreshments even though it would only be a glass of water.

Sarah's parents had anguished many hours over their daughter's strange behaviour. Malakai Miller would storm around his wife's bedroom, insisting that the child was sick in the head most probably the same condition as his mother and it would be best for everyone if she was put away. He kept reminding his wife that Sarah had been nothing but trouble since the day she was conceived. First his wife had suffered nine months of ill health and continual sickness and then after a long labour the child had been born, permanently damaging his wife who had spent the last nine years in bed suffering from some odd ailment or another. Oh yes this child had a lot to answer for. Sarah's mother would plead for her husband's leniency towards the little girl and try and reason with him, making futile excuses for her strange behaviour.

'She can't help the way she is, it's not really her fault, Malakai. She has spent so much of her childhood on her own, it would have been better if she had brothers or sisters or even friends to play with. Perhaps you could try a little harder to like her, she used to enjoy going out with you on your visits, I know that the last time you took her to church she embarrassed you but I'm sure she's learnt her lesson now and will behave herself in future. Please, Malakai, can you not try to forgive her and see it in your heart to give her another chance.'

Eliza Miller loved her only daughter but owing to her constant melancholy that left her feeling exhausted most of the time, she saw very little of the child. Her husband forbade her to see Sarah too often, explaining that the child was so neurotic and excitable that she only aggravated his wife's condition. As for his wife's suggestion that he should let the child accompany him more often when he went out, he definitely would not want his daughter to know about his whereabouts. Especially that some of his so called village duties were spent in the company of a welsh widow in Crageu who satisfied his manly needs. And of course the other reason that Eliza Miller would never understand, was the solemn vow he made to his God, that as long as he lived he would never allow the child to accompany him to church again. She would never have understood the absolute mortification and embarrassment that he had endured at the hands of their daughter.

As self-punishment he would often relive the uncomfortable ordeal even the briefest thought of that episode could make him feel physically sick. It was a long time before he felt able to go to St. Ezra's again and hold his head up high. No never again would he give her the opportunity to repeat that performance, especially in public.

Sarah would have given a very different account of that day. All had seemed well that morning, the sun was shining and Sarah was apprehensive but excited as they travelled by coach to St. Ezra's church. She felt very proud to be sitting in her father's coach especially when they drove past neighbours walking and they tipped their hats to her father who responded with a regal nod of his head.

Sarah and her father sat together in the family pew at the front of the church, she tried desperately hard to sit still and not let her bottom make strange noises, which often happened when she was tense. Her father had lectured her at great length, he explained that they would be visiting the house of The God, and as The God was King of all Kings and an extremely clever man. He was able to see and hear everything she said or did, and even know if she was having unhealthy thoughts inside her head. Sarah sat stiffly on the highly polished pew keeping her eyes firmly downcast, trying to concentrate on the gold buckles on her shoes. She was trying to understand and think pleasant thoughts about the expressionless words that were tumbling monotonously from the preacher's thin lips. Words that she could not begin to comprehend. The preacher looked like a big white bird standing high above the congregation on his pulpit bird table. Towards the end of the service his voice changed and he became excited and almost spat out his final words. For a moment, silence reigned throughout the still congregation everyone appeared to be holding their breath waiting for the preachers threats to become reality, Sarah thought all seemed to be going extremely well and she was exceptionally pleased with her good behaviour. For once she gave her father no cause to reprimand her but unfortunately just as she breathed a sigh of relief that the hand of the God had not emerged through the roof of the church, plucked her up and transported her off to hell or to wherever they stored the naughty children. She relaxed her downward gaze and stretched her arms and allowed her eyes to wander around the fascinating surroundings. Suddenly a shaft of sunlight beamed through the beautiful stained glass windows and this was the point of her downfall.

As large as life, there, in the window of multi-coloured glass was a portrait of her very special friend, Tobias. She became very excited and could not contain her emotions, she tugged at her father's arm to draw his attention away from his conversation with the preacher and make him look at the portrait of Tobias. At first her father tried to push her away and ignore her rude interruption but she did not stop there. All she wanted to do was to show her father what Tobias looked like and then perhaps he would believe that her friend really did exist. As her excited voice grew louder and louder a steel hand gripped her arm squeezing the life out of it, she looked up into her fathers red angry face, through gritted teeth he told her to be quiet and behave. Her outburst did not make her father appreciate the existence of Tobias at all. The immediate thought up-most in his mind at that moment was to remove Sarah from this house of The God as quickly and quietly as possible. This outburst was more than enough for Malakai Miller to bear especially in front to all these people. He made his apologies to the bewildered preacher and started to forcibly guide Sarah out of the pew. Just for a second he relaxed his grip on Sarah's arm and she seized the opportunity to run out of his reach and take a closer look at the picture of Tobias. It showed him holding a lamb and surrounded by small children, she rushed up to the window and began to hold a very loud one sided conversation with the facsimile of her friend. As a child she was oblivious that her excited ramblings had drawn the attention of the rest of the congregation, who had halted their exit from the church to watch the performance she was giving. It seemed at that moment to Sarah's father that the entire populations of St. Pagans if not the whole world were casting their undivided attention on him, him, the stalwart of the community the god loving respectable Malakai Miller, who was at this moment unable to quieten or control his devil possessed daughter. He would never be able to face these people again without reliving the shame of her behaviour. Not noticing or acknowledging the sympathetic glances cast towards him in his moment of humiliation, he pulled Sarah roughly away from the offending window and down the black tiled aisle. Mothers shook their heads in sympathy for this poor demented child that they had often heard about but never seen before. And Fathers nodded their heads in agreement with the action the man was asserting.

The angry man dragged his protesting, screaming, squirming daughter down the cobbled path of St.

Ezra's he took such large strides that her small feet hardly touched the ground. And when they reached the lych gate and she was still ranting and raving about the wonderful Tobias and screaming for him to help her, she was brutally thrown against the closed wooden gates. An accumulation of anger and shame had risen to the point of explosive consequences, every vein in her father's purple face appeared fit to burst. Now completely out of control, he roughly seized hold of both of her arms. He pulled her up off of the ground and spun her around to face him. He couldn't contain his pent up rage any longer. His frustration gave vent to the satisfying freedom of physically abusing his daughter. Violently, he shook the small confused child, so hard, that her brain rolled around inside her head and her eyes could not focus clearly. As her head rocked from side to side his hand came up and he sharply slapped the back of her head, making sure that it was in a place where the bruise would not show. Sarah tried to swallow the burning bile that had risen in her throat, but to no avail. Unfortunately, just as her father thrust his face down a few inches from hers and begun to spit out a myriad of venomous words, her breakfast, which had been greatly disturbed, by the violent shaking, decided to hastily vacate its warm premises in rather an undignified manner. Just for a moment there was absolute silence and the hand that gripped her so roughly released her and she dropped to the ground. Horrified and confused by what had happened she recoiled from her father's dripping face and vomit drenched coat, and stumbled dizzily still retching to the coach.

Scrambling up the steep steps she threw herself inside, making herself as small as possible in the far corner under the seat. For what seemed a lifetime she held her breath waiting for her father to enter the coach. Thankfully for Sarah, her father did not join her, the driver was given angry instructions to take the wretched child back to the house immediately and make sure that she was locked in the nursery until he returned. Malakai Miller washed his face in the water fountain that was set in the church wall, he decided to walk home across the fields worried that if he went by the footpath he might meet up with some of the congregation who had witnessed the dreadful spectacle. He could not entertain the thought of travelling home in the same coach as that witch of a child. He was so distressed by the events of the morning, that all the muscles in his legs trembled as he walked down Manor hill. Once he entered the lane behind the blacksmiths, he climbed over the stile and walked towards a copse of small trees, when he was well hidden by the overhanging branches he reached inside his jacket and pulled out a small silver flask from his pocket. Greedily he drank the contents. He sighed with relief as the burning liquid soothed his fraught nerves. Leaning on a field gate he pondered as to why God had sent him such a punishment in the form of his daughter. He'd always been a good Christian soul and carried out Gods words according to the heavenly book. He knew that before long he would either permanently damage that demon child or as he really desired, put her out of his misery.

After that occasion Malakai Miller chose not to set eyes on his daughter and instructed nurse Banks that she keep Sarah in the nursery, until arrangements could be made for her permanent departure from his home. After all he'd easily managed to achieve it with his mother it should not be too difficult to repeat the procedure with his daughter.

CHAPTER THREE

Nature's clock ticks silently moving through the ages of man
When we are small, we yearn to grow up
And when we are grown up we want to turn back the clock
And we yearn to grow down.

The clock in the nursery was not replaced, so Sarah had no idea of what time it was. Tobias said you didn't need a clock, to know the time, you just had to become aware of the world around you. Look at the sun and the shadows, the birds feeding, and you would soon be familiar with nature's time clock. In his world, there was no such thing as time, because time was only needed on this earthly plane, to organise, control, account and justify for your life's movements.

Nursey Banks noisily unlocked the nursery door and entered carrying the supper tray. Puffing and panting from the climb up the two flights of stairs she heaved herself into a chair.

'Come on hurry up and eat your food. Your father has instructed me, that as a punishment for dancing and cavorting around the room like a wild animal and breaking the clock, each evening after supper I'm to sit with you and make sure you read your bible.' She paused to catch her breath. 'You are to learn seven passages. Writing each one down seven times every evening before you go to bed. And at the end of each week I'm to listen to all the pieces that you have learnt. Your father has chosen the passages that you are going to start tonight.'

Sarah could feel the nurse's annoyance at her father's request, it would mean that she would have to spend more time with Sarah than she cared to. Usually she would rush into the room, first thing in the morning, to supervise Sarah washing and dressing and then she would bring up the breakfast tray, stoke the fire and leave, not reappearing again, until lunchtime avoiding any conversation with Sarah as possible.

The nurse had on many occasions made it perfectly clear to Sarah, that she disliked this job immensely. One minute she would be looking after this lunatic child and the next pampering to the whims of the child's mother who never left her bed. And as for the master he went from days of silence to blind rages, there must be an easier way of earning a living. Besides there were no perks in this house, like some of the other establishments she had worked in. No alcohol was ever let through the door even at Christmas time. The food was basically plain and boring with no extras to be pilfered, comforts and pleasure were not part of the master's rules. If only she could get enough money together she would leave this bloody place.

Exodus. Chapter Eight. This was one of Sarah's favourite passages from the heavenly story book.

And the lord spoke unto Moses, go unto the pharaoh, and say unto him. Thus saith the Lord.
Let my people go, that they may serve me. And if thou refuse to let them go, behold, I will spite all thy borders with frogs. And the rivers will bring forth

frogs abundantly, which shall go up and come into thine house, and into thy bedchamber, and upon thy bed.

At this point Sarah's mind drifted off vividly daydreaming. She thought how wonderful it would be to have a steady stream of green wet frogs come indoors from the garden through the front door, hop up the stairs crawl into her room and climb onto her bed. Just imagine the nurse's face if the room was filled with a green slimy mass of frogs climbing all over her feet.

With the evenings reading over, the nurse who had been dozing and quite oblivious of the passage that the girl had been reading, pulled back the bed covers and signalled for Sarah to get into bed.

The nurse suddenly gasped in horror and put her hands over her face, just for a slight moment her eyes seemed to be playing tricks on her, she could have sworn that the bed had become a seething mass of green wet slimy frogs all climbing over each other. Rubbing her eyes she looked down at the bed again, she was relieved when she saw that it was completely empty there was not a frog in sight.

'What are you up to, you little devil? I know you did that.' The nurse raised her hand to Sarah. Quickly Sarah replied.

'Nothing, I don't know what you mean. What's the matter? I don't understand.'

'You know exactly what I mean. You won't get away with it. You mark my words.'

When the nurse had left the room and noisily locked the door, Tobias materialised and plonked himself down on the bed beside Sarah.

'I don't think she liked the frogs, do you?' he said with a huge grin on his face.

'How did you do that? Will you teach me, please?'

'You can do it yourself, you just need to practise to make your imagination become reality. If you believe in something strongly enough and never doubt it or have negative thoughts, then anything is possible.'

'Will I ever be as clever as you Tobias?'

'You will be as clever as you want to be. We always have the choice to be anything we choose to be. It's just that some things don't come very easily and you have to work at them. But nothing is totally impossible.'

Life for Sarah remained unchanged for many months. She sat in her room with only the company of the miserable nurse and of course Tobias. She tried hard to learn not to talk out loud to him, especially in front of the grumpy nurse, even though sometimes she found it difficult to restrain herself from commenting or laughing at some of the antics that he performed to entertain her lonely hours in the room.

But of course there is always the straw that broke Malakai Miller's back.

This particular evening the nurse had left Sarah locked in her room sleeping soundly. Around about eleven o'clock the very foundations of the house shook with Sarah's screaming and wailing. Sarah's parents and the nurse presumed it was another one of the excitable child's nightmares and they all chose to ignore her. But Sarah was not asleep she was wide-awake and was desperately trying to wrench open the locked bedroom door. She shouted and screamed for someone to come and let her out. She kept repeating the same sentence over and over again. She insisted that she had to get out of the room so she could go to help her grandmother, who was trapped in a large house that was on fire and burning fiercely. Her haunting cries continued for a long time and penetrated every corner of the house but still no one went to the child's aid. Sarah begged for her father to help grandmother who she could see was dying trapped in a locked room, which was slowly filling with acrid smoke. But still nobody came to help Sarah. Nursey banks and Sarah's father still tried to ignore the noise upstairs that the child was creating, but after yet another half an hour of screaming and crying and the nursery door being hammered. The irate master of the house shouted for the nurse to follow him up to the nursery, half-heartedly she levered her fat body out of her comfy chair.

The poor hysterical child had been trying to get out of the locked room and as the couple made their way up to the landing there was an ear splitting sound of splintering wood.

A surge of inhuman strength rushed through Sarah's small body, her nails clawed at the door-frame ripping out great splinters of wood. Just as she managed to wrench the door open leaving the lock hanging in the broken wood, her father with the nurse cautiously hiding behind him arrived on the top landing.

They were not ready for the monstrous spectacle that crouched before them, and stepped back fearfully as Sarah crawled on all fours towards them. She appeared to have taken the stance of a wild animal, her eyes were red rimmed but tinged with orange, and they wildly glared at the couple standing in front of her. She tilted her head back so she could see them clearly and curled her lips back to reveal long white sharp teeth. A voice that did not seem to be his daughters snarled something unintelligible at him followed by a death defying snarl that echoed throughout the house. The couple were rooted to the spot with fear and utter disbelief not knowing which way to safely move. Panic stricken Sarah had now achieved her aim to get out of the room to summons her father, to help her grandmother. And now as he stood before her, she started to return to normal, still sobbing, she stood up. Her terrified father, felt much more in control of the situation once Sarah returned to a feeble small child again.

'You've got to help grandmother, she's dying in a fire. Please father.' Painful sobs burst out.

'Honestly father I can...see her.'

Still shocked from the way this mad child had appeared to change into some sort of jungle creature he didn't listen to a word Sarah was saying. Nor did he see his only daughter, wild eyed and sobbing obviously deeply distressed. All he saw was an inconvenience in his life. He had experienced more than his fair share of imbecile members of his family. For years he had witnessed his own mothers sightings and predictions and just when he'd rid himself of that problem the child had started behaving the same way. Of course it was in the bad blood, it must have been passed through him to his daughter. He honestly considered himself extremely lucky that the hereditary insanity had completely missed him out.

Looking down at the snivelling child he told the nurse that he thought it would be best if she fetched the preacher to exorcise the devil that he believed shared Sarah's body. But the nurse had insisted that a doctor was needed.

Reluctantly he agreed and then bellowed at her.

'Well don't just stand there gawking go immediately and instruct Styles to fetch the doctor, the child is hysterical and out of control.'

On reflection he considered that perhaps it was a good idea after all, at least the doctor could see her at her worst, surely this would convince him that the child's illness had deteriorated rapidly and the kindest action would be to commit her to the asylum.

The nurse delighted with the chance to leave the frightening scene on the landing, heaved her rotund body down the stairs. Sarah gaining a little strength stumbled towards her father, alarmed by her movements he quickly stepped backwards, she collapsed at his feet pleading with him for help. Her white hands tugged at his trousers legs again she mumbled to him about what she could see in her vision. With all her strength she pulled herself up and tried to move past her father, if he wouldn't help then she would go and appeal to her mother.

With a shudder and a look of sheer distaste that he had to touch this excuse for a daughter, he grabbed hold of the tear drenched black tangle of hair that brushed past his hand. Propelling his protesting daughter into the nursery he forced her down into a chair, careful not to let his grip on her hair weaken. With all her might she fought him, biting and scratching his hands until they bled. At the same time screaming for her mother to come and help.

Downstairs her mother pulled the eiderdown over her head and thrust her fingers further into her ears trying to shut out the pitiful pleas of her daughter.

Sarah screamed for Tobias to come and help her but her emotional turmoil clouded the fact that he had been beside her all the time trying to help her, but she could not hear him.

The elderly Doctor Jones made his way up the steep flights of stairs to the attic room. He certainly did not enjoy coming to this dark miserable house, apart from the long arduous journey to the outskirts of St. Pagans, when he eventually did arrive he would be given a tradesman's welcome and treated like a servant.

Sobbing miserably again, Sarah lost all the fight in her, she could hardly breath, gasping for fresh air her small body collapsed into the chair. Only then did her father release his grip on her hair and let her small deflated body fall from the chair and crumple onto the nursery floor.

'I'll thank you to sort this problem out as quickly as possible, Jones. And then I want a serious word with you in private. I will be in my study.' And Malakai Miller departed from the nursery leaving the Doctor and the nurse to manage his child. Doctor Jones uttered some sort of muffled reply, at this moment his only concern was for this frightened sick little girl who was slumped in a heap like a bundle of rags.

He had known what would be expected of him before he even entered this miserable house. He felt sad for anyone or anything with feeling that had to live in this uncompassionate household, the poor child did not fit in with the strict upbringing that her father demanded of her. She lived a punishment for her existence the rules being fire and brimstone. And fear that The God would punish you, for the sin of being a small child. Anyone who broke the harsh rules in this house would be banished as being mad. What could the girl's father expect of her, caged like a small bird, a prisoner from life, it would all take its toll, she would either adapt to the confines of the bars or as he suspected Sarah had done, yearned to be free. Creating imaginary episodes to draw attention to herself, grateful for being noticed even if it was only her father's anger that she received. And of course there was the non-existent friend that she spent so much time talking to and of course the strange predictions and the bizarre daydreams. Admittedly she behaved very much like old Hannah Miller and he put that down to Sarah spending her early years with her grandmother before the old girl was committed to the bedlam of the 'Tall Oaks' asylum.

He opened his bag and extracted a small phial, putting two drops of the vile smelling liquid onto a piece of lint, he held the pad to Sarah's nose. Instantly she coughed and spluttered and came out of her state of collapse.

As her eyes flashed open she instantly remembered the vision that she had witnessed just before she had fainted.

'Get up off the floor and stop that snivelling,' boomed the nurse.

The doctor helped Sarah to her bed.

'Sit up properly, for the doctor, will you.'

Sarah sat bolt upright, but found it difficult to control the deep sobs that racked her small body. Her raven black curls stuck to her crumpled red face still drenched with teardrops. This pitiful, bereft child with a vision inside her head so real, that no one would believe, how could she convince them that her grandmother's life really was in danger. Her eyes became wide and black as the frightening vision entered her mind again. She witnessed the black smoke curling around the crackling roof of the tall building, and then great amber flames licking the forest of chimneys, she could hear the inmates screaming to be saved. She felt their blind panic as they threw themselves at the heavily barred windows thrusting their arms out into the safety of the fresh night air grasping at freedom. The victim's lamentable cries of hopelessness filled Sarah's ears, they were pleading to be saved from the raging smoke and flames. This was only a small part of the day-mare, worse was to come. Her wonderful grandmother was sitting upright in a chair, grey smoke silently crept under the locked door, her eyes expressionless stared into the distance. Sarah shouted to her grandmother to get out of the room as quickly as possible. She saw orange flames penetrate through the wood of the locked door and burst into the room, she heard her grandmother gasp for air. But still she did not move from the chair. Somehow her senses had become magically linked to Sarah's. Hannah was sending a farewell message to her granddaughter telepathically. The familiar warm voice came into Sarah's mind space.

'Sarah...Sarah...listen to me my beautiful child, please do not be afraid, I must talk to you for I have little time left on this earth, listen carefully, my darling. I am sure by now that, you must be aware of inheriting my ability of clear seeing and the gift of healing. You must use your gifts wisely and only for the greatest good of all, cautiously using it otherwise as a last resort, to stop cruelty or an injustice. Throughout your life you will find there will often be a price to pay for your gift, as you are very different from most people. You will be teased and often taunted but remember, have faith in yourself and...If fear ever knocks on your door...And your faith answers it...There will be nobody there.'

There was a long pause and Sarah strained her ears to hear her grandmother's faint voice.

'Oh...Sarah do not worry...I am not afraid, it's a far better place that I will be travelling to...if only you could see the wondrous rainbow of lights that are here with me and your dear great grandmother has come to guide me...'

At this point Sarah screamed and screamed the doctor tried to hold her but she threw off his kind arms. She shouted at the doctor to rush quickly to help her grandmother. Doctor Jones was quite alarmed by the child's behaviour this was the worst he had ever seen her she was totally out of control and hysterical. He reached in his medicine bag for a bottle of strong sedative, two drops would soon calm her and send her off into a drug induced sleep.

Grandmother's voice was pleading with Sarah to be calm and not get into such a state, dying for her was not really the end but just the beginning of a new existence without all the cruelty and trouble of this life.

'Have a happy life my little one...I will always...love...you....We...will...meet...again...I promise...Farewell my little bird...F...are...well... I... Love...You...'

'You're all too late she's dead,' Sarah screeched wildly.

The doctor held the glass to Sarah's lips, defeated she sipped the liquid not caring any more as to what happened to her. She could not understand why no one, especially the kind doctor Jones would not listen to her pleas and help her grandmother.

The sedation worked quickly and the child's eyes became heavy and rolled back into her head as unconsciousness took her into a deep forged sleep.

The doctor watched his little patient submit to the drug. Well this was exactly what her father wanted the doctor to do, sedate her, so that she was incapable of any more outbursts or better still for Malakai Miller, commit her to one of the many institutions for difficult children, who were destined for a life of misery.

These horrendous places were worse than any workhouse. Rebellious, handicapped and young pregnant girls were all banished away from the world's eyes, locked into wards lined with cast iron beds without any proper sanitation. The care of a sort was provided by underpaid untrained staff, with very little supervision. Many of the unfortunate inmates should never have been placed in these hostile institutions, often vast amounts of money exchanged hands to bribe people in authority to take some poor misfit child whose parents found them unacceptable.

Society made very little provision for the mental or physically handicapped, the latter often with normal brains trapped inside their cruelly deformed bodies, unable to communicate and let the world know how they were treated all were imprisoned as if they were idiots.

How could he sentence Sarah to that hopeless future, once you were on the inside that is where you would spend the rest of your life, it was love and care that she needed. He doubted that she would ever achieve those scarce emotions whilst she lived with her parents. No, he decided he would stand up to the girl's father and refuse to commit her.

The nurse pulled the covers over the drugged child, her mind being pre-occupied, cunningly outlining a scheme that she was developing, a scheme that she had been nurturing, which could possibly secure her future. And tonight, could be the night to finalise the details and put her proposition to her overwrought master. If after this latest upsetting episode the Doctor still refused to get rid of the difficult child, the nurse was pretty sure that Mr High and Mighty Miller would very readily accept her plan. It was her opportunity to move out of this house for once and for all, and of course make some easy money on a regular basis. She would have to pay her poor simple sister something towards the child's keep, but the majority of the monthly figure that she had in mind to extort from the master, would be hers, after all, didn't she deserve it? She would send money for a short while to keep Gwen sweet and then, oh dear, she would tell her sister that the Miller family had moved away without a trace and that the money had stopped. She knew her simple sister well enough, that she would never throw the child out. She could see no end to the ways she would eventually be able to manipulate a few more pounds out of the child's desperate father, possibly after a few months a little emotional blackmail, threatening that if he did not cough up with the cash, then she would have to return the child to her rightful home. No more looking after rich peoples kids. She was going into a bit of luxury living for her.

Hovering outside the study door the nurse grinned, delighted at the angry exchange of voices on the other side. They were going at it like tom cats. She just managed to step aside as the doctor came striding out of the study and rushed past her with his face like thunder. As he reached the hallway and waited for Styles to fetch his overcoat there was a loud knocking at the front door. Styles handed the doctor his coat and went to answer the door. Malakai Miller emerged from his study to see the doctor and the police constable from the village in conversation.

'What do you want constable?' demanded the angry voice from the top of the stairs.

'I'm sorry to disturb you so late in the evening sir. But I'm afraid, I have some very grim news for you.'

Malakai Miller descended the stairs. 'Go on man,' he said impatiently, 'what is it? Speak up.'

'There has been a terrible tragedy,' he paused and took a deep breath before continuing. 'This very night about two hours ago a raging fire engulfed the Tall Oaks institution. There were many casualties owing to the rooms being locked up for the night and I'm sorry to say that, it is believed that your mother, Mrs Hannah Miller has perished in the inferno, the wing where her room was has been completely gutted and only the charred ruin remains. We were able to recover a few bodies from that area before it was totally destroyed. Perhaps in the morning you would come down to the mortuary and see if you could identify what we believe is your late mother's body. And then you can make arrangements for the funeral. I'm sorry to bring such bad news.'

'Alright constable, I'll see you in the morning.'

Was the only reply the man made. He showed no emotion or any form of expression on his face. He held the door open for the constable to leave.

When the door was safely closed, fervently his eyes darted to the doctor. He never mentioned a word about his mother, but in a low growling voice that only the doctor could hear he said,

'That girl's the devil himself, she caused this, and if you refuse to do something about her, then I will. She is a sorceress you cannot deny that, all evening she has been raving about my mother's death in a fire. Can't you see that she has summoned up some sort of evil and everything she has said has come true. Now she has killed my mother. What more proof do you need?'

The doctor not wishing to get caught up in anymore unpleasantness pushed past the ranting man and swiftly made his way out of the house.

When he was safely in the coach and well away from the house he mulled over the evenings strange events. You could not get away from it the child was very odd. He did not believe she could actually cause her grandmothers death, nor did he really think that she could in some odd sort of way predict the evening's catastrophe. And yet it was the second time the child had predicted an event that was just about to happen. The grandmother used to do it to. That's why she was in the asylum. No, he said to himself there was obviously a logical explanation to it, it must be a coincidence. But he wasn't altogether convinced of that line of reasoning.

Events of the evening played well into the cruel nurse's hands. After eagerly listening to her propositions, Malakai Miller agreed to the devious women's suggestion that her dear sister in Cornwall would willingly take the child off his hands, for a price of course.

To him it was a heaven sent miracle. At last he could actually see an end to the problems that had shadowed his life, he would now be rid of the two thorns in his side, his mother, god rest her troubled soul, was now dead, and his daughter would be very soon transported miles and miles away from here.

'Hallelujah,' he shouted at the top of his voice.

'Oh thank you God, thank you, I knew you would listen to your long suffering servant,' then he added as an afterthought,

'Amen.'

The heavy burden of his insane relatives had been lifted. Oh yes, his god had really listened to him and answered his prayers, not quite as quickly as he would have liked but that did not matter now. His punishment was over. God knows just about how much one of his faithful servants can take. Tonight to show his appreciation he would read two whole pages from the bible and offer an evening of endless prayers. He never really ever doubted that he was a good man and always believed that when his time came, there would be a very special place for him in the kingdom of his god's heaven.

The nurse could hardly stop herself from jumping with joy, she could not believe that her conversation with the master had gone so well. He did not argue or disagree with anything she put to him or want to negotiate the sum of money that she suggested her sister would require for the keep and schooling of Sarah. Tonight he would have agreed to two, even three times the sum. The nurse realising how readily he agreed to the amount, kicked herself for not asking for more.

Hurriedly she scrawled a letter to her sister in Cornwall and clasping it in her fat hands rushed off, down to the coach house. She bartered wet kisses and a quick fondle of her many folds of skin for the coach driver to post the letter off to Cornwall as quickly as possible.

And so on that fateful night a deal was struck that would be the turning point for Sarah's life.

Boldly the Initials S. M. stood out emblazoned in gold paint on the tin chest that sat in the middle of the nursery floor, it was nearly full to overflowing with sensible clothes. Sarah had been allowed to choose just a few of her precious possessions to take with her. And as she was under the impression that she was only going away for a short time she didn't feel the importance to collect all her treasures from the nursery cupboards. But she could not possibly dream of leaving the house without her grandmother's last gifts, given to her before she left the house to perish in that dreadful institution.

Reaching to the back of the scantily filled toy cupboard, she pulled out a small wooden box. Lifting the lid she gently unwrapped the black velvet cloth to reveal her treasured gifts. Cradling the beautiful crystal ball in both of her small hands she held it up to catch the light. The ball was perfect, not a flaw or bubble could be seen in it. Nestled in the bottom of the box was a delicate wind chime, made of gold chains and hanging down from the assorted lengths were cut crystal teardrops of various sizes. When the breeze caught the chimes the faintest tinkling of glass against glass could be heard. This was a very comforting sound to Sarah. Her grandmother used to say that when it was hung in the window, if it chimed the sound was to herald, that a new born fairy had received its wings. These were the only possessions that Sarah cared enough about to want to take away with her. Willing herself not to cry as she thought about her poor dead grandmother she tucked the box, down deep inside the chest.

Sarah had never been away from her home before

and felt a little nervous at the prospect. But she had been assured by both her parents that on account of all the frightful events that had recently occurred it was best for everyone, especially her mother whose health had deteriorated rapidly since grandmother's death. Her father explained to her that it was all for her own good, adding a little venom, that she had brought it on herself.

The lid of the chest was finally closed and the leather straps secured. The family coach stood ready in the drive outside the front door.

'Come along child, you're keeping everyone waiting.' The nurse dressed in her Sunday best was going to accompany Sarah on the long journey to Cornwall. The coach driver hauled the heavy chest onto the tailboard.

Malakai Miller stood at the front door impatient with his daughters delayed departure. He was studying his pocket watch when Sarah came down the stairs.

'Please can I say goodbye to Mother?'

'No, I don't want you upsetting her, I will tell her you said goodbye.'

She looked up the staircase expecting her mother to appear at any moment. Her father followed her gaze.

'She's resting and I think it's best if you just leave, now.' He talked to Sarah as if he was dismissing a member of staff.

'Do try and behave yourself, child,' he added.

There were no hugs or kisses. 'Goodbye father. When will I be coming home and how long am I going for?' No answer came from his pursed lips.

'Come along, we have a long journey in front of us,' the nurse took Sarah's hand and pulled her out of the front door. Sarah instinctively knew that her father was avoiding telling her the truth about how long she was going away for. She followed the nurse down the steps to the waiting coach. When she reached the bottom she turned and glanced back at the door, but it had already closed. She peered high up to the balcony windows of her mother's room, hoping to catch a glimpse of her or a least a limp wave of farewell, she was so sure her mother would never let her go without saying goodbye. The curtains at the dark windows remained closed and unmoving. She tried very hard to be brave and not to cry again, but the feeling in her throat hurt and hurt until it forced warm tears to spurt out of her eyes.

'Mummy,' she shouted at the top of her voice, and then in a strangled screech. 'Please, I promise I'll be good, don't let them take me away. Please. Mummy.'

The nurse's fingers gripped the flesh on Sarah's arm until the child screamed in pain, she was bundled roughly into the coach. The sobbing child wondered why her parents did not like her, she never really understood what she had ever done wrong and how she managed to be so troublesome.

The coach passed through the gates and out into the wide world, this was the first step for Sarah on the pathway to the journey of life.

Once again Eliza Miller forced her fingers into her ears so she could not hear the pitiful screams of her only child. Now, he had taken everything from her. The one thing that made her miserable life worth living was her daughter. She had always known her husband hated the child almost as much as he hated her.

On the day of his mother's funeral Malakai Miller returned home ready to celebrate his freedom. He found his wife's room empty, he knew she could not be far as she was unable to walk unaided. He searched every room from the attic to the cellar of the house she was nowhere to be found. Completely bewildered by her absence he notified the local police station. The local countryside was scoured to no avail.

Three weeks later fishermen found her lifeless body floating face down in a river seven miles away from St. Pagans.

CHAPTER FOUR

Some say love is like a red rose
Signifying happiness light and love
But what of the black rose in the shadows
Starved of all life's sunshine above.

The faded blue eyes blinked and splashed tears for the small child within her onto the rough paper perched on her lap. The stubby pencil had ceased to record and the aged Sarah was back now in this time space. Moses looked up at her quite unsure of what she was doing. Her claw like hands wiped away the salty streaks from her cheeks.

Just for a while she could still feel the unhappy emotions of being an unloved nine-year old child.

That was the very last time she had ever seen her parents, and of course by now they would have passed on to another world. Over the years she had tried to trace them but without a clue to the address that they had moved to after she had left, her enquiries had been fruitless.

Moses was getting impatient and was rather anxious that Sarah might have forgotten his early morning romp in the woods. Watching him bounding to the door and then back to her side she understood perfectly what he was trying to tell her. She reached for her cloak and sticks and stiffly walked to the door, by this time the dog had started barking excitedly and cavorted around the room in circles chasing his tail. As she opened the heavy oak door Moses rushed outside startling the dove family that used the porch as a cote. They were the laziest birds that Sarah had ever come across. Their fat feathered bodies didn't leave their comfy perches, just their heads moved up and down into their puffed up shoulders with their beaks opening and closing hurling abuse and insulting remarks at the noisy dog.

'I didn't notice you lazy lot in the dawn chorus this morning, was it too early for you?' Sarah did not wait for the reply and hurried on down the path, just catching sight of the dog's tail disappearing into dense undergrowth.

Sarah stood and took a deep breath savouring the wonderful fresh smell of the dew-ridden vegetation around her. Everything looked brightly coloured and refreshed in the early morning sunrise, droplets of glittering moisture decorated the herbs and wildflowers that grew in her woodland. Sarah stooped to collect the aromatic flowers of the camomile that grew so prolifically in the July sunshine.

A group of beady-eyed Jackdaws flew noisily past her, she knew exactly where they were heading. They behaved like a raiding party on the loose.

She had named the cottage 'Jackdaw Cottage' after the glossy black hooligans that every year ripped her thatched roof to shreds, stealing the material and stuffing great beaks full down the chimney pots to make their nests. Even though they were most destructive birds she felt quite sorry for them. The local farmers and game keepers took great delight in shooting them and suspending their lifeless bodies from the trees, with hope of deterring their relations from visiting. But really they did very little harm and were quite friendly birds and very easy to tame even though they did have a liking for shiny objects which they would remove from your home without always asking.

As she continued to stroll after Moses she was completely unaware that she was not alone in her recreation, in the shadows of the trees beside her walked an old enemy. His cloak blended in with the colours of the woodland. He had become so close to snatching her recently and now he was growing impatient.

Every time she closed her eyes to rest or sleep he watched her every move, standing over her he would hold his hands in front of her face feeling how strong her breath was, willing the breathing action to stop. How tempting it was to just cover her mouth and nose with his skeletal fingers, after all she was so old now it would take very little to snuff out her life just like extinguishing the flame of a candle.

Moses stopped in his tracks and started to omit a low growl. Sarah squinted her eyes trying to see what Moses was looking at. The bracken and fallen twigs crackled as the invisible reaper crept away. The voice of Tobias came into Sarah's head.

'Go back to the cottage Sarah you have walked enough today.'

'Oh, that's it spoil my walk, Tobias these days you really are becoming quite a nuisance, I will not be long I just wanted to visit the 'Willow' tree before I turn back. I have a feeling by the way you are carrying on that this could be my last chance.'

Tobias knew better than Sarah. She would pay another visit to that special place before she died. Also she would spend a little precious time in the pagoda. Carefully she trod her way through the overgrown footpath that had disappeared beneath bracken and brambles.

Eventually she reached a part of the woods, which allowed the sun to pierce through the tree-tops, a place where the grass was always fresh and new, many years ago she had named this peaceful place the fairy ring. In the centre of the grassy ring stood a magnificent Willow tree its yellow-green fronds reached right down to touch the perfect grass circle, they formed the perfect skirt of a crinoline. If you cared to part the branches and step beneath them you would have witnesses an extraordinary sight, for there in the cool sun starved darkness grew a small rose bush.

What seemed a century ago, Sarah had planted both the Willow tree and the rose cutting. They portrayed the complete sunshine and shadows of her life. The sprig of willow had been happily snapped from a far greater tree that towered above a wooden pagoda that stood not far from there in the grounds of High Markham. She had been so exceedingly happy when she had snapped off the small twig and pushed it into the centre of the fairy ring. Very quickly the twig had sprouted new shoots and established itself as a grand tree. But the rose told a different story, it marked a grave, when Sarah had planted the rose it had been the only flower left alive in a heart-breaking wreath that she had placed on the fresh mound of brown earth. It had originally been a blood red rose. Forming roots it had readily flourished where she had planted it, but over the years it had never ever bloomed again.

Sarah parted the branches of the tree to look at the small grave, she suddenly gasped in astonishment, the once barren rose bush had at last decided to flower, not a blood red rose as it should have been, but a black rose the colour of midnight. She knelt to touch its petals, they were velvety and as soft as butterfly's wings. As she took her hand away the petals loosened and slowly one by one fell to the ground like weightless teardrops. All the breath of life within her seemed to drain from her body, leaving her completely fatigued. She had known since the day she had planted the rose cutting, that the year it bloomed again would be the last year of her lifetime.

Concentrating on putting one foot in front of the other she wearily started to make her way back to the cottage, her body seemed suddenly to weigh a ton. Moses noticed his mistress leaving the woodland and ceased his game of chase which he was having with a young squirrel. Disappointed that the fun was over his tail drooped downwards, sulkily he followed his mistress back home. As they reached the garden path of the cottage the unmistakable sound of horse drawn cart could be heard trundling down the lane behind them. Still finding walking very difficult Sarah stopped to catch her breath, silently she pleaded for Tobias to give her enough strength to get inside the cottage. The approaching cart drew nearer, Sarah beckoned for Moses to go indoors. She knew that the young ginger haired boy driving the cart was very nervous about visiting Jackdaw cottage and even more worried about meeting Moses the dog.

Andrew never could get used to delivering provisions to this part of the village. His father and his grandfather before him had delivered here and they said they both felt the same way about it. Not that the old women had ever said or done him any harm it was just that you could not help but listen to the rumours and stories that were passed down through the generations and if you only believed half of them that would be enough to make you very cautious of visiting the cottage. The most frightening story Andrew had heard about the old lady was: on the nights of the full moon at the stroke of midnight she could be seen to enter the churchyard, and then turn herself into a wild striped creature. She would grow long claws and sharp fangs. People had witnessed her scratching and clawing at any unsuspecting person who might be passing through.

He was told that this was a true story straight from the disfigured mouth of one of her victims. His grandfather had said that in his youth he used to collect flour from the Mill Farm where she lived. In those days she was a beautiful young women, with long flowing black hair and sky blue eyes, people used to travel miles to buy her herbal cures and she had the uncanny knack of putting her hands on injured or sick animals and people and curing them. But then there had been a scandal and she had moved into the cottage in the woods and become quite a recluse. It was told that she cursed everyone up at the big house. Fear had kept people away from the cottage. Many times a few kind hearted village folks had tried to visit her and even the preacher himself had tried to see her, but she would always rush out at them and hurl abuse and throw curses their way. Not that she had ever behaved this way to Andrew.

The boy hastily dropped off the sacks of provisions just outside the broken gate. Sarah would wait patiently for the cart to turn around and head back up the lane. When she got her second wind she would go and drag the sacks indoors. But for now she must rest. Turning around to cross the scullery she nearly tripped over a heap of earth and broken flag stones. The rescued vixen had decided to build a lair beneath the dresser. She had dug out a fair sized hole beneath the bottom cupboard and the floor, just below where daisy had her nursery. All you could see were a pair of amber eyes glinting in the darkness of the cave. Sarah had hoped that the now healthy fox would soon take her offsprings back into the wild. She already had too much of the outside, inside. Just look at the place. On the top of the dresser amongst the cups, odd saucers, string, bottles and jars sat a broken cuckoo clock and inside where the cuckoo should have been lived a family of blue tits. It wasn't that Sarah really minded the birds. But they did take the most awful liberties.

Originally the mother bird had flown into a window pane and stunned herself, after a few days convalescing in the cottage she had preened her dishevelled feathers and without a bye or thank-you bolted out through the open door. Only to return a few days later with her husband and set up home in the cuckoo clock. Between them they produced eight blue and yellow puffballs that really had not been too much trouble until they all decided to flee the safety of their nest and practise their clumsy fledgling flying lessons around the kitchen. It was extremely lucky for the birds that Sarah had a firm arrangement with the cottage cats. The agreement was that they must only hunt for food and not as man does for pleasure and strictly outside the cottage not inside, here the inside creatures were protected, outside everything had a fair chance and after all it was nature's way. The earth provided everything man or beast ever required for their survival, you either had to hunt, reap, sow and occasionally pay for your daily food. And how Sarah had paid for her daily bread, the monthly cart of provisions sent to her through the Trevallians guilt. Oh yes she had certainly paid for it. Sometimes it used to bother her to receive this charity, but pride was not always a positive emotion, especially if through an overdose of it you lost out.

When she sensed the boy and the cart were safely down the lane she mustered up enough energy to drag the sacks into the cottage. Stopping every few feet to get her breath she managed to tug them inside the doorway, their contents spilling out onto the scullery floor. Often she became quite cross with herself, her brain had the energy to move mountains but, alas her body refused to respond to her lively organs requests.

Unpacking the sacks Sarah knew exactly what they would contain, essential provisions, cheese, flour, lard, meats, butter, potatoes and a few coppers in the bottom so she could if needs be visit the local farm and buy eggs. Gone were the days when the provisions arrived in smart wicker baskets full to overflowing with wonderful delights and luxuries. Hidden amongst the provisions would be wonderful surprises, perfumed soaps that made your skin so soft, lace handkerchiefs and exotic crystallised fruits from far off lands and aromatic perfumes in richly painted glass bottles, smelling of unusual flowers, foreign spices and coffee beans. Now these items were just memories in an old ladies head.

With everything stored away in appropriate cupboards and boxes Sarah woke up the lazy fire with a few logs and when they spluttered into life she threw a lump of lard followed by four thick pork rashers into the spluttering black iron pan that sat on the grid over the fire. Two eggs were cracked into the bubbling fat and finally a large lump of bread to soak up the tasty juices. Moses sat patiently waiting for his share eagerly anticipating his breakfast. Sarah reached for the only remaining unchipped blue and white willow plate from the paraphernalia on the dresser. Pulling open a rickety drawer she took out a beautifully worn silver knife and fork and a carefully folded blue damask napkin. Like a lady she tucked the napkin into the baggy neck of her well-worn dress and sat down to enjoy her food. Moses demolished his breakfast in one hasty gulp and then in absolute disbelief searched around the bowl for it, not understanding that he had eaten the entire breakfast in one mouthful, which he could not even remember tasting.

With the breakfast crockery washed and restored to the dresser and her cloak pockets unpacked of the herbs and mushrooms that she had collected this morning, Sarah felt she might just have enough energy to set about a few chores, though, she would have to take short breaks in between. She threw the pot of cold tealeaves over the well-worn flagstone floor, the leaves dampened down the dust that seemed to regularly enter the cottage through every nook and cranny. An army of wood lice offended by the intrusion of the tealeaves into their cosy crevice angrily marched across in front of the broom, full well knowing that Sarah would wait until they had found a safer home before she swept. With her linseed oil cloth Sarah started to polish the few bits of good furniture that she possessed. First she would begin with the poor long suffering old pine dresser and table, which was either being scrubbed with a rough bristle brush or being lovingly polished with a soft oiled cloth. Moving onto the sitting room she slowly dusted the large oak sideboard and the bookcase under the small window. Carefully she cleaned the fragile glass swan that sat on the bookcase, the thin glass was hollow and filled with a clear liquid, years ago when she had received the swan as a present she had been told that it was filled with angel's teardrops. And she never had any reason to doubt that this was not the truth.

Sarah really did believe in angels, she understood that they were the kind loving people who had died before their time. They were allowed to move onto happier realms where they became guardian angels appointed to watch over us.

Tobias appeared in the room but Sarah was so absorbed in her thoughts and dusting that she did not notice him. As he was quite an extrovert spirit he was not very happy about being ignored. A sudden gust of wind blew open the front door and a furious flurry of dust and leaves scattered all over the clean scullery floor that Sarah had just painstakingly swept. And before Sarah could reach the door to close it the leaves and dust swept themselves up into a mini tornado and wound their way back out of the cottage as quickly as they had arrived. Left in the void of the gust was a blinding pink light, it radiated from the ceiling, filling the room with a rosy glow. Sarah was bathed in the warmth and brilliance of her ghostly friend's entrance. She knew that Tobias must be lurking somewhere in the cottage. She looked around for him, but he was nowhere to be seen. Just as she went to close the scullery door something made her heart miss a beat, she had found him. He was hanging from a hook on the back of the scullery door with his arms stretched out at the sides and his chin on his chest, just as if he was hanging on a cross.

'Please, don't do that Tobias, you made me jump and you know it makes me feel so sad to see you that way.'

He glided down from the back of the door, only to hover beside her. In a very teasing voice he told Sarah that he had been on a quest, and then he stopped talking, he was waiting for her to show some interest and ask about his quest, when she didn't he carried on revealing his news in a very loud voice. He had been very busily searching through the realms of his world to see if her parents were there. He'd travelled right down from the ultimate glory of heaven, through the rainbow lands and he was pleased to inform her that her mother was most happily settled in the nursery realms, but he could find not a single trace of her father. Now interested Sarah started to listen to him. He went on. 'Because I could not find your father, that means one of two things, he is either, you know where, down there,' and he pointed to hell. 'Or as I suspect, he's in limbo, The Valley of the Lost Souls, if I'm not mistaken. He obviously does not realise that he is dead, he'll be fumbling his way through the darkness still believing he's a good man. I don't think he will even make it to the learning realms. It's likely that his miserable soul will be reborn without a choice, so he can live through another lifetime on this earth, learning the lessons that he didn't get right the first time around. Or if he is really unlucky then he will be reborn as a small animal, caged and unloved.'

Sarah thought for a moment about her cruel father she never had wished him any ill but, if you shall reap as you have sown then he will be harvesting a lot of ill fortune for a very long time, on this earth and beyond.

'By the way, Sarah, whilst I was floating through the realms searching for your lost loved ones, I stopped off at the destination station and they informed me that very soon one of their representatives will be paying you a visit. She is called Sonja, and she's going to make friends with you. In the trade we call her a doorkeeper and when your time comes to, dare I say it, Pass Over, pop off or kick the eternal bucket of life then Sonja will be with you to make your journey as trouble free and comfortable as possible.'

Tobias walked back and forward across the room with both hands holding the front of his robe as if he was wearing a teacher's gown.

'We do not expect any hitches, but every so often a soul does get a little lost or perhaps I should say mislaid, only temporary, you understand. In the past it has been known that a soul on a final journey to the ultimate glory of heaven miscalculates the distance and finds themselves doing something that they did not particularly enjoy when they lived on the earth. I can remember one instance in particular, it was unfortunate that he was a devout catholic priest and that even in death he was a bit of a tyrant. Well he missed his stop and found himself in the middle of a very loud all soul's party, you know the type of occasion wine, women and all those sort of pleasurable things. All the deceased on this realm were fun loving confirmed party goers on the earth and had chosen this very exciting destination, but this poor man really did not want to be there he found it a bit too noisy and bawdy for his liking. We did apologies to him and moved him very quickly to his chosen realm of peace and tranquillity. It turned out that his novice doorkeeper, who should have been guiding him to his correct chosen destination suffered from a very strange sense of humour and became quite fed up with the priests constant whining and righteousness. As the doorkeeper was a bit of a practical joker in his life he decided to drop the man off before his chosen stop. The doorkeeper now resides on the entertainment plane.'

'For goodness sake Tobias, you do ramble on, you hardly stop to breathe.'

'I don't need to, do I?' retorted Tobias humorously.

'There you go having the last word again. Well you can keep your, what's her name, Sonja the Doorkeeper. I'm too old to make any new spirit friends, I have enough trouble with you, but since you are here, perhaps you could just infuse me with a little extra energy. I want to get to my treasure chest at the back of the log cupboard, I've things in there that I need to sort out.'

And she made her way towards the cupboard. The doors to the log cupboard scraped the floor as she tugged them open, she sighed heavily when she looked inside and saw the amount of logs and rubbish she would have to remove before she would be able to reach her treasure.

'Oh come on Tobias please give me strength, my arms are weak and useless.'

'Leave it for now Sarah, wait until tomorrow and I will send someone to help you.'

'Like who?' replied Sarah, sarcastically.

'Have a little patience Sarah, you know full well that when a task becomes too difficult to handle it is often because the timing is wrong and obstacles are put in your way to stop you completing what you set out to do. When the time is right then you will achieve your aims. You must practise what you preach.'

'Bugger off you wise and wonderful bloody know all, go and guide someone else you're no good to me today.'

A sphere of light bounced off the walls and the grandfather clock chimed thirteen times which was a sign that Tobias was becoming annoyed. He had been a spirit guide for hundreds and hundreds of years and befriended many living mortals through their lives but Sarah was the most stubborn he had ever come across, the older she became the more difficult he found her.

There was no point to staying around whilst she was in one of these moods, he might as well do a little drifting around the realms. He always enjoyed visiting the planes where he recognised important people who had either performed wonderful deeds for humanity when they lived on the earth or became famous through their misdeeds. Today he thought he might just visit Galileo who was in his element in the spirit world, what an interesting man he was. And perhaps if he had time he would enjoy a quick conversation with the famous Leonardo da Vinci, now he was a man to be admired, obviously he had been placed to be born in the wrong century his knowledge was for a future date, a different time, for more intelligent ears. Some would say he was gifted but no, the creation station had got the, to be born date wrong, mistakes can be made even in the afterlife, after all they are only inhuman...

Tobias remembered another little trade secret that

he could divulge to Sarah sometime. He wondered if she had ever pondered on the thought as to why some people are truly gifted, almost since birth they have knowledge of a particular accomplishment, for instance famous composers and musicians who achieve with very little difficulty. Well the secret of the matter is that they are not as such gifted but they have lived on this earth before. So they had learnt their talent then but of course when you are reborn you are not supposed to remember your previous lives but as well you know some people do, the so called gifted remember the ability to play, paint or compose etc. So there, you have it, they have learnt it all in a past life.

The air crackled as the almighty wise one left the cottage.

Wearily Sarah tossed two logs from the cupboard onto the hearthrug not caring to hear the screams of the black beetles that flew through the air clinging onto the logs tightly with all their legs trembling. At this rate it would take her a week to empty the log cupboard, frustrated with the thought she flung the two logs back into the cupboard. Her independent streak made Sarah annoyed that she was unable to complete the task that she had set herself, she would give in to her useless body tonight and rest in hopes that tomorrow she would be able to reach her precious chest.

CHAPTER FIVE

Saviours are sent to you but come in many guises
Look for the signs, wait for the coincidences to begin. Trust.

The two men stood carefully scrutinising the dilapidated thatched roof. One of the men was dressed in his Sunday best suit, his white collar was buttoned so tight around his neck that his mauve face looked like it was about to burst under the shade of his small bowler hat. His companion wore hard working clothes clean but showing the signs of restoration.
Sarah heard their loud voices as she opened the door to take Moses for his early morning romp. For a little while the men were unaware that the occupant of the cottage was watching them. The posh pants was pointing a finger at her roof and the worker nodded his head in agreement to whatever they were discussing. Moses rushed down the path barking, delighted at the opportunity to scare somebody. The posh pants jumped at the sudden intrusion of the noisy dog but the young man did not budge. He put his hand down for the angry dog to smell and when Moses had sniffed the hand and decided he approved of the owner he let Jack crouch down and fondle his ears.
Sarah pulled on her boots and plodded angrily down the path, she was not only cross with the

sudden appearance of the men studying her cottage but equally angry with Moses, her so called guard dog who was now drooling over one of the enemy. You could see the apprehension on the faces of the two men as Sarah stormed down the path towards them. She was wearing a faded felt hat, which was pulled over her flowing grey hair, men's heavy boots with no laces and an extremely threadbare blue velvet cloak. They both stepped back slightly as the wild women approached them.

'Well,' snapped Sarah. 'What do you two want, then?'

They looked at one another both waiting for the first one to be brave enough to speak out.

'Cat got your tongues?' She was irritated by their silence.

'I. I am the agent acting on behalf of the estate of High Markham,' squeaked posh pants and as an afterthought, he added, 'Madam I have been instructed by the Owners solicitor to modernise this cottage and get it ready to go on the market with the rest of the estate. Mr Jack George here is the builder who is going to repair that leaking roof and carry out all the other necessary refurbishments.'

Jack smiled warmly and nodded in agreement with what the posh pants had so far said. For a moment Sarah could not utter a word, it wasn't often that she was at a loss for something to say. Her mind raced over what the agent was telling her. The estate was going to be sold and this included her cottage, she had always understood that she would have this cottage for life. Trying to move her tongue in her very dry mouth she managed to ask the posh pants for more details. At this point the young Jack butted in.

'Please don't worry Madam, we will try not to

inconvenience you too much.'

He looked at the frail old lady standing before him and found it hard to believe all the stories he had heard about her, he suspected that each time the original tale had been told a little more was added just to entertain the listener.

The panic inside Sarah subsided and she found her voice. 'When are you selling my home?'

The agent looked down his nose at the walking rag-bag, he really would like to get on with surveying the property his time was precious and besides why should he have to justify anything to this tenant who had never paid a penny rent in all the years she had lived here.

'The estate will be put on the market as soon as it's brought up to scratch. You are what we call a sitting tenant, and I understand from the solicitor that there is an agreement that states you have the place as your home until you choose to leave or you die.' He thought to himself judging by the look of her that it would not be very long. Sarah caught his latter thought. 'Don't you bet on that you cheeky bastard, I've still got some life left in me.'

The agent went very red and nervously coughed when he realised that Sarah had read his mind. Jack guessed what had happened and laughed very loudly, he liked this women she had character. The agent thought he better try a different tactic with this old hag. Very slowly he started to explain.

'Firstly we are going to patch up the roof and then paint the walls outside and clear the garden of this tangled mess,' and he pointed to the wilderness of brambles and briars. Enthusiastically he continued hoping to get on the right side of her.

'And then, when the outsides spick and span we will plumb in water pipes to the kitchen, this will save you having to use that contraption of a water pump in the rain, gas will be installed so you can have a cooker and proper lighting.' He then made his finale which he was sure would win her over.

'You will have, at great expense to the estate an inside lavvy and a bath with running hot water. There.' He stepped back feeling quite pleased with himself for delivering all that good news.

Her mind could not take in everything that had been said to her. All these new-fangled ideas, why couldn't they just leave her alone, it would not be long before the cottage would be vacant and then they could rip it apart for all she cared. Water, gas, lavies inside, she liked her lavvy in the garden she could sit in the wooden hovel and look out into the countryside, besides it was home to all sorts of creepy crawlies, great black cob spiders had spent years decorating the walls with their tapestry of webs.

Posh pants stood waiting for an answer, not receiving one he continued to try to ease a reaction or reply from Sarah.

'Well you are a very lucky lady, I expect you will find it all rather exciting, won't you?' He spoke as if he was talking to an idiot.

'Patronising sod,' she spat at him. 'It would take a lot more of a man than you, to excite me, Mr Bloody agent.'

And when she saw his face flush with embarrassment for the second time that morning she was satisfied with her curt reply. Promptly like a soldier she turned on the heels of her large boots and marched down the path into the cottage. She would have slammed the front door behind her, but she knew the door was a lot frailer than she was and would not stand it.

Once inside the cottage she calmed herself down with a swig of her elder berry and camomile rescue remedy.

Moses did not follow Sarah back into the cottage, but stayed beside Jack George who was rubbing the dogs grey muzzle, they were both lost in perfect bliss. It was not until he heard his mistress calling him in her serious grown up voice that he slowly slunk down the path and half-heartedly crawled back into his home.

'Lovely dog, Mrs,' shouted the young workmen, who was very taken up with the creature and his mistress. Sarah heard but chose to ignore the comment.

'You old traitor Moses what did you think you were up too?'

Moses thought he would do better if he put his tail between his legs and show some sort of remorse. He crawled on all fours to Sarah's side and nuzzled her hand.

'You wait until they start banging and clattering around the place, you won't be so fond of them, then.'

Calmly Sarah thought about conversation with the posh pants. It had been a long time since anyone had roused her anger so much and also a long time since she had a conversation with anyone living.

'Talk of the dead, what did you make of all that?'

Tobias hovered above the table with his legs crossed like an eastern Buddha.

'I've got troubles Tobias, please try to be serious.'

'I heard you talking to your visitors, you were not very polite, were you?'

'Why should I be polite, all these years they have left me in this cottage without ever enquiring as to whether I needed any repairs or anything and now they are going to intrude into my life and home without even asking.'

'I don't see what the problem is, you always say that changes are good for you and that nothing is permanent, altered your philosophy now, have we, to suit the occasion I presume?'

'All I want, Tobias, is to be left in peace and quiet and finish my life story, how can I do that with all the banging and crashing around me. What with gas lamps poisoning me, my candles are good enough and then there is going to be water would you believe it, actually in pipes coming indoors, the pumps got plenty of life in it yet and the waters as sweet as champagne.'

Just for a moment she drifted off remembering the real taste of champagne as cold as the winter's frost and served in cut crystal glasses. What she would not give now, to put on her blue ball gown and spend the evening dancing in the arms of a handsome young man and end the night sipping champagne, watching the sun set and the moon rise never wanting the morning to come and the spell to be broken.

For a brief moment Sarah was lost in the world of memories. Suddenly the room became very dark and Sarah couldn't see, her ears seemed to buzz and she felt as though she was falling, making a grab at the back of the chair she just managed to steady herself. As her eyes started to focus she saw a figure in the room, he was clothed completely in black she tried not to look at his face, she knew who he was and why he had come.

'Please Tobias,' she gasped, her hands trembled.

'You said I could have a little more time, I beg you, just a couple more days.' She stood pleading for her life, nearly collapsing with the pains in her chest. 'I must make arrangements for the animals they will die if I am not here to care for them.'

The shadow in the corner chuckled as he heard her pleas, cackling laughter filled the room echoing off the walls, penetrating her ears and bursting into her brain so that she could not speak properly.

The spirit of death was enjoying his battle with Tobias. The room had started to become a little lighter and the terrible laughter became fainter and finally ceased. Standing beside Tobias was a young dark haired girl, she was dressed in animal skins and had her long black hair plaited with beads and shells.

'Sarah, this is Sonja, I told you she would be here to help you on your final journey, do you remember?'

Sarah still in pain looked at Sonja through her cobweb eyes. So this really was the end of her life, she had reached the time when she could shed her ageing shell and be free, even though she looked forward to her next journey she still wanted to tidy up a few loose ends in her life and her mind.

'Sarah, we can only let you stay until All Saints Eve, make the most of the precious time you have left, that is all we can allow,' said Sonja in a strange accent.

Sarah wandered around the cottage picking up and looking at some of her favourite possessions seeing them in a new light as if she was logging every detail about them in her mind in case she forgot the comfort they gave her. She realised that she would not need any of these material reminders where she was going, for there are no pockets in a shroud. She wondered what would become of all her things when she died, would the posh pants go through them and uncaringly toss them all on a fire in the garden. Her only really valuable possessions apart from Moses were locked in the chest at the back of the log cupboard, and of course her crystal ball and chimes. It would have been nice to have found somebody to leave everything to, somebody who cared. Fate would take its course, she was sure and they would fall into the right hands.

Passing the photographs on the wall she caught the reflection of herself in the glass, she peered closely at the strangers face staring back at her. Disappointed and shocked she went to the chest of drawers, daring herself to take out the silver backed mirror that she had deliberately laid face down in the drawer many years ago never ever allowing it to see the light of day. Turning it over and holding it up in front of her face she apprehensively looked straight into the eyes of the poor old girl reflected in the mirror. Leathery weather beaten skin hung in folds around the face, Oh yes, this was, her face, she wondered when this terrible change had taken place, colourless long straggly hair wildly framed her face. And now she looked back at the poor old girl in the mirror who was now crying, tears freely flowed from the faded blue eyes, they carelessly splashed onto the wooden furniture, creating white stains in the waxed surface. She looked at the photograph of the raven haired beauty on the wall thinking was that really me, I used to be young like her.

At that moment a hand touched her shoulder, at first she thought it must be Tobias and she did not turn to look.

'I'm sorry,' the voice said. 'I did knock the door and call for you, but when there was no answer, I thought something must be wrong, so I took the liberty of coming in. Is there anything I can do?'

Jack George placed a caring hand on her arm.

'You're very upset, come and sit down and I'll make you a cup of tea, my mother always used to say that tea was the best thing if you were troubled.'

The young man showed genuine concern on his face. Sarah put down the mirror with trembling hands. Now here was the right type of person that she could really do with at this moment. Caring strong arms helped her to her rocking chair. Jack's eyes scanned the room for the kettle, he was surprised to find it hanging over the fire and not on a cooker, but then he remembered that she did not have any modern appliances. The cottage reminded him of his grandmother's old place when he was a child, he felt that time had stood still between these walls.

'I am sorry, what was your name? Please call me Sarah. I feel a lot better now, Jack, let me make you a cup of tea, please sit down, would you like herbal tea or I do have a little Indian leaves if you prefer it?'

Jack chose to sample the herbal tea, he could not quite make out the wonderful flavour, it reminded him of blackberries, elderberries and rosehip, in fact he could taste all the fruits of the hedgerows. Moses was delighted with the company, he pushed himself coyly against the boy's trousers. This did not go unnoticed by Sarah.

'Do you like animals, Jack? Moses certainly has taken a liking to you.'

'I've always been fond of all living creatures, I spent a lot of my childhood in the woods getting to know the wildlife. I did have a dog until recently, she died of old age, I had her with me for most of my life and feel quite lost without her by my side, I haven't taken a liking to another one until now.'

He rubbed the neck of Moses affectionately, Moses drooled looking up into Jack's face as if he had just fallen in love.

'I'm getting too old to run him in the woods, you would be more than welcome to take him out with you, and he really does enjoy his exercise.'

The dog knew exactly what his mistress was saying and suddenly started to leap about, it was the word O.U.T that made him so excited.

'Come on then,' said the boy. 'A quick run before it gets dark.' And the happy pair raced off down the path and into the woods.

What a weight had been lifted from Sarah. She knew that when the time came, that Jack would make a good master for Moses. This young man had been sent to help her, when he returns from the walk with Moses, she would ask him to help her pull out the chest from the log cupboard, this would solve a big problem for her.

CHAPTER SIX

A pinch of Yellow sun dust and Bucket of blue sky
Mix them together and make a summer pie.

With the rusty chest sitting on the floor and her new friend stacking the logs back in the cupboard, Sarah chatted idly. She felt as if she had known Jack all her life, he kept stopping what he was doing to listen to her with great interest. She explained about the chest and her childhood and he made the right sympathetic noises when she explained how she was banished to Cornwall.

Jack was really enjoying Sarah's company and was not in the least frightened of her, he felt it was sad that village rumours had condemned her to lead such a solitary life out here in the woods. Admittedly she was a little eccentric and seemed to live in the past, he put it down to living on her own for a long time. The cottage he found fascinating, especially the wildlife that shared the place, he could not help but notice the mice living in the sheaths of corn that hung from the ceiling, most people he knew put poison down to kill them but here they were fed.

'Come and drink your tea, Jack, you have worked so hard this evening, I don't know how to thank you.'

Jack had to duck down as he walked across the room avoiding bunches of dried flowers, herbs and of course the mouse corn that hung from the beams.

'I can honestly say Sarah that I have really enjoyed being here with you and Moses, I would like to come again and visit, if that's alright with you. Perhaps you will teach me to how make this delicious tea.'

'Next time you come all the recipes will be written down for you along with the story I've been telling you about.'

'I shall look forward to reading that.'

When Jack had left Sarah sat down, sharpened her pencil and wrote her last will and testament, at last she had someone to leave her precious things to, someone she, and not forgetting Moses, liked and trusted. She held Moses face close to hers and looked him straight in the eyes and explained to him that soon she would be leaving him and when that happened he was to go and fetch Jack. Moses listened and understood every word she said.

Sarah knelt down onto the floor beside the chest, her shaky finger outlined the letters, S. M. which were barely visible, the decayed leathers straps came undone very easily. Hesitating for just a brief moment she reached for a parcel.

Unwrapping the yellowing linen she revealed an oil painting of a very handsome man. He had a mop of blonde hair falling over his laughing blue eyes. His green velvet jacket was open, showing a gold brocade waistcoat. In his hands he held a gold-ended riding crop. Sarah gave a sad smile when she saw the laughter spilling out from the man's eyes. Oh what a man he was, what sunshine and shadows they had enjoyed together.

The next package was a beautiful azure blue velvet dress, as bright and new as the day it was made,

Sarah laid this over the back of her chair and tried to recapture the days when she had worn this dress. Pulling out a small black leather box her clumsy fingers prised open the small gold catch. The light from the fire caught the dazzling blue sapphires and ice white diamonds of the necklace and earrings that nestled on a bed of cream raw silk, who would believe they had continued to sparkle all these years shut in the dark chest, locked inside their box.

Undoing the catch on the necklace she took her time and fastened it around her throat. The earrings were a little more difficult to put on, but eventually she managed it. Like an excited child she went through the chest finding an assortment of precious treasures, pressed flowers, monogrammed handkerchiefs, books, sketches of past friends and letters that had meant so much to her when she had received them. She handled the flowers and read through the letters reliving the emotions she had felt when she first acquired them.

One parcel remained in the bottom of the chest, the smile that she wore dissolved as her trembling hands unwrapped the crumbling brown paper. Painful memories returned to her heart and she thought that she would burst with the overwhelming ache. Her breath caught in her throat as she laid out the weightless contents of the parcel.

On the rug in front of her she placed two identical pairs of lace booties and matching christening robes each with their embroidered initials on them. She gathered up the robes and buried her face in them hoping to encounter something of the babies that had once worn them, they smelt only of the lavender seeds that she had sprinkled in the chest.

She strained her senses, listening carefully, she could barely hear the echoing laughter of Luke and Rosie somewhere far in the distance.

How had she ever coped with that tragedy and survived. It was only her faith and belief that had seen her through. Sarah knew that grief was the hardest emotion you would ever have to experience in this life, the void, the loss left behind at first seems too much to be able to cope with, each stage of grief seems to last forever and the tears never seem to stop tumbling.

Trying to carry on without your loved ones seems impossible but, each day you handle it, you talk about it over and over again trying to convince yourself what really happened. Tobias said that even though the physical shell is no longer with us, that person never really dies, they live on in our hearts and minds as precious memories, never to be forgotten. You keep them alive by remembering them. The human spirit is battered and bruised by grief. But keep the spark of love alive and you will come through. The pain ebbs away eventually and that leaves the mind clearer to remember more joyful times. Our loved ones are only a whisper away. It is though they are in another room quite near to us, but we cannot enter it, just yet. You sometimes experience hearing, seeing or even smelling them, you are constantly being reminded of them, perhaps hearing a particular tune they liked or seeing a favourite flower of theirs, these are the moments of comfort. We will all meet again that we can depend on.

The treasures were returned to the chest except the blue velvet dress and the jewellery. With the mirror propped up on the mantelpiece, Sarah tried to remember how she used to pile her hair up on top of her head when she would wear the blue velvet dress. Excitedly she dragged the hairbrush through her tangled mass, time and time again she pulled at the strands until they were free. Clumsily she pushed the granite curls into place and secured them with the rusty hair grips.

Looking in the mirror she was pleased with her appearance. The face that smiled back at her was a young face with raven black hair tumbling in curls. The sapphires in her ears and cascading down from her neck matched the azure blue of the dress that hung perfectly on her once shrunken frame. In the background a ghostly waltz played. With a feeling of complete contentment Sarah turned to face Sonja and Tobias.

'Look at me Tobias, Doesn't it take you back. I'm my old self, listen, can't you hear that beautiful music?'

Cheerfully Sarah bent to caress Moses, she held his face against hers and whispered. 'Go now my boy, its time, go and find Jack.'

Moses gave her a final knowing look, he licked her hand with all the love he felt for his kind mistress, and left the cottage.

The paper and pencil on the bookcase floated into Sarah's hands. She was ready to complete the final chapters of her story. This was her last revisiting she knew she would not be returning to this world.

The wind chimes gently rang and the crystal ball filled with a purple mist which radiated out into the cottage. A handsome young man with blonde hair silently waited in the shadows for Sarah.

Young Jack George was quite surprised to see Sarah's dog Moses sitting on his doorstep so early in the morning.

'Hello Moses, whatever are you doing here?' He

reached down and tussled the fur on the dog's head.

Moses was agitated and could not keep still, he walked to the gate and then stopped and looked back at Jack, he waited just for a moment and then came back to stand in front of the young man. Jack knelt beside the dog, he noticed that his tail hung low between his legs.

'What's the matter boy are you trying to tell me something?'

CHAPTER SEVEN

The land of Merlin of fantasy and dreams
of round tables and kings and maypoles and queens.

Legend has it that long ago the devil was flying over Cornwall carrying a large boulder to block the entrance to hell. Archangel Michael challenged the devil, and a furious battle raged between the two. The boulder was dropped and where it landed became Hells stone and Archangel Michael became its patron saint of the village.

To celebrate the victory, every May the villagers hold celebrations called the fuerry dance. This is a time of thanksgiving for St. Michael and to herald the return of the life giving sun that gives fertility to man, beast and the earth.

And it was such a day that the Pendarvis family had decided to take a day off from the Mill Farm and join in the festivities.

Gwyneth polished the face of little Mary with spittle on a rag, leaving the child's cheeks red and shiny. The five year old struggled to get away from her mother's rough treatment. Sarah stood in the bedroom anxiously tugging on her new sunshine yellow dress hoping that she had not grown any more since she had finished making it. She was rather pleased with her work on the dress, it had not been an easy task, as she had barely enough material to make herself one, let alone squeeze one out for little Mary. Night after night she had sat straining her eyes, with only the light of a candle to guide her needle but she had been exceptionally pleased with the results of her hard work and now today they both were going to wear their new dresses.

Sarah tugged the dress over her head, the bodice of the dress only just managed to fit over her youthful frame. She felt slightly embarrassed and awkward about the shape her body was changing to. The fabric stretched tightly across her small protruding breasts, she should not be embarrassed, especially after living six years with this family, who had little or no pride when it came to their bodies. She should not have worried. Sarah's feelings were remnants of her puritan childhood where it was a sin to look at your body and to touch it was a greater wickedness.

Looking into the broken mirror that was propped up against the wall she was rather pleased with her reflection. She secured the dress with a white sash and pinned a coronet of fresh May blossom and Sycamore into her hair. Now she was ready to join Gwen, Janet and little Mary for their day at the Fayre.

The May sunlight shone brightly out of a crystalline blue sky as the family group walked down the lane from the farm towards the village green. To each side of them wild flowers lined the hedgerows and ditches. As they approached the village green they could hear the happy laughter from the revellers, dancers were twirling and plaiting coloured ribbons around a white hawthorn pole. By ducking in and out of the ribbons, they formed a traditional pattern around the tall pole. A group of musicians played an assortment of musical instruments. Daniel the children's father tapped his foot in time with the fast music that he belted out on his fiddle. Peter his eldest son put down his bohrain when he saw Sarah and his young sisters approaching. He handed the goat skin drum to Sarah, very confidentially she replaced Peter in the band. After a couple of very popular songs the dancers finished their display and the musicians disbanded and went to find refreshments. Daniel and Sarah joined Gwen and the children. Around the edge of the green, traders had set up stalls to sell their wares, every kind of craft could be found.

Sarah beckoned with her hands to Janet to join her to have their hair braided and plaited with fine ribbons. Janet was only ten and now totally deaf, Sarah had taught her a way to communicate with her hands so they could understand each other.

When Sarah had first arrived at the Mill Farm she was told that Janet was touched in the mind like she was. It did not take Sarah very long to realise that Janet's problem was that she could not hear, so she could not speak correctly only in an unintelligible language.

Delighted with their hair Sarah and Janet pushed their way through the crowd to find the rest of the family. They bumped into Peter who was making his way to the Pendragon Arms which was the inn on the other side of the green. He was certain that was where they would find his father and most probably his mother as well. Peter was absolutely right Daniel was standing sharing a light hearted conversation with the rest of the musicians. As he saw his eldest son approach he shouted an order to the flustered landlord, to bring his son a pint of 'The Old Local' eventually a pint of extremely cloudy cider was passed out through the door to Peter.

Gwen watched her son pour the strong liquid down his throat in one gulp, angrily she admonished Daniel for ordering the boy another pint.

'Don't worry women, he can hold his drink, just like his father,' and he thrust another tankard at his son. Who very readily accepted it.

Sarah collected up some stray tankards that had been left on the ground, she took them to the open window of the inn, the smell of stale ale and tobacco wafted out along with a noisy hubbub of conversations. Peter, eager to get away from his mother's too watchful eyes had joined a group of his friends inside the Inn and as Sarah peered into the dark interior he reached towards her to take the tankards, as he did his playful companions teased him about her. They nudged each other and laughed as they made outrageous comments about her availability, as they did about most of the young girls in the village. Hearing the lurid comments and hoping that Sarah had not, Peter turned on them abruptly and told them to be quiet. His seriousness seemed to have the opposite of the desired affect he had intended towards the group. Encouraged by the confidence the pints of 'Old Local' had given them, they continued to harry Peter.

'Hey, I wouldn't mind taking her up the Tor, look at her, just right for it isn't she. Well what do you say Peter? You gonna set me up with her then? After all we are friends.'

The group fell about in fits of inebriated laughter.

'What do you bet, he's keeping her for himself. Or he's already had her, come on tell us,' spluttered

Benjamin Fryer. 'What was she like then?'

Peter felt his temper rising as the group continued with their lurid suggestions. His face coloured, and of course this did not go unnoticed.

'Look at his face, we are right, ain't we?'

Peter, unable to tolerate any more of his friend's rotten behaviour and accusations, cast his eyes downwards, fearing they would read his mind and uncover the truth. 'She ain't my real sister really, she's just living with us,' he shouted before roughly pushing his way past the jeering group and storming out of the Inn.

Gwen noticed her eldest son leave and watched him slouch off into the crowds with his head down and his hands deep in his pockets. He's in a mood again, she thought. These days he always seemed so sullen and angry, she had tried to talk to him about his mood but that only seemed to aggravate him further. When she tried to discuss her eldest son's behaviour with Daniel, he told her that she should not keep badgering him and leave him alone or else, he would probably leave the farm and then where would they be without his help.

A shout went up for the musicians to return to the green. The procession was about to start. Daniel's eyes searched the crowds for Peter but he was nowhere to be seen so Daniel asked Sarah to play in his eldest son's place. She felt very pleased to be included in the band to lead the snake of happy folk through the village. Daniel nodded his head for Sarah to start the procession. She drummed a continual slow low note, boom, boom, boom, everyone gathered behind the singers and musicians. Slowly they rocked from side to side in rhythm to the slow drum and then the singers began the song and the march started.

We are welcoming in the summer 'o,
The terror time has gone 'o,
We gather here today to sing 'o,
A thanksgiving song 'o,

Sarah drummed the monotones tune again,

Boom...boom...boom...boom...
It's a time of warmth and fertility to the earth
The suns a wakening it's a time of rebirth,
Boom...boom...boom...boom...
We herald the coming of May 'o,
We herald the coming of May.

Marching slowly the colourful parade set off. Men, women, children and even babies were wearing wonderful handmade animal masks and fancy dress created throughout the year just for this occasion. Young virgin girls carried May flowers and sycamore hoping to attract a husband. Spinsters of the parish concealed talisman beneath their costumes in desperate anticipation of sharing their cold lonely beds. The old and sick gathered at the back of the procession, ready to receive the new seasons fertile energy into their tired and weary bodies. Raggety puppet men dressed in costumes made of strips of coloured rags danced in and out of the marchers dabbing shoulders at random with their magical Ash wands. Squeals of delight and shrieks of laughter could be heard above the music as the young men from the village sought out their intended partners from the masquerading crowd. Hoping that underneath the masks they had chosen the right girl. Weaving their way through the village the cavalcade visited local farms. The farmer's wives brought out their corn dollies and pinned them to their front doors so they could be blessed by the May sunshine. The corn dollies had been made from the stalks that were left uncut at the edge of the fields after last autumn's harvest, the spirit of the corn was driven into the remaining stalks as the field was reaped. All winter the corn dollies had been kept indoors to keep the spirit happy and warm, but now the spirit would be ploughed back into the earth to ensure a good yield.

As the powerful sun grew tired of its high position above the village and started to descend behind the hills, the marchers made their way back to the village green. Finishing touches were being made to the gigantic sacrificial fire that had been built in the middle of the green, in honour of the sun. Village wives had brought their own offerings to throw on the fire. The local butcher was roasting an ox that had been carefully fattened throughout the winter for today's sacrificial slaughter, there would be enough for everyone to have a slice of the sizzling beef which would be wrapped between slices of rough brown bread.

A great cheer rose up from the excited crowd, as the oldest inhabitant of the village ignited the fire. As the flames took hold of the dry wood it sent a shower of red sparks high into the air. Loaves of plaited bread were tossed onto the fire and swiftly devoured by the flames. Daniel threw a modest bag of flour, his contribution from Mill Farm, whilst Gwen, Janet and Mary threw greenery and flowers collected from the fields. Juniper logs were added to the fire in the conviction that the smoke from the logs would drive away demons and boughs of birch trees which were decorated with red and white rags were pitched onto the flames to safeguard against witches.

Sarah had contemplated at great length about what she would give to the spirit of the fire, in the end she had decided she wanted to give love, love of the sun the earth and every miraculous creation that dwelled on it. She had been out to the woods and collected bunches of fresh Vervain, the magical love plant, this she had woven with freshly cut white hawthorn into a small wreath. She stood before the flames and visualised, love. Love should be warm and caring, compassion for everyone good or bad, it should mean forgiving those who can't help but cause pain and suffering to others. Most of all she wished that, if you cannot help anyone, do not hurt them unless it is to stop them from committing an injustice to another living being.

Sarah saw love as a beautiful pink bubble that you could step into and feel its warmth and bathe in the emotion of happiness.

Bill Wilcox propped himself against a cart and observed the celebrations around the blaze, he was still a little intoxicated, even though he had spent a few hours sleeping his belly full of alcohol off. He had woken up huddled in a heap on the grass where he had been thrown by the angry landlord. He watched as the revellers joined hands in a large circle around the fire and danced. More and more people pushed their way in to join the circle and as it grew in size it became really noisy and boisterous with the gleeful screams of the single young girls who were pulling into the circle their intended beau's. Through the mass of jubilant faces Wilcox noticed that the small girl with the raven black hair was not attached to any particular male in the circle. He lurched forward unsteadily and stumbled awkwardly towards her. Sarah was caught up in the fun, and at first did not notice him push his way between herself and Janet, she only looked at him when she felt his tight grip on her hand, and looking up into the bloodshot eyes of the drunk she instantly felt sorry for him. He appeared to have one eye on the pot and the other up the chimney, and that led Sarah to think he was a little bit of a simpleton. She held on to his hand as the movement of the circle gained momentum, being unsteady on his feet the faster they danced the more he could not control his balance and suddenly he lurched backwards and toppled over still clutching Sarah's hand, she could not help but fall down with him. Poor thing she thought as she scrambled to her feet trying to pull the halfwit up. A great cheer went up as the dancing stopped. The boys and girls dispersed to sit in small groups around the warm embers of the fire. Janet thinking that Sarah had found a partner went off to find her mother and sister leaving Sarah with the boy.

Sarah did not feel she could just go off and leave the poor chap on his own, after all, he was a colour short of a rainbow and at this moment really did need her help. She crouched down beside him.

'Are you all right? Can I help you?' she inquired, genuinely concerned for his welfare. 'Are you with anyone, who brought you?' When he did not reply she asked more gently, 'What's your name?'

'B-Will,' he mumbled into the beautiful face that towered above him, 'B-Will Wilcox, take me home,' and he looked up into her face with the expression of a pathetic cross-eyed lost lamb.

'Where do you live? You tell me and I'll take you there, don't worry you'll be all right,' and she laid a caring hand on his shoulder.

'I'll...I'll show yer,' he said as he grasped both of Sarah's hands and she hauled him to his feet.

Bill Wilcox could not believe his good fortune, this girl was like butter in his hands. He'd often seen her with her brother at the market selling chickens. He looked at her firm young body taking in the gentle curves of her hips, his greedy eyes wandered up to take in the handfuls of perfect new breasts topped with firm nipples that protruded through the tightly stretched bodice of her sunshine yellow dress. He dribbled and licked his lips at the thought that she could be a virgin and he could have the honour of deflowering her and educating her in the delights of becoming a women. Just for one fleeting moment he thought it was a little unusual that this young girl seemed to be so attracted to him. Usually when he was overflowing with liquor he had a lot of trouble charming the women and come to think of it even when he wasn't drunk it still seemed a problem. Well everyone's fortune had to change sometimes and obviously this was his lucky night. Cleverly he played her game and explained stuttering, stupidly, that he lived just across the Wild Barrow field, and when he led her off in that direction she went quietly, like a lamb to the slaughter. His intention was to entice her away from the crowds insuring that they would not be interrupted or be within hearing distance of anyone. He knew from past experience that often these young girls led you on, they teased and encouraged you and when it came down to the business they cried off. Well that was not going to happen this time. Willingly she followed him over the style into the dark field, following the footpath she soothed him in a gentle voice. 'Come on, you'll be all right, we will soon have you home.' Like a small child she led him through the night, keeping a watchful eye out for sight of the lights of his home.

Following the footpath along the edge of the field they reached a part that was sheltered by tall overhanging trees. Bill pulled her sideways and tried to lead her through an opening in the hedge. His hand clenched around hers tightly, alarmed by the darkness and the strength of his grip Sarah tried to loosen her hand from his painful grasp.

'Just a moment, not so fast, I can't see where we are going, it's dark in here. What's the matter? Is this really the way to your house?' She tried to keep the panic from her voice, as Bill pulled her further into the dark copse. Her thoughts were interrupted by a warning voice inside her head, telling her to be very careful and that she could be in danger and she should get away from the boy as quickly as she could. Sarah was suddenly aware that she could no longer hear the music coming from the celebrations she could only just make out the distant glow from the bonfire in the night sky, they must have walked a very long way from the village. Fully alert she apprehensively looked about her trying to find her bearings, she could just make out in the darkness the steeple of the church silhouetted against the night sky.

'Are we going the right way, Bill?' she asked nervously. He did not answer.

'I think perhaps we should go back to the pathway,' again, he did not reply. She tried with all her might to pull away from his grasp. With a sudden lunge towards her he swept her off balance and pushed her down onto the ground. Winded by the sharp contact with the hard earth she gasped to speak, but before she could utter a cry for help Bill's face loomed above hers and his hungry lips covered her face with wet harsh kisses. She struggled and screamed, turning her face from one side to another trying to avoid contact with his sour lips, a powerful arm pushed its way under her chin and locked her head so she could not move. Over and over again he forced his tongue in her mouth until she thought she would choke from the taste of his foul breath. Her small frame did not stand a chance against this powerful boy, who had only one intention on his mind. Her small hands beat wildly against his back and head, she grabbed handfuls of his hair and tried to lift his face away from hers, but to no avail, he enjoyed the fight she was putting up, it made him feel powerful to inflict such fear in her. In a swift movement he covered her body with his, the weight pinned her down. His rough hands quickly ripped the yellow fabric of the tight bodice of her dress and in seconds he had found her small breasts, he pummelled at them groaning with pleasure as he fondled the young flesh. Expertly in one movement he pulled the fragments of her dress up to her waist exposing her underwear as she struggled frantically to free herself, he tore the remaining clothes from her shaking body. But just when he thought he had dominated her and was ready to give vent to the excited swelling in his groin his hand momentarily lost its grip on Sarah's mouth and neck. Seizing the opportunity Sarah wrenched her head to one side and screamed for all she was worth. Interrupted and angered by the ear splitting sound she had made he raised his fist and brought it down on the side of her head, she sank into oblivion from the sharp blow. Confident that he could now continue without her protest he rolled onto one side so he could undo the buttons on his trousers. It was then that he heard the low growling sound, at first he was not sure what creature had made it or the direction it came from. He cautiously glanced around him, the low moaning growl seemed to vibrate through his whole body, now there was no question to where the horrific snarling came from. Instantly he pushed himself off of Sarah and sank back on his heels, his trousers which were around his knees stopped him from being able to get away from the gruesome angry half human creature that crouched before him. Scrambling to his feet he tried tugging up his trousers, he turned to run but stumbled in blind panic. The whole copse was rocked by the inhuman shriek that came from Sarah's mouth. Sarah's eyelids flicked open to reveal yellow eyes with great coal black centres. The snarling grew menacingly louder and louder, frozen in terror the petrified man found he could not move, he was rooted to the spot. On all fours she crawled slowly towards him and as she moved he thought her appearance started to change. Her body was becoming large and feline like. He could have sworn that black and orange hairs sprouted from her skin and covered her body and that her face was distorted, wide with an ugly crushing jaw. The lips of the half-human, half animal curled back to reveal pure white glistening teeth. The snarling became a shrill shriek and penetrated the eardrums of the now terrified victim. He clapped his hands over his ears to shut out the inhuman sound.

The last vision he saw was the powerful muscles of the animal flex as it prepared itself to pounce. Razor sharp nails sliced and slashed and in one quick movement ripped his face into bloody shreds. He turned away from the horror and tried to shield his eyes from the sight before him. The quick paws caught him as he turned away, they peeled clothing and skin from his shoulders, he felt his own warm blood trickle down his back and soak into his trousers. The angry animal slowly stalked around him in a circle taunting him, never taking its bright eyes from his blood stained face. And after what seemed hours the wild creature slunk off into the darkness of the night.

The demented boy reached for a scrap of Sarah's yellow dress to staunch the bleeding wounds on his face, with a surge of fear he jumped to his feet and staggered towards the church hoping that somebody would be inside to help him. Eventually he reached the church, he hammered on the old oak door, it was locked, and at that moment he was to remember why it had been secured, the reason being, a few weeks before he had strolled into the open church and helped himself to the brass candlesticks and altar cross and since the robbery the church door had been locked day and night. Exhausted and in terrible pain he shrank away from the door, panic welled up inside him as he sensed that the creature was still around. He could feel Sarah's eyes watching him and penetrating his brain intruding into his head. Through blood filled eyes he nervously scanned the graveyard. A strangled sob gurgled in his throat as he caught sight of Sarah, she was standing upright now her torn clothes hardly covering her small body she was staring at him from the edge of the churchyard. She raised her arm and forked two fingers at him, the curse reached him before he reached the shelter of a large gravestone. He felt the curse enter his body, sinking to his knees he gripped his hands together and prayed for all he was worth. He asked God to save him from the wild girl and to forgive him for robbing the church. His god happened to be out at that moment and had nailed a note to the

gates of his heaven. It read: Sorry, not here at the moment. Saints, you know where to find me.
Sinners, you have to guess where I am.

CHAPTER EIGHT

She eyed her victim by the barred church doors
Pleasurably she purred as she licked his cruel taste from her claws.
Lovingly she groomed his flavour from her skin
Pleased that the sinner's God wasn't in.

As you approached Mill Farm from the narrow rough lane that wound its way up from the village, you would have been greeted by the sight of the tall post wind mill. The wooden sweeps loomed high over the farm buildings that were nestled between the hills, the sails of the mill turned to catch the constant breeze that blew between the Tors. The tall building shadowed the hotch potch of barns, stables, sheds and chicken houses that lay beneath it. A courtyard was home to a variety of fowls and a few wayward pigs that rooted vigorously between the cracks in the flagstones. From the courtyard you could mistakenly have thought that the low single storied stone building was another stable but in fact it was the living accommodation for the hardworking Pendarvis family.
The animals that inhabited the farm had much more spacious living conditions than the humans, the reason being that the good health and welfare of the creatures represented money, a meagre income that was barely enough to keep everything going through the long harsh winters.

Sarah stretched stiffly and uncurled her feet from underneath her, she had not gone to bed last night but dozed fitfully in the only comfy armchair in the house. Pulling her shawl around her trembling shoulders she crouched down on the hearth in front of the flame-less grey cinders. As she stabbed the heap of dust with the iron poker she noticed the yellow fragments of scorched fabric, a sobering reminder of the events of previous evening. She totally blamed herself, how could she have been so stupid to step into it all so easily and willingly. Gwen was always telling her she should not be so trusting that human nature was not as easy to understand as Sarah thought it was. Sarah was always making excuses for people who were cruel or committed terrible crimes, believing that there was a reasonable amount of good in everyone, it was just that we did not always notice it.

The bruise on the side of her temple made her head and jaw ache. She remembered Bill Wilcox attacking her but had no recollection of events after his fist had smashed into her face. Vaguely she recalled arriving home and taking off the fragments of her ruined dress and throwing it on the glowing ashes of the fire and then washing herself with cold water in the trough in the courtyard. Did she dream it or did she remember Peter holding towels and her night dress ready to cover her naked body. She wondered if any of the family other than Peter knew about her embarrassing arrival home. She felt really guilty and thought that somehow she must have encouraged the boy, perhaps she was to blame for his lack of control. By her own naivety she must have inadvertently egged him on and had completely misunderstood his intentions and when she suddenly started to object he must have been so frustrated and angry that he could not fulfil his urgent needs that he had lashed out at her. So in her mind she forgave him and totally took the blame. Her change of behaviour into a wild creature was completely wiped from her mind.

Gwen emerged from the communal bedroom, scratching her red skin that prickled from the course blankets she had slept under. She was surprised to see Sarah up and about so early. Bleary eyed she reached for the kettle and dipped it into the bucket of fresh water on the draining board. Scuffing her bare feet across the rough cold stone floor she noisily hung the kettle on the hook above the fire.

'Give it a rake Sarah and see if you can wake it up. I didn't expect you up so early, considering you were out so late. It was a good day, wasn't it?'

Sarah did not reply. Shuffling back across the room Gwen dipped last night's dirty mugs into a bowl of cloudy cold water, shaking the drips from them she set them down amongst the clutter on the long kitchen table.

'Did you have a good time? I brought Janet and Mary back after the bonfire party finished, Mary was asleep on her feet I had to carry her back on my own. Daniel did his usual and I presume he slept it off in the mill last night, I don't care as long as he didn't come in here with all his drunken courage and wind.' Gwen droned on and on.

'No wonder we never have enough money to go around what with my husband and son supporting the Pendragon Arms at every opportunity, they'll be the death of me, you wait and see.'

She forgot that Daniel and Peter worked on the farm every day of the week, month, and year from dawn till dusk and often when the cattle and sheep were giving birth, it could be twenty four hours before they crawled into bed.

Sarah had stopped listening to Gwen's conversation, she had heard the same repetitive words almost every morning since she had arrived at the Mill farm. You would think that Gwen ran the whole farm single-handed.

This morning Sarah had her own set of problems filling her thoughts. The most important being, how far did Bill Wilcox go after she was rendered unconscious. Most of her body felt battered and bruised but instinctively she was almost certain that she had not been raped, well at least not her body. Her mind had definitely been violated but those wounds you could not see and to heal them would take time not medicine.

She was quite unaware that the same worries were going through Peter's mind. When he had returned to the farm last night he found that Sarah was not at home, after waiting a while he grew concerned as it was out of character for her to stay out on her own. He returned to the aftermath of the days celebrations. Coming across a rabble of his friends he asked if any of them had seen Sarah. Rob assured him Sarah was most probably tucked up with the man he had seen holding her hand as she crossed the stile, he was the bloke from over the Wild Barrow fields. Alarm bells had rung in his head as he raced along the dark footpath. As he neared the break in the hedge that led to the copse at the back of the church-yard he had stood stock still, an inhuman cry penetrated his ears and touched his very soul. Shaking with fear that something dreadful was about to emerge from the churchyard he had crouched down behind a tree.

From the field of gravestones he heard a human cry of pain and shouting for help. With all the courage he could muster he nervously edged his way towards the sobbing sound, he was nervous of what he was going to stumble on. Before he could make out which direction the cries had come from he saw Sarah, crouched on all fours silently staring at the church doors. He was so distracted by her appearance that he never noticed the traumatised man lying in a heap of blood soaked clothes or hear the muffled sobs coming from his ghastly disfigured mouth. It was all like a nightmare to Peter, he had gently stood her on her feet and was so upset when he saw the dishevelled state of the remains of her clothing.

Ever since the first time he had set eyes on her that day seven years ago when she had stepped bewildered off her father's coach, she had touched a special part of his heart which from that day he had reserved only for Sarah. Knowing that one day they would share their life together, not as brother and sister but as husband and wife. Always he had acted like a big kind brother, he had helped her overcome the sadness of being rejected by her parents, he had always tried to understand her strange imaginary friend, never mocking her as the rest of the family did. And as she grew he had developed an obsessive passion for her, he had observed her silently waiting for the right moment to reveal his true intentions. He felt sure his mother had already guessed about his feelings towards Sarah. He worshipped every inch of her and the thought of any man soiling her young body made his stomach churn into a tight ball, and he knew that he would willingly kill anyone, whoever laid a hand on her. Little did he realise that he would not need to lift a finger in revenge on Sarah's behalf, because, by the church doors a man had already received a severe punishment for trying to defile her body. A chastisement he would remember every time he looked into the mirror or perhaps whenever he considered repeating the crime.

Peter had taken off his coat and wrapped it around Sarah's shoulders covering her exposed breasts. She did not utter a word as her brother scooped her up into his strong safe arms and carried her home.

When they had reached the courtyard at the farm she spoke her first words since he had found her.

'I want to wash please fetch me some soap.'

She had removed the remains of her new frock and all her other clothes. Peter returned with soap, towels, her nightdress and a warm shawl. He lowered his eyes as he passed them to her it was the first time he had seen her naked, even though the rest of the family had always stripped off in front of each other Sarah had always changed her clothes or bathed in private. She splashed the cold water from the trough all over her body and rubbed the large bar of yellow soap over every inch of her bruised skin. Time and time again she scrubbed herself from top to toe, trying to wash away the terrible memories that were vivid in her mind. She dipped her long hair into the cold water and soothed the bruise on the side of her face. Peter could not stand watching her rub herself raw, gently he removed the soap from her hands and wrapped the towels around her. He guided her indoors where he sat her down in front of the fire and rubbed her wet hair until it shone in the firelight. He slipped her nightdress over her head and covered her shoulders with the shawl, like a small frightened animal her eyes stared into the flames of the fire, she hunched forward holding the shawl closely around her. He tried to question her as to who had attacked her, but to no avail.

'Go away, please Peter. Leave me, I'm all right. Please.'

He did not know what else he could do to help. All he really wanted to do was to hold her in his arms and tell her that he loved her and make her tell him who had done such a thing. He wanted to say he would protect her from such a thing ever happening again and would gladly lay his life down for her. But he did not say any of those thoughts out loud instead, he quietly left Sarah on her own and spent a troubled sleepless night in bed.

When Janet and little Mary emerged from the bedroom Sarah then went in to get dressed. She pulled on her grey dress, the only one she now had, with a strip of braid she tied her hair back from her face, and looking into the mirror she noticed the ugly bruise. Tracing the injury with her fingertips she was filled with sad anger towards Wilcox. Ripping the tie from her hair and letting the locks tumble untidily around her face she cursed the wretched man who had tricked her. On the shelf above hers and Janet's bed she reached for a small stone bottle, she dabbed the bruise gently with Witch Hazel, the cool liquor penetrated the injury instantly soothing the discoloured skin. Holding her hands to her face she felt the energy from them calm her aching head.

Daniel frowned when the sunlight streamed in through the window of the mill and burst into his fragile brain, he always regretted the night before, the morning after. Washing out his coated mouth with a swill of cider from the hidden stone jar, he

spat onto the dusty floor. Trying not to make any sudden movement that would send the queasy nausea welling up into his mouth, he set the cogs in motion to start the millstone turning. Gwen tutted when she heard the mill's sails groaning as they caught the May morning's breeze, this meant that Daniel had only just started the mornings grinding and everyone's breakfast would be late. He had always insisted that no one sat down for breakfast until he was there as head of the table as hopefully respected head of the household. This latter conclusion on his part was a little doubtful. Gwen seemed more and more to control everyone's movements including his, well today he was certainly determined to disrupt the happy household, he would make her wait to dish up breakfast, he was fed up with her constant nagging,
'Don't drink so much, Daniel, don't spend so much, Daniel, get up Daniel, go to bed, Daniel.' She was getting like his mother not his wife. His stomach grumbled and he realised he was actually hungry, 'Damn,' he cussed loudly, perhaps he would have his protest another day when his guts were not so demanding.

Thick slices of bacon laid in rows on the black smoking griddle, Gwen had hacked them from the dismembered swine's carcass that floated in the barrel of salt in the corner of the kitchen. Not one piece of the poor home slaughtered pig would be wasted, the head would be boiled and the slush would be poured into moulds to make brawn. The trotters would be roasted with an onion and noisily sucked clean of fat and meat by the men in the family, bowls of pork dripping would be stored in the cold larder the solid fat would seal the blood, juices and jelly at the bottom, salty and savoury it would be spread sparingly on great hunks of rough bread, usually given to little Mary to grease her constant dry cough.

Daniel and Peter met up outside the house.

'Where's your good for nothing brother got himself to this morning? He was supposed to be helping me in the mill.'

'Well he's not with me, he's more trouble than his worth. I expect he has gone off down that bloody preacher's place again. Ma says he's not cut out for the hard work we give him.'

'Mamby pamby bloody girl if you ask me,' retorted the boy's father.

Both men entered the kitchen together, Janet and Mary were already sitting at the table, Sarah was still in the bedroom dreading facing the family. Peter put his head around the door, she was sitting with her crystal ball in her hands as she often did.

'Grubs up, are you coming out to eat?'

Replacing the ball in its box she reluctantly left the bedroom. The atmosphere at breakfast was very strained, Gwen was still cross with Daniel and tried not to send a word his way, but sent messages to him through Peter.

'Ask your father if he wants one rasher or two. Tell your father we need more logs for the fire,' she went on and on.

Daniel was far too hung over to start an argument with his wife, he hunched his shoulders over his food and shovelled it into his mouth praying his stomach would accept the greasy nourishment without complaint.

'Have you seen Matthew this morning Ma?' inquired Peter.

'He was up early and has gone off to help in the preacher's conservatory,' answered Gwen.

'He should bloody well be here helping his family, not playing about with his lordships fancy flowers, that's women's work,' barked Daniel.

'You leave him alone, he's not strong enough for the work you give him, he tells me that the preachers wife is very fond of him and wishes he was her son,' said Gwen proudly. It was good to think that she had something that the preacher's wife envied.

'I would not be surprised if he became a blessed bible basher himself,' said Daniel.

'Then he could really shelter himself from the world behind a frock, just like a woman. You can imagine him all dressed up in their queer clothes, hymning and praying, reading from the bible and telling us all how bad we are and how good he is.'

Everyone at the table laughed, taking advantage of the mellowing moods in the kitchen Peter asked Sarah if she was all right and had she recovered from the night before. Sarah just nodded her head hoping that he would not continue the conversation. Gwen's eyes shot to her son face.

'Why shouldn't Sarah be all right, what happened last night?'

Peter hesitated when he saw Sarah's face become ashen.

'Oh nothing,' he said quietly.

'Don't, nothing me my boy, I know when you children are trying to hide something.'

Sarah sat toying with the food on her plate, praying that Peter would not tell his mother about how he had found her with her clothes ripped. But her prayers were not answered. Peter started to describe in detail how he had found Sarah and brought her home. All eyes looked at Sarah.

'And what's the story then, my girl,' demanded

Gwen, suspicious of the circumstances that Peter had described he found her in.

'Who were you with in the churchyard at that time of night, and what had you been up too to get your new dress so ripped? Come on I want an explanation, we've been all through this before with Molly and her carryings on with the boys, I'm not going through it again with you.'

There did not seem any point in trying to justify herself, she did not for one minute think Gwen would actually believe her story. Especially the part where she had thought Bill Wilcox was a simpleton and that she had quite willingly gone off with him across the fields to the churchyard and when he got too familiar with her she cried off and he had lost his temper with her. In the grim light of day it did seem a pathetic story and one that she was sure most girls had told at one time or another to cover up their sexual cavorting. Peter was itching to know the full story and was determined not to let the questioning rest. He needed to know the truth, who had she been with and exactly what had taken place.

Gwen did not wait for an answer from Sarah but rambled on irregardless as to whether she was right or wrong.

'You just be careful young lady we don't want any more mouths to feed in this house, you just remember that when you're mucking about with the lads there is always a price to pay and don't I know it, that's how our twins Molly and Peter came about, weren't it Daniel?' He grunted in reply completely disinterested with his wife's babbling.

'Don't go on Ma, I'm sure Sarah ain't been up to anything like that, have you, Sarah?' All Peter wanted to hear Sarah say was, no, she hadn't given herself to any man and she was still pure. Sarah told Peter and his mother exactly what they wanted to hear.

'Please don't worry Gwen I haven't done anything I should not have, I helped a drunk home last night and he got a little silly, that's all, honestly. I managed to cope with him. Peter has made it all sound worse than it really was.'

Gwen really did not take too much notice of Sarah's explanation, all she was really bothered about was that the girl did not get herself pregnant as it would most probably mean something else for her to look after and feed.

Sarah needed a diversion from the current conversation and luckily enough it came. Tobias who was roaming the room aimlessly appearing and disappearing started to sing. Sarah started to laugh when she heard his dreadful singing voice.

'Don't you be a worry guts, poor old Gwen, Sarah's not getting eyes for the gentlemen.'

'That's enough of your awful voice,' said Sarah still grinning.

Tobias stopped his humorous ditty and took up the empty seat opposite Sarah. His strong hands pretended to hold a knife and fork, he began to eat an imaginary plate of food and when he finished he wiped his mouth on the back of his hand.

'Wonderful meal,' he shouted. 'The best I've tasted for many a year.'

'What are you laughing at?' asked Peter looking at Sarah's smiling face.

'Nothing you would understand.'

'Something made you laugh, was it about last night?' he said with an expression of anger on his face.

'No Peter it was nothing to do with last night now

let it rest.'

'Was it about me then?' he added quickly.

'Oh for goodness sake, just leave me alone will you, you're really starting to annoy me with all your silly questions.'

Peter really was getting on her nerves. She rose from the table collecting the dishes as she went. Peter's chair scraped the floor as he instantly jumped up and rushed to join her at the sink. He whispered urgently in her ear, 'We must talk Sarah, I've got to know who it was you were with and what went on.'

'It's none of your business Peter, now go away.'

He grabbed her arm quite roughly, startled by his behaviour she dropped the stone jug she was carrying sending it crashing to the hard floor.

'What are you two up to over there? Just look at what you have done Sarah, try not to be so clumsy. Peter isn't it time you were back out with your cows? Go on with you, out.' And Gwen shooed him out of the door with her teacloth.

As Peter went out through the door young Matthew rushed past him coming in. He seemed to be very excited about something and hardly caught his breath between words.

'Calm down Matthew, I can't understand a word you're saying when you talk so quickly,' said his mother.

Peter hearing some of his younger brother's ramblings stepped back inside the kitchen to listen.

'What's that about the churchyard, was it last night? Come on Matthew sit down, take a breath and tell us the whole story.' Peter joined Gwen and Sarah at the table.

In due course the story became clear. The preacher accompanied by his wife and Matthew had arrived to open up the church for the early morning service. When they were walking along the cobble path towards the church they heard a terrible moaning sound coming from behind a gravestone. At first the preacher had tried to ignore the awful noise saying that it was possibly a drunk sleeping off last night's celebrations, but then his wife went to investigate and found a terribly injured man, barely alive. He was crawling along the ground towards the church, begging for mercy, the preacher's wife had screamed and almost fainted when she saw the face of the man all bloody and shredded, he was a terribly frightening sight.

At this point Matthew went into excited grisly detail that made his mother wince with horror. Pleased with the effect his story was having on his Mother, the boy then proceeded to pull an ugly torturous face and groaned.

'Get on with it Matthew,' demanded Peter.

'Well, then the preacher made me run as fast as I could to fetch the constable from the village. It was really horrible, all the man kept saying over and over again was that he had been attacked by a wild creature, and then he started moaning and crying again. I ran at top speed and the officer had a job to keep up with me on the way back. They couldn't get head nor tail out of the chap, they thought that his mind had gone and the shock of the attack had most probably turned him into an absolute idiot. And do you know what else the officer said?' The group listening shook their heads. 'He said that it was not the first attack by wild creatures in the area. He reckoned the animal had escaped from a travelling menagerie that had toured the area a while ago. He's going to get a group of men together with guns and they are going to search the woods for it and I'm going with them.'

'Oh no you're not young man, you're going to stay here on the farm if there's a wild animal about, you let the constable find it, you're only a boy,' said Gwen.

'Did the constable mention the other attack by the creature?' inquired Peter.

Matthew thought for a little while then added,

'Yes, the first attack was when a woman from St. Ruthen reported that her child had been kidnapped by gypsies. The body of the child was found about a month later buried in a shallow grave in woodland. The child's mother lived in a hovel with man who gave himself the name of Spencer, he was a travelling tinker, buying and selling anything he could get his dishonest hands on.'

At this point Gwen broke in, 'I remember that story it was so sad, the heartbroken mother was the only person at the baby's funeral. It had to be held in unconsecrated ground outside the churchyard wall, because they would not allow a burial of an unchristened soul inside the church property. Something odd happened to the tinker whilst the poor woman was at the burial.'

Matthew continued the conversation. 'Yes it did, while she was away at the graveside, Spencer the tinker did not go to the child's funeral but went out hunting in the woods instead, they say while he was out he was attacked by a strange wild animal but he could never identify what it was. The badly injured man was found petrified and delirious from his terrible injuries. In between bouts of unconsciousness he begged for forgiveness. He admitted to the doctor who was summoned to stitch his wounds that the wild creature had screeched at him in a human voice saying that this was his punishment for torturing and killing the small child and then burying his body in the woods. Hence he was arrested for the baby's murder.'

Matthew was absolutely breathless when he finished his explanation of the morning's events at the church and the episode of the tinkers attack. Peter said he also had heard strange animal noises in the churchyard last night when he went to find Sarah, he added that they were lucky that the animal did not attack them, it must have happened after they had returned home. Sarah wisely remained silent.

CHAPTER NINE

The magic of the world is there for all to see
And it does not cost a penny it is absolutely free
There's the miracle of the glowing sun
That hangs in the sky each day
Which fills the plants and trees with life
With its warming solar rays

And at night if we look upward
As far as the eye can see
There is to behold another wondrous sight
A million diamonds shining bright
And the ageing man in the moon looking down
Sending his silvery light icing all around

Breathe the heady haze in the woodland
As the bluebells bow and ring
Marvel at the shy little primrose
That heralds the start of spring
Witness the winter cold brown field
Change with green arrows shooting up
And the bright red poppies sway
With their close companion the buttercup

The magic of the new born lambs
With springs upon their feet
And the golden rushing sea
That is the noisy field of wheat

And as we look through searching eyes
There is a magic all around
The miracles of nature
Are just waiting to be found

In the summer sunshine the farm became a busy bustling place. The once sodden fields had dried out and the new sown seeds had started to send their new green arrows heavenwards soaking up the sun's life giving energy. The cattle mooed contentedly as they lazily grazed on the lush new grass, they were happy to be outside in the countryside after being confined to their dark damp barns all winter. Most of the farm's livestock has given birth and increased the stock, much to Peter's satisfaction and Sarah's pleasure.

Sarah stood on the field gate surveying the landscape, she took deep breaths of the warm air which was scented with the aroma of new life. It never ceased to amaze Sarah how the barren lifeless countryside of the winter could rapidly change into colourful growth. And how small hard seeds the size of a pinhead miraculously contained the exact pattern to expand and grow into tall healthy plants, given the right amount of warmth, earth, light and moisture. It was the same with all living creatures, how incredible it was that they could reproduce miniature copies of themselves, growing seeds that formed miraculously while still inside the womb, living in water and only breathing air when they were born.

Today was the most perfect day for Sarah to collect herbs, the early morning dew on them would have dried by now. She collected her basket and silver scissors from the farm kitchen. Gwen teased her as she saw her with the small silver scissors.

'Do you really believe that you should only cut your herbs with silver, Sarah, surely it does not matter what you use?'

'Any other metal would taint the perfume and flavour Gwen, and if you pull the leaves off by hand you risk causing bruising and losing the precious oil they contain,' explained Sarah for the umpteenth time. 'And you should only sow the seeds on the night of the full moon.'

Peter watched Sarah make her way to the woodland at the back of the farm. He wished that he was not so busy and could have joined her with the herb gathering.

The woodland this morning seemed exceptionally noisy, all the birds wanted to sing and chatter at the same time. Sarah found a new patch of wild thyme and she stooped down to cut the small stems in her mind she was calculating how many varieties of wild herbs and aromatic flower petals she would need to complete the order for making her herb pillows, sachets and healing remedies. Originally, Nicola and Amy Paget the sisters that owned the small tea and cake shop had taken just a few of Sarah's natural wares to see if they would sell and of course they did sell extremely well. Sarah found that her crafts were starting to become profitable but most of all it was enjoyable. She would spend the fine days collecting all the ingredients and then in the evenings she would sit with Janet and they would sew the fabric and lace, making the cases and filling them with petals and leaves. On the wet days when she could not go out in the woods she would spend her time in the kitchen mixing and crushing roots and plants to make healing lotions and balms.

The Paget sisters were very kind to Sarah and took nothing from her for selling her goods, Sarah repaid them by going to visit their elderly father whenever his joints played up. She would take along her oils and soothe his aches and pains.

Something disturbed the birds that were feeding at Sarah's feet and they flew high up into the tree tops. Sarah stood up and looked around for the cause. Out of the corner of her eye she thought she saw something move behind the trunk of a great oak tree. She paused for a moment to see if she could sense Tobias's presence, nothing.

Moving towards the tree she was startled when her ghostly friend started to appear, but before she could talk to him he faded away only to reappear a few seconds later.

'Tobias, what do you think you are doing, you don't know whether you are coming or going do you?' she giggled.

He was still very faint and parts of him did not materialise at all. He was trying to talk to Sarah but his voice was so faint she could not hear what he was saying. It all seemed to amuse Sarah and she laughed at the hilarious comical, performance of her friend. Very soon though, the smile slid from her face. At first she felt as though somebody was holding a hand over her face and she could not breathe properly and as she gasped for air a figure shrouded from head to foot in a black cloak loomed up in front of her. The fleshless jaw of the figure opened and omitted a hell raising laugh that seemed to thunder through the whole of Sarah's body, it pierced her eardrums and rolled around inside her head until she thought that she would burst with the horror that had entered her body. Her brain reeled as she tried to concentrate on calling for Tobias to help her. But the evil presence of the Spirit of Death had drained Tobias's energy and he was powerless to help Sarah. The laughter started to subside but still the figure loomed above Sarah the smell of decaying flesh crept in to her mouth and nostrils and she swallowed hard to keep herself from retching.

'Have you guessed who I am yet, dear sweet little Sarah? Well, let me introduce myself because you are sure to come across me, often. I am all the things you dread in life, I can be disaster, cruelty, disillusion, unfairness, illness and not forgetting my ultimate gift, death. Now I am here to initiate you into the adult world, the real world where you are not sheltered by the comfortable blanket of childhood anymore. Already I believe you have had a taste of one my nasty experiences of being grown up, did that not slightly knock your beliefs of love and trust in the human race? Well if it did not, then life will, there will be many more of those lessons in store for you. To me, people like you are a challenge, all that love and light you portray is not real. Mark my words when you have gone through all my tests you will change every one does. You see your god and I are brothers, he lives up there in the holier than though bit, and well, you could say I live in the very warm cellar. We spend much of our time playing games with you humans. My followers are the evil in life they join me in hell to keep up my bad work. I guide them and teach them to satisfy my lust for seeing people suffer. But my brother works tirelessly to get the better of me. I am Evil and have no conscience so I do not care about anyone only myself. My brother thinks he is winning at the moment in the popularity stakes, but not for long, I can assure you. I poach on the young and new adults who are vulnerable and ready to follow the opposite of their mentors. Watch out for me, I am always ready to strike a bargain for your soul, remember I enjoy your darkest moments they satisfy my lust for all that is depraved.'

The Devil swept his arms around himself and dissolved laughing into the ground. For a moment the world seemed to stand still, the sun had hidden behind a dark cloud and all the birds stopped singing. Tobias started to gain power and materialised in front of Sarah. He was very concerned for her. She had knelt down on the grass, her eyes were so large and staring that he thought some lasting damage had been done. Quietly he tried to communicate with her, gently he soothed and reassured her that he was there, beside her. Eventually she wakened from the trauma that she had just experienced.

Sarah did not seem to notice or hear Tobias, she gathered up the spilled herbs and slowly put them into her basket. How could Tobias explain to her that she had been chosen by his brother, D.Evil to be a victim in his cruel game. He could only pray that her strength and courage within her would eventually tire him and he would lose interest and let her go...

Shaken by the odd incident Sarah slowly walked home, she could still hear the thunderous voice in her head and still see the grotesque face looming into hers. Tobias tried again to penetrate her mind.

'Sarah please try and listen to me, I can help you,' he waited patiently for her to answer, but she kept on walking.

'Do you remember Sarah, what your grandmother told you when she was dying? She told you that you had a gift and there would be a price to pay for it.

But most important of all she told you to have faith in yourself and that if fear knocked on your door and your faith answered it there would be nobody there. Think about it Sarah. Life is not always beautiful rainbows and sunshine, you cannot possibly have a rainbow without a rain storm. So you need to use your faith in yourself to tell you that you are all right as a person and all your intentions are for the greatest good of all. And you need to use your strength to stand by your beliefs and your courage to look the devil in the eye and handle the bad times. If we did not experience dark storms, how would we know when to recognise that the sun was shining?'

'Of course you're right again, Tobias but why when I was feeling so good about life, did something have to spoil it.'

'Each event we encounter, good or bad takes us forward in knowledge and we evolve towards being experienced in learning to live. It enables us to help others by what we have been through, we can understand people's pain and pleasure if we have sampled it ourselves at some time in our life. Is that clear to you? Don't dread the world Sarah, but live in it and fill yourself with courage and strength to conquer all the adventures good or bad that come your way.'

She felt herself fill with a newly found confidence.

'He thinks I'm a challenge does he, he has no idea what he has taken on, does he Tobias?'

Her ghostly friend drifted along beside her, happy that she had understood what he had told her.

CHAPTER TEN

Grace Trevallian pulled the bell rope beside the fireplace and waited patiently for a member of staff to answer her summons. Down below in the kitchen the group sipping tea glanced at the bell jangling on the wall, the tiresome sound intruded into their relaxation period.

'No peace for the wicked,' laughed Nellie Nap the good nature Cook.

Hodges the butler pushed the remains of a hot muffin into his mouth and wiped the butter from his chin. Buttoning up his jacket and straightening his tie he left the jovial group at the table and set off for his mistress's sitting room situated on the next floor of the house.

'I'm popping home tonight Nellie, have you any left overs for me Ma?' inquired Molly.

'If I said no, you would only go and help yourself, wouldn't you my girl?' She got up and went to gather some scraps from the servant's larder. 'I know exactly what you take from the main pantry Molly, and if Hodges catches you, you can say good-bye to your job and he won't give you a reference and then where will you be?'

Molly thought before she replied cheekily, 'Out of a job I suppose.'

'Aw, get along with you, here you are you can take these bits with you.' And Nellie passed her a brown bag. 'Mind you, your basket looks like it's quite full already.'

'Thanks Nellie. I'll see you later, goodbye,' Molly shouted hurrying to get outside the door before Hodges came back down from upstairs. Just as Molly went to close the door behind her Hodges appeared.

'Hang on minute, Molly, I want a word with you,' the girl stopped dead in her tracks, fearing the worst.

'Mrs Trevallian wants you to ask that young sister of yours, Sarah, to come to the house tomorrow afternoon. She wants her to write out a guest list and invitations in her fancy writing for the coming party. Now don't you forget.'

Sighing with relief that Hodges had not wanted to check the contents of her brimming basket Molly quickly closed the door and made off towards home.

'Sure I'll ask the lazy bitch, Mr Bloody Hodges,' she muttered to herself as she walked down the drive. 'That will be really hard work for the little lady to do.'

Molly worked quite hard at the big house, she had been living and working there since she was thirteen years old when Sarah had first moved to the farm and pushed her out. The cook Nellie had been like a second mother to her. Molly was allowed to have an evening off once a week to visit her family at Mill Farm. She always managed to take home a few bits and pieces that Nellie had given her from the pantry, also a few items that Nellie had not consented too. Her light fingers could not resist the temptation to stuff small things into her pinny pocket, items that she could sell cheaply to friends and neighbours who were always ready to purchase a bargain.

Back at the house Hodges thrust a large piece of paper towards Nellie.

'What's all this then?' She pulled her eye glasses out of her pocket to read the spiders scrawl on the paper.

'Well Nellie you're going to have your work cut out, we are going to have a party and here is your menu and all the instructions for the evening. The Master and Charles are on their way home and the Mrs is arranging a party to celebrate.' Nellie looked at the great list that Hodges had passed to her.

'I wish she would talk to me first about the menu, half of these things will be out of season and it will be really difficult to get my hands on them.'

'I'm sure my dear Nellie you will try your hardest to please Mrs Trevallian, we all put our trust in you and you never let us down.'

'I do believe you're buttering me up, Mr Hodges.'

'Would I...Would I, she also said that you can get extra help in for the night.'

'I shall need it for the week, tell her, not just the night.'

On her way home through the woodland path that lead down to Mill Farm Molly was still muttering to herself about Sarah, she really did jealously resent her spare sister and her lazy way of life, especially as she had always believed that her life changed for the worst, when the mad brat came to live at the farm. She had been pushed out to make room for her and she had worked her fingers to the bone ever since, whilst the little madam with her posh talk and special fancy writing had it very easy at the farm. If it was not for her own twin brother Peter, who idolised Sarah, she would have got rid of the bitch years ago. That easy way of life should have been hers, anyone could collect a few herbs and make stupid ointments and medicines and then sell them to unsuspecting victims.

Something amber flashed in front of Molly, as the bracken rustled Sarah appeared.

'Hello Molly. I thought I'd come to meet you, I know you don't like the woods at night.'

'How did you know I was coming?'

'I just knew.'

'Is that a bleeding flea ridden fox with you, I don't know why you associate with those vermin, they carry all sorts of diseases. If dad catches you he'll shoot it. By the way the mistress wants you up at the house tomorrow afternoon to write some invitations in your posh letters. Don't forget.' Hoitely Molly walked quickly ahead of Sarah.

Sarah and the fox stayed right behind Molly all the way down to the farm. Sarah was delighted to be asked to visit Grace Trevallian again. She had fallen in love with the glory and splendour of High Markham ever since she had first visited the house a few months ago when she had been asked to help Nellie at a garden party. She only had the job of passing around small sandwiches and appetisers but she really felt part of the occasion.

Grace Trevallian had taken an instant liking to Sarah who appeared to be a cut above the usual type of casual labour that came to the house.

This particular afternoon Grace was experiencing a terrible headache and the heat from the sun was making it far worse. She had tried to walk around the garden and be sociable by chatting with her guests but her throbbing head seemed to be overwhelming her. Just when she thought that she would have to give into the sickly pain and retire to her bed the young helper, Sarah came to stand beside her and whispered in her ear. She said that she knew she was suffering and that she could alleviate the pain in a few minutes if the mistress would care to take up the offer. Grace Trevallian was so desperate that she would have tried anything, Sarah was summoned to follow her into the house.

Once inside Sarah asked the lady to sit down on a comfortable chair and try to relax. She showed her how to breathe air in through her nose and out slowly through her mouth and when her breathing was more relaxed and calmer Sarah held one cool hand lightly on her forehead and the other on the back of her neck. Sarah quietly chatted to Grace explaining to her what she was doing. She told her about creating an image in her mind to visualise that up above their heads was a wonderful pink light and it radiated a beam that penetrated down through the top of Sarah's head filling her with its healing rays. The rays coursed through her body and she channelled them out through her hands into Grace's aching head, soothing and replacing the tension and pain with its calming healing rays maintaining balance to an unbalanced painful area. Amazingly enough after just a few minutes the woman's sickly headache had gone and the grateful lady returned to her garden party, excitedly explaining to some of her guests about the experience she had just had with the young serving girl. Some dismissed immediately what she was telling them but others listened carefully with great interest noting to get the address of the girl just in case they might need it. Even though in their circles it was more opulent to be seen to have the most expensive doctor in the areas carriage parked in your driveway.

Molly unpacked all sorts of special treats from her basket. Peter grabbed a piece of raised pie and took a mighty bite out of it, before his mother had a chance to store it in the larder, she slapped his hand.

'Leave things alone that would have made a meal for you and your father. Now go on, get out of the way I want to talk to Molly before she has to rush off back to work.'

The three women sat at the table, Molly talked at length about how dull life was at the house and how miserable the mistress had become. She hoped things would improve once the Master and his son returned to England.

A couple of times Sarah tried to join in the conversation about the Trevallian family, but Molly totally ignored Sarah and carried on talking to her mother. When Molly eventually paused to drink her tea Sarah piped in quickly.

'If ever they need any more staff at the house Molly, I wouldn't mind working there permanently.'

Molly laughed. 'You work at High Markham, don't be daft, what could you do apart from write fancy letters and muck about with your potions. They would not want the likes of you there all the time. You would never manage it Sarah, it's damn hard work, you are on your feet from morning till night, running up and down those stairs answering her ladyships bell, fetching her this and fetching her that. Besides she don't need no one else and if she did she wouldn't want anyone daft as you, she'd want someone normal,' and she added. 'Ain't that right, Ma?'

Gwen did not answer immediately, she hated it when Molly put her in an awkward position regarding Sarah's sanity. Peter saved his mother from answering.

'You don't want to work up there Sarah, you've got more than enough to do here, what with helping Ma and making your bits and pieces for the shop. You be content with doing the fancy invitations for her ladyship and leave it at that.'

'I could do all sorts of other things, Peter. I can work just as hard as Molly.'

Peter started to get a little annoyed with the thought that Sarah wanted to leave the farm. He certainly did not want her up at High Markham working where he could not see what she was getting up too.

'We like having you here, don't we Ma, she's a real help to have around isn't she?'

Gwen nodded her head in agreement with her son.

'But I could do all my jobs here a lot faster and still work at the house besides the money would come in handy.'

'That's true,' agreed Gwen.

Panicking slightly Peter added quickly, 'I think Molly is probably right,' and he hesitated before he went on. 'No one's going to employ you for long once they realise you have funny turns are they? It's hard enough for normal hard working people to get jobs, so there isn't much hope for the likes of you,' and he added quickly, 'or Janet, is there?'

'That's enough you two, don't be so cruel to the girls, they are not so bad that they can't lead nearly normal lives, Janet and Sarah do very well. So we won't hear any more about their illnesses.'

Molly could not hold her tongue especially when there was something bitter on the end of it. 'So they are going to lead normal lives are they, like go to work and get married and have children, go on Ma you've got those two for life you have. I can't see queues of eligible bachelor's knocking at the door asking, please Mrs, can we choose one of your idiots? And you saying, of course young men please do come in. Now would you like one who can't talk and can't hear but she's very good with her hands or you can have the other one who does not stop talking to herself and goes off into trances and speaks to dead people, please take your pick.' With that last entertaining statement even Sarah joined in the hysterical laughter that followed Molly's performance.

'Oh Molly you are funny,' said Sarah without any animosity towards her. 'But it's not really true, is it? I am not ill, you all know that. One day I'll show you, you just wait and see. I will get a job up at the house, I know I will. I can feel it.'

The smile rapidly dropped from Peter's face. He knew when Sarah felt so strongly about something that she wanted to happen, it usually did. He now felt quite guilty and regretted what he had said to her. Even though she did not appear to be upset by their unkind words and had joined in with their laughter. He knew her well enough to know that every hurtful word would strike deep into her heart. When he was in his twins company they always seemed to bring out the worst in each other.

'I've got to get back to work, who's going to walk with me? After all there's supposed to be a wild creature on the loose somewhere in the woods.'

'I'll walk back with you Molly,' said Sarah smiling. 'I'm not frightened of any wild creatures.'

'Well if you're going so am I,' piped in Peter jumping to his feet.

The three walked up the lane and into the woodland that surrounded High Markham. Molly and her twin chatted endlessly and Sarah tagged on behind listening to their conversation. They followed the footpath that wound up through the trees and led out to a clearing by the lake. When they reached the drive leading to the house Molly said her good-bye's and reminded Sarah to be at the house the following afternoon. Sarah watched Molly until she disappeared from view, around the back of the house, to the staff entrance.

'Come on Peter, let's go and look in the windows no one will see us.' And she started to creep up the drive making sure she stayed in the shadows of the tall cedar trees that lined the path. Peter reluctantly followed her.

'What do you want to look in the house for, Sarah? It's only full of old furniture, I wouldn't give you a penny for any of that fancy stuff or any of them frilly bits. The chairs look like they'd break if you put your arse on them.'

'Oh come on Peter do stop moaning, I like to look at all the beautiful things.'

The bright candlelight inside the house cast its beams through the windows illuminating the lawn and terraces of shrubs and trees. Sarah felt very excited hiding there in the bushes beside the windows, hoping that she would not be seen by anyone inside.

Peering through the small panes of glass in the french windows she savoured the splendour. Her eyes relished the richly decorated interior. A heavy gilt mirror hung above the carved oak fire surround reflecting the light of the tall candles that shone from the silver candelabras, which stood each side of the wide mantelpiece. Two cream silk covered sofas sat facing the fireplace, inviting you to nestle into the comfort of their feather filled cushions. Fine mahogany pieces of furniture adorned the room. Sarah absorbed every detail of the marvellous room. Peter was getting quite cold and fed up waiting for Sarah, she heard his boots scuffing the stone terrace.

'Shush,' she whispered, 'someone will hear you.'

'I'm going, are you coming or not?'

Reluctantly she left her hiding place beside the window and followed Peter, who by now was briskly striding down the drive.

'Wait for me Peter, you're walking too fast and I can't keep up with you.'

Peter pretended not to hear Sarah and carried on heading to the path that skirted the lake. Almost running Sarah caught up with him.

'Peter, whatever is the matter, have I done something wrong?' She reached for his arm and tugged him to a standstill.

'You're not in another mood with me, are you, tell me, what have I done this time?'

He thrust his hands in his pockets and looked down at the ground where he was kicking the toe of his boots at an exposed tree root.

'It's you Sarah, all the time you go on about the big house and all the wonderful things in it and your dream of living in a place like that with all that posh stuff.' He stopped and looked at her. 'It makes me feel really fed up.'

'Why should it make you feel like that, Peter? It's my dream not yours.'

So many times he had rehearsed the next part of this conversation but now the opportunity had come he was suddenly at a loss for words.

Sarah sensed there was a lot Peter wanted to say to her, she was not quite sure that she wanted to hear it but, as Tobias would say it was best to unburden the soul than store it, letting the unspoken words gain heavy black cobwebs.

The moon slipped behind a black swirling cloud, and emerged intermittently, so that the two young people by the lake were shrouded in semi-darkness, this gave Peter the confidence he needed to unburden his deepest inner thoughts on Sarah.

'I've always tried to be kind to you, Sarah, even though I sometimes tease you, I don't really mean it.' He faltered waiting for her to confirm his kindness.

'Of course you have Peter.' The lights from the mansion on the hill mesmerised her, the glow seemed to temper the damp miserable evening.

'See what I mean,' snapped Peter, making Sarah jump. 'You're not really listening to what I'm saying are you? You're like a bloody moth drawn towards the bright lights. Well you know what happens to moths, don't you? Which is what will happen to you, you'll get too near the flame and your wings will be burnt.'

'Peter, you're not being very kind now. I don't understand why you are so cross with me. Why shouldn't I want to live in a lovely house like this?'

He moved away from Sarah and sat on a fallen log and put his head in his hands. Sarah thought he was crying and could not bear his misery, she knelt down beside him putting one arm around his shoulders.

'I could never give you anything as grand as that Sarah, no matter how hard I worked, you have to be born into that sort of wealth.'

'I am sorry Peter, I'm a little confused. Why should you think that you have to provide me with a beautiful house? I don't understand why you think it's your problem.'

'Because.' His heart raced as he smelt the woodland in her hair, he moved closer to her.

'Because, because,' and his hands reached for hers.

'Sarah I love you,' he groaned. 'Oh my Sarah.'

His arms came up to encircle her.

'Just say you love me, please say you do and make my life worth living.'

Sarah was completely taken aback by this sudden declaration of his affection. She quickly took her arms away from him and stood up.

'Yes Peter, I do love you, just as I love the rest of the family, we are brother and sister.'

'You are wrong Sarah, we are not related at all. There is nothing to stop us marrying.'

'What! Marry you, for goodness sake Peter you can't be serious, what in heaven's name are you talking about? I can't marry you.' She racked her brains for something to add to lighten the rejection.

'There are lots of girls in the village that like you and most of them would be much more suitable than me. After all, as you and Molly have reminded me many times, I'm, what is it, completely barmy and on a good day half mad?' she said laughing, trying to make light of the situation.

'I've only ever wanted to be with you. I've never felt like this before about anyone. I need you Sarah. You can't say no, I've watched you for years and waited for you to grow up so we could be together. And I can look after you, after all I do understand your problems. I swear Sarah if you say no, I'll top myself. I can't even bear to think about my life without you, I've planned this ever since I first saw you. I'll never let anyone else have you Sarah.'

He reached for her hand and pulled her down to sit beside him on the log. He felt her slight resistance as he pulled her closer.

'Peter, listen carefully to what I am going to say. And please try to understand. You must realise this has come as a complete surprise to me. I have so much living to do, I am not ready to settle down yet.'

'It won't be just yet.' And he put his arms around her. 'You'll soon get used to the idea, I know you will. I'll make you really happy, honestly Sarah. I won't take no for an answer, you are mine. I'll renovate the barn, it will make a smashing home for us. And you won't have to go to work you can carry on just the same, I will let you collect your herbs and make things for the shop if you really want too. But you'll be so busy running our little home and looking after our children that you'll soon forget about those silly dreams of yours.'

He seemed to totally ignore her earlier refusal.

'Now come here and let me give you a little taste of what's to come.' Confidently he tilted her face towards him and kissed her lightly on the lips.

Drained of her strength, she did not object and this he took as a signal that she had agreed to all his demands.

Tobias stood observing the situation not entirely happy with the way the young man was behaving. Now here was someone for Sarah to be very wary of. Not only had he managed to sow the seed of doubt into her mind that questioned her sanity. He was now trying to feed off her energy, making him strong whilst she became weaker, vulnerable and more manageable, all to satisfy his own needs. He had come across this type of person many times. They were so easy to recognise, he called them psychic vampires: Weak willed, low achievers too lazy to create anything for themselves. They poach on the strength of others, usually using emotional blackmail as one of their weapons, making you feel guilty and sorry for them, manipulating you into doing something that you did not want to do. If you are aware you can sense their presence instantly: They always choose fun loving spirited people who radiate wonderful energies. And once they have chosen their victim they start the 'Poor me' performance. Sapping your energy, unburdening their troubled soul, they off load all their problems onto you, moaning and whining selfishly self-centred. And of course you being the good natured kind person you are, you feel so sorry for them and try to help. They are the people you dread seeing because when they leave you feel tired and drained.

Peter's mood had suddenly changed, he was really happy. 'Come on Sarah,' he said and yanked her to her feet. 'Let's go and tell Ma and Pa our good news.'

Her feelings for Peter at the moment were very confused and she did not want to hurt him or encourage him in any way. But she was still very young and inexperienced towards relationships with the opposite sex. Apart from the drunken Bill Wilcox most boys in the village steered well clear of her and Janet. She had often thought about the reasons why, and had come to the conclusion that she was different from most girls. She did not want to believe that she was ill or mad, even though ever since she could remember that is what she had been called. These days she tried really hard not to talk openly to Tobias, or comment on the ghostly figures of the deceased that she sometimes saw still going about their normal pattern as if they were still alive. Something inside her stirred as she thought about Peter actually liking her enough to want to marry her. A slight doubt came into her mind. Why should he want to marry her if she was as bad as he made out, when he could choose from the many girls that he had been with. At least she knew him, and nothing about her behaviour would surprise him, and she supposed you had to learn about love and men sometime in your life. After all, she was nearly eighteen. Molly had been going with men and boys since she was very young and it was only Molly's version on sex and men that Sarah had to base things on.

When they reached the outskirts of the farm Peter stopped and pulled her around to face him. His cold lips reached down to kiss her. She moved her head away.

'You'll have to be patient with me Peter. It is all happening to quickly. I don't really know what you expect from me. Can we start by just getting to know each other?'

'I'll show you everything, Sarah. Trust me.'

And he kissed her again but with much more meaning. She quite enjoyed the feeling of his lips touching hers. A new sensation deep within her stirred her emotions, she responded to his kiss by lifting her arms and placing them around his neck. She thought she could become quite interested in Peter's attentions. Even though she still felt that she should not be behaving like this with him.

He pulled her tightly to him and turned her so her back leant against the trunk of a tree. He moved his hands expertly over her, carefully caressing and awakening every part of her body. Confidently his hands hitched up the front of her skirt and slid inside her undergarments. She gasped with pleasure as his searching fingers took her to an even higher state of passion. His moist lips trailed down the side of her neck. Undoing the drawstring around the neck of her dress he exposed her small white breasts, cupping them in his hands he explored the nipples with his tongue. Moving his body against her he aroused her further. She could feel the swelling in his groin rubbing against her. She became oblivious of anything other than to satisfying the overwhelming hunger that consumed her.

As her hand searched for the buttons on his trousers, intending to free him to gratify her urgent need, he stopped abruptly and pushed her away from him. 'No Sarah don't do that, not yet,' he said in a husky voice. Rubbing a hand through his damp hair he turned away from her. 'Peter, you can't stop now, please,' she pleaded. 'Do your dress up, it's late Ma will wonder where we are.'

Sarah was too angry and frustrated to do anything other than shout.

'Peter what did I do wrong? You must tell me.'

'You did not do anything wrong, Sarah, it's just that, I don't want us to rush things.' And he started to walk away from her.

'Wait a minute, Peter, don't dash off we have to talk.'

No he really did not want to rush something that he had dreamed about for years. Many nights he had lain awake with Sarah asleep in the same room imagining that she was lying beside him as his wife, pure and unsullied by anyone and he was to teach her about the pleasures of pleasing a husband. No he would not readily let go of that dream now in a moment of unplanned fumbling in the woods.

He held her hand as if she were a small child and pulled her into step beside him.

'I told you Sarah, I will teach you everything but slowly and only when we are married can we do all the things that I have planned for us, until then we can only enjoy certain pleasures.'

Sarah wanted more, now, she wanted to experience the fulfilment of lovemaking. Her body knew something was missing and it ached for satisfaction. She did not want to lose that wonderful feeling, which only now in the cold night air was beginning to leave her. Persistent in trying to get her own way, as they neared the house Sarah pulled Peter to a standstill, in the shelter of the barn.

'What are you doing, Sarah? Come on let's get indoors it's chilly.'

'I can soon warm you up, come on,' and she opened the door of the barn and taking his hand propelled him into the darkness. He protested and tried to free his hand from hers, laughing she turned to face him.

'Peter, I want you to kiss me again before we have to go indoors, please,' she said as she pulled the neck of her dress undone, exposing her breasts. Tilting her face up to his she put her hands inside his jacket and around his neck. Angrily, he pushed her away and held her at arm's length.

'Stop it Sarah,' he hissed, 'I don't want you behaving like this, it's vulgar.'

'But I enjoyed what we did back there in the woods and I thought you enjoyed it too?' And again she thrust her arms around his neck, he shook her away.

'I did, but you must wait for me to decide when I want to teach you more.'

He pushed her away from him and stepped out of the barn and walked towards the farm house. Sarah followed him, walking slowly. What had he unleashed? No, she must not behave like this it was all wrong, he didn't want or like her to be so forward and brazen about their relationship, she was making it feel cheap and ordinary just like it was with the other girls he had been with. This time it was to be special, she was untouched, he wanted to be her teacher and in control of her initiation into the adult world. And she should be the innocent pupil waiting for her next lesson not vulgarly demanding it. A dark thought came into his mind. How could she appear to be so naturally experienced in lovemaking if she was a virgin? Before he went inside the house he turned to wait for Sarah who was sulkily trailing behind him.

'Sarah, am I the first man you've been, you know, familiar with? Have you let anyone else do what we were doing tonight?'

'Course not Peter, why do you ask?'

'I just wondered, you seem sort of used to kissing and things.'

'Oh, is that what's worrying you? Well, it just comes naturally, just like eating and breathing. That's what your sister says.'

'Don't you dare go listening to anything Molly says about the matter, I don't want you behaving like her, have you got that clear?' Sarah nodded in agreement. 'Perfectly, thank you.'

He was not really satisfied with Sarah's answer to his question. But at this moment it would have to do. He could not think of another question to ask, or another answer he would really want to hear.

CHAPTER ELEVEN

The afternoon sun penetrated the tall windows of Grace Trevallian's dayroom, she sat in the window enjoying the warming sunshine that was shining through the open balcony doors. The room overlooked the rose terraces that gently rolled down to the lake.
Occasionally she would glance down the long sweeping drive to see if Molly's sister was coming. She hoped her scatty maid had remembered to give the girl her message. A few months ago she would have written the invitations herself but her hands these days were very shaky and her writing untidy and she wanted everything to be absolutely perfect for this forthcoming party.
Her husband and only son were expected to dock at Penzance in a few months' time. Ralph her husband had only been in the Indies for the last six months but, it had been five long years since she had last seen Charles. She imagined he must have grown up an awful lot in that time. Charles was just nineteen when his father had decided that he should learn the family business and the best thing he could do was to spend a few years getting first-hand experience under the supervision of the company manager. Unfortunately just as Charles finished his apprenticeship the manager had an accident on one of the ships and so Charles was expected to stay there and run the business. When

his father had eventually received the letter from his son explaining the situation six months had passed and then it was another few months before Ralph Trevallian arrived in the Indies. In that time Charles had not only successfully managed the company but had opened up more trade routes for his father's ships.

Now not one ship ever moved from a port without a full cargo, coffee and spices would cross the seas and on return the hold would be full of wool and passengers. When his father realised the capability of his son he decided to leave him abroad to run the foreign side of the business. This had caused a lot of ill feeling between Grace and her husband. She knew that originally Charles did not want to work in his father's shipping business, he could never agree with any of his father's beliefs and tactics, especially when it came to handling the staff. Charles had always stated that he wanted to stay at High Markham and run the family estate, which his mother had inherited from her father.

He would have been most happy doing that as he had a way with ordinary hard working folk. Charles was not a loud and arrogant man like his father but his popularity with people seemed to bring out the best in them. He was a kind person, firm and fair and always genuinely interested in the welfare of others, unlike his father, who believed you obtained the best from your workers if they were constantly threatened with losing their homes and jobs.

As a child Charles was at his happiest when he was running off with the estate workers children. He often landed himself in a lot of trouble with his father who objected to his son mixing with a class of people that were beneath him. His father believed that you kept a distance between yourself and the common people.

Ralph Trevallian was quite disappointed with his son, he looked on his attitude to be a sign of weakness and spent a lot of unkind words on the boy trying to get him to react in a more aggressive manner. Charles would never take the bait that his father laid for him, he never lost his temper or returned the stream of insults. Ralph told his wife that her son had no backbone and he would never make a man of him. But after five years of hard work in the shipping trade his father could not accuse him of that anymore.

Fifty invitations carefully scribed were piled high on the leather topped desk in Grace Trevallian's drawing room. Sarah carefully cleaned the nib of the pen and replaced it on the brass inkstand. She would have finished them a lot sooner if she had been left on her own. But she had to keep stopping to answer the many questions that Mrs Trevallian asked her. The Mistress of the house was really enjoying the company of another female to converse with.

'Well done Sarah, I'm sure you have written those beautifully. Thank you for your help. My hands are so shaky and my eyes are not so good these days. I have these little eyeglasses,' and she held up a pair of gold spectacles which were hanging on a chain around her neck.

'But they are not very clear especially for writing. I was so pleased when I saw your beautiful script on the label of the headache potion you sent with Molly. I knew that if I ever needed anything specially written, then you would be the person to ask. I hope you did not mind me sending for you.' She reached up for the bell rope, which was hanging beside the fireplace and gently pulled it.

'Can you stay for tea, its ages since I have had someone young to talk to? Most of my friends are my age and full of moans and groans.'

Molly knocked the door and entered the room. She was instructed to bring a pot of tea and a selection of sandwiches and cakes. Molly's eyebrows knitted together as she furiously frowned at Sarah. The Mistress beckoned for Sarah to sit opposite, where she could see her. Molly snorted as her spare sister made herself comfortable in the green brocade chair.

The elderly lady led quite a solitary life when her husband and son were away. Since her sight had started to deteriorate she had lost her confidence to go out and socialise. She used to enjoy giving weekly afternoon bridge parties with her friends but as she now found it difficult to see the cards she had to stop playing and slowly friends had stopped visiting. Her embroidery stand stood redundant in the corner of the room just like her poetry books that used to give her so much pleasure. Hodges would occasionally offer to read to her but as he had a bland voice devoid of any feeling she found that it was an insult to the authors of such beautiful words.

'Sarah would you do me another great favour?'

'If I can,' she replied with a smile.

'Would you read a piece of poetry to me before you go?'

'I would really enjoy doing that, can I fetch the book?'

'It's right here.' And she reached down the side of her chair and produced the small red leather bound book.

'Which poem would you like me to read to you?'

'Page eighty-two, please.'

Silently she drifted through the night,
Searching for a white bright light,
Through the woodland nothing stirred,
For she is a moth and not a bird.
There is only one thing on her mind,
This night it's the light that she must find,
Her body is filled with an urgent desire
To quench her lust and feed the fire.

Sarah digested the words as she read them, strange she thought what a coincidence, Peter had said to her only the other evening that he thought she was like a moth attracted to the lights of High Markham and here she was this afternoon not unlike the moth in the poem.

Grace liked this sister of Molly the maid. She was well spoken and could read and write perfectly. She had quizzed Molly about Sarah's background and received some strange story about the girl being a nine-year old foundling appearing by coach with a gold crest on the side. Molly stated adamantly that Sarah was not a blood relation of hers at all.

'Sarah I've got a proposition to put to you, you're not in any employment at the moment are you?'

'No, not exactly, I make herb pillows, lavender bags, lotions and balms from the herbs and wildflowers that I collect in the woods. The Paget sisters sell them for me in their shop. I don't make an awful lot of money but it helps Gwen and Daniel with my keep.'

'What about you're healing gift, do you not charge for it?'

'Oh no madam, that's not work that is pleasure, it does not cost anything so how can I charge people for it. All I want to do is make people feel better.'

Grace liked the answers the girl gave her. What a joy Sarah was to have around the place, just her presence was a tonic.

'I hope you don't mind my next question. I heard that you have strange daydreams and that you can see and hear people that have entered the spirit world and you talk to them.'

Sarah felt quite embarrassed at the question and was not sure how to answer. It would be no use to deny the story as she was sure Molly had already versed Mrs Trevallian on all her peculiar accomplishments and omitted anything normal or worthy about her. Grace noticed the change in Sarah's face.

'It's all right Sarah, I do understand, let me make it perfectly clear how I feel about your unusual attributes. I'm quite used to strange occurrences. Not that I usually discuss them with anyone these days, my husband forbids any talk of anything slightly unconventional.'

'My mother used to be able to contact the dead. She would hold weekly sessions entertaining relatives and friends of the dear departed with messages from the other side. She would go into a trance state and look like she was sound asleep and then from her mouth would come strange voices of the dead, desperate to communicate with their bereaved relations who were present in the room. We used to hide under the table and listen to the gasps of surprise of her victims as we called them. I had a wonderfully exciting childhood. My mother came from a theatrical background and she followed in her parent's footsteps, always the entertainer. The house was always full of colourful eccentric people, actors, writers and poets. She used to wear brightly coloured long flowing robes and ostrich feathers in her hair. Every finger would be bedecked in rings and around her neck would be glittering jewels, one day I'll show you all her wild clothes, I still have them somewhere, I think Charles has put them in the pagoda. I've never worn any of them as my husband does not like anything ostentatious. The most exciting times as a child were when my parents held parties for all their friends, they would last all weekend, every room would have some form of entertainment going on in it, and I always enjoyed the music and poetry. Everyone would drink until they dropped and then sleep wherever they toppled until the morning, it was nothing to wake up in the morning and have to step over inebriated bodies lying asleep on the floor. In fact I met my husband as a young man at one of mother's controversial evenings. He came along with his parents, you could see that he was not enjoying the evening at all, he has always been a very serious man even then. Well he became bored with the bizarre behaviour of the so called adults and we both went outside to sit in the garden well away from the house. From that moment we got on so well and a year later we were married. His father, who was a very wealthy man, financed him to start on his own in the cargo trade. He gave him just enough money to support the cost of one ship of cargo to the Indies. And stated that from then on he would be on his own to either trade with the natives and fill the ship for its return journey or fail to conduct any business and flounder miserably. Of course this was a challenge to such a young man who was eager to succeed. And look at him now, the family business has grown so much that he is very rarely at home, he finds it very difficult to delegate some of the business matters to Charles or to any other member of his staff. He believes that if he isn't in total control at all times then the company will fail. He's not getting any younger and before long he will have to retire and leave Charles to run the whole thing. Charles takes after me and is not quite as strong and arrogant as his father would like him to be. And yet he has a good head for business and gets on extremely well with the staff. My husband believes you get loyalty and respect from your workers by filling them with fear. Charles's opinion is that you obtain the best from your employees if you pay them well and give them some respect. The idea being that if a man is paid for his services a little bit above the average and his family are well looked after then he will not want to lose his job and will be loyal to you. I think I'm inclined to regard my son's beliefs as being more acceptable.'

Sarah sat listening to Grace Trevallian with great interest she could have stayed for hours hungrily absorbing the details of the family. She was intrigued by the revelations about Mrs Trevallian's childhood, it was refreshing news, coming from such a prim and proper lady who obviously did not take after her unconventional mother.

Feeling quite relieved about disclosing her beliefs Sarah did not hesitate any further and told Mrs Trevallian everything, all about her healing with the universal energy that channelled through her. She explained about the visions and sightings that she experienced and the communications she had with spirits, finishing off with her description of her guide friend Tobias. She promised the interested Mrs Trevallian that the next time she visited she would bring her grandmother's crystal ball for her to see. Grace was memorised by the young girl sitting opposite her, she didn't want her to leave, she was a breath of fresh air.

'Oh silly me Sarah we have talked so much I nearly forgot about the offer I want to put to you. I would very much like you to consider coming here regularly to keep me company. I have a library full of wonderful books that I cannot see to read works of wonderful writers, poetry comforts me and I know you would enjoy reciting it. Do you think you might consider working for me? Of course I will pay you. And it would only be part-time to start with.'

Sarah did not need any time to think about the reply.

'Yes, I really would enjoy that, thank-you for asking me. When would you like me to start?'

Grace agreed the days with Sarah.

'There is something else I would like you to consider not immediately but for some time in the near future, but of course it totally depends on my husband's agreement.' She looked at Sarah.

'Perhaps you'd like to think about becoming my full-time companion. The work would not be too difficult but I really could do with some permanent help and company, especially when I want to go out and visit friends, which at the moment is not very often. Your help could make a tremendous difference to my life. I'm sure you will get on well with my husband and son.' She paused to let Sarah think about what she had said.

'Not now, but in the very near future, at least I have given you time to think about the position. Well I have kept you long enough today, thank-you for all you have done this afternoon and I will look forward to seeing you next week.'

Sarah was so excited to be offered the chance to live in such a grand house, to her it felt like a dream come true. Since she was abandoned to Cornwall and deserted by her parents she had never stopped believing that one day she would be lifted from the harsh conditions of Mill Farm and be returned to a more comfortable way of life. And now there was a good chance of it becoming reality. She could say goodbye to the farm and the frugal existence that she led. Here she would be a member of staff but she could enjoy the civilised comforts available. Again excitedly she agreed to Mrs Trevallians offer.

'We will have so much fun together Sarah, something I don't have much of these days.'

Sarah thanked Mrs Trevallian and said she really was looking forward to coming next Tuesday. She skipped down the vast oak staircase intent on calling into the kitchen to share her good news with Molly. She flew past the serious faces of the portraits on the high staircase wall. Abruptly she stopped at one of the paintings that caught her eye. It was not of the usual sombre clothed elderly gentleman but of a young person. A wild mop of blonde hair fell over the startlingly blue eyes that laughed at Sarah. He was dressed in a green velvet hunting jacket with a white high collared shirt that touched his chin, his jacket was open to reveal a gold brocade waistcoat, and in his hands he loosely held a silver topped hunting crop. His face seemed almost alive as Sarah smiled back at the picture, winking at him she trotted down the stairs.

Once in the hallway she could not help but look around in awe at the sheer splendour of the surroundings. On the far wall hung an enormous colourful tapestry depicting a hunting scene, and underneath it the fireplace was framed by an ornately carved oak surround topped with a heavy oak beam mantle on which pewter plates and tankards stood. The wooden floor glistened in the amber glow from the log fire that she presumed was always alight winter and summer. A strange looking woven circular rug covered the centre of the floor, the colours were brighter than anything Sarah had ever seen. Purples and reds mingled with bright blues and yellows. The pattern illustrated a design that Sarah recognised. Signs and symbols denoting the stars and planets swept around in an astrological circle. Fascinated by the colourful emblems and animals that ruled each birth sign she looked for the month of August. A magnificent roaring lion woven in gold silk thread and the words 'I WILL' marked her birth month. She was still engrossed with the rug when Hodges came across her. She jumped as she noticed him standing watching her.

'Oh sorry, I was just looking at the rug. Did it belong to Mrs Trevallians's mother?'

Hodges looked over the top of his spectacles at the young slip of a girl. His mistress had just informed him of her plans to hire the girl to read to her, and that she wanted Sarah treated with respect as she was not like the usual staff they hired at High Markham. This latter statement annoyed Hodges, he did not like having to be respectful to young inexperienced staff. You were respectful to people with class like employers and professional people, not members of the household servants.

'Yes miss, it did belong to Madam's mother. Now can I show you the way out?'

Sarah smiled, 'I really wanted to see Molly, would it be all right if I went down to the kitchen? I promise I won't keep her talking for very long.'

'Come this way then,' he said and held open the door to the downstairs kitchens.

Nellie looked up from kneading a great pile of bread dough as Hodges and Sarah entered the kitchen.

'Hello young Sarah, Hodges has told me all about you coming to work with us. I'm really pleased to have you around and by the way thanks for that chilblain ointment you sent me, it did the trick beautifully I could get me slippers back on me feet in two days.'

The kitchen door burst open and Molly struggled in carrying a basket of potatoes.

'Bloody hell Nellie, isn't it about time we got a younger gardener? Forbes can hardly dig the potatoes, let alone carry them indoors.' She put the basket down on the floor with a thud. Then she turned and caught sight of Sarah standing beside Nellie.

'What the hell do you think you're doing here?' she demanded.

'Oh, come on Molly you know why I'm here. Stop pretending. I've just written the invitations for the party. And the other reason I was here so long I think you already know about.'

'If I bloody well knew I wouldn't be asking would I?' she snapped impatiently.

Sarah hesitated for a while before she replied. 'I thought that after our conversation last night that you must have asked Mrs Trevallian about a job for me because,' and she nervously hesitated before she continued,

'Well, because this afternoon she offered me some part-time work to start with, perhaps full-time in the New Year, depending on whether her husband agrees with her having me as a companion.'

No one could have prepared Sarah for the vicious onslaught that ensued. Molly's eyes turned black as the anger rose within her.

'You think I got you a job? Well you are very much mistaken Sarah I would not recommend you to an enemy let alone a lady like Mrs Trevallian. You are the very last human being I want to see working here. Do you hear me? Its bad enough you live in what was my home until you came and pushed me out, and that everybody treats you like a lady, but now you are wheedling your way in here, in a fancy bloody position with her ladyship. Well, let me make this perfectly clear, Sarah, I might be at her beck and call but I'll be damned if I am going to be at yours. Didn't you understand what Peter and I told you last night? You're not fit to work with normal people you're too bloody dangerous and stupid to have around.'

Sarah interrupted at this point. 'Mrs Trevallian knows all about me and she does not mind honestly. She said her mother was just like me.'

'Like you, Sarah, no one could be like you there aren't any witches left are there? Well you're not working here I'll see to that and if I don't Peter will.' Molly for the first time looked away from Sarah and caught the shocked look on Nellie's face.

'I'll tell you what she's like Nellie and the things she can do. She's put a spell on my brother he's absolutely obsessed with her he can't think of anyone else even though he's had offers from some of the most beautiful girls in Hellstone. And now you see what she's done. Last night she said she really wanted a job up here at the house. Peter and me told her, no she couldn't and look what's happened, today she's been with her ladyship just a couple of hours and she is in already and with promises of a full-time position.' She paused to see Nellie's reaction. There wasn't one. Nellie thought to herself if everything Molly was saying was true the best thing that she could do was to keep on the good side of Sarah. Anyway she liked the girl irregardless of what Molly said.

At this point Hodges who had been silently observing the situation decided it was about time that he stepped in and ended this family quarrel.

'That's enough Molly, it appears to me that you are very jealous of the position that Sarah has been offered. I think that Sarah is a most suitable person to be working here, more than I can say for some of the present staff,' and he looked directly into Molly's face. 'But let me warn you Molly, Sarah works directly for Mrs Trevallian and is only answerable to her. But you and the rest of the staff apart from Nellie work under me and I do the hiring and firing. So keep that in mind. And I'll have no family disagreements under this roof or someone will have to go.'

If Molly had ever hated anyone with such venom then it was Sarah.

Biting her lip so she could not reply to Hodges remarks she stormed through the kitchen and disappeared into the china room. Embarrassed, Sarah muttered a quick good-bye and left for home. Confused, Sarah could not take in all the exciting opportunities that had been offered to her this afternoon even though they were now slightly clouded by Molly's awful outburst. There were so many thoughts racing through her head that she decided not to return home immediately. She wanted a little time on her own to clear her mind. Just before she reached the main gates she crossed over the wide drive and stepped onto a secluded narrow path. Tall unruly yew trees drooped over the path creating a shady tunnel. Sarah followed the path until it opened out into a circular garden, in the middle sat a stone walled fish pond. In the centre of it stood an ornamental bronze cherub spewing glittering water that cascaded excitedly down into the pond below disturbing large flat lily pads. Nestled into the yew hedges either side of the pond were grey stone seats which were almost hidden by overhanging branches, the perfect private place for Sarah to have solitude to indulge in her thoughts. She sat down.

Sarah watched the late afternoon's sunbeams shimmering through the trees making a mottled pattern on the trickling fountain, giving the effect of dancing flames. As she watched her eyelids started to become heavy and try as she might she could not stop her eyes from closing. The warmth and the gentle sound of the water caressed her into a very deep relaxed state. She could still hear the water and the birds singing but they started to dissolve into the distance. Between the state of awake and asleep her mind drifted into a complete visualisation of her thoughts.

She re-enacted the amazing eventful afternoon up at the house, searching her mind for deeper intuitions and coincidences.

Again she listened carefully to what Mrs Trevallian was actually saying, words that had been unspoken. Was she really saying to Sarah, I am getting old, I need some help, I am lonely, my husband and son are too busy to notice me, I will pay for your company, you and your ways remind me of my mother and my childhood. Did the old lady need to reminisce into the safety of the past?

Well it did not matter what Molly thought or said, nothing would stop her from keeping Mrs Trevallian company, she needed Sarah and strangely enough Sarah needed the old lady.

Sarah's mind now moved on to the awful conversation with Molly. She listened to every painful word over again. It had all been so unexpected, even though Molly could sometimes make nasty and silly remarks towards Sarah.

Sarah never realised that Molly really disliked her so much or harboured such spiteful resentment. Thinking about it, Sarah understood what Molly had been saying. For years poor Molly must have felt rejected and blamed all her feelings on the arrival of Sarah, to Molly Sarah had a very easy life and in her eyes had claimed Molly's rightful place within the family. And now just to make matters far worse, here she was stepping into a position at High Markham, a gentle easy position set against the hard work of a servant. Also Sarah had come between the sacred bond of twins and captured Peters heart. Molly must feel that Sarah was taking and getting everything that she wanted, envy was so destructive it made people behave irrationally. She was not sure how she could make amends and prove to Molly that nothing she had ever done was intentionally meant to hurt her. And that she loved her like an older sister. Molly's accusations were quite untrue but her beliefs were very real to her and it would prove very difficult to change her attitude towards Sarah.

A cool breeze chilled the air in the garden and Sarah shivered. Opening her eyes she stood up, she felt more at ease as she had analysed some of the confused thoughts worrying her. As she started to focus her eyes on the now dusky garden a grey mist swirled in front of them, for a split second she was in a dark smoky room and then she was back here in the garden. She sat back down on the stone seat, waiting to see if a psychic vision was going to materialise. Lights flashed in front of her eyes and a golden sphere appeared. Sarah knew she was going to experience a premonition or witness an event in future.

Instantly she found herself standing in an unfamiliar warm smoky room. The heat from the log fire illuminated the airless place. Sarah looked at her surroundings, heavy brown velvet curtains blocked out any light from the tall windows. Above the carved oak fire surround hung an enormous oil painting depicting a ferocious battle scene.

Each side of the fireplace the walls were lined from floor to ceiling with deep oak shelves containing volumes of leather bound books. As Sarah's eyes took in the details of the library she realised that she was not alone in the room. She could just make out the back of a man's head sitting in a high button backed leather chair at the desk.

As she stood in the shadows the door to the library slowly opened and a female figure in a long white nightdress crept in, Sarah gasped as she recognised the person. Molly swiftly turned the door key in the lock before she crossed the room to the man at the desk. As she pulled out the pins in her hair and it tumbled down she threw back her head and laughed provocatively at the man as he poured amber liquid into two brandy balloons.

She sat on the desk facing the man the firelight caught the teasing look in her eyes as they sipped the brandy and refilled their glasses. A hand with a thick gold ring on the little finger reached to touch Molly's breast. Molly removed the hand and slapped it playfully. Words were exchanged between them but their voices were muffled and distant and Sarah could not make out what they were saying to each other nor could she see the face of the man, she could only just make out the golden hair glinting in the firelight.

Molly held out her hand as if waiting to receive something, a coin was put into her palm and she nodded with acceptance and placed it on the table. Sarah was astonished by Molly's next move, the girl undid the ribbon around the neck of her nightdress and let it slowly slip off her shoulders and drop down around her ankles.

Sarah closed her eyes not wanting to witness the following intimate behaviour of Molly and the man. Sarah tried to come out of the psychic vision but to no avail. Molly stepped out of her nightdress and stood brazenly naked in front of the chair. Strong hands caressed her generous white breasts and her firm buttocks before they gripped her arms and pulled her down to kneel in front of him. She fumbled with the buttons on his breeches and slid her expert hand inside to caress him. He lent forward and whispered something into her ear, at which she threw her head back and laughed, and then shook her head from side to side. Another coin was put into her hand and still she shook her head, the answer being no, to the question that was being asked.

She reached to the desk behind her and picked up a gold and blue enamel snuff box, the man shook his head and instantly took it from her hands and put back on the desk. More coins were trickled into her cupped hand, but Molly wanted the snuff box in payment for his demands. He leant forward and whispered again. They both laughed at Molly's reply. Readily she accepted the handful of coins and nodded in agreement of the payment, sensually she traced the outline of her lips with the tip of her tongue then she lowered her head into the man's lap and disappeared from Sarah's view. Strong fingers ran through Molly's hair as she relieved the sexual tensions of the seated man.

Sarah could not believe her eyes and felt embarrassed to be learning about the art of sexual gratification in such a crude manner. She seemed to be locked into this vision and she could not step out of it or get back to her present earth space.

The figure in the chair stretched and groaned as Molly completed her task. Glasses were refilled with fine brandy and Molly wandered over to the fire, she stretched herself out full-length on the sheepskin hearth rug and beckoned for her partner to join her. His tall frame slowly moved across the room and he sat down beside her with one arm resting on his knee. He had shed his smoking jacket and his white shirt hung out over his breeches. The reflection of the amber flames danced a pattern on Molly's moist bare skin, she wriggled as he held his glass above her and tipped it slightly so that a small amount of brandy trickled down upon her, filling her navel and running through the thick triangle of black hair. Sarah tried to move, but her whole body seemed paralysed, usually just to concentrate on moving a limb would be enough to end the incident and come out of the vision. Even though she was aware that her physical body was still sitting on the stone seat in the garden she knew that her psychic mind was locked into a scene in the future and that even with her eyes closed she would still see the true vision. With all her power she concentrated on the garden that she was sitting in before the vision.

Eventually she drifted from the dark library back to the ornamental pond, travelling in and out of reality. A voice somewhere in the distance was calling her name. Was it in the room or was it in the garden?

Peter shook Sarah quite roughly until her eyes flashed open. Bewildered she looked up into Peter's face.

'Sarah wake up it's me, Peter. I've been looking for you everywhere.' He was so relieved to have found her, especially since Molly had told him about the argument they had with each other this afternoon.

'Goodness me Peter, I think I must have fallen asleep, whatever is the time?' Sarah stretched her arms and stood up, still slightly disorientated by the strong vision that she had experienced.

'You have been missing since you went to write the invitations this afternoon Sarah, and it's nearly nine o'clock in the evening now. I have been frantic with worry as to what had happened to you.' He paused for a moment before he continued. 'I can tell you that Molly is not at all pleased about her ladyship offering you a job and I must admit I'm not keen on the idea either.' Sarah had to think for a moment as to what Peter was talking about and then all the events of the afternoon came flooding back to her.

'Peter in heaven's name, what has it got to do with you or your spiteful sister? I will work when and where I want to, do you understand?' And with that she pushed past him and walked briskly down the path. The anger inside her grew, as she thought about the two of them taking away the wonderful feeling of euphoria that she had first experienced when Mrs Trevallian had offered her the positions.

Peter and his twin's attitude made her more than ever determined to accept all that the Trevallian family could offer her.

It was an opportunity to good to miss. After all what had she got to lose.

CHAPTER TWELVE

Gwen roughly chopped the tough turnip. She was deep in thoughts about recent events within the family. How things seemed to change all the time. She was delighted that at last Sarah had found herself a part-time job at High Markham, even though she knew it had upset Peter and Molly, she was also pleased that her son and Sarah were to be married, it was a weight off her mind. Even though Sarah had never really caused any bother for her she knew that with the girl's odd ways it would be difficult to find a man to take her on. At least Peter was used to Sarah and seemed to worship the ground she walked on.

That morning Peter discussed with his father the possibility of converting the stone barn behind the mill into a cottage for him and Sarah. Daniel thought that it was a good idea and offered to help Peter with the heavy work. He even roped in the sullen young Matthew to help much to the boy's annoyance. Matthew would much rather be down at the vicarage or helping the preacher in the church, he had no inclination to get his fair hands dirty, also he didn't like Sarah very much, he found that she was far from being a good Christian. When he had asked her why she did not go to the church, she replied that as God never visited her house she did not see why she should visit his. Matthew had told the preacher what Sarah had said and the holy man replied that she was most probably a terrible sinner and was too frightened to step inside the church. Matthew had then fed the preacher with all sorts of tales about Sarah, some were true but others were the outcome of his vivid imagination and his allegiance to God. He was convinced he had found the devil's accomplice and he was just waiting for the moment when he could save her soul and convert her to a far better way of life.

Over supper that night Peter broke the good news to Sarah about where they were going to live. She asked how long it would take before the barn was ready. Peter had reckoned that they would not be able to do very much before the winter, but come the spring he could spend every evening and part of the weekends on the building. Sarah was quite relieved to hear that, she secretly hoped that the barn would never be ready. Even though she had agreed to marry Peter she wished she had taken a little more time to think about her decision. At the moment she did not actually want to marry Peter, in fact she did not want to marry anyone. She had so many hopes and dreams in her mind to fulfil and settling down to being married with children was not top of her list.

Sarah strolled along the well-worn path that led to High Markham. It had been two months, since she had been coming to read to Mrs Trevallian. Each time she came she discovered a little more about this enormous grey house and the people who lived there. She was really looking forward to going today as yesterday Mr Trevallian and his son Charles had arrived home, also this coming Saturday was the welcoming home ball. She could not wait to meet them and hoped that Mr

Trevallian would approve of her and give his consent for her to become a live in companion for his wife.

As soon as Sarah walked into the kitchen she could feel the tense atmosphere. Dishes and plates covered every available work surface waiting to be filled with one of Nellie's creations. A whole lamb hung from a spit in front of the roaring fire, young Ned yawned as he laboriously turned the handle of the noisy mechanism rotating the headless creature. On the vast range a giant copper pan bubbled away, bright red lobsters laid lifelessly in the boiling liquid ready to be emptied of their delicious contents. On the scrubbed pine table a glazed pigs head adorned a beautiful silver platter, from his grotesque grinning mouth protruded a shiny red apple, around his throat a necklace of bright green parsley and grapes concealed the fact that his body was somewhere else in the steamy kitchen waiting to be turned into yet another creative dish.

'When I've finished upstairs, Nellie, I can come and give you some help if you like,' shouted Sarah above the commotion in the kitchen.

'Oh yes please, I could certainly do with another pair of hands, thank-you Sarah,' said the cook as she lifted an enormous side of beef from the sweltering hot ovens.

'She can do these bloody potatoes,' said Molly as she scrubbed the marble sized vegetables with a small scrubbing brush. Sarah hung her cloak behind the door and had just started to walk towards the back stairs when Hodges came down towards her.

'Ah Sarah you are just the person I want to see. The mistress won't be needing you this afternoon as she's quite busy with the families homecoming, but she asked if you could be here at mid-day tomorrow to help her get dressed for the party. And she said as she doesn't know what time you will finish your duties you can stay the night.'

'Thank-you Mr Hodges,' replied Sarah.

'If you're not going upstairs then perhaps you would care to help me lay the banqueting table in the large hall,' inquired Hodges.

Sarah followed him up through the house until they reached the vast hall that seemed to stretch the whole length of the building, double doors led through to an equally large ballroom. At each end of the hall were fireplaces the size of small rooms, each side of the iron grates were stacked with piles of oak logs. Hodges noticed her looking at the fireplaces.

'Tomorrow it will be a full-time job for Nellie's grandson Ned to keep the fires in both rooms stacked and burning all evening, it's a devilish place to try and heat.' Taking the ring of keys from his pocket he opened the door to a small anteroom that held the families valuable tableware. Sarah stared in amazement at the treasure trove. Crystal glasses, decanters and fruit dishes sparkled like diamonds, you could see your reflection in the rows of silver tureens and the cutlery looked far too good to be actually used, candlesticks and vases adorned the tall shelves. Hodges passed her a white pair of cotton gloves to put on. She looked at him quizzically awaiting an explanation.

'So you don't get finger marks on anything. Your sister Molly spent the whole of yesterday cleaning this lot.'

Boxes of silver cutlery were loaded onto a wooden trolley.

'We need fifty of everything, there will be five

courses and we need to layout separate cutlery for each course.' Something about the cutlery stirred a nostalgic thought in her mind. 'Work your way in, from the outside,' that's what her father used to say on the rare occasions that she used to eat a formal meal with him.

Hodges reached for a yard stick and started to lay the table, Sarah watched engrossed in the way he measured each setting meticulously so it was absolutely the exact distant apart and precisely opposite each other.

Sarah placed the wine glasses in position on the table precisely where Hodges told her to put them. He explained to her about different sized glasses for an assortment of wines. He surveyed her work and occasionally moved a glass a mere fraction of an inch. Molly entered the room looking very harassed, she carried armfuls of flowers and greenery, she was closely followed by Ned who was completely hidden by more flowers and long tendrils of ivy. Hodges laid a cloth down on the floor and the blooms were dropped down on to it.

'Her ladyship usually does the flowers for the tables but as she's caught up with the men, perhaps you would like to do them.'

'Are you sure you want me to arrange them, Mr Hodges?' said Sarah.

'You've done it before, surely?' inquired Hodges.

Sarah nodded her head. She thought of the stone jars of lavender and calendulas that she arranged at the farm, not quite the same as white wax lilies, fragrant pink carnations and roses that had come straight from the hot houses of High Markham. Well it could not be too difficult. From the anteroom Hodges carried the most magnificent centrepiece for the table that Sarah had ever seen.

It was made of engraved silver and crystal, it stood high off the table in three tiers. Around the lower edge were twisted and turned candleholders nestled in engraved silver vine leaves. Ned brought in a tall enamel jug of water. Hodges carefully filled the vases. Sarah set to and before she realised it she had created a beautiful cascading flower arrangement. Hodges stood back and admired the set table and the perfect floral centrepiece.

'I must go and attend to my duties upstairs, Sarah. If you would like to use the flowers that are left to fill the small vases that I've placed along the table then we will be well and truly finished. Wait here for me when you've done, I won't be long,' and off he went leaving her alone.

Just as she finished the last small posy bowl of ivy and carnations Hodges and Mrs Trevallian entered the room.

'Madam has come to inspect the table Sarah.'

Sarah stepped back politely and watched as the mistress walked around the table slowly, occasionally stopping to touch the delicate flowers.

'Hodges you have really excelled yourself this time the table looks more beautiful than I have ever seen it.'

'Thank you, Madam. Sarah here did the flowers, and extremely well I thought, but not quite as well as when you do them, Madam,' he added quickly as an afterthought. Grace Trevallian smiled pleasantly at him.

'If I'm not mistaken, Hodges I think you are flattering me.' And she laughed as she left the room. As she reached the door she stopped and asked Hodges to arrange for Ned to light the fire in her husband's study as he was meeting the estate manager this evening and as the room had been unused for so long it was sure to be damp and cold.

With the table completed and a nod of approval from Mr Hodges they both returned to the bustling kitchen. Molly had finished the potatoes and was now preparing to scrub the mud off of a sink full of carrots. Hodges looked everywhere for Ned, Nellie said that she had sent him down to the estate workers cottages to give the tenants daughters and wives a reminder to be at the house sharp at six in the morning to start preparing for the party.

'I'll go up and light the fire in the study if you like?' volunteered Sarah. 'But you will have to tell me where the room is.' Even though she had been coming to the house frequently she had still not had the opportunity to investigate the maze of passages and rooms on all the floors. He gave Sarah instructions to the whereabouts of the master's room. Molly scrubbed the carrots vigorously, angry that Sarah was becoming so involved in the running of the house.

Sarah felt quite nervous as she climbed the drafty stone stairway that ran up through the house from the kitchens. Something or someone seemed to be following her, she stopped abruptly and turned around, she was not sure if her eyes were deceiving her or a shadow stood on the stairs below her. She blinked and it seemed to merge into the dark walls. Quickly she hurried up the steps. A single candle sconce lit the dim stairway, she went past two landing doors and when she reached the third she entered a long passageway. The walls were decorated with crossed swords and shields and in the dark corners stood giant suits of armour. She tried not to look at the staring glass eyes of the animal's heads that were mounted as trophies on the walls. Eventually she came to the last door on the left before the staircase to the staff's attic rooms. She lightly tapped on the door. No reply. She waited for a while and tapped again a little louder, no answer. She turned the handle and slowly pushed the door open. Entering the cold room she realised that she had visited this chamber before, this was the room in her vision. She blushed as she remembered the behaviour of the two people in the room. It slowly became clear to her that Molly was entertaining one of the men of the house, now which one could it be, the father or the son? As she lit the candles on the mantelpiece the room sprang into life. She looked around the room for more to light. She moved over to the desk and ignited three tall flaxen coloured candles, she could not help but notice the blue and gold enamelled snuff box that in her vision Molly had wanted in payment for her sexual favours. Without thinking she picked up the ornate box and studied the family crest that was engraved upon the lid. A door along the passageway closed and footsteps came towards the study. The sudden sound made her start and as she hurriedly tried to replace the box on the desk she clumsily dropped it, the dusty contents spilled out over the carpet. Frantically she tried to scoop some of the snuff back into the box but not before the study door opened and the tall figure of Ralph Trevallian loomed in the doorway. She did not know who was more surprised herself or the master of the house. She scrambled to her feet still clutching the ornate box.

'And who might I ask are you, and why are you in my study holding my property?' he bellowed and in two strides he had reached Sarah and snatched the box from her hands. She stepped back feeling very guilty but totally innocent of any crime. 'I'm, I'm,

Sarah,' she stuttered. 'I came to light the fire.' He looked at the prepared unlit grate and raised his eyebrows.

'Well that explains a lot doesn't it?' he said sarcastically.

'I work here, I read poetry to your wife, and I am Molly's sister.' She didn't know when to stop explaining to justify her presence in his house.

'If you worked here don't you think I would know about it young lady and what were you doing with this?' And he pushed the snuff box at her. He walked between her and the door and reached for the bell rope to summons Hodges. Retiring into his chair he surveyed her petite young frame. She could feel his eyes penetrating her clothes. A new maid he thought and if he was not mistaken a virgin, a stirring in his loins brought a glint to his eyes. He was always ready for a new conquest the younger the better. The uncomfortable silence was broken by the arrival of Hodges.

Ralph Trevallian questioned Hodges about the truthfulness of Sarah's explanation to her purpose in his study. Satisfied with the reply he received, he then continued to lecture Sarah on the rules of the house and what he expected from the staff. He outlined her position in the house and emphasised in a very loud voice that she was at all times to treat the family members and the house and its contents with uttermost respect, after all she was only a paid servant. He added that if ever he had occasion to speak to her again about the matter of touching valuable objects in the house then she would be dismissed and he would make sure no one else in the whole of Cornwall would ever employ her. Dismissing them both together a very uncomfortable and embarrassed Sarah followed

Hodges down the back staircase to the kitchen.

'His bark is often worse than his bite, Sarah, don't get too upset about it. He's always like this when he comes home from abroad, it will take him a month to settle down. You wait till you meet young master Charles, you won't believe they are related.'

'What did his lordship want then?' inquired Molly, waiting for an explanation to why Hodges was summoned.

Sarah waited for Hodges to tell Molly about the awful scene in the study, but he didn't, he winked at Sarah and cleverly diverted the conversation.

Even though he knew that the nosy maid would probably find out later from her employer all about the incident with the snuffbox.

'You ought to see the wonderful flower arrangements that Sarah has created. The mistress was delighted with them, she said that she had never seen the table look so beautiful, didn't she Sarah?' said Hodges to the cook.

Molly pulled a face at Sarah and turned back to her task at the sink. Hodges thanked Sarah for her help and told her to get off home as she had another long day tomorrow.

The next morning Sarah was up bright and early, ready to get her jobs done.

'What time shall I come and meet you then?' asked Peter across the breakfast table.

'You won't need to meet me Peter, Mrs Trevallian said I could stay at the house for the night, as it will be very late before I finish.'

'I don't think that's a very good idea at all Sarah. It's bad enough that you'll be gone all bloody day, but you are not staying out all night as well. I won't have it.'

Gwen looked at her son's serious expression.

'I think Peter's right Sarah, after all you are about to be married and it's not the done thing to spend the night away like that. You're not as worldly as our Molly and would not be able to look after yourself, anything could happen, and besides Peter's been very understanding about you working there, hasn't he?'

'I'll be outside waiting for you at midnight and mind you be there,' he warned.

'I don't want to be stuck out there in the cold for hours.' He wiped his mouth on the back of his sleeve and left the kitchen. Defeated, Sarah started to help clear the table, she felt Tobias beside her and silently cursed the Pendarvis Family. Tobias scolded her for being so flippant with her thoughts. He was always warning her to be careful when she became angry or thought ill wishes because there was always the possibility that they would actually come true and then they would go three times around your head and be returned to you. As you reap so you shall sow, that was one of his many favourite sayings.

The sun was not eager to shine this misty November morning and the countryside was looking dull, lifeless and damp. Sarah's boots were becoming wet and heavy as she tramped through the woods. Up until yesterday she had really been looking forward to today but after the scene with Mr Trevallian and now Peter's insistence on her not staying the night at the house, the wind had been taken out of her sails and her happy mood had disappeared. Tobias trotted beside her in silence.

'I don't know what I'm doing or where I'm going Tobias. Surely there is more to life than this continual up and down, happy and sad, sunshine and shadows.'

'Who said it was going to be easy all the time? I think you forget the lessons I've been teaching you Sarah. If you didn't keep searching for the ultimate pot of gold and happiness at the end of the rainbow and keep finding a bucket of shite then these things would not be so dramatic when they happen. You should take life more lightly, go with the flow and stop expecting it to be wonderful all the time. Has it ever occurred to you that you expect too much too soon. You never give things a chance. You want everything to be perfect all the time. When you get so intense about things it blocks the flow and you don't see the good things that are right under your nose. Appreciate the small things that happen and slowly life will start to improve for the better. Expect a little gold now and again not a great big pot all the time.'

'Well that little lecture has really cheered me up. I am grateful for my life, honestly Tobias, it's just that nothing seems to last, something always happens to spoil it,' snapped Sarah.

If the kitchen at high Markham was chaotic yesterday then today it was a full scale war. She made straight for the back staircase. Reaching the first floor landing she met a very harassed Mrs Trevallian about to go into her suite. Sarah followed her into the sitting room.

'I'm glad you're here Sarah, I wondered whether you would come here today after my husband's obnoxious behaviour last night. I can't apologies enough. You were not the only one to be at the brunt of his ill temper. I can't believe he has upset so many people in such a short time. This morning before breakfast he had angry words with the estate manager and the gamekeeper, he's given them both a weeks' notice to get out of their homes. They both have large families and nowhere to go. It's the wrong time of year for them to be homeless and without jobs. Goodness knows what will become of them. My son tried to reason with him but he will not listen to anyone. I had forgotten how much the wellbeing of the house is disrupted when he is at home. I do hope he does not spoil this evening with half the neighbourhood coming, I don't think this party is a good idea after all.'

Sarah reached for the hair brush and slowly and soothingly brushed the unsettled women hair. The mousy grey strands became disentangled quite easily, Sarah used the tips of her fingers to massage her delicate scalp. Mrs Trevallian relaxed as Sarah soothed her tension.

'I have brought a bottle of lavender and rosemary oil with me, how about a nice aromatic bath before you get dressed? It will do you the world of good and relax you.' The mistress readily agreed.

With the mistress dressed for the party and seated in her chair sipping camomile tea, Sarah nipped into the dressing room and pulled off her own drab working clothes. She slopped some cold water into the wash bowl and washed her face and hands. She reached for the new grey dress that hung on the back of the door and carefully stepped into it, unlike the mistresses low cut dress this fitted snugly up to her chin, a fine black ribbon of scallops decorated the high neck. She pulled on the pink stockings and slipped the new grey booties on. Pleased with her reflection and the clothes that Grace had bought her, she reached into her cloak pocket and took out a small bottle filled with oil. Very carefully she pulled out the glass stopper and dabbed it behind her ears and on her wrists. The extract of oils filled the room, you could not exactly identify the perfume, it could have been citrus fruits, wild herbs or lavender and thyme. It was a complete mixture of sensual aromas. She felt a flutter in her stomach as Ralph Trevallian knocked on the door, he didn't enter but shouted that it was time that his wife was downstairs ready to greet the arrival of the first guests.

'Now remember you stay with me Sarah, I want you to enjoy yourself, you don't have to stand back with the rest of the servants.'

Sarah was not too sure about the last statement, she would much rather not be here at all let alone have to stand in a room full of complete strangers especially if they were all like Ralph Trevallian.

Charles Trevallian patiently waited on the landing for his mother to come out of her rooms. He kissed his mother's hand and told her how beautiful she looked.

'And you must be Sarah,' he said holding out his hand. 'Mother has told me all about you.'

Sarah shook his hand and bobbed a curtsy unsure of quite how she should address him. He shook her hand and smiled warmly.

'I am very pleased to meet you Sarah.'

'Likewise sir,' replied Sarah.

'Come along Mother, are you ready to meet the enemy?' He laughed heartily and guided his mother down the wide staircase. Sarah nervously followed, casually she glanced at the portraits on the stairs, she instantly knew who the face with the laughing eyes belonged to.

The sounds of the musicians tuning their instruments drowned the conversation between Mother and son as they made their entrance into the reception hall. Ralph Trevallian tipped up his goblet and drained his second glass of wine. Charles noticed his father reach for a refill and hoped that he would stay sober at least till after the dinner.

Sarah dutifully stood behind the Trevallian family as the guests arrived and their names were announced loudly by Hodges. Nicola and Amy Paget approached with their parents, they shook hands with the Trevallians and waved an acknowledgement to Sarah. Sarah bobbed a curtsy and gave them a broad smile, they giggled at her formality, Ralph Trevallian turned around to glance at Sarah and he appeared surprised to see her standing there. He whispered something to his wife and she looked flustered. Molly carefully wound her way around the room offering a tray of champagne to all the guests. Sarah watched Molly and the other staff efficiently attending to their duties and wished she had been able to join them. She felt very uncomfortable just standing beside the mistress, not actually being part of any of the proceedings or conversations. She was relieved when the dinner gong sounded and she could leave her position and retire to the ballroom and wait with the other companions whilst their employers ate their way through five courses of Nellie's creations.

Tonight she was just a temporary companion to Mrs Trevallian. Sarah wondered whether she would actually enjoy being in the position permanently.

The musicians were tuned and seated ready on the small dais waiting for the cue that dinner was over. Chairs and small tables had been set out around the edges of the vast room, leaving plenty of space in the centre for dancing. By the fireside comfortable chairs and settees had been placed for the older ladies, whose dancing days were well and truly over, they would rest their arthritic bones, gossip and catch up on the latest scandal amongst the rich and famous.

The doors swung open and the master and mistress entered the room followed by Charles and the rest of the guests. The musicians on cue struck up a waltz. The host and hostess took to the floor. Charles and Nicola Paget followed. Silk and taffeta swished around the floor sounding like autumn leaves rustling in the wind. After a few minutes Grace Trevallian was quite out of breath and stopped dancing. Her husband did not hide his annoyance as he took her elbow and hastily led her from the dance floor and deposited her on a settee. Sarah watched him as he stormed off and joined some of the older men who were smoking cigars and enjoying fine cognac at the far end of the room. Grace mopped her moist forehead with her handkerchief, she looked dreadfully flustered.

'Sarah would you please be so kind and fetch my fan from my room, it's so warm in here.'

Sarah nodded and pushed her way through the crowd of people between her and the door, as she offered an apology to one of the guests that she accidentally bumped into a strange thing happened. The double doors near her burst open with such a force that it sent them crashing back against the walls almost immediately an icy blast swept into the room. Some of the ladies squealed as the draft extinguished all but a few of the candles in the room. The musicians stopped playing and just for a moment there was complete silence in the room. Everyone turned to face the open doors trying to see who was responsible for the noisy intrusion.

Charles, his father and a few of the younger gentlemen made their way towards the doors.

Sarah recoiled in horror as she saw the shadow of the cloaked figure sweep into the room and disappear amongst the guests. She looked around anxiously to see where he was. She stood transfixed as the black shadow swirled around only stopping for a second here and there to stroke and tease unsuspecting guests with his long bony fingers. The spirit of death approached Sarah and she recoiled against the wall.

By now the men of the house had found no explanation into the cause of the incident, they had found the staff in the outer hall absolutely rooted to the spot with fear unable to tell them what had happened. It appeared that the front door had also burst open and an icy wind had engulfed them and blown out all the candles leaving them also in sudden darkness. So it was presumed even though it was a frosty and clear night, in fact a freak storm had taken place and a thunderbolt must have struck the house. Satisfied with this logical explanation Ralph Trevallian ushered everyone back into the ballroom and demanded the musicians to start earning their money and continue playing.

'Are you all right?' asked Charles as he spotted Sarah standing against the wall. He stepped towards her.

'You look like you've seen a ghost.'

She took a deep breath before she answered, still not taking her eyes off the malevolent guest, who was now standing behind Grace Trevallians chair with his bony hands resting on the frail women's shoulders.

'I think you should go to your mother, she needs

you,' said Sarah quickly.

'I think that something awful is going to happen to her.'

He glanced over to his mother who was sitting talking to Nicola and Amy's mother.

'She looks absolutely fine to me. What do you think is going to happen to her? Tell me exactly what you are you talking about, look at her, she's in her element, gossiping about some poor soul I suspect.'

The spirit of death moved his shrouded head so his evil eyes could glance in Sarah's direction, the grotesque skull grinned as he flexed his long fingers and placed them around his victim's slim throat. He tilted his chin up in defiance of Sarah. She screamed and ran towards Grace, she reached her just before the lady started choking and gasping for breath. Charles was soon at his mother's side loosening her clothes and calling for the doctor who was present somewhere in the house. Still the icy hands gripped the neck of the now very distraught women.

'He's got his hands around her throat,' warned Sarah. 'Get them off please somebody do something.'

Charles glanced at Sarah disturbed by her strange behaviour.

The Doctor knelt beside the now unconscious Grace Trevallian, he explained to her son and concerned husband that she appeared to be having some kind of seizure.

'Bargain with me Sarah,' said the Devil, 'Come on play the game. Let's see, what would you be prepared to lose if I let this women have her life? A life that is so precious to you, without her, your hopes and dreams would be dashed into oblivion wouldn't they?' He had certainly caught Sarah's attention.

'Well there is always a price to pay, you could call it a consequence or a sacrifice to be made. Let me see now.' And he tightened his grip on the white neck between his hands.

'Anything, I'll do anything, but please take your hands from her throat, please,' blurted Sarah, not letting her eyes glance away from the purple face of her mistress.

Charles and a few other people looked at Sarah as she spoke, unable to grasp what the girl was saying. The doctor sat back as he realised that he could do nothing more to save his patient.

'I'm sorry,' he said as he closed his bag and stood up.

'Let me see now, you'll have to pay a very high price for this rich one's life Sarah. Do you really want to commit yourself to a bond with me that can never be broken, just to save an old lady who has only a few years of natural life left in her at the most?'

Sarah watched in horror as Grace Trevallian's spirit left the prostrate body on the settee and stood with the rest of the concerned onlookers viewing her empty shell. The distressed and confused soul glided to stand at the side of her son and tried desperately to communicate with him, but it was hopeless. Charles was completely unaware of his mother's ghostly presence, in fact, no one could see or hear the anxious pleading of the newly departed soul except for Sarah. A dull ache filled her heart as she looked at the distraught face of her mistress's only child, begging for the doctor to do something, and then the grim realisation that his plea were in vain.

Satisfied that his opponent in the game was ready to compete, the bringer of all that is evil loosened his grip slightly and the ghostly spirit of his victim started to fade.

'Ready to play, goody, goody. Shall I take your soul instead, or shall I save that for later in the game?'

'Yes, yes,' replied Sarah, 'alright I'll do anything, please hurry up, tell me, what do you want, from me?'

'It's quite simple really. I know you do not want to marry the farmer's boy, Peter Pendarvis, you have all those hopes and dreams of having a better life. You think that he's not good enough for you, don't you? You think you radiate your so called love and light, that because you're so kind and sweet you deserve some sort of prize in life and only good things will happen to you and you will get your just reward for being so much like my brother. Well Sarah, life is not really like that. As I have already mentioned, I am here to initiate you into the real world. After tonight you will experience how it really is, you have been sheltered too long. You wait in a very short time you will change and very soon you will be ordinary like the rest of you living beings. You'll stop the holier than though business and be greedy, selfish and cruel and all the other unsaintly attributes that qualify you to be a member of my cult. It's quite simple really, I am going to break you. Tonight we have an agreement. The consequence for me allowing this life beneath my hands to continue is, Peter Pendarvis. Oh how he craves and desires to possess you, now, you will give yourself to him totally without conditions. You will marry him and love, honour and obey till death you do part. And if you break that agreement, and you will, then you will have broken my contract and there will be a consequence to pay, and then I will have some fun at your expense. You will soon join me Sarah,' he paused, just giving her enough time to think about his offer. 'Well Sarah, is it a bargain?'

Sarah watched the skeletal fingers unclasp themselves. She was the only one to hear the gurgling laughter and smell the decaying breath that reached her nostrils.

'You can have your spirit but I will have your living soul.' And with an icy cold disturbance of the air the Spirit of Death swept out of the room.

Sarah pushed her way forward and knelt beside the lifeless body on the settee. Charles was kneeling beside his mother holding her cold limp hand.

'She is alive Charles, look she's breathing.' Sarah took hold of his hand and placed it on his mother's chest. At first Charles looked blankly at Sarah not comprehending what she was saying. She repeated herself. And then slowly he understood her words and felt the slight movement beneath his hand.

'She's alive,' he shouted at the doctor who rushed forward not believing what he was hearing. He did not need his stethoscope to confirm that Grace Trevallian was alive and breathing normally. In a very short time the room was bustling with excited chatter and smiling faces. Grace Trevallian's hands went to her throat as she weakly tried to sit herself upright. Had they looked beneath her high-necked dress no one could have mistaken the purple bruises around her throat, they were the perfect shape of long grasping fingers.

Ralph Trevallian ordered the party to continue, the doctor and Charles helped Grace Trevallian to her room. She was given a light sedative to help her sleep. Charles asked Sarah if she would stay with his mother for the night. Sarah readily agreed and said she would make herself comfortable on the chaise lounge. She was so traumatised by the events of the evening that she completely forgot about Peter waiting for her outside.

She dozed fitfully for a couple of hours, waking frequently to check on her patient. In the end she sat up and tried to read a book. A couple of times Grace Trevallian stirred and opened her eyes and looked at Sarah but did not speak. On one occasion when she woke briefly, Tobias was sitting beside Sarah talking to her telepathically. Tobias suddenly became aware that the elderly lady could actually see him, she had asked Sarah whom the man was sitting beside her. But before Sarah could answer she had fallen back into a deep dream filled sleep.

In the early hours of the morning when it is neither day nor night, the time when all living things are at their lowest ebb and the temperature drops rapidly, Sarah added more logs to the fire in hopes of bringing some warmth to the deathly cold room. Outside a fine flurry of snow was settling, covering the damp ground with a sifting of icy crystals. Grey heavy clouds rolled over the Tor threatening to shed its contents over the entire village. The steady breeze of the night before had now changed into a blustery wind penetrating all the windows and doors of the old house. Sarah listened to the creaks and groans inside the house wondering whether anyone was up and about in the house yet. She strained her ears to listen for some evidence of movement.

Charles Trevallian looked at his bedside clock and decided that he couldn't stay in bed any longer. He had spent an uncomfortable night unable to sleep.

As his bare feet touched the floor he shivered and reached for his slippers and dressing gown. As it was so early he would not be able to ring for the staff to bring him a hot drink or more logs for the fire. So he crept out of his room and closed the door quietly hoping not to disturb his father or any of the guests who had stayed the night at the house. As he reached the lower landing, the floor where his mother's rooms were situated he decided to look in on her just to make sure all was well. Sarah heard the handle on the sitting room door turn slowly, she waited nervously to see who or what would appear. She sighed with relief when she saw Charles. He tiptoed over to the bed and looked closely at his peacefully sleeping mother. She smiled and nodded reassuring him that all was well. He beckoned Sarah out into the sitting room, closing the bedroom door behind him.

'You look like you have had as much sleep as I have,' he said to Sarah. 'I am going downstairs to make a pot of hot coffee would you like some? It's very good.'

Sarah nodded in agreement. She had never tasted coffee before but she did not want to show her ignorance by asking what it was like.

'I'll bring it up here, I think at the moment this must be the warmest room in the house.'

In a very short time Charles returned with a tray laden with food and a pot of the most delicious smelling liquid. He placed it down on the rug in front of the fire and Sarah joined him.

'We used to do this when I was a small boy,' he whispered and he stabbed a doorstep of bread with a toasting iron and thrust it near the hot flames.

'I'll toast the bread and you spread the butter and put the marmalade on.'

They both laughed like naughty children as the sticky butter dribbled down their chins.

'Don't you dare tell my mother that I served the coffee in tea cups and not the minute coffee cups that she uses, will you?' he begged.

As her mouth was still full of food she shook her head in reply.

They chatted easily for the next hour about his mother's condition and his trips abroad. She listened with interest as he explained in detail about the countries he had visited, places that she had only ever read about in some of his mother's books. He told her of the constant sunshine and the happy smiling dark skinned natives of the Indies, who wore vibrant coloured clothes and worked from sunrise to sunset, singing all day, as if it was a joy to be alive. She was mesmerised by the pictures he depicted of the exotic flowers and strange animals that lived in the tropical sunshine, they came alive inside her head as he cleverly described them. Sadly the magic of the moment was broken when Molly entered the room with a tray of breakfast for her mistress. She was visibly surprised to see Charles in his dressing gown sitting with Sarah in front of the fire and judging by the tray of dirty crockery they had been together for a while.

'Excuse me sir,' she said politely. 'I have a message for Sarah.'

'Let me take that tray into my mother.' He took it from Molly and went into his mother's bedroom leaving the girls together.

'You better get yourself downstairs pretty sharpish. Peter is down there, he's demanding that you come down immediately or he's coming up to get you.' She smirked as she spat out her message.

Sarah got to her feet and straightened her dress

amazed at the dreadful sticky butter stains that covered the front of the skirt.

She gently knocked on the bedroom door. Sarah asked how Grace was and explained that Peter was waiting for her in the kitchen and she would have to go home. Grace assured her that she was perfectly fit and did not know why everyone had made so much fuss. She told Sarah to run along home and hoped that Peter was not too upset at her staying the night.

Grace was familiar with Sarah's relationship with Molly's twin. They had discussed her forthcoming marriage and even though she sensed that Sarah was not at all sure about Peter she had made her mind up to go through with it. As the girl had no real family Grace had said she would like to provide the wedding for Sarah. After all she had grown very fond of this slip of a girl, if she had a daughter then she would have wanted her to be just like Sarah.

Charles thanked Sarah profusely for looking after his mother and hoped they would get the chance to talk again. He shook her hand warmly. Running down the stairs she braced herself for the ensuing onslaught that she knew she would have to endure when she saw Peter.

As she expected he stood in the kitchen with his arms folded waiting for her. His eyes were black with anger as she caught the tail end of his conversation with Molly. His eyes straight away looked at the stains down the front of her dress. Ripping her cloak off the hook he threw it at her, opened the door and pushed her out before she had time to put it on.

'Come on,' he snapped. 'Get out, now.'

Molly smiled to herself she knew her brother well

enough to know that once they were outside Sarah would be in for a lot of trouble, after all the girl deserved it, didn't she. It was a wonder that her brother had waited until this morning to come and get her. She had only just managed to stop him last night when she had given him the message from Charles that Sarah was staying the night. She had omitted to tell him the details as to why she was staying. Peter had instantly jumped to the wrong conclusions and Molly had let him and added a few untruths to really add fuel to an already raging fire.

All his worst fears concerning Sarah seemed to have come true in one single night. All along he had believed that once she was out of his sight then something like this would happen. His possessive behaviour towards Sarah blotted out all rational reasoning. In his mind, with the help of his sister everything he imagined might happen was now reality. She had spent the night at the house with that bastard Charles and he had taken what should have been his and left his dirty mark on her dress for everyone to see.

Outside the light flurry of snow had gained strength and almost become a blizzard. The wind whipped Sarah's cloak from her and chilled her to the bone. She pulled it back around her with frozen hands. She pulled her hood down over her face and bent her head against the wind and followed Peter down the drive.

He made sure that they had walked far enough from the house so no one would hear what he was going to say to Sarah. Just as they reached the main gates he turned to grab hold of her arms and spill forth all the accusations he had spent creating over the last twenty four hours. Half of his words were taken by the wind and she could not hear what he was saying. He called her a slut and a whore that she was no better than the girls on the streets. He reminded her that she had agreed to marry him and that if she broke that agreement he would make sure nobody had her. As she remained silent and did not defend herself or deny his accusations his anger rose. His hands gripped her arms and he violently shook her. Her hood came off and the icy wind released her wild black hair to fly freely in the wind. She raised her head to look up at Peter's face. Visions of the small child being violently shaken at the church gates flashed through her mind. It was all just the same, she did not know what she had actually done wrong then and she did not know what she had done wrong now. She had only experienced two men in her life and they both seemed to be the same. As the tears dripped onto her frozen face a silent shadow passed through the trees and she heard the grotesque laughter. She looked into the face of her future husband and resigned herself to the fact that she had actually chosen her own destiny, she could have let Grace Trevallian die and then she would have been free to choose. But she would have suffered guilt over being selfish and that she would not have been able to live with. Now she would adapt and make the most of the forthcoming situation. Compared with some unfortunate people's lives she was a very lucky person. A man loved her, he was prepared to look after her and provide security. She would have a nice little home and children. What more could she really expect or wish for. After all what was love. She convinced herself that her fondness for Peter would eventually grow into some sort of love. The shaking stopped and as he loosened his grip on her arms she lost her balance and flopped down in the snow. He pulled her to her feet.

'Now, listen to me Sarah, you will never visit that house again, do you hear me? If you had listened to Molly and me in the first place none of this would have happened. I don't know if I really want to take you on now, after what's happened.'

She found her voice, 'Nothing's happened, Peter, nothing at all.'

Raising her voice above the wind she related the previous evening's events. She omitted the part about the bargain with the Grim Reaper and then made all the denials that Peter expected to hear. Even though they were perfectly truthful she still felt she needed to convince Peter that nothing had happened. Just to please him she told him that she did not like Charles. This ploy certainly did the trick. In return he told her that Molly had once confided in him that Charles preferred young men for his company and he had never been with a women. Sometime later she was to realise that Molly had made up that story because Charles had refused her offers and she had been upset by his rejection.

Peter thought about all that Sarah had said. In his mind he was still not sure. Of course there was one way that he could prove that what she had told him was true. He really had desperately tried to reserve this until their wedding night but under the circumstances he might have to find out one way or the other before then.

Charles Trevallian stood looking out of his mother's balcony window. Through the driving snow he could just make out the figures at the end of the drive. He saw the girl's wild raven hair dancing in the wind and the aggressive manner of the man who was roughly shaking her. Instinctively he wanted to rush out of the house and intervene. He related to his mother what was happening outside and then he saw Sarah fall down into the snow.

'I can't watch this mother, I'll have to go out there and stop the man.'

'You can't interfere son, they are to be married. It's none of your business.'

As Sarah scrambled to her feet he turned away from the window and sat down beside his mother.

'Mother, I want you to tell me all you know about Sarah.'

'I had a feeling once you met her you would ask me this question. It's a shame you did not come home sooner Charles before Molly's dreadful brother laid claim to her.'

CHAPTER THIRTEEN

The winter had started early, the fields and surrounding countryside were becoming covered with a thick layer of frozen snow. Heavy black clouds rolled over the Tor casting dark shadows over the hills. Peter had brought the sheep down from the higher ground and confined them to a pen near the farm. The unhappy cattle had been kept in the barn for many days it seemed pointless to let them out when you could not see a blade of grass, they moaned miserably as they shifted around in the damp dark building. Already the animals had consumed a large amount of the winter food store and Peter was worried that if the bad weather continued he would soon run out. He always kept a fair amount in store for his own animals use and the surplus would be sold, he relied on the income, but this winter looked to have all the signs of being a long one and that would mean he would have to buy in.

The north-easterly wind rudely penetrated the farm cottage. All the chairs were pulled up in front of the large log fire, every so often an icy blast would blow down the chimney and the room would be engulfed in a blue haze of wood smoke making everyone eyes water and smart.

The men in the family were becoming restless and annoyed as the miserable weather stopped them from their nightly visits to The Pendragon Arms.

Daniel and Peter sat in front of the fire dozing and drinking the raw scrumpy that Sarah had made. It had not had enough time to improve and mature, but still they consumed it, complaining bitterly about its sharp taste and pulling awful faces as the raw acidity assaulted their taste buds. Gwen and Sarah sat at the table going through the pile of clothes that had to be darned and mended.

'We should really make a start on your dress soon, now that we have all this material,' said Gwen. 'I hope we have enough to make the girls matching outfits, it would be so nice to have you all in the same colour lace.'

'By the look of the amount we have we could make most of the village dresses,' replied Sarah.

'I thought it was very kind of Mrs Trevallian to send us the material, we could never have afforded such quality, could we?'

Sarah put a finger to her mouth to quieten Gwen. Gwen looked towards Peter and realised that he was dozing in the chair and had not heard her comment about the wedding material being a gift from the Trevallian family. After that disastrous weekend of the party, Sarah had written to Grace explaining that it would be best if she did not visit High Markham for a while. She did not tell her that she had been forbidden by Peter nor did she inform her about the trouble that she had been in for staying the night of the party. Grace had written back sending the letter to her with the cart boy who collected flour regularly from the farm. She told Sarah that she really understood and that they would always be friends and perhaps once she was settled and married then Peter would not object to her visiting High Markham again. But for now perhaps they could meet sometime for tea at the

Paget's teashop, to make arrangements for the wedding without Peter knowing. She would send a message via the errand boy letting her know when she would be next visiting the village.

Sarah had really missed her visits to High Markham, but very soon she had put the spare time to good use and seriously put in a lot of thought to creating and supplying healing potions to the Paget's shop. She had expanded her range to cover all sorts of ailments. Owing to the cold spell of weather it seemed everyone had some sort of ache, pain or complaint.

Recently Sarah had been considering opening a small shop of her own in the village. Nicola Paget had suggested the idea as her father owned a small property adjoining the girls' tea shop, it had recently become vacant and Nicola thought it would be a good idea for Sarah to rent the property to sell her wares and practice healing. Sarah had discussed the idea with Peter and he did not seem to object, especially when she told him that Janet could work with her. She had worked out the cost of actually renting the shop and the expected income and Peter seemed satisfied that it could bring in extra money that was well needed. The only reservation that Sarah had was to whether she would be able to supply enough stock to fill the shop. Nicola suggested that she could actually sell other people's crafts and this would complement Sarah's merchandise and fill the shelves. Sarah had made a few inquiries and very soon managed to recruit a few craftsmen eager to sell their creations. So, the plan was starting to take shape and Sarah hoped to visit the property as soon as the weather permitted her to walk down to the village. Nicola's father had said if she decided to take it on then she could have the first month rent free on the condition that she had to clean and decorate the shop herself before she could open. When she consulted Tobias he said it was an opportunity for a new adventure, it must be meant as it was all slipping into place quite easily and she should follow the path that was being opened up for her.

Sarah shivered as she scratched a small area of ice off the inside of the windows, the stone floor in the cottage was so cold on her feet that she had to stand on tip toe. She peered out through the ice covered glass at the wintry landscape. Even though the arctic conditions were treacherous it was the only time that the earth looked perfectly clean and beautiful. The full moon made the fields and trees look quite magical. Tonight she could not sleep there were so many ideas racing through her head and she had tossed and turned eventually disturbing Janet. She needed time on her own without the noisy family around her. Finally she decided to get up and make a hot drink. But now she was wide awake and really wanted to go outside and walk in the beauty of the night. Making sure not to disturb the rest of the family she gathered her clothes from the bedroom. Putting on Peter's large working boots she silently lifted the latch on the door and ventured outside.

The perfect stillness was breathtaking, she surveyed the carpet of glistening diamonds that stretched for miles before her. It was far too cold for it to snow anymore and the ground had started to freeze. Millions of crystals reflected the silvery light of the moon that hung in the midnight blue sky. The yard and the lane leading from the farm down to the village, a few weeks before, had been a brown muddy quagmire lined with rotting autumn vegetation and the trees barren and stark. Now the world had become a winter wonderland. The trees had been iced with a piping of fine crystals. High statuesque drifts lined the lane enveloping the dormant hedgerows barely leaving a narrow pathway down the lane.

The livestock grunted and shifted around as Sarah crept past the barn. Suddenly an idea came into her head, she turned and looked at the woodland behind the farm, something seemed to be pulling her attention to the trees and far beyond. No, she thought she must not go anywhere near High Markham. But the feeling to visit was overwhelming. Before she could convince herself to go back indoors she found her feet had taken her past the farm and the mill and now she was following the path up to the house.

The fear and the thought of what would happen to her if Peter caught her made her feel hot and warmed her up immensely, a voice inside her urged her to continue and convinced her that she was in the safety and freedom of the night. She told Tobias off for encouraging her to disobey Peter's definite orders. But as usual Tobias told her she was doing nothing wrong just walking in the woods, she wasn't actually going to knock on the door of High Markham and ask to go in, was she?

'Come on,' he mused, 'Where's your sense of adventure, who knows what's ahead of you unless you find out. If your fear turns you back, you could miss a wonderful exciting new experience. Live Sarah, don't let fear keep you within the security of what you know.' Then he was off on one of his talks. He walked back and forward in front of her trying to gain her undivided attention. 'Life is like a crossroads. You can stand in the middle for all eternity. You can see the paths leading out away from you but through your own fear you think you would rather stay safe and secure in the middle never finding out what's at the end of the pathways but always wondering. Well now let me give you an example.'

'Do I have any choice,' said Sarah, her words coming out in clouds of misty breath, which was soon engulfed into the cold night air.

'Well you have the choice to listen or the choice to ignore what I'm saying.'

'All right, all right get it over with.'

'At the moment, like I have just said you feel you are standing in the middle of a crossroads. There are four roads leading away from you, north, south, east and west. Each one has a signpost, HOPES and DREAMS is one, TRY ME, MYSTERY TOUR another, TRUST ME, D. EVIL and the last, DEEP BLUE SEA. You seem to believe only one path leads to your happiness, but do you know which one. Your fear of choosing the wrong one stops you from trying any of them. So you stay safely at a standstill in the centre, sometimes nearly taking the chance. Now let me give you some advice. Life is full of opportunities, if the path you have chosen turns out to be a dead end, what is the worst thing that can happen to you, you just turn around and go back to the centre and start again. But at least you will have tried it and will not always be wondering what would have happened if you had taken it. Then it would have become one of your future regrets, which are only mistakes we have made in the past. What if I told you that every path you take will lead to an adventure, a new episode, and that whatever path you take will be right for you at that time.'

He stopped for a moment to let her think about what he had said.

'So you are telling me to let go of the fear of getting things wrong and do what my instinct tells me to do at the time, and it's all right if I do get things wrong. What has all this got to do with you edging me on to visit High Markham when you know that I am forbidden by Peter to go anywhere near the place?'

'It's his fear that stops you from going not yours you are just afraid of him, we should not expect to manipulate others human's lives with our own fears. Anyway if you don't go now you might miss an adventure, and it's the adventures in our youth that fill us with memories that keep us company when we reach the autumn of our life. We must grow old without any regrets that we did not take the chance. Only have regrets for the things we have done not the things we haven't.'

They both had now reached the lake, the dark grey mansion loomed above them high up on the hill. The surface of the lake had turned to ice and the moon reflected on the grey mirror. At this moment Sarah could believe that she was the only person alive on this earth, perfect tranquillity engulfed her how peaceful the world seemed especially after being confined to the cramped noisy farmhouse for the last few weeks. She pulled her cloak around her tightly against the cold and sat down on a fallen tree trunk, as her eyes grew accustom to the moonlight she could just make out the silhouettes of a pair of deer desperately clawing at the ground in search of food. High in the trees a dark pair of wings beat silently as the night bird spied its prey and prepared to swoop on a small water rodent that had cautiously emerged from the frozen bank of the lake. Sarah turned her head as she strained her ears to listen to a distant sound coming from the direction of the house. It sounded like a dog barking or could it be a fox. Again she heard the sound nearer this time and accompanied by the voice of a man. Sarah quickly jumped up and turned back to the pathway intending to seek shelter from the trees and not be seen by whoever was now approaching her at great speed. But before she achieved her aim a black spaniel churned its way through the snow and rushed towards her. The barking dog was so excited at finding Sarah that he jumped up at her and nearly knocked her over, she patted him and rubbed his long curly ears and told him to be quiet as the noise he was making was enough to wake the dead. The deep barking continued and the sound bounced off the trees and echoed around the lake. The mass of black unruly fur playfully cavorted around Sarah's feet, each time she reached down to seize his collar with a hope of being able to silence the death defying sound he was making, the dog thought she wanted to play a game with him and became more boisterous. A shrill whistle from the direction of the terraces pierced the air and the dog stopped dead still in his tracks, he looked at Sarah and hesitated for just one second before he raced off back up to his master. Charles Trevallian quietly scolded the dog and ordered him to stay by his side as he continued his walk. At first he thought Rufus had become excited by a rabbit or fox but as he knelt down beside the dog a familiar fragrance of woodland herbs filled his senses, instantly he knew who the dog had been barking at. He hurried his stride through the crisp snow and took the path that led down to the lake. Sarah sensed the man and the dog coming towards her, she wondered who could possibly be about at this time of night in such freezing conditions. Again the dog greeted her and she returned the affection.

'Well fancy meeting you at this time of night,' said Charles.

'This is the first time I've bumped into a human being, we usually meet plenty of wildlife and occasionally scare a poacher but we have never had anyone to talk to before have we Rufus?' And he stooped and ruffled the dog's fur.

'Same here,' said Sarah. 'Do you often walk at night, can't you sleep either?'

'Let's keep walking,' he said.' The cold seeps into your marrow if you stand still too long.' And he held her elbow and guided her along the path beside the lake. 'I expect you're going to recommend to me to purchase one of your famous herb pillows that my mother curls up with at night, aren't you?'

Sarah laughed. 'I'll send one up to you, free of charge.' She added.

'I hear that you are going to open a shop of your own very soon. It sounds a very exciting enterprise. And I'm sure you will do very well and my mother will most probably be your best customer. She regrets not seeing you anymore.'

'I also miss visiting your mother, I've grown very fond of her, she's a very kind lady, at least you are at home now and she has got your company.'

'Not for long I'm afraid, I still have the family fortunes to attend to abroad. In fact already I feel I have neglected them too much and directly after Christmas I must return and sort out some new trade routes that are being opened. Well I must not bore you with talk of my business. Tell me, what are your plans for the future apart from having the most popular Cure-all shop in Cornwall?'

They had walked almost around the outskirts of the frozen lake. She told Charles about her ambition to help and heal people and all the earth's living creatures. She told him about her dream of having a sanctuary where she could take in all life's waifs and strays, handicapped and ill-treated children, abandoned babies, young people who found themselves on the streets. Passionately she described how she could offer a purpose and self-worth to most of society's rejections.

Charles listened with great interest and was genuinely enthusiastic about her ideas. She told him about the asylum where her grandmother and many other people had died and about how everyone treated Janet as if she was mad and yet she was only deaf. She had become so absorbed in the intensity of the conversation that she had not realised that they had now walked well away from the lake and had followed a trail that she had not taken before. The woodland seemed to close in around them and the branches of the tall trees reached down to touch them both. Charles noticed her apprehension as she realised that the place was unfamiliar to her.

'Have you never visited the pagoda, Sarah? When I was a small boy I used to hide away in there for hours. Mother would know where I was but she would never tell my father. It's just through this clearing.'

The path widened and opened out, forming a circular clearing. Even though all around them the ground was completely covered with snow, in the centre of the area sat a circle of fine green grass, not a flake of snow or ice touched it. He caught

Sarah's expression of complete bewilderment.

'It's always been like this. I don't know why,' puzzled Charles.

'Sarah knelt down and ran her fingers through the new green grass. It's a fairy ring,' she said quite seriously. 'A magic circle, the earth's energies are very good in this spot, if you feel it, you will see that the ground is much warmer here than the rest of the woodland. There will be some very good ley lines under this earth,' and she promptly started to take off the heavy boots of Peters that she had been wearing. Charles started to laugh. 'What in heaven's name do you think you are doing? You'll freeze to death. You look like you're about to paddle your feet in the sea.'

'Oh come on, take your boots off and join me,' and she stepped into the circle. 'It's lovely and warm, honestly.' Rufus joined her but his master didn't. He just stood watching the cavorting pair with a very amused look on his face.

'You are nothing but a scaredy cat,' she shouted to him.

'No I'm not.'

'Oh come on no one can see you, only me and I won't tell anyone, honestly.'

'It's absolute madness to take off your boots in these freezing conditions.'

'And we thought you were a big strong man, didn't we Rufus?' she teased. 'Now do I look cold,' she questioned as she threw off her coat and scarf.

'Feel my hand,' and she stretched her hand towards him. As he cautiously felt her fingers she instantly gripped his hand and roughly pulled him into the warm circle. Caught by utter surprise he stumbled and fell taking Sarah down with him. Rufus who was so excited by the human's behaviour, he thought this was a new game and playfully started to attack the two prostrate figures. The more Sarah tried to push the dog away the more Rufus nuzzled and nipped her and the more she screamed and laughed the more Charles went into spasms of hysterics. The tears dripped down both their faces as they tried to get to their feet. Every time Charles tried to give a sharp command for the dog to stop he was racked by more laughter. He made a grab for the dog's collar and managed to subdue the excited canine's behaviour. Sarah remained seated on the grass her feet and knees of her stockings were green with grass stains she was absolutely exhausted from laughing, she tried to wipe away the tears from her face.

Charles handed her a fine linen handkerchief, she wiped her eyes and blew her nose on it before she realised that it was such a beautiful item. 'Oh sorry,' she said as she looked at the mess she had made of the exquisite monogrammed handkerchief. 'I think that I had better wash this before I return it to you,' and she popped it into the pocket of her dress.

'Well Sarah I can't remember when I last laughed so much, of course you are right, this circle is really warm, how strange.'

'See, I told you so.'

'Now you sound just like my mother.' He stepped out of the circle and held his hand out to her.

'Come I want to show you my sanctuary.'

Nestled beneath an enormous willow tree sat an extraordinary building. The dome of the roof was made of glass and the wooden roof frame swept down to the six sides of the pentagon shaped structure, it then curled up into a roll at the edges and was topped with a golden spheres. The outside walls were black marble with oriental designs painted on them. The roof of the front porch was supported by two black pillars which framed the enormous oak doors. Sarah was fascinated by the building and could not believe that she had never been to this part of the estate before.

Charles reached underneath one of the stone urns that sat at the entrance, and extracted a large wrought iron key. With a clank and a rattle the key turned and he pushed open the heavy oak doors. He held out his hand, took hers and led her inside.

The stars and frozen moonlight shone brightly through the glass-domed roof of the pagoda, casting an eerie blue light throughout the white marbled room. As Charles put tinder to the fire Sarah felt a shiver enter her body. It felt like fear and yet it also felt like excitement. This place even though she had never been here before felt really familiar to her as if all her life she had been looking for a special place and now she had suddenly found it a place where you could feel safe to live in for the rest of your life and a place that you would just as happy to die in when the time came.

Charles lit the candles in the gilt sconces that were backed by tall gothic mirrors. All six sections of the walls had identical mirrors and candle sconces. When all the candles were lit they reflected into the mirrors opposite casting an illusion that the room was full of hundreds of mirrors and twice as many candles. The strangely shaped room harboured an assortment of elaborately decorated furniture that had been collected by Charles's grandparents on their many visits to far off lands. Sarah nervously took a seat by the fireside. She sat on a heavy brocade chaise lounge that mimicked the golden colour of the roaring flames. Charles was opening the doors of an elegantly painted black and red Chinese cupboard.

'I'm afraid we only have champagne or brandy, which would you prefer?'

Sarah had never tasted either of the drinks that he offered. She hesitated slightly before she answered. 'Perhaps Champagne, no Brandy, no champagne, Oh you decide I can't make up my mind.' The cork on the champagne bottle burst out into the room and Sarah gasped as the golden liquid bubbled excitedly out of the bottle and onto the white marble floor. Two tall crystal champagne flutes were filled with the lively liquid and placed on a small side table.

'I don't think we will need an ice bucket tonight, it's perfectly chilled already,' he took a sip.

'I must admit it is my favourite drink. It always makes me feel happy and content and it soothes my senses. The world always seems a better place after a couple of glasses of champagne. Well, are you going to try yours or just watch me drink mine?'

Sarah coughed as the bubbles rushed up the back of her throat and burst into her nose. She was mesmerised by the glass in her hand, the crystal had been cut into so many angles that the prisms of light danced off in all directions, all the colours of the rainbow were cupped in her hand, reminding Sarah of her grandmother's wind chimes.

'Well what do you think of my sanctuary? My grandfather had it built for my grandmother. It was constructed upon the lines of something oriental that she had seen on her travels. My father used to say that she had it built as a boudoir so she could entertain her stream of lovers without my grandfather knowing, I think she spent a lot of her time here when she wanted to be on her own. Or when she was doing one of her card readings and she wanted privacy. In fact in the back room I have kept some of my grandmother's things just as she left them. It gives me great comfort to see them. I was very fond of her even though she was quite eccentric.'

Sarah was walking around the pagoda looking at all the fine pieces of furniture, she stopped to answer his question.

'I like your sanctuary very much. It is the most beautiful place that I have ever been in, I feel very safe here.' Charles got up and joined her.

'That's a very strange thing to say. Don't you feel safe at the farm?'

She answered very quickly.

'Oh yes I do,' she didn't want to give him the impression that there was anything wrong in her life. So many people she knew were only too ready to unburden their soul and make people feel sorry for them. Also she had her pride, if she admitted she was not altogether happy then she was saying that she had failed in some way. So her policy was to always say everything was fine. Charles did not pursue the question any further.

'I used to spend hours here at night looking up at the star filled sky.' And he looked up to the glass-domed ceiling. Sarah followed his gaze. A million dazzling stars and many bright planets hung from the midnight blue sky, the more her eyes grew accustom to the night sky the deeper she could see into the universe.

'I find this is the perfect place to get complete peace. I can stargaze with my telescope, read and sometimes catch up on my writing.'

'What do you write?'

'Oh nothing very clever I'm afraid, just a few bits

of poetry that never makes much sense.'

'I didn't know that you wrote poetry, your mother's never mentioned it.'

'My mother will not acknowledge that I write poetry, as you well know she likes the traditional poets, whose works are quite hard to understand. I am what you would call a modern poet. I write about things that touch my heart or make me angry. Mother says I get far too passionate about too many lost causes.'

'I would like to read some of your work some time.'

'Well if you really want to, but it's not that good. It's in the other room in the desk, come I'll show you. And Sarah please feel free to come here anytime you like, you know where the key is hidden. I'm sure you will get as much pleasure from this magical place as I do.'

'Thank you Charles that is a very kind offer, it's comforting to know that I have somewhere I can go if I need a little peace and quiet.'

'Mind you I doubt that you will have a lot of spare time on your hands to come here, what with the setting up of your business and your forthcoming marriage to arrange. My mother is getting very excited about the wedding. She has a long list of things that she wants to discuss with you. As it's a little difficult for you to visit her at the moment she thought perhaps she could come down to the farm and see you there. Do you think that would present a problem with the family?' He purposely did not say Peter.

Sarah was deep in thought and he waited patiently for her reply.

'What were you thinking about Sarah, you were far away there for a moment?'

'Oh sorry, I feel this room is so familiar it's uncanny, what were you asking me?' He repeated the question, as she followed him into the small room.

'I'll have to have a word with Peter and see if it's all right and then I'll send a message to your mother.' Sarah's eyes scanned the small room it was crammed with furniture and strange objects. Colourful scarves of oriental origin adorned the walls. Two Painted Chinese vases stood on the shelves above the bed they contained plumes of tall black ostrich feathers. The bed itself was covered in a bright purple silk throw over which was highly decorated with embroidered symbols in gold thread.

'Look at all these things,' said Charles. 'I don't know why I have kept them so long. I suppose it's because I was so fond of her. Sometimes when I'm in here I feel so close to her. Do you sense her at all, Sarah?'

'You will have to give me something of hers to hold, something that she was very attached to.'

Charles went to the dressing table drawer and pulled out a black leather box. As he opened the clasp and exposed the contents the light from the candles caught the diamonds and sapphires in the box and radiated a glittering reflection out into the room. Sarah gasped as her eyes absorbed such beauty. Charles dropped the waterfall necklace into her hands. She closed her eyes and took a few deep breaths to still her mind. In a very short time a vision started to appear. Far in the distance of her mind she could hear music playing, she strained her ears to listen and as she did the music grew louder. Somewhere an orchestra played a ghostly waltz. The notes were hypnotic. Charles intently watched the expression on Sarah's face. 'What do you see Sarah, tell me?'

'Can't you hear the music Charles it's wonderful, my heart is filled with such happiness I can't describe it to you. Just a minute, I can see someone.'

'Go on,' said Charles. 'Tell me who is it.'

'I don't know who she is, but she is very beautiful. She is wearing a velvet dress the colour of azure blue and around her neck are the jewels that I am holding.' Sarah drifted off again into the magical scene.

'She is dancing to the music, she is here in the pagoda.' Sarah was so overcome with emotion that tears started to fill her eyes. A feeling of absolute love that she had never experienced before filled every inch of her body. She closed her eyes and the music played louder and louder. She could feel her body wanting to dance and sway, mesmerised by the liquid rhythm.

'Sarah, you are getting upset, what is the matter?' He took the jewels from her hands.

'I saw a lady she was so beautiful, I think it must have been your grandmother. She was so real.'

'Just a moment,' said Charles, 'I want to show you something, is this the dress?' And he went to the wardrobe and pulled out the very same blue velvet dress.

Sarah held the dress to her. 'Oh yes, this is it. So it was your grandmother.'

'Did she say anything to you, perhaps a message for me?'

'Sorry no, she was just dancing to the most beautiful music on this earth. Next time I'll try and contact her for you.'

'Why don't you try the dress and the jewellery on,

I'm sure it will be a perfect fit,' and he left the room. 'I promise I won't look.'

Sarah hesitated not really knowing what to do. But she was drawn to the glittering jewels and the incredible blue dress. Quickly she pulled off her threadbare clothes and boots and slipped the dress on. Of course Charles was right it fitted perfectly. Reaching inside the wardrobe she took out a pair of velvet shoes that matched the dress, they were exactly the correct size. As if she was being urged on by some unforeseen force, she opened a drawer in the dressing table and took out a silver hairbrush and hair pins. With a flick of her wrist her wild raven locks were piled expertly high on top of her head, she allowed just a few ringlets to cascade onto her white slender neck. As she turned around Charles appeared in the doorway. Standing silently behind her he fastened the waterfall of diamonds and sapphires around her neck. He turned her around to face him. His hands lingered gently on her shoulders. She thought she was standing too close to him and nervously tried to step away from him but her feet refused to move. The melodious tune that she heard a few moments ago started to creep into the room and fill the pagoda. Charles led her out of the room. He took her in his arms.

'I can't dance, not properly.'

'Oh yes you can, trust me.'

As if she was caught up in a magical dream she fell in step with him. His mop of blonde hair fell over his eyes as he looked down at her. He could not help but notice that her eyes were the same azure blue as the dress she was wearing. All Sarah's nervousness had left her, she waltzed around the white marble floor as if it was the most natural thing to be doing in the early hours of a winter morning. The music seemed to penetrate deep within her very soul, awakening a part of her that had been dormant a very long time. Her body glided in harmony with the strong arms that held her. The couple radiated golden threads of pure love from the passion that entwined them. If only Sarah had realised that the strength of their love would have been so potent that nothing could ever have come between them. Not the truly righteous Tobias or his devil of a brother the spirit of Evil. If she had known this she could have chosen a very different pathway for her life. But as far as she was concerned her bargain with the spirit of death was not negotiable she had given her word. Driven by unforeseen forces the couple continued to dance, mesmerised by each other. Sarah tilted her chin upwards ready to receive a gentle kiss from Charles. Her heart felt suddenly free from the barbed wire that seemed to have encased it all her life. She responded to her soul mate with all the genuine passion that she could reveal. At last she felt this is where she was meant to be. The music started to fade into the distance and as it ebbed the couple stopped embracing and starred at each other. Grim reality pushed its way into Sarah's mind. Charles was so overcome with emotion that he could not speak. He held Sarah at arm's length, trying to find the right words to express himself. The magic of the last hour started to disappear and was slowly being replaced by fear of what she had been doing. Still the couple remained speechless. Embarrassed by Charles's silence Sarah pulled herself away from his arms and hurried to the small room to change out of the dress. Charles stood rubbing his forehead in utter amazement and confusion unable to understand the strong feelings he was now experiencing. He'd had a few relationships, here and abroad, but never before had he felt such overwhelming love for any one person. And never before had he been so spellbound. He felt he was suffering from some sort of shock. In the small room Sarah had the sensation of becoming hot and cold, she was also confused but embarrassed by her own forward behaviour and she quickly took off the velvet dress and returned the jewels to their leather box. Replacing the blue slippers with Peter's work boots made her want to cry. She pulled her cloak around her and left the room, she could not look Charles in the face. Quickly she blurted out. 'Thank you for letting me try on the dress and your grandmothers jewels but I really must be going.' He stepped forward to stop her.

'Please Sarah you can't leave yet. There is so much we need to talk about, before I leave England. Please I implore you Sarah stay and listen to what I have to say to you it could change our lives.' Flustered and frightened she pushed past him and made for the door.

'No, I'm sorry, I can't. I should never have come. If Peter knew I was here my life would not be worth living.'

'I can't let you marry that man Sarah, I know you don't love him. You will be just letting yourself in for a life of misery.'

'You don't understand what you are talking about Charles. I have to marry him,' and she was gone.

For a long time he stood at the open door of the pagoda, but he knew it was no use to go after her she was running like the wind and would be well on her way into the woods by now. He walked back into the pagoda and stood in front of one of the tall mirrors. 'Well grandmother, what do you think of her, isn't she the right person for me.' A handsome lady looked back at him with a broad smile on her face.

'She will do very nicely my dear boy, but as you know in the world I live in there is no such thing as time so I cannot tell you when I can manage to manipulate events for you. Just be patient and go with the flow for the moment.'

'But she's about to marry somebody else.'

'In the past marriage has never stopped partners from falling out of love with each other or in love with another, besides, forbidden fruit often tastes much sweeter. Trust my dear Charles. If it's right the universe will provide...'

CHAPTER FOURTEEN

Deep icy slush and thick brown mud covered the centre of the village. The slow thawing snow had run off the higher ground and gushed down the lane flooding the main street. Horse drawn carts slowly pushed their way through the frozen quagmire gouging deep furrows making it more treacherous than when it was solid with three feet of snow. Peter urged the horses forward, they strained and heaved, blowing hot steam from their nostrils. Under the extreme weight of the laden cart the wooden wheels creaked and groaned as they slowly turned and sunk deeper and deeper into the mud.

Peter and Sarah had braved the slightly improved conditions this particular morning to come down to the village, Peter wanted to collect stone and window frames from Appleton's builders yard so Daniel and him could make a start on the barn conversion. They both had a little time to spare as it was too wet to work out in the fields. He had dropped Sarah off at their new venture. At last she had made her mind up and decided to open her curious little shop, selling just about everything and anything, she was eager to open in time for Christmas. Peter did not mind what she sold as long as it made money, something that they really needed at this moment.

The shop was situated in the main street. It was

not very wide, but it was long and narrow. On one side it adjoined Nicola Paget's Tea shop and on the other side was an archway with wrought iron gates, through these was a long cobbled alleyway leading to the undertakers and funeral parlour. It was a family business run by Elisha Moore and his spinster sister Alison. The brother and sister reminded Sarah of the walking dead. They were both very tall and extremely thin. Sarah reckoned she had seen more flesh on a dog bone than they had between them. They both had the same waxy embalmed look about them, and it was rumoured that they were both addicted to the intoxicating fluid that they worked with. A couple of times Sarah had smiled and waved a greeting to them as they passed her shop window, but neither managed to offer any kind of acknowledgement at all which convinced Sarah even more that they were not of this world. Tobias had reassured her that they definitely were not of his world either, because no one was that miserable where he lived.

Quite often when there was a funeral next door Sarah would look up and see the dear departed follow their empty body to their own funeral. She thought if only the grieving families realised that the body in the coffin was just the vehicle for the soul to live on this material plane and that when you died the soul was happy and free to move on into the other realms of your spiritual journey.

Sarah rubbed the condensation off the inside of the shop window and peered through to look at Peter who was still struggling with the well laden cart. She would be most surprised if he managed to get back up the steep lane to Mill Farm with the amount of materials he had loaded into the cart. He smiled and waved at her when he saw her watching. She waved back at him. Recently he had been in reasonable humour and had started to become quite interested in the shop. She had to admit she was getting a little excited about their forthcoming wedding and the new little cottage that Peter and Daniel were building for them. They had spent the last month planning the interior of the cottage. It was going to be quite a lot bigger than she had first thought. She would have a kitchen come living room with a separate small scullery which would have a tub built into it for boiling the washing and heating the water. It would also enable them to have some privacy to take a bath. The stable part of the barn would be split into two to provide two small bedrooms instead of one large one. One for Peter and herself and one for the children when they came along which Peter was sure would happen almost immediately. Through the side door of the barn Peter was going to build a sheltered earth closet.

With Janet's help Sarah had made calico curtains for the new home. They had to roughly guess the size the windows would eventually be. Sarah had embroidered bluebells and primroses on the hems of the curtains and plaited blue and yellow ribbons to act as tie backs. At the moment they were working on a patchwork quilt, they had great fun identifying all the different squares of material, there was a piece of Mary's baby dress, remnants of Janet's petticoats and Gwen's apron and pieces of very expensive brocade fabric that Nicola had given to Sarah.

Grace had really been very thoughtful and provided Sarah with all sorts of useful things for her bottom drawer. She had asked Nellie to sort out the cupboards in the kitchens at High Markham and had given Sarah, iron pots and pans, a few odd willow pattern plates and a box of assorted kitchen utensils and cutlery. To Sarah's delight, when she rummaged through the box she had found a matching knife and fork in silver plate. She had carefully wrapped the pair up in a damask napkin and stored them away carefully, planning only to use them on special occasions.

The wedding had been arranged to take place in March. The church had been booked and Peter had finally agreed to allow Grace to arrange a reception in the Tythe barn on the estate. Peter was still not very keen on Sarah visiting the house but he had mellowed a little towards the old lady. After all she was footing a lot of the bills that occurred with the wedding. And he really did want to have a wedding that he and Sarah would always remember and of course would be the envy of his friends.

Since that strangely wonderful evening in the pagoda Sarah had not seen Charles at all not even a glimpse of him in the village. She had been quite happy to put that episode well behind her. One of the reasons was that she was totally embarrassed by the episode. She could only remember a small part of the evening, she presumed that she must have been intoxicated by the champagne and hoped she had not done anything more than dance, dressed in his grandmothers clothes, what a fool she must of looked to him. She expected that he had decided to keep well out of her way. The other reason was Nicola had mentioned that her mother and Grace had been discussing how nice it would be if Nicola and Charles were to become friends. Nicola was most eager for that to happen and had recently confided in Sarah that she had always had a soft spot for Charles. She mentioned that on the evening of the party at the house he had asked her to dance twice and he only asked all the other girls for one dance each. Sarah thought of the feel of his arms around her, as they had waltzed around the pagoda. Why had she thought anymore in to it? After all it was only a dance. Sarah had listened intently to Nicola and came to realise that Charles was most probably still laughing at her silly behaviour. She hoped that he had not told his mother.

The shop walls had been colour washed with an earthenware paint to give it a natural appearance. Either side the walls were covered with pine shelves. Down the centre of the shop was a long table covered in a dark red cloth, on the table was an assortment of Sarah lotions, potions and parchments. The shelves held a variety of handmade crafts and the far wall was covered in shelves full of interesting books. Carefully Sarah unpacked the small stone jars of balms and lotions, she placed them on the pine shelves that stretched across the walls. In small baskets she laid lavender bags she had made out of floral fabric edged with locally handmade lace. The herb pillows were scattered along the pine counter where she also kept the scales for weighing her herbal tea leaves. There were lace edged handkerchiefs, collars, love potions in small coloured glass bottles and sycamore wands. Talisman crafted out of clay and good luck charms hung by red ribbon from brass hooks on the oak mantle above the roaring fire. In a wooden box beneath the counter she had a selection of magical Angel wish bags. They were beautiful drawstring bags made from fabric almost as fine as the gossamer of fairies wings, inside the bags were an assortment of wonderful objects to bring you positive thoughts and actions, love, luck, courage, healing and strength. There was a heavenly white angel feather tied with ribbon and encircled by a piece of parchment containing a special blessing from the angels, three white candles and three wish spells, a lucky love pebble, a small bag of special stones, amethyst, rose quartz, tiger-eye, aventurine, all with individual meanings and a sea shell to represent the ever changing ebb and flow of life. These bags were unique gifts for very special people.

Long red velvet curtains enclosed a private area at the back of the shop where Sarah could take customers for healing. Hanging just behind the curtains were her grandmothers prized crystal wind chimes. Whenever the door opened the breeze would cause the air to stir and the chimes would ring.

The heavy iron bell above the door rattled and clanged as Nicola came into the shop carrying a steaming hot cup of tea for Sarah.

'I thought you could most probably do with a drink. My word you have been busy it all looks wonderful and so interesting.' said Nicola as she wandered around the shop picking up Love potions and pimple cream.

'I saw Peter struggling up the hill, is all that stone in the cart for your little cottage.' Sarah nodded in agreement.

'Thanks for this tea Nicola, it was just what I needed. I haven't any hot water at the moment, I can't seem to get the range out the back working. Peter said he might come back later and look at it for me. Luckily the fire was easy to light in this room.'

'Have you had any customers yet?'

'No, I'm not really open, I have still got quite a lot of goods to unpack,' and she pointed to the crates at the back of the shop.

'I'm not very busy at the moment, Amy's decided to come to work today so would you like me to help you?' offered Nicola. Sarah readily agreed.

The two girls carried the crates from the back of the shop. They unpacked a selection of small framed watercolours of wildlife and local landscapes painted by Evelyn Templin the blacksmiths wife. Sarah said they were her particular favourite pieces to have in the shop. She had fallen in love with the beautifully detailed portrayals of foxes and badgers and hoped that she would be able to eventually purchase one if not more for her new home.

Out of the crate came six ornately designed hand carved love spoons, each one containing a different number of beads in the handle. These were bought or carved and given to your wife to be, the amount of beads in the handle were to predict how many children you would have. Sarah tied red ribbon to the handles and hung them along the brass hooks of the dresser. The shelves of the dresser contained jars of relish, mint sauce and unusual mustards, each jar lid had a pretty fabric mop cap on it. Janet had crocheted beaded fly covers for milk jugs and white cotton cake doilies. The shop was starting to take shape.

'I think you will be ready to open for Christmas Sarah. You've plenty of stock too. And once you are open people are sure to come in with their crafts for you to sell.'

'Yes you're right. It's all taking shape, I'm going to have a word with Peter and see if we can open next Monday.'

The light was starting to fade and Sarah lit the candles in the shop.

'I really ought to get back next door and help clear up before closing time,' said Nicola. 'You just know that Amy won't bother.' And she went to leave. Sarah thanked her for the help she had given her and went to open the door, as she put her hand on the handle the door flew open and the large bell made such a din which startled both of them. A young woman burst into the shop. Her shawl was pulled tightly around her head and her skirt and feet were covered in mud.

'Oh sorry my shoes are in a terrible mess and I've walked it all over your clean floor.' Both the girls looked down at the mud splattered floor. Sarah stepped forward. 'Please don't worry about the floor it will soon mop clean. Can I help you at all?'

The girl looked nervously from Sarah to Nicola.

'Which one of you does the healing, you know with your hands.'

'I'll be off Sarah,' said Nicola. 'It looks like you have just got your first customer.'

'How can I help you? Do come and sit by the fire you look absolutely perished.'

The girl who looked to be in her mid-twenties declined the offer to take a seat as she said she could not stop as she had left her children at home unattended.

'Well it's like this,' she began. 'Firstly I must tell you that we haven't any money to pay you. The doctor has stopped coming to see my son because we owe him so much and we can't pay him. When I heard that you did healing I thought you might come and look at him. That is my son, Christopher. He just sits day after day his legs are so weak, the doctor said that he's a cripple and he will never be able to walk or get around, I have to carry him everywhere. The doctor used to give me a medicine that would keep him quiet so he would sleep most of the day and night, he was never any trouble, but since I can't pay the doctors fee we haven't had the medicine and he just sits and screams and cries most of the day and half the night. My husband says if I don't keep him quiet he's going to leave me. He can't get his sleep. He's the new gamekeeper for the big house and we've only just moved into Keepers cottage. If he can't sleep then he can't do his job properly. He is out in the estate most of the day and all times of the night checking for poachers. Yesterday the estate manager found him asleep in the woods and he was given a very severe warning and was told that if he caught him again he would have to inform the master. I am at my wits end. Please help us.' She stopped abruptly and took a deep breath, she had hardly paused to breathe between sentences, panting she eagerly awaited Sarah's reply.

'The best thing I can do is come and see him, Keepers cottage, you say? Yes I think I know how to get there.'

'Can you just give me something to quieten him till you see him?'

'Well I do have tisanes of valerian, but that is not recommended for children I would much rather come and see him first. And please don't worry, there will not be any charge for the visit. Now how about tomorrow at, let's see, mid-day, is that all right for you?'

'Yes, thank-you so much.'

Sandra Wicks left the shop and hurried off down the muddy path with her face down against the cold breeze, she nearly bumped into Peter.

'Was that your first customer I saw leaving?' he inquired as he entered the shop.

'Well, you could say that,' replied Sarah.

'Didn't she buy anything then?'

'No, not really Peter, I'm going to look at her son tomorrow.'

'How much will you charge her for that, remember your times money now Sarah, you have got overheads to pay.'

'I know, I know,' she replied slightly ruffled.

'If you're ready I'm going back to the farm in about half an hour. I have just got to pick up some wood from George and then I'll be ready.'

'All right I can finish the rest of the unpacking in the morning. Can you look at the range, today?'

'No, it will have to be tomorrow,' he replied and dived out the door before his ears received Sarah's reply.

When they arrived back home the family were all gathered around the table. Daniel was filling a glass bowl with oil from a stone jug.

'What are you doing Pa? Would you give me a hand to unload the wood?'

'Hang on a minute son, come and look at this, you'll be pleased to know we will not have to use candles anymore. We have ourselves an oil lamp,' and he screwed the wick back on the container and lit it, flames roared high and the startled Daniel quickly turned the wick down and placed the glass funnel over the flames. They all sat mesmerised by the new appliance.

'Oh Daniel its wonderful look at the light it gives out,' exclaimed Gwen.

'How safe is it?' she nervously inquired.

'Well, it's best not to carry it around whilst it's alight,' he said.

'Where did you get that from, then?' asked Peter.
'We could do with one of those, couldn't we Sarah?' Sarah nodded her head.
'It is yours, the old lady sent it down for you. The boy said they were everywhere up at the house in all the rooms, apparently our Molly's going mad, she's been given the job of filling them up, cleaning and lighting them. We thought you wouldn't mind if we used it till you both moved out.'
'I must thank Grace for all the things she is doing for us, she is so kind,' said Sarah.
'It's nothing to her is it?' said Peter. 'Look at all the things the rich buggers got, she can spare it. Makes you wonder why she does it though.'
'Because she's a very good friend Peter, that's why,' Sarah replied angrily.
'More like she feels sorry for you, little rich kid who lost everything and has to live with the likes of us peasants. You're her little charity case eases her conscience about having so much and being so bloody greedy. I expect she discusses her patronising noble deeds with her ladies circle. Well I don't mind, just keep the riches coming, everything will be gratefully received by yours truly, perhaps we should make a list of all the things we want and give it to her.'
'Oh Peter how can you say such things.'
'Well it's the truth she'd give you anything including her own son. Or have you already had him and she's suffering guilt, that's why she gives us so much.'
Sarah felt a little hot at Peter's remark. What did he know? Or think he knew. Could he have seen her go to the pagoda? Tobias came into her mind.
'Ignore it Sarah he's antagonising you. Don't give him the benefit of thinking he has the power to

distress and disturb your emotions. It's all to do with control and power, you know. I really must explain it all to you more clearly some time. But just as a brief example, if he is aware that he can distress you with a few words that he knows will upset you, then he will have gained power over you by being able to control the change in your emotions by using those certain words, for example, accusing you of being near Charles Trevallian. He is aware that the name 'Charles' is enough to upset you so every time he thinks he might be losing a little bit of power and control over you and you need putting in your place, out he comes with the old routine. He's found a weak link in your strong chain. Some men like a woman to be weak and that way they can control them. So, if you can be strong and not react to the remark and let him see that it has no effect on you then eventually he will stop playing the power game.'

'Considering that was one of your brief examples Tobias it certainly took quite a while.'

'What did you say?' snapped Peter.

'She was talking to, you know who,' said Gwen.

'Now that's enough you two, no more of that Peter, you two should be happy, your weddings only four months away. Come and give me a hand Sarah, suppers all but ready.'

Sarah felt very uncomfortable about all the things that Grace was doing for her and made up her mind that she would talk to her about it soon. She realised that Grace was acting as a mother figure towards her and she really did appreciate everything that she had done for them, but she had an uneasy feeling that somehow they were taking advantage of the old ladies kindness.

CHAPTER FIFTEEN

Keepers Cottage nestled lazily in the middle of woodland on the outskirts of the vast High Markham estate. Sandra Wicks looked untidy and slightly harassed when she pulled open the door. She balanced a snotty nosed baby on her hip and a small infant gripped tightly to her worn skirt. Sarah stepped into the steamy kitchen of the small cottage. A fire roared under a boiler in the corner of the kitchen and the water inside bubbled and gurgled. Piles of bed linen and clothes were strewn over the wet stone floor waiting their turn in the copper. A large mangle stood over an overflowing tin bath, ready to squeeze the water out of the well washed clothes.

'Please excuse the mess,' said Sandra, 'I just can't find enough hours in the day to complete all the things that need doing. The children seem to take up so much of my time.' She led Sarah through to the living room. A large clothes horse full of dripping clothes stood in front of the roaring fire. Sandra cleared a space on the settee and brushed off the bread crumbs.

'Please take a seat, can I get you something to drink?'

'No thank you. Is this the little boy with the bad legs,' inquired Sarah looking at the baby in her arms.

'No, he's upstairs, I try and keep him out of my

husband's way and he's due home for his lunch soon.' She put the baby into a small basket crib that sat on a chair. The little girl hanging onto her started to cry when her mother pushed her away.

'Stay with the nice lady Rachel, I won't be a minute, I'll just go up and get Christopher,' and she opened the stairs door and disappeared. Sarah tried to talk to the little girl but she hid her face behind the settee. Moments later Sandra reappeared at the foot of the stairs carrying a small blonde haired boy. She flopped him down on the floor in front of Sarah. He looked to be about three years old.

'Well there you are, this is Christopher. Say hello to the lady. He can talk but he doesn't always want to.'

Sarah watched as the little boy rolled over on to his front and pulled himself along the floor. From what Sarah could see of his legs they appeared to be quite normal but, he did not attempt to move them or stand up. Sarah knelt on the floor beside him. 'Hello Christopher, my name is Sarah, your mummy has asked me to come along to meet you.'

The boy took no notice of Sarah and carried on dragging himself around the floor. 'Can he stand up at all?' asked Sarah.

'If you hold him up he can, but he can't walk.'

'I would like to have a really good look at his legs,' said Sarah.

Sandra caught up with the boy and rolled him over onto his back, the child let out a piercing scream and thrashed his arms at his mother. She carried on struggling with him ignoring the ear splitting noise he was making, eventually she removed his trousers. Sarah carefully felt the small limbs even though they appeared to be perfectly normal the muscles on his thin thighs and calves were more or less extinct. Through nearly three years of lack of movement and any exercise they had withered and lost their elasticity. Sarah examined them carefully.

'It will take quite a while to strengthen his legs but I don't see any reason why he should not be able to walk. Of course he won't be able to run quite as well as the other children but I am sure with your help Sandra we can improve his quality of life. Look it's quite easy, all you have to do is make sure he exercises the muscles.' Sarah placed the palms of her hands on the soles of Christopher's feet. She pushed against his feet and his legs moved very easily at the knees, 'Now Christopher I know you can understand me. I want you to push your feet against my hands.' At first the boy totally ignored what Sarah had said, and looked at her blankly. 'I know how to make you move young man.' And she tickled him under his arms. She received the reaction she was looking for. He squealed with delight and pushed her hands away from him with his feet. 'Ah, so you can move your legs,' said Sarah happily. She massaged Christopher's legs using one of her home made rubbing oils. Whilst she did this she concentrated deeply on channelling healing energy out through her hands and into the lazy dormant muscles. The boy remained quiet and very still. Sandra Wicks watched her young son with interest. She was pleasantly surprised and relieved to see him so relaxed.

'I think that you could stand up now if you really wanted to.'

Sarah reached for a small trolley that the other child used to cart wooden bricks around in. 'Can I go out into your garden and see if I can find some heavy rocks to put into the trolley, Sandra? I don't want it to tip over when he pulls himself up and puts his full weight against it.'

The damp cold air outside was creating a swirling grey mist that appeared to be seeping from the almost frozen muddy earth, even though it was only just after three o'clock in the afternoon, the yellow tinged daylight was declining over the tall barren trees that surrounded the cottage. Careful not to slip on the mossy ground Sarah searched the muddy overgrown garden for something heavy enough to steady the little boy's walking trolley. At the back of the cottage beside the water pump Sarah found the exact stones that she had been searching for. After a lot of pulling, puffing, blowing and tugging she eventually removed the moss covered lumps of sandstone from their snug damp quarters. A toad that had thought itself safely sheltered for the winter, shuddered slightly as his warty skin was exposed to the dank winters air. With little enthusiasm he crawled over the moist earth intent on finding another unoccupied stone to provide him with shelter for the next few winter months. The stones fitted perfectly into the trolley. 'You will have to find something to cover these with. They are really wet and muddy, but they are just what we need.' Christopher sat in silence curiously watching every move Sarah made.

'Come along then young man, let's see if you can stand up,' said Sarah as she pulled Christopher to his feet. Very shakily his small hands tightly gripped the trolley handle. Sarah's gentle hands supported his weak legs. The boy's mother stood in amazement as her son stood upright without help for the first time in his life. Very slowly Sarah pushed the trolley forward. Instinctively Christopher swung his right foot forward and as the trolley moved away from him his left foot followed. All of a sudden the peace in the cottage was broken by a piercing scream coming from the little boy. For a moment Sarah was surprised by the noise. But when she looked at his face she realised it was not a scream of pain or frustration but a sound of joy. He was actually squealing with delight. Very soon everyone in the room was joining in with Christopher's laughter.

'I don't know how to thank you,' said Sandra. 'We have got a long way to go yet,' replied Sarah. 'His legs need to be strengthened by regular massage and a daily exercise program. If you like I'll call by tomorrow and bring you a supply of massage oils and show you how to use them.' Sandra Wicks could not thank Sarah enough and was very happy for Sarah to visit again.

Word travelled fast about the progress that the small boy had made, thanks to Sarah's healing hands and herbal oils. The next few weeks flew by. Peter had eventually managed to mend the range in the back of the shop allowing Sarah to use the warm room for healing. She had covered a small day bed with a soft sheepskin rug and made the small area look and feel as comforting as possible.

Very soon the little shop became an extremely popular place. Sarah was not sure whether her popularity was down to her helping young Christopher Wicks or as she suspected, something to do with Grace Trevallian and her son Charles. Her diary for healing was becoming full with the names of some very well to do ladies of Hellstone. Often the ladies would mention that they had been recommended to visit by Charles. Sarah made a mental note to thank him when she next saw him. Sarah with young Janet's help was kept busy for the best part of the day. Peter was more than pleased with the increased income that the shop was making. Already the money had swiftly disappeared presumably on materials for the reconstruction of their new home. With Daniel's help they had made good progress and already you could see the outline of Sarah and Peter's first home.

At last the bridesmaid dresses were completed and folded carefully and placed in Sarah's tin chest, which was the only clean and safe place to keep them. The wedding dress was still in a state of chaotic completion, most of the pieces were tacked together and only needed Sarah to find the time to finish the final stitching and sow the trimmings on. Sarah had been so busy with opening the shop for Christmas and making her balms and cures in the evenings that she really had not found the time to get on with any sewing. She was very grateful to Grace, who had offered to have her own seamstress make the dress to save Sarah time but Sarah had decided it would be fitting to make her own bridal gown. Grace had been worried in case it was Peter who had stopped Sarah from taking up her offer but this time Sarah's excuse was genuine. At the moment Peter quite readily agreed to most of Sarah's requests without an argument. In fact over the last few weeks he seemed to be growing quite distant and preoccupied, he had supported her tremendously with the shop and had worked hard planning their little home but he seemed to spend more and more nights away from the farm. Sarah was a little concerned and mentioned her worries to his mother, Gwen said that she thought he was making the most of being single and he would soon settle down once they were both married.

Christmas Day was now only a week away and Sarah had made up her mind that as soon as it was over she would get the fine details of the wedding sorted out. This coming Saturday was the Christmas party in the Tythe barn given by the Trevallians for all the staff, tenants and estate workers. Usually only the men of the Pendarvis family attended and enjoyed the merriment. They would come home with Christmas Fayre supplied by the Trevallians. Previous Christmases it had been a couple of joints of meat, poultry, fruit from the orchards and a bottle of wine from the estate vineyards. This year it was going to be slightly different all the females from the family were going by request of the Trevallians. At first Daniel and Peter were not that pleased with the idea of the women being there to keep an eye on them. But Gwen had talked them around to it. She pointed out that it was a long time since she and the girls had been to any gathering of this sort and that she looked forward to meeting some of the workers wives that she had not seen for quite a while. It would give her the opportunity to invite them to Peter and Sarah's wedding. Gwen was rather impressed by all the fine arrangements that had been made for her son's wedding. It was going to be just the occasion that she would have wished for him. She would be pleased when it was all over and Peter had moved into the barn with Sarah. Recently she'd had enough of his annoying behaviour especially when he and Molly his twin got together.

Sarah rubbed her sore eyes. The light from the oil lamp was just as irritating to her eyes, as sewing by the light of a candle. At long last it looked as though her wedding dress was near to completion.

For the last few hours she had been stitching small pink bows and embroidered rosebuds around the lace hem of the dress. Tonight was the occasion of the workers and tenants Christmas party. Sarah had not been too bothered about going along and as young Mary had started a rather nasty head cold she had volunteered to stay at home with the sickly child, who was now sleeping peacefully after a mug of herbal cold cure.

Sarah could hardly keep her eyes open, the warmth from the fire made her feel very relaxed and sleepy. She laid the finished dress onto the table behind her and settled herself back into the chair. A few more days and it would be the New Year. She thought of the coming year ahead, she expected it to be quite an eventful year. What with her marriage to Peter and the move into their own little home also the challenge of making her shop into a really successful healing centre. There was still a lot that she wanted to achieve as far as the business was concerned. Oh yes it looked as though there were going to be lots of changes. Her eyes became heavy as she reflected on all that had occurred in the last year, life was not too bad at the moment. She considered herself to be a very lucky person. When you think all the things that had happened since she came to this strange little hamlet called Hellstone. In fact she could hardly remember the days long ago when she had been brought to this farm by nursey Banks, Gwen's awful older sister. A strange feeling came over Sarah and she felt herself drift off into another time another place on her psychic see-saw. She was back being a small child, she was standing in her mother's bedroom at home, she was alone but she could smell the perfume her mother wore. Looking around her she could see all the things that she remembered about her mother's room. Walking over to the bed she touched the crisp clean white cotton sheets. She knelt and trailed a finger outlining the heavy lace patterned border. She buried her face into the snowy brightness and lost herself in the smell of lavender bags and cool linen. Walking over to the glossy polished dressing table she reached for a small glass swan filled with a clear liquid, it used to be one of her mother's most treasured possessions. She had once told Sarah that it was a secret to who had given it to her but it was before she had married Sarah's father, she had been told that the swan was filled with angel's tears. And the person who had given it to her had loved her very much. But her marriage to Malakai Miller had already been arranged by her parents. And her first and only sweetheart had left the country and she never heard from him again. Slowly the room became misty and Sarah lost the so very real vision of her childhood home. The wick in the oil lamp started to smoke as the oil ran out, the only light came from the red embers of the fire. Too comfortable and warm to move, Sarah thought about her position here at Mill Farm.

The whole Pendarvis family had been very kind to her really. It was only Peter's possessive behaviour and his sister's jealousy that spoilt it at times, she supposed that she should be grateful that at least Peter cared enough to be possessive. For a brief moment she let her mind wander into fantasy land. If's and But's and And's. The land of how things could have been different. Perhaps her pathway would have been different IF her father had loved her AND her Mother had not been so frail and frightened and stood up for herself. BUT it all happened. Fate has sealed her path. She realised that she couldn't change the past only let it go and live for now and go forward.

Sarah could hear their voices long before the party revellers reached the front door, Gwen stumbled into the kitchen first closely followed by a very inebriated Daniel who was singing at the top of his tone-deaf voice. Janet who was deaf but not dumb was making a very strange sound indeed, she obviously knew what she was gabbling about. Sarah could not help but laugh as the family tried to get themselves in some sort sensible order.

'Well you look like you have all had a very good time,' said Sarah as she helped the wide-eyed Gwen into a chair. Daniel placed a very shabby parcel onto the table, mumbled something and stumbled into the bedroom. Janet was very cautiously trying to balance the kettle on the fire. 'Here,' said Sarah, taking it from her, 'Let me do that, before you have an accident.' Janet sunk down on a stool at the table and rested her chin on her hands and seemed to stare into nothingness.

'How is Mary?' enquired Gwen.

Sarah explained that the child was sleeping peacefully and she expected her to feel a lot better in the morning, which was not so very far away.

'Come along,' said Sarah. 'It's already Christmas day and we haven't been to bed yet. Four hours and it will be morning and we will be getting up again.' She presumed that as Peter did not come in with the others, that he must be checking that the livestock were all secure for the night. She poured herself a cup of hedgerow tea, whilst she waited for Peter's return, carefully she wrapped her wedding dress in stiff brown paper, it would be counted as unlucky for Peter to see the finished piece before the day. Tomorrow she would safely place her dress in her trunk with the girls' dresses.

Sarah didn't know how long she had dozed by the fire but when she tried to move her head her neck had set itself in a very uncomfortable position. Stiffly she made her way to the bedroom and climbed in beside the soundly sleeping Janet. It seemed that Sarah had only just dropped off to sleep when she was awoken by little Mary furiously tugging at her arm. This morning the excited child obviously felt a lot better and was now eager to open the gifts that hung on the bough of fir tree that Sarah had brought in from the cold.

The fir was to symbolise everlasting life, the gifts to represent sacrifices to the spirits of the earth and trees. Sarah had made all her gifts for the family and friends some were very pretty but others were quite misshapen and amusing.

It was a very quiet Christmas morning. Daniel and Gwen had both chosen not to have any breakfast they sat quietly sipping their tea nursing sore heads. Janet was unusually cheerful and told Sarah that she had really enjoyed the party she had been dancing all evening mostly with young Tim and she had arranged to meet him again down in the village sometime next week. Sarah asked Janet in sign language, who was at the party and did all the Trevallians attend. Janet replied that Mr Trevallian only appeared briefly to give out the Christmas money to the estate workers and that he disappeared as soon as he had finished but Charles had stayed at the party all evening enjoying himself dancing with the staff from the house. Sarah asked what had happened to Peter. Janet looked away from Sarah's gaze. She signed to Sarah that she did not see him leave, but he was not with them when they came home, she expected that he had gone drinking with his rowdy friends and most probably slept it off at one of their houses.

Just before lunch Sarah handed out the gifts to the family. She placed Peter's on his empty chair. No one mentioned his absence. Daniel and Gwen were delighted with their present of a very colourful rag rug which straight away replaced the threadbare one in front of the fire. Daniel tried on his scarf and Gwen was amused at the apron. Very quickly little Mary stretched out on the rug and began to play with the doll that Sarah had made her, it was dressed in a wedding dress that was identical to her own. Janet was delighted with the red velvet hat and muff that had been made from an old curtain that once adorned the windows at High Markham.

There was still no sign of Peter when Molly joined the family for Christmas lunch. She had brought with her a basket overflowing with pies, puddings, sweets and biscuits. There was a bottle of vintage port from the cellars of her employers and a large piece of stilton cheese that smelt as though it was past its best. Totally ignoring Sarah she gave small gifts to her family. Sarah could not believe her eyes when the girl gave her mother the small enamelled snuff box that Sarah had seen Molly ask Ralph Trevallian for in that sordid vision. A wooden box containing large cigars was her present for her father and small coloured glass bottles of cologne for Janet and Mary. She did not have a gift for Sarah. Sarah gave Molly a set of lace collar and cuffs, Molly did not acknowledge the gift and tossed them over to her Mother. 'They're yours.' Was all she said.

'I suppose I better give you these,' said Molly through pinched lips.

'I had to promise that I would.' Begrudgingly she slapped a small parcel onto the table.

'Is it for me? Who is it from?'

'Open it and you'll bloody well find out won't you,' said Molly and plonked herself down heavily at the table. Sarah picked up the small parcel that was wrapped in tissue and tied with fine gold cord.

'I think it must be from Grace,' she said quietly.

'No one else would send you a present like that would they now? You really have wormed your way into her affection haven't you? You get everything you want. Well make the most of it because the Masters getting wise to you and your little game. I told him you're not the sweet little Miss Innocence that you want us all to believe that you are. I don't know what Peter sees in you, I reckon you bewitched him just the same as you did to her ladyship.'

Sarah chose to ignore Molly's outburst, she had heard the same conversation so many times before that she was becoming immune to the accusations.

A small card dropped out from the wrapping. It read;

'My dear Sarah, I do hope you have a wonderful Christmas, these pearls are something I thought you could wear on your wedding day. My mother gave them to me on mine.' Sincere wishes. Grace.

Sarah opened the leather case to expose a dark blue velvet lining and nestled in the cloth sat a perfect single string of natural cream pearls. Molly tutted as Sarah extracted them from the box. 'I didn't think that she would be giving you anything normal, like she gave me, a bloody bar of stinking lavender soap and six handkerchiefs with the lace so hard that you'll cut your nose into shreds if you dare to use them. Not that I really care, I'll always have the last laugh on her bloody ladyship. One of these days she'll push me too far and I'll tell her and her precious namby-pamby son a few things about the Master of the house and me. That will soon wipe the smiles of their bloody faces. You wait and see.'

'That's enough Molly we don't want to spoil Christmas day do we? It's bad enough that Peters not here,' said Gwen, looking a little agitated.

'Let's get on with dinner shall we or that goose will have melted into a pan of grease and be the size of a pigeon.'

Peters head ached as the cart trundled along the muddy tracks every time it went over a bump and jolted, his whole body heaved and he wretched over the side. Surely he thought he must of already lost the contents of his stomach a few times since the party last night. His head was still filled with feathers and he had to concentrate to remember the events of last evening. He had left the party just before ten, when he and Colin the stable hand had been escorted quietly off the premises. He seemed to remember having a go at Molly's boss, old man Trevallian. He didn't think he was being unreasonable when he'd caught his Lordship out the back of the barn with his sister's skirts up around her waist. Why shouldn't the bloke pay a few bob for him to keep quiet? After all he could afford it. Peter couldn't believe his luck, there was no argument at all when he threatened to tell Charlie boy and his mother, very quickly a few pounds had been placed in his hand. And just as quickly he had been escorted from the party. What an easy way of making money that was. It certainly beat working on the farm. He thought he would leave it a few weeks and then perhaps with Molly's help they could get a few more pounds. The money he had made last night had been well spent, first they had travelled to their favourite gaming house with hopes of doubling their money and then when they had their fill of alcohol and lost most of their ill-gotten gains. Colin had suggested they visit his recently widowed sister's house, her elderly late husband had left her a fair sized farmhouse and about ten acres of land just to the north of Penzance. When they'd arrived it was a little after midnight and Colin and Peter were well on their way to being totally intoxicated. Colin's sister who did not appear to be a women in mourning explained that she had rented out her spare rooms to a few of her girlfriends, apparently they were unfairly evicted from their accommodation making them all temporary homeless, after the house they had been renting was closed by the local magistrate.

Peter could hardly keep upright when he'd stumbled up the stairs to Jane's bedroom, she had to help him every step of the way. Only once did his conscience send an alarm signal to his brain but that was short lived owing to the expert hands that were slowly arousing him. And now in the grim light of day he still did not feel as though he had cheated on Sarah. He had just experienced a night to remember not only with Colin's sister but he had ended up with the attention of a couple of her friends. Never again would one woman at a time be enough. In his head he justified his actions by making excuses, after all he wasn't married yet, he was still free to do just what he liked. And he wasn't really sure anymore whether he wanted to marry that barmy girl after all. She thought herself to be so prim so proper she was a damn liar. She'd been cheating on him for ages. And now he had the proof. Last night at the party Molly had told him that she was pretty sure that Charles and Sarah had been seeing each other. Also the old lady was always asking about Sarah and the wedding. She was quite sure that the last time Sarah had visited the house she had seen her go into Charles's bedroom and it was ages before she came out. Even Ralph had told Molly that he wanted Sarah to be married to Peter as soon as possible because he was worried that Charles was interested in the strange girl. So in the light of last night he didn't think that his behaviour was too bad. In fact he thought he might just go back and visit Jane again, her sexual activities really appealed to him. Also that big farm was all hers and she really needed someone to help her run it. Mind you she had made it clear that whoever came to live there would have to have a tidy amount of money to support her and the lifestyle she was accustom to.

The track to Mill Farm loomed up in front of them. Peter suddenly remembered that it was Christmas morning.

'Bloody Hell Colin its Christmas day, my Ma's going to kill me.'

'I'm sure you'll invent a very convincing story for your mother, mind you I don't know how you'll explain that.' And he pointed to Peter's throat.

'What?'

'You'd better cover it up before you go in,' said Colin.

'Cover what up, what the bloody hell are you talking about?'

'That bloody mark on your neck, my sister certainly took a liking to you didn't she? By the look of you, she nearly flipping well gobbled you up and sucked the life out of you.'

Peter pulled up his collar to cover the bite mark and gave a sly laugh. 'She can eat as much as she likes of me and so can her friends.'

'Steady on, you're due to be married soon,' said Colin.

'Well,' smirked Peter. 'It's only Wedlock, not a bloody padlock.'

His shoulders sank when he climbed down from the cart. He hoped his mother wouldn't give him too much of a hard time about missing Christmas morning. Sarah definitely wouldn't once she heard the sad tale he had to tell.

Everyone's eyes in the room starred at Peter as he entered the kitchen. 'Merry Christmas to all of you,' he shouted. 'You won't believe what happened to me last night.' And he reeled off a very convincing explanation about Colin's sister being in serious trouble and how he went with Colin to Penzance to help her. Then adding more lies to the story that the cart had broken down and the shaft had split and struck him a blow to the side of his neck causing a terrible bruise. At that point he dramatically pulled his collar down to expose his neck and reveal the fiery bruise. And finally how awful it was to have to wait until this morning to get it repaired, knowing that he had missed Christmas morning with his family and future wife.

'Oh you poor thing Peter, what a terrible night you've had, we were worried about you. That was so kind of you to help Colin, is his sister alright now?' enquired Sarah. Quite easily she believed Peter's incredible story, and did not doubt one word of it. Very readily she praised him for being such a good friend to Colin and his sister. She was very proud of his selflessness. Lovingly Sarah bathed and soothed the bruise on his neck with cool witch hazel tincture. Peter smiled pathetically as he tucked into his well-dried out Christmas dinner. His twin Molly never said a word but looked across the table into her brothers lying eyes and further into his lying soul, she understood exactly what he had been up to. They both grinned knowingly.

The girls cleared the table to make room for the tasty assortment of puddings and sweets that Molly had brought from the house. When they could eat no more Peter and his father opened the bottle of vintage port. The women started on the wine that Sarah had made with the elderberry flowers earlier in the year. It looked so clear and harmless but after the second glass they all seemed to have fits of the giggles.

Mary went off to play with her new toys and Janet sat with Gwen and Molly trying to lip-read their whispered conversation. Sarah who was feeling very happy decided to put her gift from Grace into her tin chest. Slowly it was becoming her chest of treasures.

Very quietly she pulled the awkward object from beneath her bed and pulled the leather straps that undid the buckles. In the chest the very first item was her wedding dress wrapped carefully in brown paper, just three months now and she would be wearing the dress down the aisle, a little thrill of excitement entered her body and she blushed at the thought of becoming Mrs Pendarvis.

She placed her dress and the bridesmaid's dresses on the bunk. Right at the very bottom was the box containing her grandmother's crystal ball, the crystal chimes were now hanging in her shop. Something soft caught her hand and she pulled out Charles's monogrammed handkerchief. Gold embroidered letters C.T reflected the candle flame in the room and just for a moment she could have sworn that she heard ghostly waltz music being played by an invisible orchestra. A rainbow of dancing lights and a swirl of white robes entered the room.

'Hello my dear friend I wondered whether you would be here today. I know this is a very special occasion for you. Most people don't seem to realise that Christmas is the opportunity to be part of the biggest Birthday party ever,' said Sarah in a silent voice. In an equally silent voice Tobias replied. 'How could I not visit you, today of all days. These special days don't really matter too much to us when we have crossed over to this part of our journey. But as so many people insist on celebrating it as a festival I suppose I really ought to acknowledge it. Even though the way it is becoming is not quite to my liking. It is a very nice gesture to give gifts to each other but I feel it is all getting way out of hand. And look at how some of you earth dwellers stuff your poor bodies with every kind of rich food and drink almost to the point of obscene greed just because it is Christmas. We sometimes forget that half of the world's population cannot find food for one meal a week. I would much prefer it if people gave each other gifts that really mattered and lasted a lifetime.'

'What do you mean?' said Sarah, quizzically.

'Your world seems to be fast becoming ruled by Pleasure, Power, Greed and Hate, this is not how I envisaged the New World to be.'

'I suppose you would only be happy if everyone was a follower of your particular cult.'

'Not at all, it's faith that is important. All cults and religions have good parts and bad parts and of course your beliefs are personal to you. My particular cult happens to be one of the most popular and I think that is because it has a good set of rules to abide by. Compassion and kindness play a big part in it.'

'Oh come on Tobias don't you think that it ought to be updated slightly, some of the things that are mentioned in the book are a little bit difficult to believe in.'

'Well I do admit that there will come a time when my religion will take a bit of a hammering. Owing to man's incorrect interpretation of Christianity we will lose our popularity and that will be a time when some folk who are left without a faith or belief will become vulnerable and lost. Many years ago the very same thing happened to your pagan beliefs Sarah. As I have already mentioned the time will be when the earth reaches the twenty-first century. That is when there will be a revival in the old ways. Then all the cures and remedies that have been long forgotten including healing with your hands, collecting bark from trees and roots of flowers to make potions with to cure all ills, will be as popular as they were centuries before. But of course it will be scientists who invent them not witches or pagans. But no one could possibly mind who invents cures as long as the sick are healed. Up till that time science will always take the easiest route and always provide the easiest logical explanation to everything.'

'I hope you are right my dear friend. I shall be long gone when this revival takes place. I dare say I might be travelling around the realms with you.'

'God forbid,' said Tobias and they both laughed very loudly.

'Are you still trying to convert me to your

Christianity or have you given up on me?'

'You are more of a Christian than some preachers I know of. It's the way you conduct your life that matters. Your attitude toward fellow human beings, that's what it is all about not being seen to be a do gooder but silently working for the greatest good of all, really if I was to sum it all up, love that is what the heart of the matter really is, to love unconditionally. That is how I became one of the greatest healers of all time. I learnt to love. I would sacrifice my life again and again just to have left part of me behind so that mankind would always remember my love and compassion. And to teach my beliefs to their children and on to their children, so, I live on, I will never be forgotten, I never died. I live on in the very depths of people's hearts.' As Tobias uttered those words tears filled his eyes and he could hardly go on. Sarah saw the love and compassion in his eyes and through to his very soul and she was filled with the most incredible feelings of sadness.

'Tobias my dear friend, if you were flesh and bones I would hold you so tight, all I can do is thank you for loving me so much. I wish I could go back in time with you and stop the terrible torture that you endured.'

'It was all part of my journey to benefit mankind.'

'Would you say it was worth all that pain and suffering you went through, Tobias?'

'Of course it was I could never doubt that. Pain goes quickly. Death is nothing, just ends and new beginnings. But I know that I changed the world. I gave the word humanity a meaning. Man then wrote a new set of rules to end barbaric behaviour. Oh yes it was worth it, every spot of blood I shed was absorbed into the earth and in its place rose a new consciousness that would reshape man's attitudes towards each other.'

'I'm intrigued to how you became my friend and guide.'

'Well there is no mystery to it, Sarah. My father sent me to earth the moment you were born. I came to help you on your journey through your life, it was a task that I chose. Unfortunately you are already aware that I have a twin brother. Who is a complete opposite of myself in looks as well as deeds. The reason we are so dissimilar is so you can know what good really is. Without the devil misbehaving inside some of us, we would not know what bad is. It would be like heaven all the time if nobody did anything bad or evil. So to know who I am you have to experience my brother's bad behaviour. It's a continual game of actions and reactions. If you didn't have unkindness no one would be aware of kindness. Without hate how would we recognise love? It would be a very strange place if everyone floated around being sickly sweet all the time.' He looked down into Sarah's eyes. 'Don't look so sad, I'm here. Okay not quite as wholesome as I was, admittedly I'm a little bit faint in places but as you know, if you believe in me then I am with you throughout the whole of your life.'

Tobias reached out a strong hand and brushed Sarah's cheek with his fingers.

She felt the power of his touch. A great strength filled her body.

'I can't imagine what I would do without you as my friend Tobias.'

'Let us not get gloomy Sarah after all it should be a day to rejoice. It's my birthday. Why not have a little look in your crystal ball. I know for a fact that the weather outside is very cold and bleak but if you go ball gazing I think you could be in for a nice surprise.'

With her hands cupped Sarah cradled the crystal ball. At first all she could see was her own reflection, her eyes became heavy and she was sure she was going to fall asleep the voices of the family in the other room became fainter and fainter. As her head started to droop she felt herself falling forward and then tumbling in slow motion. With a very gentle bump she landed onto a patch of grass. It was bright luscious green and spongy to touch, she floated to her feet. She was standing in a summer garden which was surrounded by a high stone wall. Creeping up and over the walls were white, pink and purple Clematis flowers, their large delicate heads swaying slightly in the warm breeze that licked Sarah's face. The sky above was so clear and blue providing a perfect background for the white doves that flew silently overhead on the thermals of warm air. Tall rose bushes were smothered with thousands of apple scented pink blooms that filled the air with a mysterious fragrance, their perfume blended with the grey and purple lavender bushes that edged the narrow stone path. Hollyhocks and foxgloves stood like soldiers exhibiting their perfect blooms.

In the centre of the garden stood a tree covered in white blossom. Its branches reaching down to the ground like a wedding veil. If you looked really closely you could make out the presence of two people sitting on a white wrought iron seat beneath the tree. Sarah could feel the sun's warmth penetrate the top of her head and spread soothing warmth throughout the whole of her body. All tensions left her body and she experienced a feeling of total relaxation and well-being. The couple in the garden appeared not to notice Sarah. She slowly walked towards them. To her great surprise she was looking into the youthful face of her grandmother. She was dressed in a pure white lace dress with a pink satin ribbon around the waist. The hem of the dress was edged with tiny embroidered rose buds. Her beautiful hair was piled high above her head and cascaded in long ringlets down her back. In her arms she held a small child, a little girl with a mass of beautiful golden hair, she was also dressed in white lace and pink rosebuds. Beside her grandmother sat another lady but her face was covered by a large sun hat held onto her head by a blue chiffon scarf, a small boy with golden locks sat on her lap. Suddenly with a squeal of delight the children leapt down onto the grass and started to play with the snowflakes of blossom that the breeze was blowing off the magnificent tree. An immense feeling of contentment welled up inside Sarah, she knelt down onto the grass and sleepily relaxed into the warmth of the sunny afternoon. What a beautiful visualisation this was and such a release from the pressures and tensions of everyday worries that seemed to play such a large part in her life. Often when Sarah was healing she would use this type of creative visualisations to still her patient's minds and make them relax. It was far easier to heal someone who was totally calm and peaceful. Every part of your delicate system functions more accurately when the brain instructs the lungs to breathe more calmly, then the heart beats in a more relaxed fashion which makes your blood pressure become more stable. Also a relaxed state gives the inner healing soldiers the opportunity to get on with their job without being worn out by worries and tensions.

Sarah was now so relaxed she felt as though she could stay in this enchanted garden for the rest of her life.

The children scampered and played, their laughter filled the air and echoed around the high stone walls. The lady who sat next to Sarah's grandmother slowly arose from the seat and glided toward where Sarah was sitting. Sarah gasped with surprise as she recognised the face that was looking at her from beneath the beautiful white hat. Her mother held out a hand to Sarah and helped her to her feet. Sarah saw her mother as she had never seen her before. Her body was free of pain and all the lines of sadness had been erased. She was a perfect picture of health. Words caught in Sarah's throat. There was so much she wanted to say. There were not many days in her life when she had not thought about her mother and what had become of her at the hands of Malakai Miller. And yet in this dream she was here in front of her as if it was real life. Part of her brain warned her, this is just a daydream, don't believe what you are seeing. Anything is possible when you create a daydream. You control it totally from beginning to end. Daydreaming is your private safe place only you can enter.

A voice that resembled a well forgotten familiarity and warmth entered the space inside her head which was reserved as a sanctuary. The voice trickled like a stream of sparkling water. 'I have waited so many years to see you. I have gone over and over your disappearance and what I would say to you if ever I saw you again. Somehow I felt that I was to blame for your father's dislike of you. I tried many times to stop him from treating you so badly. He never had any patience with you or me. I think that his religion made him a very hard man to please. In one way I was relieved when he said you had left. He wouldn't tell me where you had gone. All he would say was that it was for your own good. What I have to tell you now is the honest truth. And if I lie my soul will never rest in peace. You do not know how much I loved you. You were the very bright light in my very dull life. When you entered my life I felt so fulfilled I thought my heart would burst with joy. But very quickly the joy turned to such sadness. Your father was very jealous of you. He resented the amount of time I spent nursing you and then he blamed you for my ill health. In fact he was to blame for my ill health. The only way I could stop him from his perverted abuse was to remain too ill to be of any use to him. My ill health was my security from his most humiliating conduct. But Sarah I loved you so much, you were part of me. When you were just three months old he convinced the doctor that I was a very unstable person and not mentally fit enough to bring up a child. He put it to me that if I loved you enough for your own good I should let a nurse look after you. Your grandmother here,' and she pointed to the serene lady gathering roses. 'She owned the house then and lived upstairs in her apartments, she also suffered failing health and Nurse Banks was brought into to look after all three of us. The rest I am sure is carved in your memory for eternity.'

Sarah felt her mother's small cool pale hands clasp hers and raise them to her lips. Please can you forgive me Sarah? I know that I should have stood up for you more but I was selfish it was easier to let him do just as he wanted. His temper as I am sure you remember was a fearful thing. If only I could turn the clock back I would do things so differently. The vision in front of Sarah was starting to fade.

'Wait please wait, don't go yet mother I have got so many questions to ask you.'

The scene in the garden changed the glowing sun disappeared behind a grey rain cloud and the gentle breeze became a gusty wind. The once green leaves on the tree turned autumnal brown. The figures in the garden started to dissolve and fade away.

The crystal ball was now a clear glass sphere perched on Sarah's lap. She blinked as her eyes became accustom to the dim light in the bedroom.

'Tobias did you see the vision as well. You must have done. Please say you did?'

'You saw what you wanted to. It is nothing to do with me. It was your imagination, your vision.'

'Whether that vision was real or not Tobias, I am happy to have been given the opportunity to confront her after all this time. And as you say I heard what I wanted to and if that makes me feel better about past events then it cannot be wrong.'

They were interrupted by Gwen, she entered the bedroom carrying Mary who was fast asleep, she laid the child onto her bed, and Janet wearily followed her mother and climbed into the bed she shared with Sarah. In the other room Daniel noisily scrapped out the ashes from underneath the fire and banked it up for the night. Tobias watched the family enter the small room and when he thought that there wasn't enough space even for a ghostly spirit he twirled about a bit and left the room via the ceiling. Sarah grinned to herself and climbed into bed beside Janet who was already snoring very loudly, Peter did not come to bed he decided to have a last check on the livestock before turning in. Often he slept out in the stables with the comfort of warm hay and the company of his cache of strong Ale. He would wake when the cockerel shouted or when his father doused him with a bucket of freezing cold water. These days he complained that the bedroom he shared with the rest of the family was far too crowded and noisy.

After what felt like hours Sarah was still wide awake. Somewhere in the distance the church clock struck another hour, but still Sarah's eyes would not close and give in to sleep, straining her ears she could hear the faint sound of a dog barking. She recognised the bark and knew exactly who would be walking his dog at this late hour. She tried to stop her thoughts from recalling the night in the pagoda for fear that she would be tempted to go and repeat the episode. But try as she may she found herself listening to a whispering voice inside her head. The voice gently spoke words of encouragement to her, it was gently enticing her to get out of bed and make her way to the pagoda in the woods. It was a mysterious voice that almost hypnotised her, she found it very hard to resist the suggestion that was being made to her. The voice was urging and coaxing her to go out into the dead of night and meet Charles at the pagoda. A thought entered her head that brought her abruptly to her senses. Peter was somewhere outside and the chances of him seeing her at this time of night were almost a certainty. She must try and concentrate on something else and not give any further attention to this disturbing intrusive voice. The voice slightly frightened her it was very persuasive, before she could control the movements she had crept out of bed and was heading for the front door. It was as if an unknown force was sweeping her along. With all her strength she willed herself to sit down on a chair. Over and over she tried to avert her mind to concentrate on the events of the day. At last she was back in control of her actions. What a strange Christmas day it had been. It had not been really unpleasant at all, but she could not say that she had enjoyed it as much as other years. These days everyone indoors always seemed to be short tempered with each other. The farmhouse was far too small for such a growing family. Things would surely start to improve when she and Peter moved out and left more space. She was aware that at the moment she was quite sensitive, the amazing vision of her mother and grandmother had made her recollect her early childhood years, she had thought so much about her mother recently, more so as the wedding grew nearer. It would have been so nice to have her mother around to share it with. Gwen was always very kind to her but she was Peter's mother so it was difficult to share private thoughts and worries with her. There was always Grace who had helped her tremendously but Sarah felt it would be very unfair to unburden herself onto such a dear elderly lady.

Outside in the damp night air, creatures came out of hiding intent on enjoying the solitude of the darkness, all too soon they scampered back into their safe woodland quarters. Charles Trevallian and his dog very noisily tramped through the undergrowth. It was Christmas evening and he could not remember a Christmas day more tense and uncomfortable as this one had been. His father had made sure that today he was going to be the only member of the household to enjoy themselves. He had started with his obnoxious behaviour at breakfast, complaining that the food was cold and it was about time that his wife sorted out the staff. He moaned that the cook was too old for the job and the food was becoming boring and was always cold when he received it. His wife had pointed out that had he arrived at the table a little earlier each morning then the food would always be piping hot as it was when she arrived. After her statement Ralph Trevallians face grew purple with rage and he had left his chair so quickly that it flew backwards across the floor and tipped over a side table that displayed a collection of small marble figurines. He then stormed down the stairs and supplied the cook and the rest of the staff with a myriad of verbal assault. From then on the day seemed to go so slowly. Charles had to wait until his father had shut himself in his study with a bottle of brandy, before he could apologies to everyone. He noticed that Molly seemed to be taking some strange delight in seeing the rest of the staff in so much trouble. Apparently she was not included in the reprimand. He was rather pleased that she would be going home for the afternoon. But before she went she was called to the study and spent rather a long time with his father behind the locked door. Charles knew what was going on between his father and the maid, he just hoped his mother didn't. Charles and his mother had then spent the afternoon entertaining the Paget family. He and Nicola had managed to escape from the house and take the horses down to ride on the beach. The day was very cold and windy and the sand had whipped up into their eyes and faces making it very difficult to see where they were going, but the ride was exhilarating. They had ridden to a sheltered cove and sat on the damp rocks skimming pebbles across the disturbed water. Strangely enough they had talked very little about each other. The conversation always seemed to end up with Sarah as the topic. In fact Charles had learnt an awful lot about Sarah from Nicola. And the more he heard the more he liked. He was secretly willing Nicola to tell him that Sarah did not want to marry Peter but that information was not forthcoming. The afternoon seemed like an eternity. He was glad when it was time to ride home. His mother had retired to her suite quite early and his father was left snoring loudly in his study and not expected to sober up before Boxing Day. Charles was so restless and felt frustrated with the way his life was going or more to the point not going. When he could stand the house no longer he had taken the dog and walked the perimeter of the vast estate. And now here he was at the pagoda and still feeling very alone. He had a yearning to return to warmer climates. In fact over the next few weeks he must ensure that his vessel was sea worthy and ready for the return journey. He loved England especially Cornwall but his passion was the sunshine and the beautiful people of the Indies. You could not compare the way of life abroad with life here in England. He thought of this Cornish coast, the rugged rocks and the raging cold sea that was always greedy to wreck your ship and devour you and your cargo. The calm blue seas that surrounded the island where he lived abroad were just as treacherous at times but were silent in their beauty.

Resisting the urge to rush out of the door and run through the night to the pagoda, as the persistent voice was encouraging her to do, Sarah lit a candle and sat down at the table. A cold draft came from under the ill-fitting front door and she tucked her feet up into her nightdress. Pulling her shawl tightly around her cold shoulders she reached for a pencil and scrap of paper. Finding it very hard to concentrate she focused her mind on what dear Tobias had talked about earlier in the evening. Her pencil scratched the surface of the paper and what appeared was a piece of poetry that burst forth from the depths of her compassionate heart.

Please teach me to love
Touch my heart with true love
Don't let my words of comfort be empty
Or ever let greed overcome sharing
Never let me hurt if I cannot help
Please let me hear unspoken cries
Guide me truthfully
And then I will learn how to love

In the face of fear give me courage
When I am faced with tasks so great
Don't let me turn my back and walk away
Give me my purpose, my pathway, my reason for being
Teach me to love without rules and conditions
To love saints and sinners
Let my acts be unselfish without expected rewards
And my deeds silently administer and then - I will truly know how to love.

CHAPTER SIXTEEN

All too soon the laurel, fir and ivy were being removed from the farm cottage. This was a particularly happy time for Sarah. She loved the beginning of the New Year. Everything living was getting ready to reproduce again. Soon she would be able to see new buds forming on many of the plants and trees in the woodland. The cycle of life would be starting again after the long winters rest.
It would be many weeks before the first day of spring when the evenings would become lighter and the birds and wildlife would enjoy the beginning of warmth returning to the earth.
The New Year had started with vengeance January had brought strong gales that let nothing stand in their way. The whole landscape had been changed by the loss of many trees. Groups of villagers had gathered with their saws and axes to clear the paths and roads. There would be no shortage of logs this winter. Luckily Daniel had secured the sweeps of the mill and no damage had been done. One extremely treacherous night the roof of the cattle sheds had rattled itself loose and taken flight and Peter had found the mangled remains of the corrugated iron panels spread over the fields the next morning. All the men including Matthew had spent many hours over the last few weeks securing the outbuildings and clearing debris from the yard. Down in the harbour many ships

had lost masts and rigging, the Trevallian's vessel was no exception, luckily it was an extremely sound ship and had only suffered minimal damage. Fortunately Charles would not be delayed for too long. The fitters reckoned they would be able to finish the work in three weeks.

Grace Trevallian was overjoyed to think that her son would be able to stay home for a little longer. She secretly dreaded him leaving especially as her husband was not going with him. Charles had promised her that he would speak to his father about hiring a companion to keep her company. Unbeknown to his mother Charles had spoken to his father and his father had said it was a good idea, and then he had suggested that Molly be promoted to the position. Charles had tried to talk his father out of it but he was adamant that she was a good choice for the position. Charles could not imagine how his mother would take to that suggestion. What she really needed was someone like Sarah who was bright and intelligent who could appreciate his mother's frail health and keep her mind occupied with interesting conversation. But he knew that was out of the question it was too late to ask her to work at the house. Her little shop was becoming very successful and Sarah was fast making a name for herself. Quite a few of his mother's cronies swore by the perfumed oils that she sold. No one could quite make out the ingredients the oils consisted of but they were the most extraordinary fragrance. Once you had experienced the exciting aroma you could recognise it anywhere. And you had the urgent compulsion to own it. According to Nicola it was so popular that there was a waiting list of names, for people who wanted to buy it. Sarah could not create enough of the oils to satisfy the ladies of Hellstone. Charles suspected that they contained a alchemy of natural extracts of herbs and woodland flowers blended to form an ancient magical recipe.

The wind snatched at Sarah's hair making the wild black strands fly in all direction. She was trying to build a low dry stone wall around her new herb garden at the back of the farm. The windmill cast great shadows over the small plot of bare earth, she knew that in the summer the sun would be high over the mill and it would give some useful shade. Many of her herbs were wild and grew in the woodland around Hellstone, she knew of every flower and plant in the area for quite a few miles. Each day she would harvest from a different part of the estate so she never exhausted any one place. Some of the plants grew twice as strongly once Sarah had culled them, they benefited immensely from the attention she gave them. One of the plants that she needed to grow in her garden was to be lavender. She used this kind grey and purple plant more than any other. Albert the gardener, who tended the Paget's gardens, had offered, come the autumn, he would harvest the great mass of purple lavender bushes that grew there, he also gave Sarah the address of a friend of his who worked for one of the great lavender growers in Norfolk. If business continued to expand as it had in the last month, then she would certainly have to consider approaching the growers.

She stepped back to admire the rickety creation that was supposed to resemble a wall, she laughed to herself at all the cracks and crevices, it seemed such a simple easy job when she had first started, but obviously there was a lot more to this art than she realised. At least the woodlice and other strange little creatures would have plenty of caves to hide in.

Today was Sunday and Sarah's little shop would be closed all day, this was not really a day off work for Sarah because this afternoon she had promised to have tea at Nicola's house. Mrs Paget had been suffering for a long time with sore aching bones and desperately wanted to try the healing that she had heard so much about from her friends. Sarah always enjoyed Nicola's company, it was great fun having their businesses so close to each other. Often when it was busy Nicola would pop in and help Sarah, she said she much preferred to work in the strange little shop of treasures, than selling tea and cakes to rich fat old ladies.

Peter with the help of Matthew was laying the flagstone floor in his new home. Matthew grumbled and groaned as they lifted the heavy stones off the cart. He would much rather have been helping the preacher's wife with her flower arranging and the visiting of the sick in the parish. He hated getting his hands soiled and more than that he passionately disliked having to be at Mill Farm helping his brother make a home for his future mad wife. No amount of persuasion could make Matthew change his attitude towards Sarah. She had never actually done anything to ever upset or harm him but he could barely tolerate being in the same room as her, when this did happen he would nervously reach his hand inside his shirt to grasp protection from the crucifix that he wore close to his skin. The preacher had instructed him to beware of the girl, she was not of the same religion as good people and Matthew believed every word the messenger of the Lord told him, it was God's law. He had on many occasions witnessed her madness. All he could pray for was that when she entered the church to marry his brother God would capture her soiled soul and cleanse it as he had many other sinners. The boy nearly jumped out of his skin as Sarah put her head around the door to see how Peter was getting on.

'Hello, you two. Well, you really are getting on with the floor. It looks so different. It's nice to see you here helping, thank-you Matthew.' And she smiled at him. His eyes immediately darted downwards to stare at the floor, he was fearful that if he looked into her face he would be turned into a pillar of salt or catch whatever it was she was suffering from.

'I'm off to clean myself up and then ride over to visit Nicola for the afternoon, I shouldn't be home too late, I'll try and get back before darkness.'

Peter was puffing and blowing as he was struggling to place an odd shaped piece of stone into the earth floor, he did not really take too much notice of what Sarah was saying, he vacantly nodded his head in agreement as she disappeared from the doorway.

The white horse trotted silently through the countryside needing very little control or directions from his rider. The barren fields and winter woodland rolled past as they continued on their journey together. Sarah very rarely rode the fine white horse that she had been given by a grateful farmer in payment for treating his team of ailing coach horses. They had become lifeless and ill through the wrong diet and the damp conditions that they were being kept in. Sarah had to remind the farmer that horses have to work so hard and should be treated with respect. They should have the best of fresh body building foods and not be left with their feet in water or mud. Animals were slightly different from humans, they often responded extremely well to touch healing and it was always a joy for Sarah to see nature's dumb creatures relax and repair so quickly. This magnificent white horse had taken a liking to Sarah when he was just a youngster and not broken for riding. When she had first saddled the young nervous horse she took the time to talk to him in a hushed voice, explaining exactly every single movement she was making and to the reasons why. She knew he was aware and had completely understood every word she had whispered into his soft pink ears. So, when the first time came for Sarah to climb onto his firm back he knew just what to expect and he behaved calmly and confidently. From that day onwards they became the very closest of friends and to this day always communicated telepathically.

From this vantage point high above the village of Marazion, Sarah looked down upon the restless grey sea that was edged by the constantly moving golden sands. She paused for a moment to admire the magnificent view of St. Michael's Mount emerging majestically from the ocean. The great mound of rugged rocks topped with a magnificent house soothed the otherwise sombre Cornish horizon. Far in the distance she could just make out the outline of the bay of Penzance, the docks where the Trevallian's ship was still waiting for completion of the storm damage. An angry blast of air coming in from the sea hastened Sarah to guide her mount inland and continue the last stretch of her journey. Very soon she was trotting up the drive to Nicola's home. The white cottage stood out brightly amongst the dreary grey countryside. The wooden beamed building was a grand specimen of another age and had been kept in immaculate repair. Mr Paget was a property owner and made his wealth from renting premises to local businessmen, most of the village shops were owned by the family. He was a very kind man and was well respected amongst the community as being very fair in business unlike his neighbour Ralph Trevallian. Sarah turned from the driveway and led her horse to the stables at the back of the building. She was surprised to see Charles's horse and the groom preparing Nicola's horse for a ride. As she approached the back of the house she could hear raised voices coming from the day room. She paid a greeting to the kitchen staff and made her way through the house to where the voices were coming from.

'Oh, take no notice of these two,' said Mrs Paget as Sarah entered the room.

'They have been arguing throughout all of lunchtime.'

Sarah stooped to kiss the elderly lady on the cheek. Nicola and Charles both stopped arguing when they saw Sarah. Nicola beamed with pleasure when she saw Sarah and rushed to her and gave her a tight hug. Charles approached her and bowed his head and kissed the back of her hand.

'I'm so glad you are here, you must convince Charles to stop his father from renting out those derelict stables to all those poor people, it's not right, something must be done about it.'

Sarah looked at both the young friends with a quizzical expression on her face.

'I'm sorry I don't know what you're talking about Nicola,' and she looked at her directly for an explanation. But Charles butted in before anyone else could speak.

'It's nothing she's got her facts wrong. I keep trying to explain that the derelict stables she refers to have been vacant for a very long time. The last entry I saw in the estate books regarding that property was, that the buildings were condemned and the tenants were re-housed in the workhouses and the property was sold off for some development. That was a few years ago.'

'And I say you are wrong. I have heard on good authority that the place is no better than a slum, young children and elderly people are dying there in the most disgusting and unhealthy conditions. It is far worse that you would expect any animal to live in.' With that last statement Nicola was so frustrated that he would not believe what she was saying, that she burst into tears and rushed out of the room. Charles looked absolutely bewildered and fled after her.

'Oh, dear,' said Nicola's mother, 'let's get on with my healing shall we, I'm sure they will both sort it out.'

Sarah unpacked her bag and placed her rubbing oils on a clean white cloth. She really wanted to run after Nicola and demand she tell her exactly what she was talking about, it sounded absolutely dreadful. But she must keep out of it at the moment and get on with the purpose of her visit.

The old lady relaxed as Sarah massaged the healing oils into her bony joints, as the warmth penetrated the thin layer of delicate skin the pain started to subside. Warmth was a great healer for soothing painful joints. Nicola's mother slept peacefully in her cosy fireside chair.

A young girl brought in a tray of light refreshments and silently put them down on the low table beside Sarah. Moments later Charles and

Nicola entered the room both dressed in their outdoor clothes.

'We were going for a ride along the beach,' whispered Nicola. 'But we have decided to go to look for the stables instead.'

'We thought you might like to join us,' said Charles quietly. 'But we must go soon before it gets dark.'

Sarah tiptoed out of the room and retrieved her cloak and boots from the cloakroom. The wind had died down and the afternoon had turned damp with a cold chill in the air. She had no idea where they were going. Charles and Nicola led the way and Sarah followed almost silently on her snow white horse. If the mystical unicorns were real Sarah felt sure her horse would have been one, he held himself so proudly and had no sense of an ill temper at all. As they rode she enjoyed the warmth that radiated from his strong body.

They must have trotted constantly for almost forty minutes, they started to slow down as they approached a small hamlet of thatched cottages. Grey smoke idly swirled from the huge square chimneys, the lack of breeze created smoky fumes at street level.

At the end of the muddy road they turned into a narrow uneven lane, the hedgerows were so overgrown that there was only just enough room for a single horse to pass.

Charles kept looking back to make sure Sarah was still behind.

'We will be there in about fifteen minutes Sarah, I know it will be a wasted journey but I have to satisfy this young lady that I am not lying.'

The muddy lane became so uneven and overgrown that they decided to dismount and walk the short distance to the clearing where the stables used to be. The horses remained safely tied to a tree.

'Come on,' urged Charles. And he put out both arms for the girls to hold onto.

'You will have to apologies to me in a minute you know,' he teased.

'I really hope you are right,' smiled Nicola.

Sarah was still in the dark about the argument but she was enjoying the banter between the two. She thought how well they got on in each other's company. The lane became slightly wider and they entered a clearing. The three of them stopped walking abruptly and stared at the ghastly body of a decomposing dog that was sprawled across the pathway. Nicola made a gasping sound and looked away. Charles's face became very serious as he looked at the derelict stables in front of him. He left the girls and walked forward. Smoke from damp braziers caught in their throats and permeated their clothes. A nauseous aroma filled their nostrils and caused their eyes to water. Sarah hastily followed Charles. Her mind was being invaded by the souls and disturbed spirits of the many dead and dying. She was looking at the emaciated bodies of many poor creatures. Never had she witnessed anything like this before. Each hovel she looked into held its own separate nightmare. Bundles of rags which were small children were barely moving with very little sign of life. Inside her head screamed the pitiful voices of long dead mothers and children who even after death howled pitifully for their loved ones. She could hardly breathe as she witnessed the spirit of a mother trying to tell someone where her young child was. Charles stood stock still as he watched Sarah communicating with the dead. She talked fluently to someone he could not see but he could hear. A cold chill ran down his back as the Spirit of Death had a party. No one could have been prepared for the full horror that was revealed that winter's day, it was as if every poor and destitute soul with their mother's, father's, children and grandparents had ended up in this hell-hole. Silence gripped the group. As if in a trance Sarah entered a dark hut and rooted around through the bundles of living human nightmares. She found the body of the mother whose spirit had pleaded with her to save her child, cradled in the arms of this poor dead soul she found the barely breathing body of a new born child. Carefully she undid the stiff cold skeletal arms that had held the infant. But as she reached to save the small life she felt the child pass on to be with its mother. Charles and Sarah held each other's hands tightly as they walked through the small pathway between the hovels. Young and old men turned to look at them as they walked through. There were no windows in these derelict stables. Roofs had long caved in, ship's canvas and corrugated iron seemed to be the materials that held the place together. There was no sanitation, human excrement ran down the centre of the pathway. The people that had managed to survive were filthy and covered with scabs and sores. Sickness was prevalent and Sarah knew something would have to be done immediately if these lives were to be saved. Charles looked in humble disbelief at the heaps of human rags that sat staring unblinking at the smoky fires. A young man with a limp hobbled towards them. Charles was immediately at Sarah's side.

'Come to look, ave yer? Bugger off. We don't want your sort coming here gloating. Bloody do gooders.

Make yer feel better does it. Earn you place in heaven.' Sarah felt tears of sadness spring into her eyes.

'That's it lady have a good cry at our expense. Well your bloody tears won't put food in my kid's mouths will it? What do yer want? Oh, I know another Sunday afternoon bible basher. Let me see now what did the last soul saviour say. Trust in the Lord and he will save your soul, she said she'd come back and help us and oh yes she did. She came and what do you think she bought us?' he paused to let them try and guess. 'Well she did not bring us food which is what we really needed and she did not bring us warm clothes which would have helped the small children and old folks, no, she brought us bars and bars of bloody soap she said a clean body was a healthy body.'

The young man's face changed from anger to such sadness. He bit his lip to try and stop the grief that was rising in his throat and making his voice falter. Emotion overcame him as he tried to tell them what had happened. Three times he started to explain and each time tears washed down his stained face leaving clean streams of pink flesh. He took a deep breath and swallowed before he began.

'Do you know what happened to my four year old son?' The couple shook their heads. 'He was so excited that the lady had bought him a gift, he was so grateful to her he could not stop thanking her and kissing her hands, she really felt good when she left here,' he hesitated again. 'That night he slept with the box of soap cradled tightly in his arms. I hadn't realised he didn't know it was soap and not food, and in the middle of that night he must have been so hungry that he opened the box and took bites out of all of the bars of rose scented soap. He was so ill for days and then like the rest of the little ones here he caught the disease from the bad water and he died, he's buried over there next to his mother and his baby sister.' He pointed to a mound of earth amongst many. The young man found his anger again.

'So what are you people going to promise to bring us, food, clothes, clean water, medicine? They are things that we need. You people feed waste food to your pigs that would keep everyone here alive for weeks.'

Charles waited for an appropriate moment and stepped forward. 'I am so sorry to intrude, believe me I honestly thought that this part of the Trevallian estate had been cleared of occupation years ago.'

'Don't mention that bloody name to me or to anyone else here. You wouldn't believe the stories I could tell you about that family. It's them that are to blame for all of this.' And he swept his arms around him. 'The authorities are well aware of the way we are living, but they are open to bribery and corruption. Let's face it the rich always stick together when it comes to acknowledging the poor. We don't exist. We have no voice.'

Very bravely Charles told him that he was a Trevallian. And his father's name was Ralph and they had once owned the stables and the land but it had been sold off a very long time ago. The man's reaction was slow to come and Charles braced himself to receive it.

'Then you my dear friend and I are half-brothers, we share the same father. But I can guarantee he treats your mother a lot differently than he did mine when she was alive. And I am afraid I have to correct you, this lot is still owned by you and your father. And I hold you and him responsible for all these sad lives and all of the unnecessary deaths. I suppose you could call this place, staff accommodation or the estate's retirement home, I have lived here all my life. Some of them who have long passed on had worked all their good years for the Trevallian family. Didn't you ever wonder what happened to your nurse and your grandmother's companion? They were all here living in absolute squalor and being charged for the privilege. As soon as your father got my mother pregnant she was sent here to live like a gypsy, no-one would ever believe her, when she said that Ralph Trevallian was my father. She told me that she was threatened with prison if she did not retract the accusations she had made. My mother could prove that she was telling the truth, I have your family birthmark on my shoulder and if I am not mistaken you have the very same mark on yours.'

Charles listened carefully to every word that was spat at him. He could not argue with anything that was said. His eyes swept over the human debris that littered the muddy alley in front of him. Great bundles of rags slightly moved to prove they were still alive, Sarah knelt down beside a very old lady she held her small grimy hand in hers. She put her face close to the matted mass of hair desperately trying to hear the words that were being whispered. The only word that she could make out was 'Help me.'

'I will help you,' she said. 'I am going now but I will be back in the morning with help.'

Sarah turned to Charles unable to say a word. She just shook her head in absolute disbelief and sadness. Silently they walked back to where Nicola was waiting. Charles caught the angry expression on Sarah's face, her eyes had become quite strange and menacing and just for a brief moment he thought her features had changed. Sarah had never felt such utter contempt and hatred for anyone as much as she did for Charles's father. At this moment all she could think of was the terrible inhuman situation that he had let these people live in. He must have been fully aware of the misery he had caused and allowed. Before she could tell Charles what she thought of his father he had answered all her unasked questions.

'I can only apologies to you both for the sight you have had to witness this afternoon. And Nicola I am so sorry that I ever doubted you when you said this was happening. I can honestly say with my hand on my heart that I knew nothing about this at all, as far as I was concerned the land did not belong to my family. I feel so responsible for such misery. When I get back home I promise you both that everything humanly possible will be done for the people who remain here.'

Sarah looked straight into his eyes and through to his very soul and she knew he spoke the truth. The journey back to Nicola's house was in stunned silence. No one felt like supper. Sarah gathered her basket and made a polite excuse for her sudden departure. Charles disappeared into the house with Nicola so Sarah took the opportunity to ride home with just herself for company. She had decided no matter what Ralph Trevallian action was she was going to go back tomorrow with food and clothes and someone in authority who could help those poor people.

Later that evening the kitchen staff stood stock still in absolute admiration and amazement as they listened to the young master's usually gentle voice bellowing at his father. Never before had such a blazing row shaken the very foundations of the house. They could not begin to wonder what on earth had prompted such a furious exchange. Molly had been in the master's study when the door had suddenly burst open and Charles had stormed in and ordered her to leave, she was quite upset that his father had not corrected him for his rude intrusion. Before she had time to fasten her gaping bodice Charles had propelled her roughly out into the passageway. After that, all she could hear was the young man's accusations and anger over something that he had seen that afternoon. As far as Molly could make out Charles had been out at the Paget's house for tea.

Grace Trevallian sat in awe listening to her son's anger. She felt very proud of him, she was not sure what the problem had been between the two men but it was obvious that it must have been very important for her son to react this way. She heard her husband's loud voice shout.

'They are vermin son, liars, cheats, thieves, all criminals, scum of the earth. Don't get involved in things you know nothing about.'

She could barely hear her sons muffled reply. And then her husband's again.

'Alright, I'll sort it in the morning,' followed by, 'I'll do it tonight then, just calm down it's none of your concern or that bloody interfering girls business, I don't know why you associate yourself with her. Keep away from her she's nothing but a bloody nuisance, can't you see she's certainly trying to worm her way in here. What with your mother's infatuation with her and now you. Pull yourself together son. The likes of us do not mix with the likes of her and her lot, it like trying to mix oil and water. And after all son believe me I know what I'm talking about. Just use them for your own personal gratification, they expect you to. It's what they deserve, servant, to serve, see what I mean.' And he looked at his son expecting him to readily agree with what he had just said.

'You disgust me father, I will never agree with your attitude and treatment towards fellow human beings. You can't keep using and abusing everyone and everything you come across. There must come a time when it's all got to stop.'

The raised voices subsided and Grace heard the study door open. Her husband's voice slightly croaky assured his son that by the morning the situation would be resolved. The sudden clanging from the study bell made the staff in the kitchen jump. Hodges quickly adjusted his attire and hastily climbed the backstairs to the study.

Minutes later he came down with a letter to be delivered post haste. As he put on his riding coat, questions were thrown at him but, being a true professional he adamantly refused to divulge to the nosy staff who the letter was for or where he was taking it.

Charles and Rufus left the house and made their way to the pagoda. He had decided that he would not stay another night under the same roof as his father. Hopefully he would only have to remain in England for a few more weeks. And then with his ship repaired he would head for the Indies with no intention of ever returning. There was nothing to hold him here apart from someone who he knew would never free herself to go with him, someone who was completely unaware of his affections.

The next day broke with solemn grey skies. Fine rain lazily dropped onto the already sodden ground. Sarah and Janet had been up for hours, they had packed food and clothing into baskets and wooden boxes. Given more time they could have collected a lot more.

Last night Peter and Daniel had helped the girls stack churns of fresh milk and clean water onto the cart after Sarah nagged the socks off of them. Sarah was impatient to leave. Peter had insisted that she wait for the daylight. He was not really very interested in the story Sarah had related to him yesterday evening on her return from the Paget's. He was far more concerned as to whether Sarah had been paid for her healing visit.

Sarah and Janet kept their heads down against the fine rain as they trundled off into the countryside. They made very little progress on the deep furrowed muddy lane. A few times they thought that the carts wheels were stuck firmly. But with gentle coaxing of the horses they managed to continue their slow journey. By cart it seemed to take twice as long as it had the day before. Sarah was very conscious of a whispering voice in her ear, it had been there most of the night but she was head strong and chose to ignore it. Tobias was now giving her a little warning to discontinue the journey.

'Go back. Go back Sarah,' he whispered. He had put a few hurdles in her way to make her change her mind about going but she was ignoring his advice. Janet read Sarah's lips as she spoke to her invisible friend, many times Janet had tried to see the person that Sarah so often had a conversation with but she never ever caught a glimpse of them. The rain started to become much heavier and the wind roared noisily through the treetops. Dark clouds appeared and seemed to gather ready for a storm. The girls pulled their cloaks around them and huddled together. The horses reared as the first flash of blue lightening closely followed by a great clap of thunder burst out of the angry skies. Sarah hoped the clothes and food in the cart would remain dry.

Tobias's warning voice was drowned out by the torrential rain. The storm seemed to last for the whole length of the journey. As they approached the road leading to the lane where the hovels were the path was blocked by two large farm carts and a carriage. Sarah stopped the horse and climbed down, her feet sank into the deep puddles. She was quite relieved to see that help had already arrived, she told Janet to stay where she was and look after the cart. As Sarah trod carefully on firmer ground Tobias managed to get her to listen to him. He told her to go back there was nothing that she could do. In her mind she argued with him that she had come to help, she had promised the old lady that she would return and she was definitely not going to break that promise for anyone including him. Quite unexpectedly a stern hand gripped Sarah's shoulder and a burly man stopped her in her tracks.

'I can't let you go any further miss, go back to your cart please,' and he pushed her slightly backwards.

She explained that she had come to help she had promised to bring food and clothes. Another scruffy looking man joined them.

'Aren't you the girl from the Mill, the one who's going to marry young Peter?'

'Get away from here, there's nothing anyone can do for these poor souls now. It's just a matter of clearing up the bodies. Everyone is dead. It looks like an epidemic of some sort or the bad water got all of them, old, young kids, babies the lot. The sight and the smells bloody horrendous, we are clearing them all out and burning the remains of the buildings. So there is nothing for you to be doing here unless you're a preacher and want to say a few words before we get rid of them.'

Sarah's head reeled as she took in what the man had said. Before she could ask any more questions a fully laden cart covered in tarpaulin rattled its way down the narrow lane it was coming towards them. Sarah stepped back to let it pass. You could not mistake the contents of the cart the stench was unbelievable. Sarah's eyes blurred as she saw the spirits of the dead walk freely behind the grotesque funeral procession, following the vehicles for their souls to their communal resting place in a lime filled trench away from the eyes of decent people. They would never offend Ralph Trevallian ever again. The problem of yesterday had been well and truly solved. Sarah returned to Janet her heart was heavy, she could not believe that they had all died so quickly. She asked Tobias what had happened.

'Last night men came on behalf of the Trevallians with food and water. And when they came back this morning everyone was dead. I think they expected that to happen, the water they bought was not healthy. But, no-one will ever be able to prove that they were poisoned.'

Back at High Markham Ralph Trevallian received the news he had been waiting for. Later in the day he held his head in his hands when he related to his shocked son the details of the sad story about an epidemic claiming them all.

The reply was, 'I don't believe you father I never will, you are a cruel ruthless man who I shall never trust again as long as I live. I am ashamed to share the same name as you.'

Sarah's journey back home was made with a very heavy heart. All the assurances of help that they had made to these forgotten people were empty words of unfilled promises. They all must have been so pleased when the carts arrived late last night delivering food and much needed water. They would never have guessed as they quenched their thirst and filled their bloated stomachs that all the gifts of help were laced with enough poison to wipe out the whole of the encampment.

The hooded figure the Spirit of Death and Ralph Trevallian had certainly danced hand in hand last night, they both belonged to the same cult, which was devoid of any guilt or conscience.

That evening at the dinner table Sarah related the story. Peter and Daniel said it was as much as they would expect from that lot up at the house. Daniel felt the poor souls were better off and he knew about the place it had been used for a long time but he did not realise that it had become that depraved. Sarah said that the whole incident should be reported to the authorities.

'Don't waste your time, they are all in it together. There are two laws, one for them and one for the likes of us. Best you forget it Sarah, there's much more important things to fill your mind with. The wedding is only four weeks away and I hope you've got it all sorted. And don't you go upsetting her ladyship till afterwards, I've got a lot of friends coming to the party and I've promised them a really posh do and I don't want to disappoint them.'

'How many have you invited, Peter? I thought we were only going to invite family and a few close friends,' said Sarah.

'That was when I was paying for everything. Things are different now.'

She was slightly upset that he had not consulted her about the changes, she had already told Grace how many were to be catered for. She explained this to Peter and suggested that they pay for the extra guests by using some of their savings. This statement seemed to irk him even more.

'Don't you go bloody sulking about it Sarah, you're lucky to be getting wed at all, be grateful. Besides who were you going to invite, it's not as if you've got a great big family supporting you, is it?'

'I have a family out there somewhere, you know that Peter,' she retorted.

'They did not want you, remember, they paid to have you taken away. If they had wanted you they would have come and got you.'

'They don't know where I am,' she said feeling defeated. 'They kept me until I was nine, they must of loved me for some of that time,' she paused and then added, 'don't you think so, Peter?'

'They knew where you were. They couldn't of cared less.'

'Don't Peter. I know what you're saying is true. I am sorry I have upset you but please don't say anymore horrible things to me.'

'Well,' he snapped. 'We are your family and you should make the most of it, I could still change my mind and then where would you be, an old maid of the parish,' he said and then added laughing, 'a daft old maid of the parish.' Silently he sighed with relief. At least he had diverted her mind from the subject of using some of their savings for the wedding.

Each week Sarah gave him the profit from the

shop to save for their future and each week he spent it on being entertained by Jane Parminter and supporting the gambling houses in Penzance. Unbeknown to Sarah he had proposed to Jane just a few months ago, she had told him to save his proposal until he could afford to keep her in the style her late husband used to. Until then he was still welcome to visit and pay for her sexual favours. He never begrudged the coins he always left her on the bedside cupboard. It amused him that his wife to be was paying the bill for his personal entertainment. He had dreamed of what he could do with that farm and the vast amount of land that Jane owned. He could make it pay but he needed capital before she would consider his offer. Well perhaps it wouldn't be long before he might be coming into some money.

'Are you coming down for a pint, Pa?' he said as he put on his jacket. Daniel very readily joined him.

'Don't either of you be too late,' said Gwen, 'you both have to get up early tomorrow.' As they slammed the door Gwen heard them shout something that she could not understand. 'Oh well they'll be the ones with the sore head in the morning not me.'

She knew her son would not be back tonight. He and his father would fill themselves with ale and then Daniel would stagger home and fall into bed and Peter would return in the morning.

Sarah was very unsettled and still very angry and a little confused with the events of the last twenty-four hours. This afternoon Charles had come into the shop to talk to her about the tragedy. He had been visually upset by the whole proceedings and went to great lengths to explain to her, what he thought had really happened. When she had cried with such sadness he had put his strong arms around her and comforted her. At that point something inside her stirred, she could only describe it as though she was being enveloped in a warm soft bubble. She experienced a great sense of security and wellbeing. How long they remained together she did not know. But the spell was only broken when Nicola noisily entered the shop. Just for a moment the three embarrassed friends stood in silence. Sarah had withdrawn from Charles's arms very quickly which made the scene look all the more suspicious. There was a stunned awkward silence before anyone spoke. Charles had looked directly into Sarah's eyes searching for the emotion that he had sensed just a few moments before. As if she knew what he was looking for Sarah cast her eyes towards Nicola. Who was sure she had just experienced a very intimate moment between two of her very good friends. Who would of thought it. No wonder he never really took any notice of her, all along it was Sarah that he was interested in. Now things became a lot clearer. Sarah caught the thoughts in Nicola's mind.

'You are wrong Nicola, what you are thinking is not true.'

Charles frowned unable to quite grasp the conversation between the two girls.

'Have I missed something, somewhere?'

'No.' Laughed Sarah. 'Nicola thought she had caught us in a compromising situation.'

'Oh,' smiled Charles.

'Charles was just comforting me after I stupidly got upset,' explained Sarah.

'I think we all need to get together over this,' said Nicola. 'It's been an awful shock for all of us. Why don't we meet at my house one evening?'

'How about both of you coming to my place, at least it will be quiet there. Not the house, I have moved out from there into the pagoda.'

'That is really a very good idea Charles, don't you think so Sarah? I have often wondered what the inside of your sanctuary looked like. When shall we come?'

'Let me see, how about Friday evening about eight is that alright with both of you?'

'I will bring cakes and scones.'

'You will need something to wash them down with. Shall I chill some champagne?' offered Charles.

For a moment Sarah was deep in thought. 'I'll bring Candle Spells and Wishes,' she added.

'Ooh,' shrieked Nicola. 'What an evening that will be.'

'I shall look forward to seeing you both on Friday,' said Charles. 'I must say goodbye now, I am off to check on the progress report with the ship fitters. And I must be in Penzance before dark.'

'I'll come down to your farm to pick you up Sarah,' said Nicola.

'Don't worry about coming to Mill Farm, its right out of your way besides I know a short cut through the woods and I can be there in a very short time.'

The friends all departed agreeing to meet on Friday evening. At first Sarah regretted making the arrangements but then after this evening, listening to Peter and the way he made her feel perhaps it would do her good to go out to see friends. After all Peter was away every Friday night and recently only returned home Sunday afternoons. She hoped that when they were married he would stay at home more and not want to spend so much time out with his friends.

CHAPTER SEVENTEEN

I AM PLEASED TO ANNOUNCE
THAT FROM THE 1ST FEBRUARY
APPOINTMENTS ARE BEING TAKEN

Sarah pinned the hand-written card to the inside of the shop window so that everyone passing would be able to read it. Unfortunately the very first person to stop and squint at the words was Matthew's hero, the short sighted Preacher. After fumbling into his pockets he eventually located his spectacles. A deep frown furrowed his sweaty brow as he read the message. He huffed and sighed when he had finally digested the news. Outside of the pulpit and without the courage of his gin bottle he was not a very confident man. The only reason he was here was because of a joint letter of complaint that he had received from a few of his well to do parishioners, people that were influential and he could not afford to ignore their views on the matter. If he was really truthful as long as the girl kept well out of his way he was not too bothered. Mind you, he was always telling Matthew to steer clear of her and take no notice of her ramblings. He had said it a hundred times but still the boy would go on and on about her. The boy seemed obsessed by her practices. As far as he was concerned, if she managed to cure a few of his moaning members of his congregation and it kept them away from his church door then he could not complain about her. Recently his love of the Juniper Berry very much outweighed any real or long lasting interest or affection for anyone. The long-term effect of continual saturation of his once lively brain had now started to take its toll. More and more he relied on Matthew and his own wife to prepare the sermons and services also to keep him informed of daily-expected events, such as weddings and funerals.

High blood pressure highlighted his cheeks as he pushed open the shop door.

'Hello,' said Sarah, smiling. 'It's nice to see you, have you come to talk about the wedding.'

He wished that she was not such a happy person. It was always easier to deal with somebody who did not keep smiling at you.

He looked at Janet and then at Sarah. 'Is there somewhere we can talk in private?'

'Do come through,' said Sarah, holding open the curtain to the healing room. 'Take a seat.' And she pointed to the feather cushioned chair.

He sunk down into the softness and was glad to take the weight of his shaky legs. Sarah looked at the man and could see he was quite troubled she could also feel that there was a serious deep-rooted problem like a black cloud hanging over him. She knew about his alcohol problem but felt there was something playing on his mind causing him to drink to conceal reality. 'Can I get you anything?' she asked.

'No, no thank you. I am afraid I've not come on a social visit. I need to have a serious talk with you.' He stopped abruptly as the bell on the door jangled loudly and made him start.

'Don't worry Janet will look after them. What is it

that you have to say to me?' She could not believe that this man out of his surroundings was so unsure of himself. In the pulpit he always seemed to be loud and confident. Sarah had never really liked or disliked the man. She always felt he was providing a worthwhile service for his customers that needed it.

He took a deep breath and began to stutter and stumble over his words. Sarah listened carefully and tried to decipher the actual cause of complaint. She raised her hand to stop the man from going any further.

Just as she did this Tobias materialised, he was wearing white robes and for some strange reason he had tall white-feathered angel wings towering above him. She shook her head in disbelief at the spectacle in the corner, how could she take this poor man in the chair seriously when she had Tobias imitating an Archangel behind him. She tried to look away from the truly magnificent presence. If only the preacher could have seen her ghostly companion. Before she could take full control of the situation a broad smile started to spread across her face. Taking a deep breath and trying to concentrate on the immediate situation she made herself look into the purpose of the preachers visit. 'So what you are trying to tell me is this. Ralph Trevallian and some of his friends have complained to you about my shop and my methods of helping people, am I correct?' she knew she was and continued, 'Let me see, did he say something along the lines of, she's absolutely mad, or was it she's an evil women or perhaps his favourite, she's a witch? I am sure it was something very similar. So, that is why you are here? Do tell me what you expect me to do about it.' Not that she paused long enough to let the man answer. 'My policy is never to harm if I cannot help. And I am sure, if you just take the time to talk to a few of the people that I visit they will assure you that I cause them no ill effects. The whole purpose of my shop and the nature of it is to provide a positive service so people can take responsibility for themselves by choosing a natural method. I am not against orthodox medicine, my way is not an alternative but with correct guidance it works well alongside it, as a complimentary medicine. Of course we must give credit to our medical profession after all they spend years studying the workings of the body. Surely we cannot put total accountability for our illnesses onto the doctor's shoulders. After all it is our body and we must take control of it. I think nature and science should go hand in hand. In time they will rediscover cures for many illnesses by looking at what nature provides for us as for religion and faiths I cannot say whether one belief is any better than another, it is what personally suits you best. I see people from all walks of life and they all have one thing in common, one faith and that is the belief that they all want to be well again. And to me that is all that matters. And it is nothing to do with sorcery or witchcraft, it is as natural as the energy from the sun that we can all feel but nobody can really explain how it got there.' The silent preacher could not argue with Sarah, his muddled mind needed a drink he had virtually lost all sensible contact with Sarah once he had sat down in the chair.

Voices in the shop brought the man's befuddled mind back to the reason he was here. He sat rubbing his sweaty hands together. The voices in the shop made him feel very nervous. You could not mistake the voices of Grace Trevallian and her son Charles.

'Oh, sorry,' said Charles as he peeked around the curtain. 'I did not realise you had a customer.' He grinned in amusement when he saw who was sitting in the chair.

'Oh it's alright Charles I am not working. But, it looks as though I'm in a lot of trouble.'

'Really Sarah, tell me more,' and he entered the back room. The nervous Preacher quickly removed himself from the chair.

'Your father and a few other stalwarts in the village have sent a letter of complaint to the church about my behaviour and what I practice in the shop.'

Before Charles could answer his mother pushed past him and stood in front of the very harassed Preacher. At this point Tobias found the amount of people in the small room too much and took refuge in the funeral parlour next door.

'Well I hope you are going to totally ignore my husband's misguided views about this young lady,' said Grace. 'My husband knows nothing about the truth of the matter at all. I am afraid he is being encouraged to behave so badly by Molly, Sarah's very jealous half-sister. Who is very friendly with my husband. That girl would go to any means to discredit Sarah and I will not stand by and let this happen. Now get along with you and stay where you belong and don't meddle in things you know nothing about. Or you will have me and most of the ladies of Hellstone to contend with.'

The embarrassed man could not leave the shop quick enough. Tobias watched his father's sad representative scurry around the corner and into the alleyway, hiding in the shadows the man emptied the contents of his hip flask into his eager thirsty mouth. What in Heaven's name was he going to tell Trevallian? He could not possibly tell him how frightened he was of his frail looking wife.

Back inside the shop Charles was congratulating his Mother on her very assertive behaviour.

'I cannot believe you sometimes Mother you portray this gentle little lady and yet underneath that eggshell exterior hides a strong wild stranger.'

'Thank you son, I think having Sarah around me has given me confidence to cope with difficult situations.' She turned to Sarah. 'You have helped me so much, physically and mentally I can never thank you enough.'

'Grace you are embarrassing me. I've got an awful lot of bad points too. By the way you've come for your appointment haven't you? Let's get on before it gets too dark to see what we're doing.'

'I'll wait for you next door at Nicola's mother, I am off to sample her fresh cream cakes. Call me when you are ready to leave. And Sarah don't forget Friday evening,' and he was gone.

'Oh before I forget Sarah, we have had an old friend of Charles staying at the house, he's been taking pictures of Charles and myself, with a really wonderful contraption. Well, I was so impressed with the results that I have asked him to take pictures of you at the wedding so you will always have a wonderful record of the day.'

'Grace that sounds absolutely amazing, you have done so much for us already how can I ever repay you?'

'You have already repaid me a thousand times just with your youthful company and all the care you give me. I can honestly say, you are one of the people that I know, in any situation I could turn to and truly trust. I mean it when I say, you are just like a daughter to me. I know I am not the same as your real mother but it has given me great joy to make some of the arrangements for your wedding. You really are worth it. Bless you Sarah.' And Grace kissed her cheek.

'Perhaps one day you will be doing it for Charles and Nicola.'

'I think Nicola and her parents would really like that to take place. But Charles only looks on Nicola as friend nothing else. I would not be surprised if he has a sweetheart out in the Indies, all of a sudden he seems very eager to return.'

'When will he be off then?' asked Sarah.

'Well there has been another delay by the fitters. It could be one month or at the very most two. Between you and me Sarah, I wish my husband would go back and my son would stay here and manage the estate. He would make a much better job of it and I would have his company.'

'Yes I can understand that.'

Grace nestled into the comfort of the chair and Sarah gently coaxed her to relax. The temperature in the room rose as the healing session began. The crystal chimes hanging in the window swayed gently, creating a faint but very pleasing sound. Light from the tall candles reflected in the teardrop prisms causing a rainbow of coloured lights to radiate from them, creating a spectacular pattern on the white washed walls of the room. For twenty minutes the elderly lady relaxed and received channelled energy. She felt a warmth spreading through her entire body.

'Breathe in to the count of five,' said Sarah in a very quiet voice. 'And as you breathe out to the count of five I want you to imagine that you are pushing out all impurities and illness. If you give your disease or complaint a dark colour so that when you breathe in you visualise beautiful clean crystal air filling your lungs and permeating the whole of your body. And when you breath out you visualise great clouds of misty dark breathe pushing out, leaving your body healthy and well.'

Sarah very carefully placed her hands on Grace's head with the lightness of a feather. In her mind she saw a healing light radiate through her fingers and enter Grace. The extra healing energy stimulated the depleted system enabling it to rebalance and repair any illness. Thus assisting the inbuilt repair procedure that we all have.

Sarah was always amazed as to how the human body could repair and regenerate new cells if the others were damaged. She would point out how we sometimes actually heal ourselves. Look what happens when we cut or gash ourselves almost immediately the flesh starts to regenerate and within a few weeks only a scar is left behind.

Janet waited for the healing session to end before she brought in a tray of refreshments. She poured two cups of elderflower tea and placed a plate of shortbread on the side table.

'Thank you Sarah, that was wonderful. I feel absolutely relaxed and my nerves which were on edge when I came in are now very nicely sedated. Before I go I must purchase some of your lavender bags and perhaps Janet would weigh me up half a pound of your elderflower tea, I promised Nellie that I would bring some back with me. Hodges and Nellie are so looking forward to your wedding, it was kind of you to ask Hodges to give you away, he has bought a new suit and goes over what he has to say and do a dozen times a day. The kitchen staff are finding it all so very entertaining.'

Sarah laughed at her last comment. Hodges and Nellie had become quite special people to her and she was pleased that they would be there to support her.

'Well if you would like to let my son know I am ready to leave. I shall look forward to seeing you next week.'

CHAPTER TWENTY

Make a pillowcase with white cotton approximately one-foot square, leave open one end. Fill with the following:
Use equal amounts of, Lavender, Lemon Balm, Peppermint, Angelica, Bergamot, Rosemary & Thyme, mix together the dried ingredients and fill the pillowcase.
Stitch the open end closed.
Make a pillow slip out of floral or velvet fabric, decorate or embroider to your own taste.

Janet tightly held the damp hand of little Mary. They were patiently waiting their turn to be served. You could never become bored in this shop, from floor to ceiling the shelves and glass fronted cupboards were stocked with every possible item that a women could possibly need. Whether it is for sewing or wearing, Browns was the best drapers and haberdashery that you could find for at least twenty miles. Janet had come today with a long list of items that Sarah required. Top of the list was five yards of narrow white lace, to edge floral lavender bags, next were two reels of white cotton and three yards of red velvet to make small soft pillows filled with aromatic herbs to tuck under your head when you needed to relax. Janet also wanted a length of cream ribbon to make little hidden surprises for Sarah's wedding dress.

A very rotund lady who was being served could not make up her mind whether she wanted pink drawers or cream ones, Janet giggled as Ruby, the humorous shop assistant, held up an enormous pair of pink bloomers so the customer could view them more clearly. Very quickly Janet pulled a straight face as the lady looked around to see who was laughing. Mary wandered off to look at the glass-fronted drawers that were full of brightly coloured buttons, beads and threads, above the counter hung cards of needles, hairgrips, elastic and shoelaces. You could have spent a whole day in the shop and still not discover everything. At last the lady chose one pair of each of the coloured bloomers, Ruby carefully wrapped them in brown paper and tied the parcel with string.

Janet handed over her list for Ruby to read. The girl was quite aware that Janet couldn't hear a word and made sure that she was facing her when she spoke. Janet read the girl's lips. She was saying that she was pleased to have received an invitation to Sarah's wedding and was really looking forward to it. She said how lucky Peter and Sarah were to have so much help with making all the arrangements and organising everything. Also how nice it was to see Mrs Trevallian so happy. It had given the old lady something to occupy her time with, after all she led a very miserable life with that awful husband of hers. Janet watched the words form on Rubies lips and nodded with agreement. She too was looking forward to the wedding she could not wait to wear the beautiful lace dress that Sarah had made her. She secretly hoped that perhaps she too would soon be able to find a young man and get married like Sarah.

Carefully all the items were measured out using

the long brass ruler that edged the glass topped counter. Janet counted out the right money and thanked Ruby for her goods. She thought they would take a slow walk back to the shop and if Mary behaved herself she would take her into Nicola's teashop and buy her a gingerbread man. The shop next to the drapers was an amazing shop called The Gallery, it contained oil paintings, watercolours, books and it was a printers and stationers. Janet loved the smell of the oils and old books, Elizabeth Waterhouse owned the shop, she was a small girl with flowing wild curly red hair. She sat on a very tall stool behind a small oak desk and it would be no surprise to find her with strange objects protruding from her unruly mop of hair, it could be a paintbrush or piece of charcoal. She was a very knowledgeable person and would help you to find any particular book you were looking for, Sarah always said this was her favourite shop. It was Elizabeth who had helped Sarah to perfect her handwriting. The shop also offered a service of writing or printing anything of importance, business cards, invitations, and letters on crested notepaper in fact any correspondence and anything artistic. It also specialised in books that had already been read and were sold for a small amount of their original worth. Elizabeth said she wanted to create a scheme to lend out books to people who could not afford to buy them and for a small cost could hire them. After all once a book was read it often became no use to the owner, so she offered to buy the books from them for a small fee and this way created shelves and shelves of second hand books for her lending library. She had three members of staff to help out in the shop. Her cousin Steven was one of the artists who designed the letter headings and formal invitations he also was a superb artist and specialised in christening portraits. He was becoming increasingly worried by the new invention of the camera. His cousin had told him that if that was the way that things were going then they would have to update themselves and purchase one of the pieces of equipment. He was not quite as keen as she was. The other two members of staff were local boys who were given apprenticeships to become printers and bookbinders. It was one of these young chaps that Janet had her eye on, the other eye being on Tim.

The two sisters climbed up the well-trodden steps and pulled open the half glass door to the shop. A musty welcoming smell of old words and spent oils spilled out into the street. Tall brightly coloured oil lamps lit the shop casting long shadows in the dark corners of the small room. Steep shiny wooden stairs twisted and disappeared up into the ceiling leading you to further treasures in the studio above. On the high staircase walls hung framed watercolours, mainly small portraits. In the attic rooms stood easels with large canvases sitting on them. Some pictures were completed and were being left to dry and others were waiting for the subject to finish their sitting.

Elizabeth looked over the top of her small spectacles and smiled as the girls entered the shop. She knew exactly why they were there. She looked at her watch and nodded to Janet. 'All right I suppose it is their lunchtime but remember fifteen minutes only and no noise.'

The girls opened a small door tucked under the staircase, it led down into the basement that housed the workshop where the apprentice boys worked. Janet had brought the boys some lunch. From her basket she brought out a piece of cloth, in it was wrapped two fresh bread rolls and a large lump of cheese. From Mary's basket she produced a can of cow's milk. The boy with the ginger hair and freckled face blushed brightly when he saw Janet. They went to sit together on a long bench. He wrote something on a slate and the two of them laughed as Janet erased his words and replaced them with her message.

Mary patiently sat on the floor playing with chalk and thin strips of paper that lay beneath the glinting blade of the guillotine.

All too soon the boys break time was over and Elizabeth's voice reminded the girls it was time for them to leave.

The outside air struck cold on their faces as the girls left the warmth of the basement. Janet turned Mary towards her and reached down, and buttoned up her coat and pulled the hood up over her head.

They both scurried past the butchers shop holding their breath against inhaling the smell of dried blood and sawdust. Mary hated the sight of the decapitated heads of the pigs lined up sightless and lifeless in the window of the shop with their pink legless feet piled high upon a tray. They crossed the road, drawn by the light coming from the shop of curios. Two elderly spinster sisters owned the shop, they both dressed entirely in black clothes from head to toe. It also appeared that they each wore every necklace or row of beads that came into the shop. How they ever kept upright under the weight of their adornment no one ever knew. One of the sisters was the expert in old objects and jewellery the other one looked after the financial side of the business. The girls were not allowed into the shop on their own but took great delight in looking at the window display that changed most frequently. You could not put a finger between all the interesting articles.

They stood pointing to odd things that they discovered. The first item Janet saw was a small glass locket with a lock of hair coiled inside it, she wondered who that had belonged to. Beside it was a collection of small wooden dolls just minute enough to live in the doll's house at the back of the display. Silver pots, pens and jewellery nestled on velvet cushions. One beaded cushion was in royal celebration and was used to house a great variety of hatpins.

The wind whipped around the girls' legs causing them to turn away from the keen breeze. Janet and Mary just managed to shelter in the doorway of the shop as the dark sky released its heavy burden of hailstones upon them. Looking through the shop door Janet could see inside, it looked really cosy. One of the sisters saw them sheltering and called them inside but made them promise to stand just inside the door on the mat and to not touch anything.

A few customers were half-heartedly browsing, really waiting until the storm passed before they left the shop. Janet recognised the voice of the man being served at the counter.

'Yes, thank you, I like that, it will do very nicely. Could you make sure that you package it soundly as it looks extremely fragile. Do you know the history of it?' The women shook her head. 'Nothing I'm afraid, we bought it at an auction along with quite a few other unusual pieces.'

She wrapped up his purchase using vast amounts of paper and then placed it carefully into a small straw filled box. Charles paid at the cash desk and collected the box. As he turned he saw the girls standing just inside the door.

'Where are you two off to?' He waited for their reply. 'If you would like to wait a little while I will take you home. The carriage is just outside, you both go and get inside, I won't be long, all I have to do now is collect a hat my mother ordered from the shop next door.'

Janet smiled and nodded in agreement. Mary was very excited about the prospect of riding in the coach.

The interior of the coach was clean and shiny. The leather seats smelt of saddle polish and Mary slid across them from one side to the other. Janet laughed at her antics. Charles arrived with an extremely large hat box and instructed the driver to take the girls home to Mill Farm. As they neared the end of the muddy main street they saw Sarah locking the door of the shop, Charles called for the driver to stop the coach. The angry wind seized Charles's words and whipped them away from his mouth as he tried desperately to shout a message to Sarah. When she saw the girls inside the coach she guessed what the lost message was. She had been just about ready to make her way home and seeing the extreme weather conditions was very pleased to accept his offer. The hood of her cloak flapped against the back of her neck leaving her long hair to play wildly in the turbulent air. Charles had seen that wild raven hair escape into the air once before. He pushed that event to the far corner of his mind before it stirred well-buried memories. She was really amused to see Janet and Mary sitting inside the coach trying to look like ladies. Charles held her elbow and helped her up the steps. He fought against the wind to close the door. The carriage rocked and swayed as it was buffeted by the turbulence. The horses were quite frightened by the noise and the odd movement of air. The driver reined them in tightly to control their skittish behaviour. The hail had turned to cold heavy rain, which lashed against the windows of the coach blurring their vision. Sarah felt really sorry for the driver of the coach who was outside in all the inclement elements. She thanked Charles for picking up the girls, she said that Peter had promised to collect her from the shop on his way back from the market but he must have been held up.

'I was in Penzance this morning and I could have sworn I saw him in the Swan Hotel.'

'No,' said Sarah. 'You must be mistaken, he set off to travel to the market late yesterday evening. He has gone to buy more stock for the farm, we've had a lot of bad luck with the animals this winter. The continual damp has caused all sorts of problems.'

'Oh,' said Charles deciding not to pursue the matter of Peter's whereabouts.

'I suppose you will be glad to return to a country with kinder weather,' said Sarah.

'I must admit the winter in England is not the kindest I have experienced. I think it would suit me to spend the summers here and the winters away, that would be an agreeable combination.'

The girls screamed as the coach lurched to one side and for a moment they thought it would topple over. The driver shouted a stern command to the wild-eyed chestnuts to hold steady. There was a loud crack as one of the four metal bound wheels splintered and buckled.

'Oh, what an awkward time for the wheel to break,' said Charles. 'The weather could not have been much worse.'

'Never mind, I am sure a few drops of rain will not hurt us,' said Sarah. 'We usually walk everywhere, come on girls your moment in the life of luxury is over, out you come.' And she jumped down out of the warm coach and into the sticky brown glinting mess that resembled the lane. The girls followed her.

'I can't apologise enough,' said Charles. 'If you would care to wait I'll get the wheel changed.'

'Please don't worry we are nearly half way home it won't take us long.'

'I'll walk with you and then I can take a short cut through the woods at the back of your farm to the stables and send the boy out with another wheel.' He instructed the driver to stay with the coach and said he would be back within the hour.

They all set off together, Sarah and the girls were quite used to the journey but you could tell Charles was struggling slightly especially when she took them over the stile and across the fields.

'I hope you know where you are going,' he said.

'No,' said Sarah jokingly. 'I don't.' She looked down at Charles's boots and trousers. He was absolutely plastered in thick mud and after walking through the rough fields that were usually used for grazing he would be wearing a very aromatic substance on his boots. Sarah laughed at the thought of it.

'Do tell me Sarah, what do you think is so funny?'

She giggled as she looked at his usually thick mop of blonde hair, black with rainwater and stuck closely to his forehead so that his noble nose protruded from the wet curtain of tresses.

The ground started to become steeper as they approached the Mill Farm fields. You could see the huge white sails of the windmill looming out of the night sky. Sarah suddenly had a thought.

'I have an idea, save you having to walk all the way back to your stables why not let me take you back in our cart.'

'I can't let you do that Sarah. Perhaps I could borrow your cart and return it when mine is mended. Do you think your father would mind?'

'I'll go and ask. And by the way he is not my father he is Peter's father,' she said.

'Oh sorry, I stand corrected.'

Daniel was still in the Mill and said he did not mind if Charles borrowed the cart as long as it was back before the morning. He said if Peter was around, ask him to help prepare the horse. Sarah popped into the kitchen to ask Gwen where Peter was. She was helping young Mary get out of her wet clothes. Gwen said Peter was in the stables somewhere.

He was not very sociable when Sarah found him. He said he had only just returned from the market and had not had time to pick her up from the shop. He was very much the worse for wear and really could not understand any words Sarah was saying. His friend Colin was with him and they looked like they had been drinking heavily most of the afternoon. He mumbled something to Sarah about celebrating, but she did not stop long enough to listen. Had she stayed longer she would have witnessed Peter boasting about his sexual conquests with Jane Parminter in a luxurious room at the Swan Hotel last night. Paid for by Sarah's savings that were supposedly at the bottom of her treasure chest.

With Sarah's help they prepared the cart. Sarah insisted that she drove them to High Markham.

That way she could return the cart to the farm. She knew that the mood Peter was now in she would be best to stay out of the way. Charles noticed a sudden change in Sarah's mood.

'Was it all right to use the cart? I'll make sure Daniel is recompensed for his kindness.'

'Oh yes that was fine, he did not mind.'

The next question Charles asked was lost as the wind increased and threatened to become a gale.

They both bent their heads downward against the ever-increasing torrent of rain that was thrashing their bodies. He reached across and took the reins from Sarah. In front of them a tree crackled and splintered as a blue flash of lightening completed its journey to earth and destroyed the giant oak. He halted the horse just as the tree crashed down in front of them barring their path through the woods. Calmly he turned the horse to the left and took the narrow lane that led to the pagoda. Sarah instantly recognised where they were heading and she was glad that they could find shelter. The horse and cart almost stood still as the strong gale stopped them from moving forward. Boughs and branches were torn carelessly from the trees and dashed to the ground. Charles tethered the horse on the sheltered side of the pagoda. Hand in hand they both ran as fast as they could towards the door of the pagoda. The lightening gathered speed and became almost a constant flash. The storm appeared to be all around them, the wind roared like the sound of an angry sea with waves crashing about their very ears. Sarah was becoming very frightened by the violent conditions. Within a few seconds the heavy oak doors were unlocked and they both ran inside. Breathless from the awful journey Sarah sank down on the chaise longue trying to catch her breath, she shivered as her wet clothes chilled and clung to her body. Charles reached for a bottle and poured them both a large brandy, he sipped his as he lit the fire. The oak logs spluttered and spat as the flames from the tinder coaxed them into ignition. He went to the small bedroom and pulled a couple of sheepskin rugs from the bed. He passed them to Sarah. Without any embarrassment she peeled off her wet clothes and draped a rug around her shoulders. She threw the sopping bundle onto the marble hearth. Charles came out from the back room wearing dry clothes, he had dressed in a long white over-shirt and tight black breeches his wet hair hung loosely over his face. Outside the storm raged bits of debris dropped onto the glass roof causing Sarah to start, trees outside crashed and snapped under the pressure from the bluster.

'It's alright Sarah we are safe here nothing will harm you.' And he sat down beside her.

'If you want some dry clothes please feel free to use grandma's they are all hanging in there.' And he pointed to the small back room. He got up and moved to where he could stand behind her, with a soft towel he gently started to dry her raven black hair, the tresses looked almost unreal when they were so very wet. She relaxed and leant back against the gold brocade and enjoyed the feeling of his hands gently caressing her head. Not for one moment did it occur to her that she should not be in this situation with this particular person. His warm strong hands travelled down to caress and massage her taught neck and shoulders with each movement she felt herself relax into a state of absolute pleasure. As she turned her back towards him the sheepskin rug that had covered her slipped down around her waist exposing her naked body. For a brief moment Charles stopped what he was doing and looked at her slightly moist olive skin. The perfume that had always bewitched him curled into a spiral and penetrated his very soul. At this moment he knew that he would not be able to account for any of his actions. As if he was being hypnotised by the aroma of hedgerows and woodland spices he felt detached from sanity and driven by some external influence. In a dream he watched Sarah turn to face him and hold out her hand, he reached for it but it seemed to be just out of his grasp. Small cold beads of sweat formed on his brow and top lip. He saw her naked body glistening in the half-light from the fire. As if he was wearing lead boots he struggled to walk around to sit beside her. Her black hair tumbled over her breasts, eyes as blue as the ocean reflected the flames of the candlelit room. She glowed with an inner light not a gentle light but a wild untamed power. What was happening to him, he tried to stop himself but someone or something was controlling his actions?

Sarah was overwhelmed by the feelings that she was experiencing. Never before had she felt this way. Strong arms enveloped her making her feel warm and very safe. The white crisp cotton of his shirt stuck to her damp glistening skin. Very gently his cool moist lips were pressed against hers, she turned and responded to the eager messages she was receiving. His lips traced the outline of her jaw and travelled into her hair and down her slender neck. She felt her body awakening to his demands. Very slowly he aroused every sense within her. She unbuttoned his shirt and nestled her bare breasts into his tanned chest. His strong hands expertly explored and awoke Sarah to a new meaning to making love. All her experiences so far had been very clumsy petting to gratify Peter's needs. Charles sensed that this was the first time that Sarah had been involved this far with a man and he wanted it to be an experience that she would find memorable and enjoyable. Not for one moment did he think of the consequences. All he knew was that this was right for them both. Lips that tasted cool and sweet returned his kisses. His strong hands were as gentle as an angel's feather as they caressed every part of her hungry body, awakening her into the realms of passion. The storm outside raged wildly but inside the pagoda it was becoming warmer and warmer as the sexual excitement between the two lovers rose to a height of overwhelming desire. Both were lost in the magical world that can only be created by satisfying the needs of two hungry lovers. She clasped her hands around his neck as his powerful arms carried her lightweight frame to his bed, gently he lovingly covered her body with his. She arched her back like a wild cat and received him. Slowly her body reacted to the gentle arousing movements his body was making. For a moment just before they entered into the depths of their lovemaking, they both witnessed a faint ghostly orchestra playing far away in the distance of the night. Many times they made love and slept and woke again in each other's arms. When all the candles had burnt down and the wind outside had quelled Sarah awoke. A smile crossed her face as she remembered all that had happened. She looked at the tanned body of Charles sprawled face down on the feather mattress. On his shoulder was a perfect red strawberry birth mark, she traced the outline with her tongue. He stirred for a brief moment but did not wake up, it was more than she could do to stop herself from running her hands down the wiry muscles of his back or smooth his mop of hair off of his face. She silently sauntered around the room looking at all his grandmother's belongings, she found herself opening the door of the small wardrobe and reaching inside she pulled out the dress she had worn on the last occasion. She slipped her naked body into it and found the matching shoes. Sitting in front of the bevelled mirror she piled her raven locks into tumbling ringlets. On the dressing table was the box with the sapphires and diamond necklace and earrings. She did not realise that Charles was awake until she felt his cool hands fasten the cascade of gems around her throat, his lips brushed her neck as he gently put the earrings into place. She looked into the mirror at their reflections, he was dressed in the outfit that he had been wearing in the portrait on the stairs at High Markham. By some unforeseen force she glided to her feet, they both entered the main room of the pagoda, his arms enveloped her and the wonderful music began. He was the first to speak as they glided around the marble floor.

'Sarah I have to tell you that from the first moment that I saw you I fell deeply in love with you. I have not been able to think of anything else. I want to beg you not to marry Peter but to come away with me. We can make a new start together, I know you will love the sunshine and the people.' He lovingly brushed her hair with his lips and waited for her to respond to his request. After such a magical night how could she ever refuse?

'You don't have to give me your reply now, please give yourself time to think about my proposal. I am willing to wait as long as it takes. I realise this has put you in a difficult situation as it's so near to the wedding.' He paused, he was frightened to ask if she felt the same way about him. The music became so faint that it was only a whisper in the far distance. Still they were locked in each other's arms. The music died away and the starkness of reality started to creep over Sarah, she looked into the eyes of her soul mate and a great sadness swept up into the very core of her being. If there was a way that she could have left with Charles this very minute then she would have done but she knew once she left the pagoda she would be back into the same life and destiny as she had left outside the doors the night before. His eyes searched hers for some sign to say there was hope for a future together.

'Charles, what we have here together is one of the most precious things that we could possibly ever experience. I know that I will always love you, wherever we both are throughout the universe we will never be parted from that golden thread that we have bound together on this earthly plane. Nothing can ever take that from us. I have promised to marry Peter and there would be grave consequences if I didn't, I could not begin to explain them to you but I have to go ahead with the wedding.'

Charles felt his body drain of all his emotions. For the first time in his life he loved somebody so much but he could not persuade her to join him.

'Sarah, I will leave that invitation open to you for the rest of your life. Whether you are married or old and grey I will always wait for you and when the time is right I know you will come to me and we will be together. But in the meantime my ship will be leaving very soon and if you change your mind and want to join me just find your way to the quay. I'm going to stay at the Swan Hotel in Penzance until the ship is ready, I don't think it would be fair on either of us for me to remain in Hellstone. Remember this place is as much yours as mine and you will always be safe here and close to me. Here, take this key. The dress and the jewels are yours they were always meant to belong to you.' She shook her head. 'Don't argue with me please, I know they will be safe with you. I will write you a letter of ownership and leave them with my mother. Remember you can always trust her as if she was your own mother.'

'Oh Charles,' said Sarah tracing the outline of his sad face with her fingers. 'If only I had met you a long time ago before Peter laid claim to me, things could have turned out so differently. Who knows what is in store for either of us as my friend Tobias says, nothing is permanent everything changes.' She stepped away from him and retrieved her crumpled old clothes from the hearth. The magic of the night disappeared and all too soon the wonderful spell that had been cast was broken. Heartbroken lips dusted her brow as she reached up to kiss Charles goodbye. So very soon she was standing outside the pagoda surveying the storm's destruction on the surrounding woodland. As she passed the magical fairy ring with its bright new grass, she picked up a broken willow twig and planted it in the centre of the ring. She turned to face Charles. 'This will grow and one day it will be a magnificent specimen, it will be our tree in our magic circle and it will always remind me of the precious moments we have had together.' Charles stepped forward and pulled her to him, holding her so tightly. 'I don't think I can let you go Sarah,' he said in a voice shaking with emotion. Her heart was heavy and aching as she released herself from his grip and pushed him away, holding him at arm's length.

'I cannot begin to tell you how I feel except that it would be unfair of me to give you false hope.' She felt her eyes fill with warm tears. 'I cannot begin to explain to you the reasons for my marriage to Peter but please believe me Charles I don't feel I have any choice at the moment, the consequences would be too hard for me to bear.' Charles reached for her hand. 'What if I could give you a very solid reason with proof as to why you should not marry him.' She held up her hand. 'It doesn't matter what he's done or what he is, I for one know he has not been loyal to me, but then neither have I, now. I will keep my side of the bargain. I gave my word.'

He looked at her face and realised that as he loved her so much he had to let her go, it was not fair to put her under so much pressure. Deep inside he knew that she did love him as much as he loved her and that the reason why she refused him must have been very important and very serious. He wondered who had such a hold on her surely it wasn't Peter?

She found the horse and cart still intact. Tobias was nowhere to be seen. Even though she knew she would be in for a lecture later. She did not care. Last night was something that she would never ever forget. A sacred bond had been made. Where ever she was and whoever she was with no one could ever take that memory away from her. As she climbed into the cart she turned to look at Charles, he did not wave but watched her until the cart disappeared from view. As she lost sight of the pagoda an eerie sound filled her ears and just for a moment she was not sure whether it was the echoes of last night's gale or the ghostly cackle of an evil presence. Very quickly she reached the clearing that led to Mill Farm, she was relieved to see the farm buildings and the sails on the mill were still intact.

Gwen was coming from the stables with an empty bucket.

'Morning Sarah, I am glad you did not try to get back with the coach, what an awful night it was. The driver had to stay here for the night, he's only just left.'

Sarah suddenly remembered why she had the cart.

'I've just woken up that lazy husband to be of yours, it's surprising what a bucket of cold water will do to a hangover.'

They both laughed as they entered the kitchen.

'Men,' said Gwen shaking her head. 'You can't live with them and you can't live without them.'

Peter staggered in through the door he needed to clean himself up and change his clothes.

'Cor I feel rough, get us a mug of tea Ma.' He looked at Sarah. 'I see you brought the cart back then, what happened to you last night?'

'Oh nothing really, I spent the night with Charles at the pagoda.' 'Oh ha, bloody ha Sarah. It's a bit too early in the morning for jokes like that.' And he swigged the hot tea that Sarah had just passed to him. 'I knew you wouldn't believe me.' 'Yeah, yeah, yeah,' he said as he went out the door. 'See you later, I'm off to sort these bloody cows out. They're knee deep in shite.'

CHAPTER TWENTYONE

Wedlock's a Padlock
Just you wait and see
He'll pop the ring on your finger
And throw away the key.

Peter splashed freezing cold water from the horse trough all over his face and arms. His friend and best man to be Colin, shivered, as he stood watching his friend. He was trying to muster enough courage to copy the uncomfortable proceedings. This morning Gwen had given the men strict instructions to keep well away from the house, Sarah had moved her bridal gown and all her possessions into the barn cottage so she could get ready in peace. There had been a slight frost in the dark hours of the morning, but the day was promising to be a perfect first day of spring for Sarah and Peter's wedding day.

'Come on you two, your breakfast's on the table you've just got enough time to eat it.'

Peter and Colin ambled into the kitchen. Breakfast was the last thing on their minds. Neither of them had actually been to bed since yesterday. Last night they had only meant to have a few drinks but then a few friends had joined them and before they realised what was happening the evening had stretched out longer and longer. They had arrived home just as the sun was rising over the Tor. Gwen left them to eat the plates of fried bacon, sausages and eggs and went next door to the barn cottage to see how Sarah was getting on with her preparations for her special day.

Colin looked about him before he spoke to make sure no one was within earshot.

He looked directly at Peter across the table.

'Are you sure you want to go through with this. Don't you feel the slightest bit guilty over what you are doing? It's not too late to call a halt to it,' he said as he shovelled the complete egg yolk into his mouth.

'I don't feel bad about it at all. She's a bloody headcase, always will be, it runs in her family.'

'I reckon she's alright, she doesn't seem to be too bad.'

Peter smiled at his friend. 'You fancy her for yourself do yer?'

His friend blushed. 'Shut up, will you.'

'All I want is to get today over and done with and then we'll all be happy. Don't forget you and your sister stand to benefit from this, not just me.' Colin thought about the financial mess his sister was in. And how she was banking on Peter getting money from marrying the girl so she could keep the farm. But, it still did not seem the right way to be doing things. Greed was like lust, it had its own invisible driving force. Reason never came into it. He could see what his sister and friend had in common, neither had any conscience.

Matthew pushed and pulled the elderly preacher to his feet, he could not believe that today of all days his hero had taken a liquid breakfast. What a week it had been at the vicarage. Yesterday four solemn faced men from the church had visited the preacher, they had been shown into the parlour.

That's how Matthew knew it must be serious. No ordinary person ever got to see the inside of the dark room, some hours later they left and so did the preacher's wife with a small suitcase. The man had not offered to tell Matthew anything about the visit, but had taken a large supply of gin with him into the vestry. When the few people who made up the evening congregation came to take their seats in the church they were greeted by the uncontrollable sobs of a very troubled man. Matthew had quickly instructed the organist to play loudly to drown out the embarrassing sounds. With a little persuasion he managed to calm things down. He explained to the group of old ladies that sat with their eyes glued to him that the preacher had been taken poorly and that he would be taking the service which he promptly did with great confidence.

Matthew poured another glass of water it disappeared very quickly down the parched throat. Like guiding a small child he coaxed the drunk to take more of the tasteless liquid. He hoped that if he took enough it would dilute the amount of gin that was swirling around inside the man. Luckily there was a few hours to go before the man was expected to perform the ceremony for his brother and Sarah.

Grace Trevallian sat patiently waiting for Molly to come and help her prepare for Sarah's wedding. If she was not mistaken the maid was purposely trying to be difficult. Things had been very strained between herself and the girl since Charles had gone to stay in Penzance, Grace felt quite vulnerable without him here. Even with her husband at the house she did not feel entirely comfortable with the girl's behaviour. Many times recently she felt that her authority was being questioned. It was such a shame that Charles had decided to stay away from home, she could only guess it was to oversee the rebuilding of the ship. He said he would call to see her before he sailed. There was a knock on the door and Hodges entered with a tray of tea. She questioned him to the whereabouts of Molly, after all it was getting late and she wanted to arrive at the church in good time. Steven, Charles's friend had arrived over an hour ago with his picture taking equipment and was patiently waiting in the conservatory. Earlier this morning Grace had sent flowers from the hot house down to the church for the preacher's wife to arrange for the wedding. She was a little surprised when the message came back informing her that the women was not there and could she send for someone else to arrange them. Very quickly she had sent a message to one of the ladies on the church flower rota. She hoped the day would be perfect for Sarah and tried not to think too much about the man she was going to marry.

Sarah and Tobias looked at the reflection in the mirror only one of them could be seen.

'I hope I'm doing the right thing Tobias?' she said surveying her beautiful dress.

'How will you know if you don't take the chance.'

'I wish my mother could be here with me, I feel very alone. I thought when today came it would feel very different, aren't I suppose to feel overjoyed and happy because I don't. I feel that a lead weight is waiting to drop out of the sky onto my head.'

At that moment Gwen and the girls burst into the room. They squealed with delight when they saw Sarah in her dress. She thanked them for the surprise lover's knots that they had hidden inside the skirt.

Daniel's voice interrupted the girls' laughter. He

awkwardly pushed into the room his arms full of delicate long stemmed pink roses explaining that they had been sent down from the house.

Gwen pinned the fine cream lace veil over Sarah's face. It was held in place by a coronet of dill and daisies that Sarah had woven into a circle of may blossom.

The veil symbolised a pagan belief that you should cover the brides face unless she bewitched the wrong man or even worse lose her psychic powers.

Sarah smiled when she saw Janet and Mary looking identical in cream lace dresses. She had made them small posies of wild herbs and spring blossoms. Grace Trevallian's coach arrived in the courtyard outside. You could hardly recognise the man in the dark suit and tall hat. Hodges got out to greet Sarah, he held out his hand to help her up into the coach, the girls sat opposite her. She did not remember much of the short journey to the church and was surprised that they reached it so soon. She took a few deep breaths and smiled nervously as she clung tightly to Hodges arm. Her new shoes silently led her up the church path. The smell of heavily bee's waxed wood greeted their nostrils as they entered the small church porch. As the tall pipes of the organ bellowed out discordant sounds that were supposed to resemble Sarah's chosen piece of music, a sharp breeze entered the church disturbing the still air and slamming the heavy oaks doors shut. The crash startled the congregation. Matthew held his breath, convinced that the wrath of God was about to interrupt the following proceedings. Fifteen minutes later the boy sighed with relief as the church bells pealed loudly in celebration of the betrothal of Peter and Sarah.

The sky was crystal clear and the most amazing

blue. The sun shone brightly, kindly overlooking the wedding party that wound its way out of the church door. The couple ducked and squealed with laughter as they were showered with rice and flower petals. In his after wedding speech the preacher had insisted that no one should throw corn in the vicinity of the church. It had the annoying habit of nestling in just about every nook and cranny in the church path and yard, lying dormant for a while and then sending forth to the heavens bright green arrows. The elderly arthritic graveyard keeper had complained bitterly about the extra amount of work that the corn made so, it was decided to ban this form of celebration.

Matthew sighed with relief that the service was over and the preacher had more or less got the ceremony correct, he had stood beside the poor man just in case he needed to prompt him.

This morning all his fears about Sarah being totally unsuitable for his brother had been erased by the events of the last twenty-four hours at the vicarage. He only remembered his fears when the church door had suddenly closed with such a loud bang. All along he was convinced the Almighty surely would disapprove of the union and send some sort of sign of his displeasure, hopefully during the wedding ceremony, perhaps a thunderbolt or a flash of lightening but no, nothing so demonstrative. Well he was not really surprised it was all changing and he was becoming very disillusioned with the church and religion. He did not know what religion was coming to, since he'd been helping at the church it had all changed. It did not seem to matter how bad you were there was always a place for you in the Kingdom of Heaven, Murderers, Thieves and Witches. In fact anyone as long as you sold your soul and repented your sins to his divine mercy then you joined the club and you were in, a fully-fledged member. No punishment, in at the top, getting all the benefits. Well at this rate you won't need Hell because no one will be down there in the eternal fire, they will all be up in heaven forgiven.

Peter was getting impatient with hanging around waiting for the idiot with the camera to finish arranging everyone. Grace Trevallian had certainly wasted a lot of money on this he thought. Well, more fool her.

Molly watched her brother fidgeting. She could see he was finding it really difficult to keep still, his patience was running out. She caught Sarah's gaze and smirked slyly at her. She knew her twin was up to something but she was not sure what it was, only that it would soon wipe the smile off the girl's face.

Steven looked at the bride and he could see exactly who had taken his friends heart. At first he had thought that it was Nicola or Amy. He could place a very safe bet that he was right. He created and captured the image of the happy smiling couple, a picture that would be a constant reminder of the day's events. In his mind he had to remember the colours of the dress and flowers so that when he returned to the studio Elizabeth could add the colours to the developed picture. He had promised Charles's mother that he would frame one of the pictures and send it to the couple.

A great cheer went up as the couple jumped over the chimney sweeps pile of ashes, which were laid across the path, this was a custom that was to ensure their fertility. Peter's rowdy friends nudged each other and heckled Peter as he led Sarah back through the ashes for a second time. Friends and neighbours formed an archway of arms for the couple to walk through. The procession wound its way down the church path. A cart was waiting outside the lych-gate it had been decorated with flowers and ribbons even the horse had blossom in his mane. Peter helped Sarah climb up into the cart, he sat down beside her and edged on by his noisy friends he put his arms around Sarah and planted a passionate kiss on her lips. A loud cheer roared through the countryside. Surprised by the sudden attention Sarah slipped off of the narrow seat. This made the high-spirited youths laugh even more. Peter embarrassed by Sarah's stupidity in front of his friends promptly pulled her roughly back onto the seat. He snarled at the driver to hurry up and get to the party, as he needed a bloody good drink. The driver, who had been very uncomfortable sitting for so long in his stiff Sunday best, woke the patient horses with a gentle whisper of the whip and they slowly ambled their way up to the Tythe barn at High Markham.

Sarah was absolutely delighted when she stepped into the barn. The heavy oak beams that supported the roof had been decorated with boughs of blackthorn blossom and dried flowers and fruits. The long tables that held an amazing selection of savoury and sweet dishes were decorated with the first of the seasons primroses. How hard the staff of the house had worked to create all this. Sarah was very grateful to them and of course her dear friend Grace.

Peter and Sarah stood each side of the doorway and greeted their guests. Gwen and Daniel were very happy with the marriage but not Molly, she stood behind her seated mistress, she was becoming increasingly annoyed by the constant chatter about how wonderful the wedding had turned out and what a truly kind person Sarah was. She thought, if the women mentioned the girl's name once more, it would take very little effort to lean forward and squeeze her hands tightly around the old goats throat.

The barn was now packed tightly with happy people eating and drinking. The couple led the dancing, Peter had not had enough drinks inside him to really enjoy the music from the band. He made a half-hearted effort to move his feet in time with Sarah's but all he succeeded in doing was kicking dust over the bottom of her dress. As soon as more people started to join in the dancing Peter and Sarah sat down at their table with the family. An assortment of wedding gifts had been placed on their table, paper parcels, and boxes of produce and flagons of cider. Sarah saw Grace sitting on her own, she went over to ask her to join them. Grace declined the offer and said she would be retiring very soon, as it had been a long day and tomorrow she was travelling down to Penzance to say goodbye to Charles. His ship was now repaired and ready to sail a lot earlier than she thought it would be. Sarah thanked her for all that she had done for them and said she would visit as soon as she could.

Peter felt very comfortable and happy as he sampled the fine brandy that his sister had smuggled out of the house. He reclined on the straw bales that edged the dance floor. He lit a cigar that came with the brandy, clouds of smoke spiralled around his head. This is the life he thought, very soon he would be able to have brandy and cigars all the time just like his bloody lordship.

Sarah felt very happy and extremely lucky that the

day had gone so well, what a wonderful wedding it had been. She looked at Peter at last he was relaxed. Light from candles caught the band of silver on her finger, it sparkled like a star, I am Mrs Peter Pendarvis, she thought, how strange, I am a married woman. 'Sarah Pendarvis,' she said within her head and smiled to herself as she looked at her new husband.

Daniel drove the cart down the narrow uneven lane, he had managed to fit all of the family into it. He was fortunate to have the helpful light of a full moon to guide him home. He was slightly inebriated but not as much as his son, who was asleep across the back seat. A dark cloud rolled across the moon causing the light to disappear, Daniel squinted his eyes to make out the road ahead. 'Who's there?' he shouted as he thought he saw a figure run alongside the cart. 'What's the matter?' asked his wife. 'Oh, nothing,' he replied as he tightened the reins on the horses. They had started to behave skittishly, dancing a little from side to side trying to avoid something. Again out of the corner of his eye Daniel saw a dark hooded shadow gliding through the woodland at a distance from the cart. Sarah had seen the figure, he had been watching all evening, waiting in the darkness. Daniel froze as his eardrums nearly burst as the inhuman figure omitted a terrifying sound. It was the cry of an animal screaming with terror and pain. Sarah thought she was the only one to hear the haunting laughter of the Shadow of Death.

Suddenly sober, Daniel vowed he would never touch another drop of alcohol ever again.

Sarah helped Peter down from the cart. The door of their new home was already unlocked when the couple entered it and Sarah could see the reason why, somebody had decorated the small interior with flowers and good luck charms. Peter sunk down into a chair, whilst Sarah went on a tour of discovery, she related her findings to Peter. Going into the bedroom she thought she would just pull the eiderdown back to check if anyone had tampered with the bed and sure enough the sheets had been made into an apple pie bed, she was just remaking the bed when Peter stumbled through the door. He wobbled unsteadily towards her. She turned to face him. She had hoped that she would have had the time to change into the cotton and lace night dress that she had laid out on the bed. Peter pulled at the ribbons that gathered her wedding dress around her neck. The dress slipped off her shoulders and with Sarah's help slid to the floor. Peter's eyes watched her impatiently as she stood in front of him in her under-slip. He stepped forward and buried his head into her shoulder, his warm hands encircled her and pulled the back of her slip down to her waist. 'Just a minute, Peter,' said Sarah, 'let me step out of my clothes.' But he was lost driven by alcohol and his own desire. He pulled her to the bed, his mouth covering hers she tried to respond but it was all happening to fast. He forced his tongue between her lips and explored her mouth, his heavy weight pinned her to the bed, all she could do to respond was put her hands on his shoulders to ease his heavy body from her so she could breathe. Peter was so desperate to satisfy himself he completely ignored her needs. He did not bother to remove his clothes but just exposed the part of his body that needed to be fulfilled. With his knee he pushed her legs apart and with one quick movement he pinned her to the mattress. His searching body found its goal and he thrust himself into her, intruding selfishly. His movements gathered momentum as he built up a sweat trying to obtain his needs.

'Move girl, move,' he said through gritted teeth.

'You're like a bloody wet fish.' She tried to join in the painful act but found the whole procedure very distressing. He was pleased to think she was so naive on their wedding night. A while back he would have been a happy man to think that she was a virgin and that he was the first man to take her. Now it didn't seem to matter too much. At least he was proud to know that he had had her before that bastard Trevallian. His body spent and satisfied he withdrew sharply from Sarah and rolled off of her, he laid face down on the pillow and stretched one heavy arm across her.

Lying beside him Sarah could not have been more wide-awake than she was. She was frightened to move in case she woke him and would have to go through that dreadful ordeal again. She had no idea that it was going to be so awful, stupidly she had expected it to be the same as it was with Charles. She was so tense and rigid that she found it impossible to relax, all she wanted to do was get out of bed and run into the woods. From the bed she could just see out of the high windows, as she lay there she saw the moon move across the sky on its journey to far off lands. She saw the night sky turn to a deep azure blue as the sun started to rise on the eastern horizon.

The body beside her stirred, grunted and turned over, a hand moved up over her stomach and grasped her breast she felt the urgent hard probing of her husband who was now rested and refreshed and ready to repeat his performance of the wedding night. His hands gripped her buttocks as he penetrated her and forced her to move to the same rhythm as himself.

'You need some practise, my girl,' he said as beads of sweat trickled down his forehead and dropped into Sarah's hair. 'You are my wife now and you have to please me. I can do whatever I like with you and you have to obey, remember the words of the ceremony. Some girls scream with joy when I get into bed with them. They can't get enough of me.'

She did not want to hear about his other lovers. They must have been strange girls to enjoy such behaviour.

'You are so rough and quick Peter, I might enjoy it more if you took your time and were more gentle.'
He ignored her remark and gripped her nipple between his teeth, she wriggled beneath him, he took it as a sign of enjoyment, he rolled over and pulled her on top of him, his hands encircled her small waist. He admired the firmness of her youthful body. Her raven hair fell down over his face as he drew her down, she felt him release within her. He playfully slapped her backside and pushed her away from him. 'Now that was better,' he said smiling. 'We'll try that again later.' He stood up and stretched his naked body.

'I shall need a good breakfast this morning Sarah after all this exercise I've got the appetite of a horse.' And the bloody manners thought Sarah.

As she lit the range and set the kettle, she thought about last night, Peter was most probably right she needed practise and of course deep down she knew that lovemaking could be a lot better than yesterday's experience. She would try really hard to please him and then perhaps they could both enjoy it.

CHAPTER TWENTYTWO

As you entered the large room it was very difficult to notice that there was a small-shrivelled man sitting behind the large oak desk. He sat hidden by box folders and parcels of documents bound with string, that were piled so high occupying every inch of available space and obscuring his view of the door. He had forbidden anyone including his own son to meddle with or move any of the papers. He was the only person who could understand his filing system and if asked could put his hand instantly on the particular folder required. The tall dark wooden panelled walls had been preserved over the years with the pungent clouds of pipe smoke that spiralled from the elderly occupier of the office. The pipe was a habit that his son detested. The carpet and curtains had lost their entire colour to ready rubbed shag and now blended in nicely with the walls and high ceiling. Marcus Pingale likened his father's office to a cave, he also found his father's techniques at being a solicitor extremely prehistoric. Pingale senior operated his side of the business as if it was an old boys club, sometimes barely keeping within the law. Father and son argued often about their different interpretations of legal procedures.

They were both qualified in their field but were poles apart in their views.

This particular morning Marcus had opened a

letter from a Mr Peter Pendarvis from Hellstone, claiming that he was now the lawful husband of Sarah Pendarvis, nee Miller. Enclosed was their wedding certificate and now he was claiming the inheritance of his wife. Marcus had asked his father if he knew anything about it. And what was revealed was a very strange story. The father said he would notify the bank to release the amount that had been in trust for the girl. Marcus had insisted that the couple should come in person to receive it. His father said it was really not necessary for them to visit the office, as he had been handling the case for years. He knew the girl's guardian, a woman called Banks, she has been successfully running a small orphanage and baby farm for years, and he had often handled her legal papers, usually when a child was placed with new parents. In fact she had been in touch with him only a few weeks ago and told him that the girl in question was about to be married and requested that the company prepare the necessary documents to release the invested amount to her charges new husband, Mr Peter Pendarvis. Marcus stood his ground and insisted to his father that he would like to meet the couple in person before he handed over anything. So, a letter was sent to Mrs Banks requesting that the couple along with herself attended an appointment on the twentieth of May. The file number SM.365 nestled amongst the unruly mass of papers, it seemed an age before the old man's shaky fingers located it. Marcus left the gloomy main office and made himself comfortable in his light spacious room. He opened the file and removed the contents, it all seemed quite straightforward. There was a bank account totally controlled by Pingale & Son. The company authorised monthly amounts to be paid to the legal guardian, Mrs Banks, who had been elected by the girl's father to take custody of her. The allowance was increased as the child grew and needed more for education, clothes etc. It was stated that when the girl married the residue of the money and all the interest it had accrued would be transferred to an account in her husband's name. So, his father was right.

It was all quite straight forward. He carried on reading the original draft from a solicitor in Wales. He wondered why the girl had been sent to Cornwall in the first place. He shook his head, as he couldn't find any explanation to the reason for her to travel so far. A Malakai Miller had signed the papers authorising her into the care of Mrs Banks. There was nothing more of interest in the file, just a birth certificate and a letter from a doctor Jones explaining the child's mental status. Something was not quite right about this case. Marcus read the file through again, more carefully this time hoping that whatever was bothering him would come to light, but nothing. He stood looking out of the tall window looking down onto the busy street below. Surely the girl had not stayed at her guardian's house all this time. Well he would soon find out the answers to his questions.

Jane sat at the table opposite Peter she was getting very bored with the repetitive instructions that he was giving her.

'You're not listening to me are you?' he said.

'I am, I am,' she insisted angrily as she pulled her cardigan over her scantily clad body.

'If you don't pay attention and get this right, we are both going to be in a lot of trouble and bloody well broke.'

She sat down again at the table and tried to copy

Sarah's signature. Great blots of black ink splattered over the table and the paper she was writing on.

'I hope this is all worth it. Do you honestly think they know what mark your wife makes on paper, when would they have seen her signature? Come to think of it they have never met her have they? She could even make a cross for her name.'

'Don't be daft, my aunt's been drawing money for her education for the past few years. She must be able to write her name.'

'Your aunt she's a devil isn't she? How much have you got to give her out of the settlement? Not too much I hope. She makes more than enough out of that dreadful children's farm, I don't think it should be allowed. She doesn't care who the children go to as long as she gets the money for them. Anything could happen to them after they have left her and who would know?' She fell silent for a moment, thinking about her last statement.

Peter saw her sad face and realised she had a lot more in common with Sarah than he realised. He put his arm around her. 'Come on don't dwell on it, I'm sure they all go to quite decent people, after all they're not given away just to anybody, the people who buy them must be quite rich.'

'So with your reckoning rich people aren't cruel to their children.'

'No,' he said impatiently. 'I mean if you buy something it's usually because you want it.'

Their disagreement was interrupted by one of the girls who lived and worked with Jane bringing in one of her customers. They nodded heads in a brief hello as the middle-aged gentleman was taken upstairs to one of the bedrooms. They were both still at the table twenty minutes later when the red faced man huffed and puffed as he made his way down the stairs. Jane followed him into the small hallway.

'I do hope you have enjoyed yourself Sir?' She enquired with a business like smile on her face. She opened a wooden box on the table and held out her hand, waiting for the man to part with his money and pay for his services.

She went back to the table and continued to practise forging the signature that would enable her to give up the trade of satisfying lust for cash.

When she had first met her then elderly husband she had been working in one of the gaming houses and supplying favours to the customers. Her husband had found her there and fallen in love with her. One of the most memorable moments in her life was when he had asked her to marry him. She had readily agreed and moved into the farm, leaving behind her sordid past. For five years she had been so very happy living the life of a farmer's wife. She had learned to love him and the farm very much but unfortunately her happiness was to end when he contacted a fever that he had caught from the rats that seemed to overrun the barns and outbuildings. It was then that her brother Colin started to come down and help her run the farm whenever he could. He often brought with him his friend Peter. Both the men would work from night until the morning but that was not enough. Bills were coming in and she could not meet the payments. The doctor had said he could do no more for her ailing husband. Before he died he made her promise to keep the farm as he had put his heart and soul into it since he was a small boy. It had been in his family for many generations. Peter had become a very good friend to her, he was also desperate to own his own farm. He would often just ride around the outskirts of the acres of land and visualise the day when he would become owner. And now with his sham of a marriage to Sarah he had the opportunity to claim her inheritance which enabled him to raise the money that they both needed to keep and maintain the farm. She did not care that he was bound to another women, emotional commitment was not what she was looking for, financial commitment was what she needed. She would be content with the insight that she could run a respectable home again without her girlfriends using it to live off immoral earnings. Peter had a good sound working knowledge of farming and that is just what she wanted. She dipped the pen in the small pot of ink and created a very good signature that matched the one on the piece of card in front of her.

'That will do,' said Peter, 'you can hardly tell the difference. Now all you have to do is remember all that I have told you, just in case they ask you any questions about yourself.'

'Are you really sure she has no idea about her family leaving her this money?'

'Of course I am sure, as far as she's concerned her family stopped sending money for her upkeep years ago.'

CHAPTER TWENTYTHREE

Ghosts and Ghouls and naive fools.

High up in the tops of the trees perched plump purple and grey wood pigeons, they were making the most of the last of the warm evening sunshine before it set and left the woods in twilight. Sarah had enjoyed her day very much. She was extremely tired but now looking at her small vegetable and herb garden she felt it was worth all the effort that she had put into it. Grace had visited today and brought her a wonderful picture of the wedding, she had decided to place it on the fire breast in the living room. Their home was now taking shape and becoming more comfortable, she had worked really hard to achieve so much in such a short time.
The wedding had only been five weeks ago and how quickly those days had flown by, the weather was becoming warmer and more settled she looked forward to the long summer days when she could walk in the woods without being tied up in woollens and heavy boots. Opening the range door she took the lid off the earthenware casserole and tried the tenderness of the mutton with a fork. The meat had been stewing all day, she had added carrots, onions, turnips and potatoes, and now she was going to add large fluffy suet dumplings. This was Peter's favourite meal and she hoped it tasted as good as his mothers. He had been away for a couple of days

but she did not mind she was used to it. It was a shame that he had so much business to attend to away from home. As the evening cast long shadows on the wall Sarah lit the oil lamp and pulled the curtains. Tobias wandered around the room, she was pleased to see him. He said that he had been to the small chapel that was in the grounds of the big house and he had seen a few of his friends, they often hung around churches and graveyards, not to frighten people but they were usually the quietest places to meet at night. The graveyard there was quite overgrown, it was surrounded with railings that had once been painted black but now they were rusty red with black peeling paint. He did dislike seeing untidy memorials to the dead. It did not seem a fitting tribute to rest the vehicle for your soul in unattended and unloved ground.

'You seem very morose this evening,' said Sarah. 'Has someone upset you?'

'We spirits and ghosts do not have the emotion to be upset Sarah that we leave to you earth dwellers. I can be serious or amusing or when I really want to, be absolutely terrifying. Rattling chains, white hooded cloaks the lot, especially in graveyards at night. Certainly keeps people out of our meeting places.' He then hovered in front of the picture on the wall.

'Isn't that a wonderful present, I cannot believe you can capture a moment in life, only using light. I shall always remember that picture being taken it was the best day of my life. I have saved the bouquet of flowers I carried by hanging them up to dry and I shall keep them forever and ever in my treasure chest along with my headdress. I am so lucky, Tobias, look at everything I've got, a husband who loves me, a whole family,' she looked around her, 'A lovely home and Tobias do you already know my secret? I haven't told anyone yet, but I am so excited.' Her eyes glistened with tears of joy. She looked so innocent and trusting that, Tobias reached down and laid a gentle hand on her shoulder. She whispered like a small child sharing a very important secret with her best friend.

'I am going to have a baby. I can't believe it, but I know I am right. Peter will be delighted, this is something he has always talked about and we have our dear little home to bring up our children in.'

Tobias smiled down at his charge, she would make a good mother and give her children all the love that they would ever need and that would give them something that money could never buy. Love and compassion for fellow beings you could not purchase no matter how rich you were and without love for yourself and each other we couldn't grow through life but we would only stand still in endless shadows of selfishness and self-pity.

Outside a dog barked loudly at first Sarah thought it was the black and white collie of Peter's that lived in the barn, a very unsociable creature. She seemed to recognise the sound. She went out into the yard and as she did Rufus, Charles's black spaniel jumped up at her and nearly knocked her over.

'Down boy down,' she shouted with laughter in her voice. 'What are you doing here? I thought you were going back with your master.'

She looked around in the semi-darkness wondering just for a moment whether he was with his master. She could not see anyone outside. The dog followed her indoors and made himself at home as if he had always lived there, very quickly he spread himself out on the rug in front of the range. Oh well, she thought at least I have some good company for the evening. Tomorrow she would return him to the house. But for now it looked as though Peter would be away for another night so Rufus and Sarah could share the mutton casserole and her good news.

Sarah awoke in the early hours of the next morning, a feeling of nausea crept over her. Through the half-light of the spring morning she tiptoed over the cold stone floor and went out to the earth closet at the back of the cottage. She had heard about the sickness that you got when you were expecting a child so she was not too worried.

Peter entered the cottage and was surprised that Sarah was not there. He had started his journey back to Hellstone in the early hours of this morning and was now in need of a good breakfast. He did not think to look for Sarah when he found her missing, he promptly left the cottage hoping to cadge a meal off his mother. Sarah was surprised to find Peter's coat on the chair and guessed he had gone to see his family. Rufus scratched at the door, worried in case Sarah had forgotten about him.

'So, where have you been this time?' asked his father. 'And what kept you so long, you are not spending enough time here doing your work but your quick enough to take your share out of the place. All you are doing is making me work twice as hard.' He paused for a moment to take a slurp of his steaming hot tea and then he continued, 'I don't know what you are up to young man but I want you here at all times. I can't run the place single handed, it's not as if your brother shows any interest in the place. Sarah's been helping with the feeds in between running her shop and sorting out your new home. You don't know how lucky you are.' And he pushed his chair back noisily and stormed off to the mill.

Peter was most surprised to hear his father talk to him in that tone and looked at his mother for some sort of support. She remained silently kneading a great mound of brown bread dough. Annoyed by her stoic attitude he decided to forget the idea of having a cooked breakfast and also left with a clatter of his chair on the stone floor. In the courtyard he saw Sarah, she was throwing handfuls of grain to the scraggy hens that had managed to survive the winter without ending up in the oven or sold at the market. Her face lit up when she saw him walking towards her. He instantly forgot about his father's earlier lecture.

'Oh, Peter,' she said excitedly, 'I am so pleased you are home safely.' And she flung her arms around him. 'How did your visit go, did you buy any new livestock?'

He wriggled out of her grasp and smiled at her shaking his head.

'No, there's not much about at the moment. You have to be at the auctions really early to put in a bid for the good animals. And would you believe it, all that money you gave me to use, I had stolen from me pocket whilst I was there. I had to borrow the money to buy food,' and he added, 'Sorry,' in a small voice.

'You poor thing, what an awful thing to happen,' said Sarah. 'The main thing is you're home safely. Don't worry about the money I have a little more put by, you could use it next time you go. Come on inside and let me make you breakfast you must be starving.'

He was a little surprised to see the dog sitting on the rug by the range. She explained that she would take Rufus back to the house later when she went to work.

Peter enjoyed his breakfast of eggs, bacon, sausage, hot muffins and wild strawberry jam, he refused the offer of tea explaining to Sarah that he must get on with his duties at the farm.

'It really is so good to see you,' she said reaching for his hands. 'Before you go I have something that I have to tell you.' He stopped in the doorway and waited. A few seconds later he did not know what to say in reply to Sarah's unexpected news. For a moment his mind could not take in what she had said. He looked at her in complete shock.

'Are you sure, isn't it a bit soon to be certain about it?'

'Course I am sure. There is no doubt in my mind at all. By Christmas time we will be parents.'

Peter did not know quite what to say to Sarah, half of him was pleased to think that he was going to be a father and the other half shocked that this had happened now. It had not even occurred to him that this could happen. The fact was that he and Jane had planned out their future and it certainly did not include Sarah and definitely not children. He was left a little confused by his own feelings and needed time on his own to think.

'Have you told Ma yet?' He waited for her reply.

'I'll go and tell her she's going to be a grandma that will cheer her up.'

'Just a minute Peter, are you pleased?'

'Of course I am. It's just such a surprise.'

Sarah held him tightly. 'I am so pleased for us, I have started sewing small garments already. Shall we both go and tell your mother our good news.'

He nodded his head in agreement, she linked her arm in his and steered him off towards the mill.

Everyone was delighted at the couple's news even Grace Trevallian was pleased when Sarah told her later that day when she took Rufus back to the house. Grace said she hoped that Sarah would keep the dog, as her husband disliked it immensely. He said it was a useless gun dog and should be put down. Sarah was more than happy to take the fellow home with her.

Rufus sat at the back of the shop quite happy to watch Sarah stock her shelves with pots of pure honey. The honey was as sweet as honey could possibly be. Last summer she had placed hives around the meadows where an abundance of clover grew, knowing that the bees would be so happy and their produce absolutely wonderful. She had made lace caps for the honey pots and tied them with lilac ribbon. Her little shop was becoming quite crowded, her customers said that the amount in the shop made it more interesting. She hoped that she would be able to continue to work well into her pregnancy. The money from the shop was well needed, some she managed to save for their future but a lot was used by Peter to subsidise the farm. Poor Daniel was not getting any younger and found the work at the mill and on the farm exhausting. She hoped that someday Peter and her would make enough money between the shop and the farm so Daniel and Gwen could retire and let Peter hire some young strong labourers.

She placed pots of mint jelly and bottles of elderflower cordial beside the honey just leaving enough room for a few jars of mustard relish. As she had a few minutes to spare before her next healing session she thought she would call next door to share her news with Nicola. They calculated on their fingers when they thought the baby would be born and both agreed it would be around late November or early December time. Nicola was so pleased for her friend and said she would make a wonderful mother. She said she was going to attempt to crochet something but she was not very good at the craft so it would most probably be a shawl, as it would be the easiest shape to do and she hoped the child would not be two years old before she finished it. This made both the girls laugh. Sarah said a shawl would be wonderful especially if it was made by Nicola although she hoped there would not be too many missed stitches in it, creating holes where there should not be.

The morning in the shop went quite quickly. Janet arrived at lunchtime so Sarah could go off on her home visits. Her first stop was to go and say goodbye to Sandra Wicks and her family. They were leaving Keepers Cottage and going to live in Devon where they would live in much larger accommodation, Sandra was going to be housekeeper and her husband game warden for a private estate with deer parks and trout streams. Sarah was really pleased for the family. And thought the new position would be much healthier for them and their children. Christopher had grown so much since Sarah had last seen him. Even though he still walked a little awkwardly he managed to move around perfectly well on his own. She was sure he would flourish once he had space around him. Sandra held yet another baby on her hip and the previous baby was now the new replacement toddler clinging to the folds of her skirt. Sarah presented Sandra with a basket of gifts. Tea, lavender soap, hedgerow oils and small carved toys for the children and for their new home a clay talisman to bring them good luck. She wished them the best of luck and hugged each of the children before she made a tearful farewell.

Her next visit was to deliver rubbing oils to a farmer who suffered from excruciating back trouble. He had asked for a large pot as he said he also used it to rub the legs of his lame horses and his wife's bunions. Sarah enjoyed her afternoon visits, she met such a variety of interesting people most of whom were very pleasant and looked forward to seeing her.

The weather on her journey back from the hillside farm changed as it often did in May. Suddenly the perfect blue sky was interrupted by a fast passing wisp of a black cloud that emptied its contents of heavy hailstones angrily down upon its innocent victims below. Sarah sheltered under a nearby oak tree hoping that the storm would soon pass. She watched as small blue and yellow birds gathered waxy lamb's wool from the fields and flew into a small hole beneath a branch in the tree. She made a note in her mind to tell Peter about the amount of wool that was hanging from the blackthorn bushes in the field. Sheep often caught terrible parasites that bored into their skin and caused dreadful irritation. They relieved the appalling itching by rubbing themselves against hedges and walls. If the condition was neglected eventually the animal would be in such a poor state it would succumb to a variety of infections often proving fatal. Perhaps Peter had not had enough time to dip them. The rain stopped and so quickly the sun burst through and steamed off the moisture from the countryside. She stopped for just a moment on the narrow bridge over the noisy stream of clear water that tumbled down from the Tor. The water cascaded on its never ceasing journey down through Mill

Farm and onto the village. The clean water was as clear as crystals and tasted cold and sweet. Sarah used the natural liquid in a lot of her tonics and lotions and also drank pints of it herself each day. She thoroughly believed this cleansed your system. On her way down from the hill she thought she would just quickly call in see Peter before she returned to close the shop. She was very surprised to see Matthew helping his brother clean out the pigs stys. She knew the boy detested anything to do with the farm or any form of hard work.

'Hello stranger,' she called to him, 'What brings you here?' The boy looked up sheepishly but did not answer. Instead Peter spoke for him.

'The preacher has been arrested and is in the jail.'
'Whatever for?' said Sarah.
Peter looked at his brother before he answered.
'Dunno too much do we Matthew?' And he paused to throw a bucket of water over the smelly stones.
'He,' and he nodded in Matthew's direction.
'Thinks it might be something to do with the old sop refusing to leave the vicarage so the new bloke could move in.'

The boy kept his head down but shook it in agreement with his brother.

'Matthew's moving back home. So he can start getting used to working for a living. Me and Pa have enough to do, so another set of hands will certainly help. Do you hear that boy. From now on you can work hard with your hands to keep a meal in your belly and not with your bloody fancy words.'

Again the boy did not answer but nodded, keeping his head down.

Sarah was pleased that at last Daniel and Peter had a little more help. She still felt a little sorry for

Matthew he was not the sort of person to work physically hard he had more of a studious nature, a life in the church was much more suitable for the sensitive boy. As for the preacher, poor man, she knew he had a problem with alcohol but she couldn't begin to wonder what he had possibly done to be taken into custody.

As Sarah passed the mill she could not help but hear Daniel coughing he was almost choking, she climbed the steep steps and peered into the gloomy interior of the dusty mill. Daniel looked up as he heard the door open. He was sitting on a sack of grain and spitting into a piece of rag. Beads of sweat trickled down his red face as he gasped to get his breath. He was annoyed to see Sarah standing there watching him and motioned for her to go away.

'Can I get you anything, perhaps a drink of water or something to soothe your cough?'

In between hacks he told her there was nothing he wanted, just to be left alone.

She was aware that since Christmas he had been ailing for something, she had mentioned to Gwen that she thought it was serious enough for him to see the village physician. She had even offered to pay for the visit, but Gwen had reassured her that Daniel was alright and said that he had just one of those winter colds that won't go away until midsummer. Sarah was pretty sure that it was more than that. She had given him a bottle of her soothing cough recipe but she noticed that it sat firmly undisturbed on the shelf where she had left it.

She looked at the expression on Daniel's face, he was adamant that she should leave him alone. She waved goodbye to Peter and Matthew as she trotted off down to the village, as she passed her little home she could not resist a quick look at her garden. Already her vegetables were growing really well, she looked forward to using the herbs and cooking the fresh produce.

CHAPTER TWENTYFOUR

The two ladies in the coach sat opposite each other in absolute silence. Peter and his aunt Maisie had exhausted Jane with their intense schooling of information into the background details of Sarah's life. Jane was fed up and sick and tired of the whole procedure and hoped that the amount of money that Peter inherited was going to make all her effort worthwhile. At least once this morning was over and the necessary documents at Pingale and Sons signed, Peter would be able to clear her debts to the bank and get on with restocking her breeding herd. Without Peter knowing she had already sold off some of her land to neighbouring farmers, it still left her with a very sizeable property and allowed her to pay off a small amount of her outstanding mortgage. The manager of the bank had made himself clear that in no uncertain terms was he going to allow her to continue to accumulate so much debt. He had allowed her three months to clear all the outstanding amounts she owed. And if she did not comply with the request he warned her that he would not hesitate to seize the farm and all its contents.

'Now,' said Peter, 'Remember all that I have told you.'

She nodded her head in acknowledgement. And she went through the details word for word. Maisie Banks was not at all nervous she knew the old solicitor so well, this morning's visit was only to appease young Marcus.

The coach drew to a halt in the narrow alleyway outside the tall stone building owned by the Pingale family. Marcus watched the arrival of the group from his father's grimy office window.

'Please take a seat,' he said. 'My father will be with you in a moment. Can I get you some refreshments?'

'No thanks, my dear,' said Peter's aunt to the young man's kind offer. 'We are in rather a hurry, will your father be long?'

As she finished her sentence the elderly gentleman's voice could be heard calling his son into his office. There was a moment's silence and then Marcus beckoned to them to enter the dismal room. The old nurse fondly grasped the bony body of Pingale senior and hugged him to her buxom body. For an instant it looked as though he would be enveloped by her surplus flesh and disappear forever, lost in the folds of her bosom. Finally she released the little man and he flopped down in his chair quite reddened by the enjoyable experience. A little wide-eyed and flustered he flicked over various documents trying to find the correct folder.

'Here father,' said his son. 'I have it.' And he passed the brown box folder over to him.

Marcus stepped back and watched the threesome confidently sign the documents. His father witnessed the signatures with his own. All the relevant papers were given to Peter Pendarvis with an explanation as to the procedure for collecting the capital from the bank. They had already been instructed to open an account in Peter's name, all he had to do was produce the letter of authorisation from the solicitors to enable him to access a withdrawal. Marcus felt quite annoyed that he could find no discrepancies in the answers to the questions that he had asked the young lady. His father offered farewell greetings and the visit ended quite abruptly. Again Marcus watched from the office window as the group climbed back into the waiting coach. Something at the back of his mind caused an irritation, for the moment he could not put his finger on it. And then as the coach pulled away it came to him. Not one of them had showed any emotion when they saw the amount that was involved, not a smile of pleasure or even a grunt of disappointment, in fact nothing as if they were all guarding their true emotions. He knew if he had suddenly inherited that amount of money he would certainly of been smiling.

Peter handed over the envelope to the smartly dressed manager of the small bank. He waited patiently whilst the man read the enclosed letter. He offered Peter a seat. Peter had left his aunt and Jane sitting in the Swan Hotel waiting for his return. He had booked them all in for one night. Jane and Peter were to have the best room in the place, he had ordered dinner for two in their room with a bottle of the very best champagne. There was a definite spring in his step when he left the bank, for the very first time in his life he had money in his pocket not just a few bob but pounds and there was more to come. He felt he was somebody now, not just a farm labourer he was a man of means. Soon he would be a partner in Jane's farm and would be able to work hard and know it would be for filling his own pocket and not anyone else's.

Tomorrow he would transfer money to pay off Jane's debts and then have his name put on the deeds as joint owner of the property. Tonight he would pay his aunt for her part in the crime and then before he returned to the hotel he was going to visit the gaming house where he owed so much money and settle his debts. He could not tolerate having to look over his shoulder anymore when he was in Penzance, waiting for someone to attack him from the shadows. As the owner of the gaming house had repeatedly threatened to do if Peter failed to sort out his account.

He pushed his way through the ladies on offer and made his way to a door at the back of the long hallway. A group of scruffy red eyed men looked up at him as he entered the smoky windowless room. Very quickly their eyes returned to the cards on the table. A short fat man in a dirty white shirt rolled up his sleeves and motioned to an ape in the corner when he saw Peter come towards him. Peter proudly threw a handful of money towards the men.

'I want my I.O.U back. Go on don't just look at it, count it, it's all there.' And he pushed the heap towards the surprised proprietor.

The money was counted and a slip of paper was given to Peter. All was going well until he turned to leave, his eye caught the dice rolling along the green baize cloth. A thrill of excitement caused a shiver to run through him. Only for a short instance did he try to stop himself from extracting coins from his pocket and placing a bet on the outcome of the deadly cubes. With the click of his fingers he ordered drinks all round from the barmaid hovering behind him. He gave her a handsome tip and claimed a handful of her buttocks when she draped herself across him to refill his tankard.

Jane pulled the heavy damask bedspread over her and nestled between the white starched sheets. The empty champagne bottle lay on the red carpet, she had made a noble effort at eating the dinner for two but had succumbed to her bed after draining the green bottle of luscious liquid. At first when Peter had not returned she had felt a little angry but then she thought she would just carry on as normal. As he was paying she might as well enjoy what he was providing.

Maisie Banks had found her way down to the kitchens of the hotel and was enjoying a meal with some of the staff. She did not know that her nephew was out and about with a vast amount of their money in his pockets and that at this moment he was hardly sober enough to remain standing and that his loose mouth had advertised the fact that he was a man of means and carrying some of his wealth in his trousers.

Peter certainly did not arrive back at the hotel that night. In fact he was taken to his home in Hellstone by a man who thought he was doing him a favour. The unfortunate incident that occurred, left Jane and his aunt with a lot of explaining to do to the manager of the hotel when the next day he realised that Peter had disappeared and the women could not pay their bill.

Peter had left the gaming house quite pleased with himself considering that he still had money in his pockets. He was looking forward to spending the night with Jane at the hotel. With his hands deep into his pockets he thought he would walk the few streets to the hotel. He strolled through the narrow cobbled alleyways not really sure of his bearings, occasionally a coach and horses pushed its way past and he would have to step quickly back against the walls of the dark buildings. Just where the street started to wind its way uphill to the hotel a cart full of young people tried to pass a coach with an elderly occupant in. The coach brushed past Peter and caused him to stumble forward and hit his head heavily on the cobbles, the blow knocked him unconscious. Fortunately the driver of the coach saw the incident and stopped to tend to him. He was lifted into the coach, the gentleman insisted that Peter be taken to his home. Inside the coach he was laid on a seat and his head bound with a handkerchief. Every time he started to regain consciousness he would weave between concussion and inebriation. After papers were found in his pocket with his name and address on it was decided that the least the driver could do was to see him safely home to Hellstone.

Sarah snapped part of the long sticky stems off the bluebells that she had picked earlier and placed the flowers in a brown pot on the kitchen table. While Peter had been resting, she had been out for her early morning jaunt in the fields and woodlands. The walk had been quite magical and such a wonderful tonic for her. How quickly the warmth of the spring sunshine had encouraged the earth to wake up. In the woods as far as the eye could see stretched a heady lilac blue haze that contained the most amazing aroma of springtime. Nestled beneath the residue of last autumns leaves sprung the shy little yellow primrose that pushed itself upwards to bask in the new light. Thick black buds protruded from the finger like branches of the rowan trees that had waited so patiently to decorate their bareness. The willow switch that she had planted in the centre of the fairy ring was adorned with fresh green droplets of new growth and promised to be a most magnificent tree. Just a few yards away the parent weeping willow stood tall like a sentinel, its long sweeping arms guarding the pagoda that was hidden beneath it. So many times Sarah had been tempted to take a look inside but always she had managed to stop herself from entering and remembering, for fear of causing discontent with her marriage to Peter.

Indoors Sarah sipped her elderflower tea and waited for the sickness to subside she knew it was perfectly natural to feel this way in the early months of pregnancy. Already she had taken out the waistbands on her skirts and had started to make herself fuller dresses, at this rate the baby would be a giant by November.

Peter groaned loudly as he tried to turn over in bed, Sarah was quickly at his side.

'Lie still Peter, I'll change your dressing and get you something to wet your lips.'

He did not argue or open his eyes. He had been laying here for days wafting in and out of consciousness sometimes babbling on about things Sarah did not understand.

A really nice old gentleman had brought him home and apologised profoundly to Sarah for the accident, he had given her a hand full of documents that he had found on Peter and said they should be kept in a safe place. Sarah had only glanced at them briefly and pushed them into her chest for safekeeping. The only thing that did surprise her was the vast amount of money that Peter had in his pocket she had never seen so much and wondered where he had got it all from. But all the questions would have to wait until he had fully recovered.

Peter winced as she applied a new dressing to the ugly wound on his forehead. Very slowly his eyes opened and then squinted tightly together blinded by the bright light from the sunshine that pierced its way into the bedroom. For a moment she thought he was going to wake up but no, his eyes closed and he sank back into the dream world where he had spent most of the last week, the place where you go to let your body and mind repair. Quietly she left the room and pulled the door closed. Janet was sitting in the kitchen waiting for Sarah, each day she came in to sit with her brother whilst Sarah and Matthew tried to get some of the important jobs on the farm done. At first Sarah had refused to leave Peter's bedside, she had sat with him throughout the day and all through the night, but the last few days she felt able to leave him for a short while. What he needed now was time to rest, which would encourage his body to generate new healthy flesh and heal the wound to his head. She pulled on her cold boots and made her way across the yard to the cattle sheds. She quite enjoyed milking the cows, the grassy smell and the warmth of the gentle creatures was quite comforting to her. Their black and white smooth bodies shifted lazily around, knowingly they ambled into their own milking stalls where they stood patiently waiting to be relieved of their full udders. A soft mewing sound of contentment echoed around the wooden walls of the milking sheds as Sarah and Gwen worked their way through the herd who were always pleased to share their produce.

Matthew was becoming quite helpful on the farm he really tried hard with the jobs he was given but he was still painfully quiet and would not waste words with anyone. He had been given the task of emptying the pales of freshly pulled milk into the clean churns and then to make sure that they were standing out at the gate ready to be collected. Some mornings if Gwen managed to finish her work in the dairy kitchen early enough she would give Sarah a hand with the milking, in turn Sarah would be obliged to offer to help Gwen out by making the butter and cheese. At the moment Sarah could not find enough hours in the day to carry out all the extra tasks that were expected from her. Since Peter's accident she had neglected the shop and missed quite a lot of her regular healing visits.

Peter tried to focus his eyes on anything in the room that did not move around. He attempted to try and sit up but winced loudly as a sharp stabbing pain split his forehead into two and caused him to sink back onto the pillows. A wave of nausea seared through him causing his empty stomach to heave, he lay perfectly still until the feeling passed. He half opened his eyes and squinted at the unfamiliar surroundings as his eyes grew accustom to the brightness of the daylight he thought he recognised some of the objects in the room. Various things that looked familiar gave him a clue to where he was. A strong scent of bluebells penetrated his brain and he started to remember where he was but for the life of him he could not begin to understand why his head hurt so much and why he felt so weak. Questions began to race through his head and something far at the back of his mind made him feel very anxious but he could not for the life of him understand these strange feelings. Fatigue overwhelmed him and he dozed fitfully, vividly being thrust between reality and the dream world of nightmares. One minute he would wake up with a terrible start, his mind was racing and heart pounding fit to burst, sweat oozing from every pore and as it cooled with the icy temperature of the room he was left shivering between damp sheets.

Not sure whether it was real or a dream he held his breath as he saw Sarah enter the room, she was carrying a tray but she was not alone. He could not quite make out who the man was with her, he appeared to be gliding along, his feet were not touching the ground. Everything that happened appeared to be in slow motion. The man's clothes were very strange, he wore long white robes that were as weightless as a cloud and seemed to float in a breeze along with the man's mane of long grey flowing hair. Sarah and the strange figure were in some sort of conversation with each other but it did not matter how hard Peter strained his ears he could not hear a single word. Sarah and her friend seemed to be ignoring him, he tried to talk to Sarah but she ignored him and carried on chatting away to the man. Sarah came towards him with a tray in her hands, she sat down on the bed beside him and started to feed him, slowly she slipped a spoonful of broth between his open lips, he stared up into her blue eyes and shouted at her, he tried to move to show her he was alive. Suddenly it occurred to him that he was not shouting and not moving because he was still in a vivid dream and unable to awake from it, somehow he was in his body but unable to move a muscle or make a sound he seemed paralysed.

'If I was alive and air-breathing as you are, then I think I would enjoy your chicken broth,' said Tobias to Sarah.

'If you were alive my friend I would give you some but as you're not then I won't waste it. I do hope he wakes up soon Tobias, he needs to get some good wholesome food inside him to build himself up. I can't believe he has lost so much weight in such a short time.'

Peter could hear every single word that Sarah was saying but still he couldn't move not even blink an eyelid.

Whilst Sarah was talking she placed one hand over the top of Peter's head and the other gently on his chest, he felt her soft hands touch him. She closed her eyes and took a deep breath in, and then very slowly out, each breath relaxed her more and more enabling her to concentrate her entire mind and body on channelling healing energy into Peter's weak lifeless form. For the very first time Peter felt the power of Sarah's healing. A glowing vibration entered his body and pushed its way through every inch inside him spiralling right down to his feet and coursing to his toes that tingled with the new found energy. Even though he was weak he started to feel lighter and the wound on his head stopped the constant throbbing that had exhausted him.

Tobias hovered silently watchful in the corner of the room. He was not really interested in the recovery of the patient, even though he was supposed to give out love and light to saints and sinners he sometimes bordered on rebelling against the rules especially if he thought the person really did not deserve his compassion. He could not help but remember, we shall reap what we shall sow and it will increase thrice before it returns to you. He had heard the silent pleas of the prostrate man lost in his nightmare world but he chose to let him find his own way out. Tobias knew that Peter had changed so rapidly towards Sarah that there had to be some other influence towards his bad behaviour, as the boy had once absolutely worshiped her to the point of complete adoration and he would never have had eyes for any other. But things had changed and Tobias knew that events were only going to get worse. He was also aware as to who was responsible for changing the attitude of the young man towards Sarah. Peter was merely an innocent person being used as a weapon against all that is good. Tobias was the spiritual guardian of Sarah and all that stood for compassion and kindness, his brother the Evil one was now the spiritual guardian of Peter and all that was cold and cruel.

Peter started to become very relaxed and at last the dreadful dream came to an end and he was able to open his eyes. Sarah was so pleased to see him back in the living world she hugged him tightly, tears of joy trickled down her face. She propped him up on some pillows and held a cup of cool water to his mouth. He sipped it and enjoyed the cool liquid refreshing his parched mouth and cracked lips, at first his head started to swim but slowly his eyes began to focus and after a while he could see perfectly well.

'Why am I here, what has happened to me?' he asked Sarah. 'How long have I been in bed?' He looked down at the thin muscles on his once strong arms.

Sarah explained as much as she knew and could not really elaborate on it too much, even though she had this sudden vision of him in a dark room accompanied by his aunt and a strange young woman. Peter's eyes darkened as he heard Sarah describe the meeting at the solicitor's office. Luckily his face could go no paler than it already was.

Peter seemed very vague and could not remember anything that Sarah said. Not the accident or the reason why he was in Penzance. Sarah went to the chest and brought out the papers that had been found on him. He took them from her and started to go through them very slowly, the anxiety he had felt before started to well up inside him, he tried to swallow the feeling of panic. Everything flooded back to him, the meeting with the solicitors, the hotel, Jane and his aunt, and oh Christ the money. Sarah watched his expression change.

'It's alright there is nothing to worry about the injury to your head is healing nicely. And we've all managed to run the farm whilst you have been unwell not quite as well as you do but all the important jobs have been done. We have been so worried about you, can't you remember anything that happened?' Peter looked at Sarah hardly hearing what she was saying.

'Another thing Peter, you were carrying a lot of money I haven't touched any of it, it's in my chest for safe keeping, where did it come from, is it yours?'

Peter's mind was not up to thinking up a convincing answer.

'I'm not sure about that,' he said. 'I need time to think.'

Gwen was really pleased to see her son making such good progress and would be very pleased when he was well enough to take up his duties on the farm. Matthew was also happy to hear that his brother was on the mend and would soon be able to return to work. He did not think that he could carry on much longer working so hard from early in the morning until long after nightfall.

Maisey Banks sat opposite her niece at the table

and listened intently to what the girl was saying. The old nurse had experienced a very uncomfortable journey up from Penzance. Her main priority for the visit was to find out exactly what had happened to Peter, it had been nearly a month since the night he had disappeared from the hotel. His twin Molly now knew all about the deceitful episode of Sarah's inheritance and explained to her aunt about Peter's accident. The women screwed up her eyes and watched Molly intently as she questioned her about the money that Peter had drawn from the bank before he had the accident. Molly was not too sure about its whereabouts but suggested that she could visit Peter at Mill Farm and try and find out for herself. The old nurse persuaded Molly to go with her and they both set off together.

A shiver ran down Sarah's spine as she recognised the two women coming across the yard. What a spiteful combination of miserable souls they made. Gwen also saw her sister and her eldest daughter arriving and came over to greet them. Sarah stood back as the couple totally ignored her and pushed their way into her little home, Molly demanded to see her brother in private. Sarah thought it was best to leave the family on their own, she decided to do a little more hoeing of her vegetable garden and then she could sow more seeds. Ten minutes later, Gwen came out to the garden and called to Sarah,

'Would you like a glass of cider Sarah? I have to fetch some for my sister. It is so kind of her to come to see how Peter is, she's a very good nurse you know.'

Sarah chose to ignore the last remark after all she had first-hand experience to how good a nurse Peter's aunt was.

'No thank you Gwen, I'll wait until I go indoors to make Peter's lunch.'

Gwen was back within minutes carrying a heavy stone jug, a very short time later Molly and her aunt abruptly decided to leave, making noisy excuses as to why they couldn't stay any longer. Sarah could not help but overhear the conversation and felt their reasons were false and not really that convincing. When she entered the bedroom the first thing she noticed was the lid on her chest was slightly open showing a small gap. She looked at Peter and decided this was not the right time to say anything about it, he was slumped lop sided in a chair and looked very tired and drawn.

'Would you like me to help you back into bed Peter? I think you have been up long enough today you look absolutely drained.' He nodded in agreement. She helped him out of the chair and back into bed. She pulled the warm eiderdown up over him and tucked him in.

'You have a little sleep Peter and when you wake up I'll have a nice bowl of hot soup ready for you.' Sarah looked at the ugly purple scar that had started to form on his head, gently she trailed the odd shape with her fingertips he murmured something and closed his eyes.

'Sweet dreams,' she said as she kissed his forehead.

Again he whispered to her, this time she thought she understood the words. 'I'm Sorry, Sarah,' and then even more faintly. 'I did love you.'

CHAPTER TWENTYFIVE

White soft crystals of sand stretched either side of the beach house, the ribbon of land was interrupted only by small clearings of tall green palms that created a cool oasis, giving a welcome shade from the constant radiating warmth of the tropical sunshine. From the veranda Charles could look out onto the great spread of azure blue sea that rolled away far into the distance and eventually merged with the clear blue sky that formed a canopy over this bright and beautiful country. He rested his pen on the desk and leant forward on his elbows, cupping his chin in his hands he let his mind experience the luxury of daydreaming. This colourful yet wild place encouraged passion and talk of lovers and dreams of romance. A family group of parents, grandparents and a variety of children shrieked and laughed as they enjoyed an afternoon of diving and fishing. The happy noise that enveloped the silence of Charles's house made him feel sad and quite envious of the family life that he felt deprived of.

The people on the beach were far from wealthy and lived mainly hand to mouth and yet they possessed something that no amount of money could ever buy. He had a great wealth of assets but would sacrifice everything to have just one minute of the complete emotion of pure love that shone in the eyes of the people before him.

A slight breeze rustled the notepaper that sat naked on the table in front of him. So many times he had dipped his pen in the ink and it had dried before he managed to create one single mark. He had spent far too much time deliberating on what he would say to Sarah that he had completely lost the point of the communication. He found it very hard to understand why she had married the man that she did, it was obvious that she did not love him. Charles would still become flushed with emotions when he gave space to reliving the night that they had shared in the pagoda. He was so sure that they had experienced something so special that nothing could possibly come between them, but it did and now she shared her life with a man who was cruel and deceitful.

A dark skinned girl dressed in a bright colourful dress, wearing a matching turban on her head placed a glass jug of freshly squeezed fruit juice on the table beside him, he nodded a thank you, and she returned to the task of preparing the evening meal. He always ate his meals outside on the veranda overlooking the great expanse of sea, as he could not bear to sit at the long mahogany table on his own staring at the echoing emptiness of the room.

A small brown lizard attracted Charles's attention, it swished its tail from side to side as it ran across the top rail of the veranda. With great speed a long tongue protruded from its smiling mouth, uncurled and encircled a large spider that had thought itself hidden by the purple flowering bougainvillea that cascaded over the tiled canopy roof. It scurried back across the rail with its mouth overflowing with black hairy wriggling legs.

Night time came early in this heaven scent country,

first the sun gave a dying performance of rich colours from bright orange to dark scarlet and in its final throws deep fiery red, greatly magnified by the clear atmosphere. At the precise moment of sunset an unnatural silence gripped the island, every bird in the trees stopped their busy evening chatter. Creatures of the forests held their breath and waited for man to retire before they explored their night time world.

Charles lit the lanterns that hung over the porch and returned to the table, he reached for his pen, tonight was the right time to write to Sarah.

My dear Sarah,

I do hope this letter finds you well and enjoying married life. I am so sorry that I missed your wedding but the communication I had from my mother explained it all in great detail, it certainly sounded like a grand affair.

I left in such a hurry that I completely forgot to give you the present I had bought you. I cannot honestly say it was a wedding present for you and your husband, I bought it with only you in mind.

I think most fondly of you at times and cherish the memories we made together and mourn for the loss of your love and how things could have been between us. I could not tell you face to face but I want you to know that I will always love you with a passion that no man can possibly match, you are my sun and moon and stars and all that completes my world. I will always be here for you Sarah whether it is on this earth or in the realms of immortality, I am your soul mate and nothing can ever change that, I will wait for you. Not a day goes by when you are not forefront in my thoughts.

If you have visited our sanctuary, the pagoda, then

you will have already seen my gift for you. It is in the black box that sits on the dressing table in the small room. I hope you like it, I am sure you will. Please use the pagoda as often as you want to and air grandmother's clothes and jewellery for me.

I hope to return to England next spring and will look forward to seeing you. In the meantime it would be nice to hear from you. Mother writes often she would be only too happy to send the letter with hers. I am hoping that next year when I have visited my home that my mother will accompany me back here, I am sure the warm weather and healthy lifestyle will do her the world of good. If you feel you would like to be her travelling companion I am sure she would be delighted to make arrangements for you to come too.

Let me tell you a little about the place. My house is made of wood and not particularly grand but very comfortable. I spend most of my time outside sitting on the veranda wasting time staring at the white sand and blue sea that constantly moves and sifts the sand and shells that form the beach and my garden. The house and porch are covered in climbing flowering vines that wind and weave their way around every post and push their strong branches under the tiles on the porch roof. Odd little creatures live in the density of the vines. I have enclosed a couple of sketches I made of them so you can understand what I am talking about. The floors throughout the house are made of cool marble and encourage you to go barefoot something I know you would enjoy. My furniture is rustic to say the least and made by local craftsman. Everything here runs at a much slower pace than in England, the natives seem to enjoy life more and spend so much time just being alive and not trying to make money and justify their existence. I have learnt so much from them. Their values are very different to how mine were but you will be pleased to hear that I am changing my views on what is important in this life, it certainly is not material objects. As I write this letter a slither of a new silvery moon has just appeared on the far horizon. Just think Sarah, we are thousands of miles apart living in different parts of the world and yet we both gaze on the same moon that rolls around the universe.

I look forward so much to hearing from you.

All my love and affection.

Yours Charles.

Sarah giggled as she squashed her enormous body into a chair, she wished her arms were a lot longer as she could hardly reach across her stomach to the cup of tea on the table.

'My goodness me,' said Grace as she entered the room and greeted Sarah.

'You really have grown an awful lot since I last saw you.'

'I know,' replied Sarah, 'My appetite has increased so much, I can't stop eating.'

'I am so pleased, Nellie has been busy baking cakes and scones all morning. She wanted to make sure she cooked your favourites.'

The door opened and Ralph Trevallian started to come into the room, he was carrying a large envelope. He looked at Sarah and rudely ignored her.

'Your son sent you this,' he said and he thrust the package onto the table and promptly left the room.

'Oh how nice,' said Grace with a smile, 'I love

hearing from Charles,' she said happily. 'Perhaps after tea you would read his letter to me.'

Peter rested on his pitchfork. The heat of the day was getting to him. It didn't matter where he went on the farm there was nowhere in the shade or cool. All his chores seem to take twice as long as usual since he had the accident. Even though the wound had healed extremely well he frequently suffered from overwhelming exhaustion. Mind you he was still trying to lead two lives and that was tiring without all the physical work that the two farms demanded from him. Recently he had started to wonder whether he was doing the right thing. Really he did not feel he had a choice anymore, now he had become so deeply financially involved with Jane's farm that he could not really afford to let it all go. Especially as it was his chance to own property and not be beholding to anyone. Jane had started to give him a hard time and he knew her well enough to know that she would not wait too long for him to leave Sarah.

'Are you going to support that bloody fork all day or are you going to get on with some work?' bellowed Daniel from the dark doorway of the mill. Peter uttered an oath and turned his back towards his angry father and ambled into the airless cowshed and continued to move manure sodden straw from the floors.

Sarah felt the late summer sunshine on the top of her head as she enjoyed her walk home from High Markham. In her hand she clutched the letter that Grace had given her she had opened it and read it very quickly. She laughed to herself when she had read the part about travelling abroad with Grace next spring. Obviously Charles did not know that she was about to become a mother and was now quite settled with Peter. Sometimes you have to let adventures end and go. She hadn't told Grace what Charles had written in her letter only that it was nice to receive news from him.

Sarah passed the ever growing willow switch and was amazed by it's incredible size and unusual shape, the fairy ring of lush fresh grass had also increased in diameter and formed a perfect edging for such a magnificent tree. She stepped beneath the branches and under the crinoline skirt of willow wands. The tree formed a canopy, dappled sunlight danced through the branches but the grass was cool beneath her feet. She rested her heavy body for a while and leant against the rough trunk of the small tree. She could almost feel the spirit of the tree moving and hear the energy of the tree flowing. She gained great comfort from being in the presence of such amazing creations of nature.

She was not sure how long she stayed beneath the boughs each moment she was there seemed to refresh her and give her a new surge of energy. She decided that it was time to leave, she was startled to hear a whisper of a voice calling her name. She looked all around her trying to find the owner of the voice. No one appeared to be around.

'Come on Tobias, where are you? I can hear you.'
She fully expected her friend to appear. Nothing not even the crack of a twig or the sound of a bird, the woodland was very still. Again the voice called her name, it seemed to be coming from the pagoda. Who could possibly be there? The doors silently swung open as Sarah approached the building, she had not set foot in here since she had spent the night with Charles. Instantly the candles on the walls burst into flames and lit the whole room. She looked around her, everything appeared the same

as when she had last been there. The marble floor made the whole place cool, a welcome relief from the outside temperature. Perhaps she would just stop a while and read the letter from Charles. At least this place was quite private. She sat with the letter in her hands.

'You are my sun and moon and stars,' he had written, such romance coming from a man. If things had been different in her life then she would have been very honoured by his affection. She could not even begin to think about the love of any man other than Peter the father of her unborn child. A movement within her reminded her of the life that was forming inside her and how she must provide a warm and loving home for the innocent new soul that she carried. After her own sad childhood she had made a promise that whenever she had children they would know what love and security meant and not ever experience fear and abandonment as she had done.

She left the letter in the writing bureau it would be safe there. Gingerly she opened the door of the small anteroom at the back of the pagoda. The deep rich colours of the wall hangings of oriental fabric and clothes made the room spring into life. As Charles had said a small black box was perched on the dressing table waiting to be claimed. Before she opened it she could feel a million emotions flowing through her body rippling and cascading causing a wave and rush of sunshine and shadows. As she sat down on the soft feather bed with the box held between her hands she felt great beads of sweat burst out of her head, her stomach churned and her mind reeled backwards to a confused mixture of vivid memories of childhood, and more recent memories, of laying in Charles's strong arms and the smell of his tanned skin moving against her as they made love. For a brief moment she allowed her mind to indulge and relive the special moment when they became soul mates. Shakily she opened the black box and stared at the contents, dried rose petals filled the box and cushioned the fragile contents. Carefully she thrust her hand down into the mysterious container, she was inquisitive to reveal the present. Her fingers felt a very cold and yet familiar object, tears sprung to her eyes as she extracted the present, she gasped in surprise as she opened her hand to reveal her mother's Venetian glass swan that was filled with angel's teardrops. How in heaven's name had Charles managed to find this amazing gift. She looked in sheer disbelief at the clear glass glittering in the candlelight. Sarah held the present to her heart and rocked back and forward on the bed. Strong arms entwined her and she nestled her head into the shoulder that supported her. A handkerchief was placed in her hand, she wiped away the tears and looked up as she started to speak. It was then that she realised that there were no strong arms about her because she was alone in the room, there wasn't anybody here with her she was quite alone. Her heart missed a beat as she looked at the fine piece of crumpled damp fabric in her hand, it bore the initials C.T. whatever was happening to her, she placed the precious swan back into the box, nervous that she would drop the treasure and it would be lost for ever. She found it hard to believe that Charles was not in the pagoda, she had felt him so closely. His letter that Grace had given her was a welcome surprise it was so good to hear from him. He was aware that she had married Peter but he did not know she was expecting a child. She would write to him and tell him all her news about the baby and Peter's accident and also to thank him so much for the wonderful present. Somewhere within the very heart of the pagoda came the sound of an orchestra playing a magical waltz, Sarah smiled at the recognition of the beautiful melody, she lingered for a moment just to capture the fond memories that flooded into her head and pleased her very soul. As she passed the mirrors on the wall she could have sworn that she saw a figure in one of them looking out at her. All she could identify was that the woman was wearing the azure blue dress that hung in the wardrobe, the dress that fitted her so perfectly.

As she walked through the woods she found it quite hard to remember all the things that had happened in the pagoda, the further she got away from the strange place the more the memories were erased from her mind. By the time she reached the Mill Farm she could hardly recollect any of the afternoon after she left Graces house.

Gwen greeted Sarah. 'Peter's gone off with Colin, he didn't say where he was going but I expect he'll be back by the morning. Don't sit in there on your own, come and have some supper with us, I could do with a good chat and we can do our sewing together.'

Sarah agreed and said she would join Gwen as soon as she had watered her garden and taken Rufus for his run over the fields. Once inside she went to the bedroom and placed the swan in the bottom of her chest with her other treasures. She already had one handkerchief of Charles's in the chest, she folded the other one and put them together, really she should return them to him. Tonight she would write her letter to him and give it to Grace, she would not be able to give him an answer to some of his questions and she thought he most probably was a little home sick and was not really serious about his intentions. For a brief moment she wondered how different things might have been. The child within her moved and reminded her of the responsibility of being a faithful wife and caring mother. She let the wild daydreams subside and silently reprimanded herself for not appreciating how lucky she was with a husband and roof over her head.

Rufus lay down in front of his mistress with his head on his paws, he watched with eager anticipation waiting for the moment when she would go to the door and call his name.

'Come on, Rufus,' shouted Sarah.

The black mess of fur leapt into the air and skidded across the floor, his back legs caught up the front ones as he bounded out of the door and across the yard. A flurry of chickens and feathers took to the air as he raced through them and made for the open fields. Sarah waved to Daniel and Matthew as she passed the mill.

She noticed that the wildflowers were beginning to form an almost hand painted carpet throughout the hedgerows and borders of the fields. Man could never achieve such perfect colours and natural patterns as nature could. High upon the Tor she picked a grassy mound and rested her tired fat body. She cupped her hand over her eyes to shadow the bright evening sunshine and surveyed the amazing landscape that fell away far below her. In the distance she could see the rolling patchworks fields leading down to the green-blue sea that stretched far over the horizon. Grey rugged rocks edged the moving water and separated the land from the sea. The innocent waves caressed the rocks as if they were harmless friends but you could not live in these parts and not respect the treacherous rocks that lured many an innocent sailor to fight for his life and try to save his scuttled craft. Far out to sea the devil's rocks patiently hid beneath the surface awaiting their victims. Sarah was not particularly fond of the sea, the great mass frightened her and held no fascination other than a curiosity as to the nature of the strange creatures that lived beneath its ever-moving tides. Rufus rushed from the top to the very bottom of the hillside, he clumsily chased the rabbits and their families until they disappeared beneath the ground safe in their tunnels. A few adult males stood their ground and the dog soon backed off unsure of what his next move should be. Sarah reprimanded him for his behaviour and he very guiltily sat down beside her and put his snout under her hand, she caressed his long furry ears as he leant against her. High above in the clear blueness a sky lark demanded the attention of all below. Sarah strained her eyes to make out the shrill sound and locate the small bird as she watched it dive down with great speed and land on its nest in the next field.

Sarah's eyes travelled far along the coastline she could almost see the grey shadows of the faraway fishing villages and the white sails of the boats as they left the docks on the evening tide. She wondered where her husband was going this evening, could it be to Penzance? Gwen had said that he told her that he often helped his friend Colin on his sister's farm. Apparently her husband had died and she was finding it hard to manage all the work on her own. Sarah was very proud of Peter offering to help the poor women also it explained why he went to Penzance so often. If only Peter had told her she would not have worried so much and suspected him of visiting the gaming houses.

Jane stood with her hands on her hips, her cheeks glowed with temper.

'You promised me that you would settle all the debts on this place as soon as you'd been to the bank and that was months ago, and now look,' she thrust a letter into Peter's face, 'another letter from the bank. It's your fault that there isn't enough coming in Peter, you have got to stop giving your aunt any more, she's greedy and I think she's had more than enough. Why are you still paying her? All she did was set up the meeting with that old bedfellow of hers. We could have done it without her help. After all it was what was owed to you. More of a dowry than an inheritance.' She paused for breath and started folding bed linen that was drying around the fire.

Peter read the letter and placed it down on the desk in front of him. He walked towards Jane. 'Oh come on Jane give us a cuddle, it'll all be alright just you wait and see.'

'I wish I felt as confident about things as you do Peter,' she gave a gesture of a struggle to get out of his arms, but stayed enfolded. 'And while we are talking about serious things, when are you going to make an honest woman of me. I can't put your name on the deeds until you do.'

'It won't be long,' he assured her.

'What are we waiting for Peter?'

'Leave her and move in with me permanently, you said that you didn't care for her anymore so why stay. Your parents treat you like a farm hand, at least here everything you do will benefit us.' She wriggled out of his arms and stood at a distance facing him.

'I have been thinking,' said Peter, 'Can't we get your girls to have a few more customers and then we could charge them extra for the use of their rooms.'

'I thought that we had agreed to stop renting out the rooms when you move in. I don't want to share it with them any longer than we have to. I want us to be a respectable family.'

'Where will they go?'

'I'll find them somewhere it can't be that difficult. There are plenty of places to rent down in the town. Your aunt said she owned a property there somewhere, ask her. She's got no conscience and won't mind living off immoral earnings.'

'You're right,' said Peter. 'It's about time I sorted myself out. I've just been putting off the inevitable.'

'Are you getting cold feet about leaving?' demanded Jane with her eyes blazing at Peter.

'Course not. I promise by December everything will be sorted.'

'I bet you're hanging on to see her baby, aren't you? Well what about mine surely it's more important than hers is? Remember Peter that you are not legally married to her, you owe her nothing,' she paused for a moment, 'she does know about the preacher doesn't she?'

'No, she doesn't, it's not common knowledge, I only know about it because old Pingale told my aunt in confidence but I'm sure Sarah will soon find out, once her grand friend hears of it. As for the child my Ma will help bring it up, she's had enough practise with us lot. She wouldn't refuse a home to her own grandchild.'

Just for a brief moment a sentimental thought

fleeted through Peter's mind. It did not stay long enough for him to suffer the emotion of guilt.

The thought of getting married again so soon really did unnerve him. But nothing was going to stop him from becoming a gentleman farmer not even a bad case of frighteners. His aunt had assured him that he was doing nothing wrong. After all he wasn't married to Sarah, he supposed it was quite a stroke of luck that the old preacher had been an impostor for years. The only qualification the old man actually had was for being a confirmed alcoholic and grand impersonator. The authorities were reluctant to admit to the truth, as it would mean that all the weddings, christenings and funerals that he conducted were null and void. All the records and registers had completely disappeared from the church, no one knew if correct documents ever did exist.

'Well then, I'll set the date shall I?' She watched Peter's expression change.

'Don't worry I told you it won't be a grand affair I've only mentioned it to a few close friends. It will be quite unusual to be married by the captain of a ship. At least he'll be real. And I have been thinking as far as old Pingale goes, if he ever finds out he'll think we are marrying again because of the first one being void. After all the silly man was stupid enough to believe I was Sarah.'

She grasped the lapels on Peter's jacket and pulled him towards her and kissed him passionately. 'I can't wait for us to be together,' she whispered in his ear, he melted in her arms. In this state he would have agreed to anything.

Gwen was woken abruptly by a sharp knocking on her door. Sarah had been awake most of the night with the most awful cramps in her stomach. They had started in the early hours of yesterday morning and niggled for most of the day, her waters had now broken and even though the baby was very early she was sure it was well on its way to being born. Gwen looked at Sarah's face and realised what was happening she roused Janet and they hurried Sarah back to her bed. Gwen was annoyed that her son was not there with his wife at such an important moment.

With each pain Sarah took a breath and panted like a dog, she counted until the next pain coursed through her. Throughout the night Janet made endless cups of herbal tea, the blackened kettle never stopped boiling. In between contractions the women chatted about whether it was going to be a boy or girl and what were the names that Sarah and Peter had chosen.

'I can't believe that it can take so long for a baby to be born,' said Sarah.

'After each one I used to say to Daniel that is it, no more. But very soon I would be pregnant again. It wasn't until after Mary that I realised how not to have any more and by then Daniel was too old to be bothered to try and make anymore.' With this announcement Sarah and Gwen ended up laughing.

The pains were very frequent now and Sarah could feel the baby moving down inside her eager to start its adventure of life outside the safety of her womb. Her whole body was trying desperately to expel the new infant.

'Push down, Sarah I can see the head.'

'I am, I am,' shouted Sarah.

Her body arched and distorted as she took a deep breath and she pushed with all her might, for a moment nothing happened and then just as Sarah fell back exhausted on the pillows the baby slid out at last and made its arrival into this world.

'It's a little boy,' said Gwen as she tied and severed the cord of her first grandchild. She wrapped him in a cotton blanket and handed him to his mother.

'Give him to me please,' said Sarah as she reached for the blonde haired baby boy. Tears fell down her face as she looked at the perfect little person that she had being growing inside her for all these months. Her one worry was that as he was born earlier than he should be, he would not have been cooked properly but her worries were allayed as she counted all his fingers, toes and bits and pieces, they were all where they should have been.

'I wish Peter was here he will be so pleased it's a little boy.'

'I am quite cross with him Sarah, he's away more than he's here at the moment, I don't know what's the matter with him.'

Before Sarah could answer she was gripped with the most excruciating pain and nearly doubled up with its severity. Gwen reached forward and passed the baby to Janet to hold, for a moment she was really concerned that Sarah was haemorrhaging but very quickly she realised what the problem was.

'Push Sarah there's another baby on the way I can see its head.'

'Oh crumbs,' said Sarah. 'I'm having twins.'

Another blonde baby made its way into the world.

'A girl,' said Gwen and handed her to Sarah.

'Oh Gwen, I don't believe it a matching pair. Peter will be so surprised not just one but two.' She cradled them in the crook of each arm.

'I'll start to clear up and then I'm sure you could do with a rest, Janet and I will take turns to sleep in with you until Peter gets home, you're going to have your hands full for a while.'

'By the way,' she asked, 'what are you going to name them?'

Sarah looked from one angel face to the other. 'Our son will be called Luke and our daughter Rosie. I think their names suit them already don't you?'

Gwen nodded in approval. She helped Sarah wash and change her nightdress and took the soiled linen off the bed. Janet sat staring at the tiny forms that already behaved as if they had been on the earth an awful long time. Their little lungs bellowed out identical cries. 'They are expelling the devil,' said Gwen, 'and at least we know their lungs are strong. Considering they are so early, they are perfectly formed.'

'They will have to sleep top to tail in the crib as it's only a single,' said Sarah. 'It won't matter whilst they are so small, as soon as Peter gets back he can start making a double one.'

She could not wait for Peter to see his children. The twins nestled into each other as she placed them in the crib beside the bed. Gwen had lovingly washed and carefully dried both her grandchildren and then dressed them in warm cotton nighties that Sarah had sewn. Tobias appeared in the room and stood in a corner, Sarah was too tired to talk to him but she took comfort from his presence. She needed to rest but she found it difficult to take her eyes off of her beautiful children, what a gift they were, both shared the same beauty, blue eyes and an amazing mass of blonde curls, as she drifted off into the world of dreams a disturbing thought fleeted through her mind. Exhaustion took over and erased the memory of it sending it somewhere far away to be stored until ready to be dealt with.

Peter arrived back at the farm in the early hours of the next morning, he had intended to sneak in and retrieve all of his clothes and a few possessions that he wanted to take with him. Also he was sure that there must be some money in the house that Sarah had most probably tucked away. He knew her shop had been doing very well and she could soon replace anything he took. He could not believe his eyes when he opened his door and found his mother and sister there and then walking into the bedroom to find that he was the father of twins. A boy and a girl. He stood for a long time trying to understand the situation, there were so many questions he wanted to ask. Quietly as not to wake Sarah he left the room.

Daylight pushed its way through the windows and lit up the whole of the bedroom. The twins woke at the same time as their mother and both demanded to be fed. Sarah sat in a chair beside the crib and reached for Rosie, she was slightly smaller than Luke and Sarah thought she would feed her first. Instantly the little girl stopped crying as she nestled her face into the comfort of her mother's breast. Gwen came into the room.

'So you are all awake together.' She picked up Luke and cradled him, instantly he stopped shouting. 'You slept so soundly, Sarah. Peter came back and he saw the babies, he decided to sleep at our place, he did not want to disturb you all. He was very quiet I think he was in a state of shock. Like the rest of us, he thought you were due next month and only expecting one. I said I would call him when you were awake.'

'Thank you Gwen I'll just wash my face and brush my hair I don't want him to see me looking a mess.'

Luke had a healthy appetite and had no trouble feeding, his little cheeks glowed as Sarah fed him. When he could not possibly have room for another mouthful of milk Sarah popped him back into his crib. She looked out of the window to see if Peter was coming. After a while she opened the front door and called to Matthew who was feeding the chickens in the yard.

'You are an uncle now Matthew, would you like to come and look at your niece and nephew?'

The boy waved and shouted something about coming later, when he had finished all his jobs.

'Do you know where Peter is?' she asked the boy but he acted as if he had not heard the question.

As she went to close the door she saw Gwen come out of the barn. She waved when she saw Sarah watching.

'You shouldn't be on your feet Sarah, go back to bed. I'll be over in a minute, has Peter been in yet?'

Sarah shook her head and closed the door. She was beginning to feel a little disappointed that he was not around the cottage with her and the babies.

In fact Peter was leaning on a style looking across the fields at nothing in particular. He was avoiding going to see the babies and Sarah. He just wanted to walk away and try and forget about everything here. His life was not here at Mill Farm anymore, he had spent his youth slogging himself to death on this dilapidated farm. And what for, nothing, it would never be his.

'Peter, where have you been? I've looked for you everywhere. Sarah's awake, come and see her and those beautiful babies of yours.'

Following his mother across the farmyard he scraped the mud off his boots before he entered his cottage. He looked around the room, he felt at a distance from everything here, nothing seemed familiar anymore, including his family and Sarah. Sarah held her arms out to him as he walked towards her he bent down and held her briefly trying to avoid looking into the crib. Sarah could hardly contain her excitement and thought she would burst with pleasure as she placed Rosie in Peter's arms. She laughed at how awkwardly he held his daughter, she held their son. She took Peter's silence, as that he was so overwhelmed with pleasure that he could not speak. He held his son in the same way.

'Well then Peter, what do you think of them?' He was at a loss for words. They were just babies noisy at that. Babies were women's work.

'Sarah I been meaning to talk to you about a business deal that I have been offered.'

'I thought there was something on your mind. Has it got anything to do with you being away from home so much?' Peter nodded. But he still declined to tell her the exact truth.

He began with a perfectly reasonable explanation that she could not possibly disagree with.

'I have the chance to be a partner in a farm. It's quite run down at the moment and will take a hell of a lot of work to restore it, if it's to be profitable. It has an amazing amount of land that has been neglected for years. It means I shall be away for a long period of time but in the end it will be worth it, we will be able to bring these two up in much bigger surroundings and own a place of our own.' With each sentence he hoped he convinced Sarah more and more that it was the right thing for him to be doing. And of course it was going to be hard work but he was going to make the sacrifice for Sarah and the kids.

'Oh Peter if that's what you want then I can't stop you,' she thought for a moment, 'When are you going? I'll really miss you. How often will you be coming home?'

'I'll try and get home as often as I can but the sooner I get on with it the sooner I'll be finished.'

There was so much she wanted to ask but before she could Luke started bellowing and demanded his mother's undivided attention. Peter felt the conversation with Sarah was going a lot better than he had expected it to so he decided to take advantage of Sarah's mind being occupied by the noisy baby and ask for money.

'There is just one thing worrying me Sarah. I need as much money as possible to put into this venture, have you got any tucked away? After all you've got the shop as an income and I'm sure Ma will help out if you can't manage.'

'You know I have, Peter. I have been saving it for our future.'

'Well I reckon this could be the right time to invest it then,' he said confidently.

Sarah laid her son down on the bed and crossed the room to her chest, reaching down inside it she pulled out a black cloth bag and handed it to Peter. He took it from her and was amazed at the weight of it, considering he'd been dipping into it on various occasions.

'What did your parents say about you leaving?'

'They don't mind, they have got Matthew to slog his guts out now, haven't they?'

'Is it Colin's sister's place?'

'No,' said Peter a little surprised that she should know about Jane's farm. 'Look I'll have to make a move soon I want to be on the road before it gets too late.' He bent forward and kissed her forehead.

'Peter, you are leaving us aren't you, you're not coming back?' He did not answer.

'Remember I know these things, don't I. This day should be the happiest day of our lives and you are going to abandon me and your children.'

'Here you go again making a fuss, you're wrong, I think you're a bit sensitive after all you have just given birth to these two. I'll be back as soon as I can. After all it's quite a long way away I can't keep coming back and forward every day, I've got work to do there.' As he walked away from his wife and children he sighed with relief that at last he'd got out of the situation and away from Sarah's accusing eyes.

Over the next few months Sarah was kept so busy with feeding and changing that she did not have time to miss Peter. She did not know what she would have done without Janet's help, the girl did the washing and the cooking and had offered to look after the twins when Sarah opened the shop again. The latter she was going to have to think about pretty soon as her funds were getting very low and she could not expect Daniel and Gwen to help, they had enough trouble trying to make ends meet. Luke and Rosie were flourishing and had grown so much already, they had very different personalities. Luke was much more confident and quite a lot bigger than his delicate sister, Rosie was very small and dainty, she became upset more easily than her brother, they both had a mass of blonde curls, forget-me-not blue eyes and a rosy complexion. They were inseparable and hated to be apart, Sarah had also found something very different about Luke and it had started to cause her many sleepless nights, at first it was just her secret but now she feared that Molly had noticed and would cause trouble. Tobias had told Sarah that the truth will always come out when you least expect it. Sarah had noticed a faint red mark on Luke's shoulder and decided to keep an eye on it, after a few weeks it had started to become darker and slightly larger, it was then that Sarah recognised the mark. She had seen the identical birthmark before in the privacy of the pagoda, she had traced it with her tongue on the shoulder of Charles Trevallian. When she sat down and started to think about events it all became very clear. The twins were not born early they were on time and it was no surprise that they didn't resemble any of Peter's family, they were not his children. Molly had recently visited whilst Janet was bathing the twins and had seen Luke's birthmark. She did not say anything she did not have to. Sarah knew that Molly's lover also had the mark on him, she had seen it in the explicit vision she had of Molly and Charles's father in the study.

Sarah felt it was only a matter of time before her sister-in-law decided to inform her employer of her discovery. Sarah felt that it would come as no surprise to Grace, every time she saw the children she commented on how much they reminded her of her son when he was a baby. Sarah wished she could just pick Luke and Rosie up and fly away with them to somewhere that nobody knew her and where she could make a fresh start for her and the twins.

CHAPTER TWENTYSIX

Grace Trevallian moved quite quickly from her sitting room towards her husband's study. It sounded as though he was having a brainstorm, his voice was so distorted with anger that it was hard to recognise it as his. He almost pulled the bell-rope from the ceiling.

'For goodness sake, Ralph you'll make yourself ill, whatever is the matter?'

She looked from her husband to Molly. Her husband sat down heavily at his desk surprised by his wife's entrance.

'Will you kindly tell me what the problem is? I heard you mention Charles's name what has happened?' She stared at Molly. 'Does any of this concern you, if not, kindly leave the room and get back to your duties I'm sure they could do with some help in the kitchen.'

Ralph poured himself a large brandy. 'Before you drink that I want you to tell me exactly what is going on.'

'I'll tell you what is happening that bloody stupid girl that you feel so sorry for is about to try and ruin the Trevallian name. I knew that something like this would happen if you encouraged her,' he paused briefly to take a deep breath. 'I'll not have this sort of scandal ruin my son's life. Everyone knows the girl's touched in the head. Molly had already warned me to watch out for her because her own husband had walked out on her and now she's looking for a rich replacement. Well I'll see her and those bastard children in hell first. I bet I'm not wrong that she doesn't know who the real father is.'

Grace listened intently to every word her husband said. Secretly she had suspected the twins might belong to their son, the family resemblance was too great to be a coincidence and if it were true then she knew her son would be overjoyed with the news.

'You will do nothing until Charles gets back,' said Grace, 'It's his problem not yours.'

'The girl's a witch and a compulsive liar, if anything she has bewitched him.'

'Don't talk such poppycock that sort of thing went out in the Middle Ages.'

'Many a man's life has hung in shreds by the accusations of thwarted women. Those sort of women are for one use only, it's common knowledge that young men in Charles position get their pleasure from the local commoners, but it stops there.'

'Don't you dare have any more to do with that girl she is trouble.'

'My dear husband you will not tell me who I can talk to and who I can't. I would have thought you knew me well enough by now to know you tell me nothing. And by the way talking of indiscretions try closing the door next time you entertain the staff in your room.' Grace left her husband's room very pleased with herself that she had stood up to her husband.

When Sarah heard the coach arrive she knew it would be the Trevallians. 'Come in,' she shouted in reply to the gentle knock on the door.

'I know why you are here Grace. It did not take Molly long to tell you did it?'

'I want to hear it from you Sarah I know you will not lie to me. Is my son the father of your children, are they my grandchildren?' She moved towards them. Luke was delighted to see her smiling face and very readily chuckled. Before Sarah could reply.

Grace spoke again. 'Even with my failing eyesight I can see they are my son's, you cannot mistake those beautiful blonde curls. Which one has the family birthmark?'

'Luke,' was all Sarah said.

'Charles should be on his way home and I know he will want to do what is best for you and the babies. According to Molly, Peter is not coming back. At least he won't be a problem. Is there anything you need that I can bring you?'

Sarah shook her head. 'No thank-you, we have all we want. It was kind of you to come, I never intended this to happen to you or your family. I hope that it does not cause too much trouble. I really think the best thing to do would be to move away from Hellstone and let everyone get on with their lives.'

'I will not hear of any such thing and I know Charles won't. He will be absolutely delighted when I tell him about the twins. Promise me you will not go anywhere until you have seen him.'

Sarah promised her friend but was still not sure if staying here was the wisest thing.

When Grace had left she thought about what Molly had said. It was really true then, that Peter was not coming back. In the light of things she couldn't blame him.

Ralph Trevallian thought he was being terribly

clever when he arranged to meet Charles at the dock office. He wanted to warn his son about the accusations that had been made against him. He was so confident that his son would feel the same way as he did towards the blessed girl. Not for one minute did he take into account the stupid boy's misplaced pleasure when he learnt about Sarah and the birth of twins. There were so many questions that Charles wanted to ask, that his father could not answer. Harsh words were exchanged when Ralph Trevallian said only that very morning he had taken steps to get the matter sorted out. He told Charles that he was pretty sure it was a matter of pure extortion and she should be put away for it. Molly had told him that her brother the girl's husband had left, so she was really desperate to find someone else to support her and the children. Charles disagreed with his father and said he would not discuss another word with him about the matter until he had talked to Sarah.

Charles left his father standing on the quayside almost purple with anger and frustration that his son had fell under the insane girl's spell, as his son turned his back and walked away the irate man shouted hysterically.

'I will not stand by and let my son and my wife be deceived any longer by that girl. I will find a way to stop this injustice. I have the power and I have the money.' The threatening words were wasted on the young man's ears and fell flat amongst the stranger's passing by, apart from one person, who was sitting very comfortably in the captain's quarters of a naval ship, she was waiting to be witness to a marriage. She laughed as she recognised the angry voice.

Sarah dozed in her rocking chair, Rosie and Luke

were both fast asleep snuggled closely together. This morning the sun had shone brightly and she had taken them out in their perambulator, they had trundled over the rough paths and through the woodland. She had introduced them to all the wonders of nature and began to teach them the names of all the creatures that joined them on their walk. They watched the birds flying high above the trees and gurgled with delight as the soft beige doves flew down to perch on their hands. Rufus rushed about excitedly through the undergrowth disturbing anything that moved only stopping when a red fox strolled out of the bracken and frightened the life out of him, it casually walked beside Sarah and appeared to be a lot better behaved than the excitable spaniel. She picked wildflowers, blossom and early catkins which she tickled the twin's noses with, the happy little souls exploded with chuckles of delight. The cold fresh air brought a wash of colour to their cheeks and their laughter made their sky blue eyes sparkle. When the path became too rugged to travel any further she turned the pram around and took a different route home. She was pleased that she had visited the woods again, out there with nature she felt very relaxed and at peace, recently she'd had more than enough of people, they only seemed to give her problems or make matters worse. She now yearned for time to let herself heal the hurts and enjoy the most wonderful of gifts, her beautiful children.

The candles had now burnt down and the only light in the room was a slight amber glow from a few remaining embers. A friendly shadow sat at the table with his ghostly head resting on his elbows.

'I can tell what you are thinking Sarah, but you are not on your own, really. I am always here beside you even though sometimes you can't see me. I know that you feel everything in your life has gone wrong. But things will change, wait and see.'

'I know, I suppose Peter was off on his own adventure and it did not include me. And of course I had my adventure with Charles and now I have to face the consequences.'

'Just a minute I think you are getting a little confused. Nothing happens as a punishment because you think you misbehaved. You don't deserve things that go wrong unless you dished out some cruelty that is unfair, then as we've said before, it leaves you and gathers speed, multiplies times three and then bounces back to you when you least expect it. Perhaps fate decided that your first adventure say with Peter was not for a long period of your life and that was the end of it. Now you have already a clue with the birth of the twins to give you a step into the next adventure. Nothing ever happens by chance, it is all meant to be. And as I keep telling you, only have regrets of the things you have done in your life not the things you haven't. When you are young and youthful like yourself you think that your life will last forever and you cannot envisage that one day you will see that your life is perishable and you cannot look forward to many years into the future. You must always live life to the full. Live for today as if it is the very last day of your life.'

'I am going to keep a journal Tobias with all your wise and wonderful philosophies in.'

'You should write a book about your life including all your lotions and potions Sarah it would be so interesting especially in the future when your healing and remedies become popular again.'

'When I have the time,' she replied. 'At the

moment I have two very boisterous children to bring up and a living to make.' She stifled a yawn with the back of her hand.

Her head rested on the back of her chair and she let her mind free itself to play in the realms of dreamland. She slept for a long time imagining that she was flying like a bird high above the village, she could look down on the miniature buildings and swoop low over the church she was weightless and free of any earthly worries. She travelled far into the distance and over the sea, the night sky was a mass of a million diamond stars and it did not matter how high she flew they were always beyond her reach. She hovered over St. Michael's Mount and saw the lights beaming from the tall windows. She flew over farms and towns eventually finding herself high above the village where she was born, hovering over the castle she looked down upon the winding river that travelled relentlessly through the grounds never ceasing constantly moving on, passing by this place only once on its endless journey. She carried on weightlessly gliding over the spire of the church and the thatched white cottages she floated above the trees surrounding the tall house where she had spent the first nine years of her life. Not a sign of life came from the black windows, an eerie silence gripped the night air. As she moved down to take a closer look she could see that the house was in a state of ruin. The once grey slate roof had long ago collapsed and fallen through into the attic exposing the skeleton of rafters that were weathered and rotten. The remaining glass in the windows was cracked and broken and the wooden frames weathered and worn resembling driftwood, the front door had ungraciously fallen from its hinges and its remains lay among piles of autumn leaves that were gathered on the marble-floored hallway. She thought of the rage her father would have shown if he had seen the disgusting state of his once elegant house. Down in the garden sat the carved stone gargoyle seat, tendrils of ivy snaked itself through the ornate masonry. Sarah peered into her nursery window, the room seemed so much smaller than she remembered, her iron bedstead had succumbed to times erosion and had become a rusty sculpture standing in the centre of the floor. The toy cupboard door hung open revealing the remnants of the toys and books that Sarah had left behind all that time ago. Sarah's body soared up into the night sky and started to travel back home, she flew with the owls and joined the bats on their jaunt. A loud sound intruded into her dream and she felt herself falling back to earth. All too soon she sensed her astral body return to her physical shell and end her night time journey

She woke up with a start and realised that the sound in her dream was someone knocking very hard on the front door. Rufus reached the door before she did and cavorted excitedly, impatient for her to open it. At first she could not recognise the dark figure silhouetted against the night sky. Charles knelt down, his strong hands rubbed the dog's ears, standing upright his gentle eyes looked down into Sarah's face, her heart leapt a beat but then thumped so hard inside her chest that she imagined that the whole of the world would be able to hear it. Without a word he stepped forward and encircled her with his arms, holding her as if he would never ever let her go again. He had dreamed about this moment so often that he could not believe that it was not a dream.

He kissed her hair and buried his face in the

hypnotic aroma that had so often haunted him. He stepped inside the door and kicked it closed with his foot. He pulled another handkerchief from his pocket and dried her eyes.

'That's three I've got now,' she said with a smile on her face. 'Handkerchief's,' she added in answer to his puzzled expression.

'Oh. I see you do this just to steal my handkerchiefs.'

Sarah stepped away from him. 'I don't have to ask why you are here do I? Let me make it clear to you Charles all this is none of my doing, I will lay no claim to you or your family, honestly. I would never have contacted you or told a soul,' she paused and waited for his reaction.

'Well I can only thank God that it has all come out.' He reached for Sarah's hand again. 'I am sorry you have had to go through such difficult times with your short marriage but I can honestly say that I am delighted with the outcome. When are you going to let me see our children?'

Sarah took his hand and led him into the small dark bedroom, she lit a lamp and watched him as he knelt down beside the crib. He was mesmerised by the two identical figures sleeping peacefully, emotion filled his throat and stopped him from speaking a word. His long tanned fingers lifted their small hands and touched their rosebud cheeks. Just for a moment Luke stirred and opened his eyes, briefly he glanced at his father, a little smile lit up his face but very quickly his heavy lids closed again and he cuddled up to his sister. Charles and Sarah crept out of the room.

Sarah broke the silence. 'It was very good of you to come and see us, thank-you Charles.'

'You don't have to thank me Sarah, they are a

beautiful gift. I am so sorry for what has happened to you but I am willing to make amends.' She started to talk but he held his hand up to stop her.

'Hear me out please, Sarah. I want you to listen to what I have to say. Let's sit down.' They seated themselves at the table.

'I understand that Peter has deserted you and the twins, did he know that they were not his?'

'No he didn't but I expect he soon will, Molly denied that she knows where he is but I am absolutely certain that she does.'

'It really doesn't matter, no one will dispute that they are mine. You cannot stay here any longer. I want you, Luke and Rosie to move into Keepers Cottage as soon as you possibly can, I will arrange for the move.' Sarah was very surprised. 'It will be far more spacious for you all and I will make sure you have everything you need. I expect there are all sorts of questions that you want to ask me.'

'I can't see your father permitting it Charles.'

'Keepers Cottage belongs to my mother and she was the one who suggested the idea.'

'Will you be moving in with us?'

'You have been through a lot Sarah and I would not dream of causing any more pressure in your life. At the moment the most important thing is to get you all settled and happy. We'll take the future as it comes. Shall I leave you to think about what I have suggested?'

Sarah answered quite quickly. Putting her twins first she very readily agreed to move away from Mill Farm and into the cottage in the woods.

'Will tomorrow be too soon for you?'

'That will be fine,' she smiled at him.

'Just bring the things that are yours and you cannot bear to leave. Keepers Cottage has been decorated and is completely furnished but you can change anything you want to.' He stood up, but really wanted to stay for fear that when he left she would change her mind. When he reached the door he turned around, walked back and kissed her lightly on the lips. 'Will you be alright if I leave you on your own tonight or would you like me to stay? I could sleep on the floor.'

'No thank-you Charles I will be fine I have been on my own one way or another for quite a while, you get back home and I will see you in the morning.'

Gwen watched the rider mount his horse and leave Mill Farm. She knew exactly who it was and part of her was relieved. If her daughter Molly was right then it was best for Sarah and the twins to have the Trevallian family look after their own kin. And besides her son was gone and would never come home now. She had always looked on Sarah as a daughter and nothing would ever come between them, not even this. Peter never did deserve her she was just slightly different from the rest of them but not in an unkind way, she was special. Poor Sarah, so far life had treated her a little unkindly even though she would be the last to complain. Her clouds always had silver linings and her cup was always half full, never half-empty. Gwen hoped Sarah would find the happiness she deserved.

Sarah never slept that night but watched the moon ride high over the village of Hellstone, as the sun rose she looked up at the tall sweeps of the mill standing still in the early morning light, she would miss this place. Time to leave nothing but memories behind and go forward on a new adventure, as Tobias would say.

At eight the next morning as true as his word Charles arrived with his coach, closely followed by an empty wagon ready to take all of Sarah's and the twins possessions to Keeper's Cottage. Sarah only packed the things that belonged to her and the twins, she left behind anything that was Peters or belonged to his family. Charles helped the driver lift Sarah's heavy treasure chest onto the wagon along with the few pieces of furniture that Grace had given her.

Slowly Sarah's eyes scanned the rooms for the last time, a pang of sadness welled up inside her and she felt warm tears fill her eyes and tumble down her cheeks. Charles waited patiently allowing Sarah to take as much time as possible to say goodbye to Gwen and the rest of the family. It was decided that Janet would accompany Sarah and help with the move and perhaps stay at the cottage for a while until Sarah and the twins had settled.

Daniel stood beside Gwen and Matthew in the courtyard and watched the coach leave the farm. He would miss Sarah and the twins, they were all so full of life but he was glad that they would be away from here. Something had happened to change his son he had become unkind towards Sarah and the twins, in fact both his eldest children had turned out selfish and cruel and took great delight in causing as much misery as possible. Molly had taken such pleasure in breaking the news to her mother about the twin's father and revelled in it even more, when she relayed the spiteful gossip about the uproar it had caused in the Trevallian household between Ralph and Mrs Trevallian.

Everything you could possible need was here inside the cottage, Charles and his mother had been so busy filling the place with all the things that they thought would be useful. In the small larder the marble shelf contained butter, cheeses, pies and fruit tarts all made by the staff of the house. Bacon, chicken and fresh fish were outside in the meat safe. On the windowsills and small tables were placed pots of wildflowers and blossoms. Inside the kitchen a pine dresser stood, its shelves were laden with blue and white willow pattern china, the drawers had tablecloths and cutlery in. A basket of fresh vegetables sat on the shelf underneath. Passing through the kitchen you came across the small sitting room, in front of the large fireplace was a comfy couch and a long pine table was standing behind it, under a small window was an oak bookcase filled with books that Grace had brought from her own library. Sarah was taken aback by the generosity of Charles and his mother. Eventually all her possessions were brought into the cottage and put into cupboards and drawers, her chest with all her special treasures in fitted perfectly at the back of the log cupboard beside the fire. From this room a small doorway hid the narrow dark oak staircase that wound its way up to two small dormer bedrooms. In the main bedroom sat a washstand with a jug and basin on it, perfumed soap sat in a dish alongside coloured glass bottles of cologne. A pile of thick towels filled the two top cupboards of a tall boy. Matching curtains and bedspreads had been carefully selected, it amazed Sarah that all this had been achieved so quickly.

Charles watched in delight as Sarah explored her new home and he hoped that she would be happy living here. He was certainly happy that she and his children were away from Mill Farm.

'When you are ready,' said Charles. 'I will take you into town and buy you and the twins new clothes, try to make a list of anything that I might have forgotten to bring you.'

Charles was holding Rosie and Luke lay in his grandmother's arms, Sarah looked from one person to the other. There was definitely a family resemblance between them all. You could see both Grace and Charles in Rosie and Luke.

'Thank-you both for all that you have done for us,' said Sarah. 'I.'

Charles put up his hand to stop her saying anymore. 'You don't have to thank us Sarah it's as much as you all deserve. Come on Mother, we must be off and let Sarah and the children settle in.'

'We will see you in the morning,' said Grace. 'And I'll send one of the boys down tomorrow to clear the garden, I know you will want to grow your own plants.'

There were lots of kisses and farewells before they left. Charles held back and let his mother go on in front he turned to Sarah and reached for her hand.

'I can't tell you how happy you have made me. I am just so sorry I was not with you sooner. I don't know what has happened to your husband but I fully intend to find out and notify him of my intentions and my rights as father of the twins. Also it has come to my notice that your wedding might not be legal, it appears the preacher might not be what he made out to be. If I'm not wrong he was an impostor.'

Sarah put her hand to her mouth in surprise.

'Don't worry I'll get to the bottom of it. If it's true then you are not actually married to Peter and that will make things much easier for all of us.' He kissed Sarah lightly on the lips. 'I will see you in the morning.' And he left. Sarah waived until the coach was out of sight. She thought of what Charles had said about the preacher and wondered if it could possibly be true. For a moment she felt a little sorry for Peter and herself, they had both enjoyed the wedding so much, she reached for their photograph, the memento of their day, it was in a basket carefully wrapped in paper. The couple looked radiant and she remembered back, after all it was only a short time ago. She knew for that moment when the camera captured Peter and her, they could not have been happier. She did not replace the frame back in the basket but left it out to remind her that her short time with Peter was not all bad. Sarah believed too often we let the good moments become obliterated by the miserable episodes and end up believing there wasn't anything happy at all in the past adventure.

The cottage nestled itself comfortably around the little family and very soon it felt like it had been their home forever. Janet offered to look after the children in the daytime so Sarah could carry on with her healing and the shop. Grace had said she would also like to have Rosie and Luke at High Markham for one day each week. Preferably when her husband was up in town.

Every day Charles visited Sarah and the twins bringing them toys and presents that he thought they needed. He wanted to make the most of them before he had to travel back to his business abroad, this time it would be so different, he was determined to make plans for Sarah and his children to eventually follow him. Already he had arranged for an architect and builder to depart ahead of him and make a start on building a fine family house for them all.

CHAPTER TWENTYSEVEN

The two women stood on the grand staircase having a good-natured argument.

'I can't take it from you Grace,' said Sarah.

'Of course you can. I've seen you stop on these stairs and admire it often enough.'

'But surely you want to keep it, there will be a very empty place if you take it down and give it to me.'

'It will be a constant reminder of Charles for you and the twins when he is away. And then when you join him abroad, you can take it with you. I have other portraits of him and I hope to have more of you all as a family. I must say Sarah I am so glad that you have both decided to make a fresh start together far away from here. And I think it was very wise of you to wait until these two are little bit older before you take them on such a long and uncomfortable journey. I will miss you all but Charles assures me that I can come and stay with you as often as I like.'

'What's all this talk about?' asked Charles as he entered his mother's drawing room. He sat down on the rug with the twins, they both giggled with delight when he scooped them up in his arms. His mother explained about giving Sarah the painting and he laughed.

'I must say I do look rather handsome in it. I've come to take you all out for a ride, the weather is so beautiful I thought I would take the afternoon off and spend it with my wonderful family.'

Sarah gathered up all the bits and pieces that accompanied the twins wherever they went. Yesterday Grace had given them both silver rattles as christening presents, Rosie let Sarah take hers away from her and put it in the basket, but Luke held onto his tightly and refused to let it be removed from his fingers.

Sarah thanked Grace for a lovely afternoon and Charles helped Sarah take the twins down to his coach. She had been up at the house for the afternoon mainly to let Grace play with the twins. Yesterday the twins had been christened at the church. It had taken Charles quite a while to persuade Sarah to go ahead with the Christian service. But he wanted them to be christened while he was still here in England. The occasion had been marred by Ralph Trevallian rowing furiously with Charles, as usual it was about Sarah and the children. There was not a chance that he would ever except that they were his grandchildren. He threatened that they would never inherit anything from the Trevallian estate and neither would Charles all the time he was involved with Sarah. He still insisted that this was all a ploy to make money between the slut and her so called husband. Charles tried every form of reasoning with his father but without managing to change the old man's views on the situation. The only concession Charles managed was an agreement from his father to leave Sarah and the children alone to live in Keepers Cottage until he managed to return to England to fetch them.

The afternoon and the fresh air had absolutely tired out Luke and Rosie, they had been carried in asleep from the coach and put straight into their bed. Sarah sat down at the table and poured a cup of coffee for Charles and herself, they had all enjoyed a wonderful afternoon at the sea. The August sunshine was so warm and the sea air was so clean that it quickly relaxed and calmed you. Janet had left a note on the dresser to say that she had returned to the farm to help Gwen as she had been suffering from a severe cold but would be back in the morning. Sarah thought with Janet's absence that it would be an ideal opportunity to ask Charles to stay to tea and he had readily agreed.

Sarah was a little surprised to notice Tobias busily hovering around her garden, first he was at the window looking in and then peering through the climbing roses over the arbour. She wondered what the old soul wanted or was he just keeping an eye on her. Usually he respected her privacy. He knew when and where to appear. Charles noticed her watching the old man.

'Who is he, a friend of yours?'

'You can see Tobias. I don't believe it,' said Sarah.

'Oh I know who he is now. I have seen him so often when I'm in your company, does he trail about beside you all the time or is it just when I'm around.'

'No. Gosh I'm confused now, no one ever believes in Tobias, they say I make him up and that I am mad and he is really created by my imagination all because I never had a real father to love me. If you can see him why have you never mentioned him before?' she asked.

'I thought it was best not to. I knew there would be a time when I could talk about him freely to you. He seems to be quite a friendly apparition doesn't he?'

Sarah nodded in agreement not sure whether she

really wanted to share Tobias with Charles. After all he had always been her private guide even though she had always suspected that he was not quite exclusive to her that he might share himself equally between an awful lot of people.

The honeysuckle that climbed over the porch radiated its wonderful aroma in through the open front door.

'Shall we sit in the garden for a while?'

'That would be nice,' answered Charles.

They both strolled out into the garden and took a seat beneath the rose arbour. Tobias slipped quietly away into the woodland that surrounded the cottage, silently he patrolled the shadows.

Bees still buzzed around the ripe garden and birds fed greedily on the aphids and grubs that adorned the stems of the roses. The summer evening was filled with the perfume of a cottage garden and the sounds of busy wildlife, Sarah felt contented and safe tucked in the arms of Charles. They sat silently together, she noticed his heart beat a little faster and his breath become stronger as he buried his face in her hair, she grew warmer and her pulse raced, once before she had felt this way towards Charles. He tried to pull himself away from the lingering kiss that locked them together.

'We must talk Sarah and make things clear between us.'

She pulled his shirt collars towards her and demanded another kiss.

'In a minute,' she mumbled before his cool lips covered hers.

His hands searched for an opening to her bodice and quickly his fingers moved gently on her warm skin, he nestled his head against her bare breasts and kissed them slowly. She held him to her. Her body reacted to his caress and a feeling of desperation welled up inside her, every part of her throbbed with a sensation that needed to be satisfied. His hands removed the rest of her clothes and delved deeply to please her. She made an effort to stop and retreat to the privacy of the cottage but their passion was not to be delayed. Above their heads the night sky rumbled over the tops of the trees and privacy was granted to the couple below. Sarah lay naked on the grass her body covered by Charles, his hands moved expertly around the magical areas of her body that she never knew existed, she was taken on a journey that she had only ever once slightly travelled before. It could have been hours that they were locked in each other's arms. Sarah did not want the magic of the evening to disappear for fear it would never return, they covered themselves with their cast off clothes. As the dawn approached and the light came from the eastern sky they made their way into the cottage and quietly climbed into bed. They made love again not so urgently and passionate but more gentle and sensually exploring every part of each other's body taking them to a new height of fulfilment. A powerful vibration ran through Sarah's inner self and no words needed to be spoken between the two neither needed to say the words I love you but both whispered them constantly to each other.

Two pure white doves sat on the open windowsill and looked into the sun washed bedroom at the couple locked in each other's arms. Charles kissed a trail down Sarah's bare spine, she twitched and sleepily pulled herself up on one elbow, her raven hair tumbled down over her face and brushed blue black strands across Charles.

'I have checked on the twins,' he said. 'They're quite happy playing downstairs with Janet.'

'Oh no, Janet knows you stayed here the night?'

'Don't worry, she is well aware of what has been happening, you don't realise how loyal she is to you and how devoted she is to Rosie and Luke.'

Sarah climbed out of bed, Charles grabbed her hand and pulled her back down into the soft feathers.

'Not so quickly. I have brought these from the pagoda for you, I was surprised you left them there. I wanted to give them to you last night but somehow I was led astray and my mind was completely taken off the subject.'

He reached for his jacket that was lying on the floor. They both sat up in bed, Charles watched Sarah as she opened the familiar box. Bright sapphires and diamonds caught the daylight and dazzled their eyes.

'Let me help you put them on.'

He carefully secured the safety chain on the cascading waterfall of ice white and azure blue stones, he reached for the silver mirror on the table.

'Look.'

Sarah's long fingers touched the jewels around her neck. She looked at her reflection, 'I can't wear these with my nightdress can I?'

'Just one minute Madam,' and he leapt off the bed and opened the wardrobe door. There on a hanger was the azure blue dress. She put her hands to her cheeks in astonishment.

'I didn't know you had put the dress in the wardrobe? Oh Charles what can I say.'

'Absolutely nothing,' and he caught her up in his arms and kissed her with such passion that they could hardly stop themselves from returning to bed and repeating last night's performance.

Playfully she pushed him away from her and sat down on the bottom of the bed. He thought how wonderful she looked wearing her nightdress and the jewels.

'Today we must discuss all the details about our future,' said Charles, 'I don't ever want to let you out of my sight, I can't bear the thought of going away without the three of you with me.'

'Let's get ourselves up and dressed first,' said Sarah, 'and then we can have a lazy day in the garden and sort out everything we need to.'

Sarah leaned out of the dormer window and marvelled at the bright orange and red nasturtiums that had managed to climb all the way up the walls and into the thatching. A group of Jackdaws argued noisily above the chimney pots and pulled at the long reeds that made up the roof covering. Charles joined Sarah at the window.

'Charles, would you mind if I renamed the cottage?'

'Of course I don't mind. What were you thinking of calling it?'

'I thought Jackdaw Cottage would be rather nice.'

'Most appropriate,' he said laughing as he watched the black demons pull the stuffing off of the roof.

Squeals and giggles could be heard from somewhere in the garden. Janet had placed the twins on a blanket under the shade of a tall rowan tree. They were just ten months old and now managed to crawl everywhere. Luke had started to pull himself up and walk unsteadily around the furniture but little Rosie was quite content to sit and watch her brother.

Sarah and Charles were so in love that they could

hardly think of anything else but each other. All the sad events of Sarah's past were outweighed by her overwhelming happiness. Even though she had loved Peter she had never ever felt this way about another human being apart for the pure love she felt for Luke and Rosie.

'Please try to concentrate on what I am saying,' said Charles. Sarah was watching the pink petals of the bramble blossom fall like snowflakes and cover the ground below them, already you could see the small green fruit starting to form for the autumn's crop of blackberries. The garden was alive with colour, bright red geraniums filled the window boxes, orange calendula marigolds and wild camomile flopped lazily over the stone pathway.

Sarah picked a bunch of roses and put them in a jug on the outdoor table that she and Charles were sitting at.

Eventually she sat down at the table opposite Charles and looked deeply into his eyes and through to his soul. She bathed in the knowledge of his true and honest intentions towards her and the children. Charles reached forward and held her hand. He was pleased to see that already a new light shone from Sarah's eyes, a bright aliveness that he had not noticed before.

Sarah was in a far too romantic mood to apply her mind to anything other than being in love.

'Will you marry me?' said Charles to Sarah.

This question had the desired effect, Sarah instantly stopped daydreaming and looked at Charles. Her bright blue eyes stared at his face.

'Will you marry me?' he repeated.

'Yes, yes I will marry you Charles, but what about my marriage to Peter?'

'I have engaged a solicitor to prepare the necessary

legal documents to obtain an annulment of your previous marriage. With your permission of course, Peter will have to be notified as well so he can also give his consent. It is one of the requirements laid down by the law. And once that is over we will be free to be married.'

'How long will all of this take?'

'Hopefully six months at the most but definitely by the time you and the twins leave England.'

'We will be able to have the most beautiful wedding on the beach outside our house. How do you feel about that?'

Sarah was overwhelmed by all the new plans that were being arranged for her, Luke and Rosie.

'I don't know how you will find out where Peter is. I am certain that Molly does know of his whereabouts but I doubt whether she will tell you.'

'I have already asked her but she denies any knowledge of him. Even though my mother was sure that she had seen him in the grounds of the house but you know what her eyesight is like.'

'It's strange you should say that but I was convinced that I could feel his presence the other day. I was so sure that if I turned around quickly I would have seen him watching me.'

'The next thing on the agenda is.'

'You make it all sound so official,' and she leant across the table and planted a very wet kiss directly onto his lips.

He wiped it away with the back of his hand.

'As I was saying, the twins will be a year in a few months' time, shall I arrange a passage for you three for the New Year perhaps in the spring? Do you think they will be old enough to travel that distance and will you be able to manage them?'

'What a nice new adventure it will be for the New

Year. I am sure they will be just the right age. They will be eating proper food by then and be much easier to care for.'

Sarah sighed with relief at last she felt more hopeful and positive about the future for her children and herself.

'When do you intend to leave?'

'I need to leave the beginning of October to complete my business liabilities. A lot of people rely on me for the food in their stomachs and I would dislike myself immensely if I ever let them down. They are ordinary hard working folk who are completely loyal to me and I give them my respect and a fair wage in payment for that.'

Sarah listened again to the description of the country far across the sea that she would be taking their children to. She would miss the countryside of England and the wildlife but Charles assured her that she would never believe the colourful and unusual creatures that she would see. Also the exotic flowers that grew in pots in the hot houses of High Markham grew wildly and freely in his sunshine paradise and she would be able to just reach out and pick them whenever she chose.

She would not need winter clothes or heavy boots, her home would be a grand house with many rooms and the garden would stretch out to meet the blue rolling sea. He said that when he arrived there the house should be progressing well and near ready for completion. He would keep the small beach house and they could use it for a studio just like he had used the pagoda. Sarah's mind travelled and saw all the things that Charles had told her about, she felt that already she knew it so well and she was just returning to a familiar place that had always been at the very back of her mind.

That night Sarah would not let Charles return to High Markham and insisted that he stay at the cottage with her, he did not need a lot of persuading. In the middle of the night Charles woke up and stretched his arm across to Sarah's side of the bed, it was empty he rose and looked out of the window into the starry night. There down in the garden he saw Sarah standing with her white nightgown billowing in the cool breeze and her dark hair reflecting the light of the moon. Her arm was outstretched, through the woodland came a red fox as he approached, Sarah knelt down and caressed him like she would Rufus. He saw the fox nuzzle his nose into her hair and wag his tail with pleasure at her greeting, very soon a heavy stocky creature ambled through the woodland crackling the undergrowth as he came. A black badger joined the fox and patiently waited to have his white blaze scratched. As Charles watched more and more wild creatures surrounded Sarah, she sat amongst them and touched each in turn. Eventually she stood up and each creature slowly returned to the wilderness of the woods. Charles watched in absolute amazement. A cold chill ran down his spine as just for a moment he thought he saw a figure standing far back in the shadows. He was ready to run down into the garden to give chase, but with the blink of an eye it was gone and in its place stood the untidy trunk of a silver birch tree. He rubbed his eyes and looked out again there was nothing.

Sarah crept up the stairs looked in on the twins and then climbed into bed beside Charles. She nestled her cool body into his side, he put an arm around her and pulled her closer to him. He buried his face into her cold hair and breathed in the aroma of the night. He lay awake for a long time thinking about all the changes that had happened recently. He considered himself to be a very lucky man.

CHAPTER TWENTYEIGHT

The tall masts on the ship creaked as the sails flapped noisily in the south-east wind. Sarah waved frantically straining her eyes to catch the last glimpse of Charles as the vessel slowly disappeared away into the vast stretch of water. With tear filled eyes she returned to Janet and the twins in the waiting coach, she summoned to the driver that she was ready to return home.

The twins slept soundly for most of the journey, Sarah could not help but be sad, she was certainly going to miss Charles, they had become almost inseparable. She knew how quickly time passed and hoped it would not be long before she was packing her faithful trunk ready to leave England.

The coach started its steep climb up the hill to the village. Sarah started to feel uneasy she looked around her for the reason. It was not long before it became apparent. Up the road she could see that a large crowd of people had gathered outside her shop, she asked the driver to hurry up, as something must be very wrong. She could see Nicola standing looking at the windows. Sarah hastily climbed out of the coach, she summoned Janet to stay with the children. She could not help but feel an unwelcome shadow walking closely beside her. She stood with the rest of the villagers and looked in horror at the terrible state of her shop. All the windows had been smashed and the front door had been wrenched off the hinges and was now straddled across the broken counter, she stepped over the piles of broken glass and was amazed at the amount of destruction inside the place. Every pot of lotion, relish and balm had been flung at the far wall, their contents had slid down to the floor and created a disgusting messy heap. Books and pictures had been destroyed, lace mats and corn dollies were trampled into herb sauces and tea leaves. The beautiful Angel wish bags were scattered about the room, their secret contents exposed for all to see. The wooden counter was in two halves, hacked and splintered wood formed ghastly sculptures like broken bones. The worst part of it all was the red sticky paint that dripped like blood all over the walls, she stood back and read the menacing words. Bloody witch, slut whore and finally in capitals across the ceiling, BURN HER.

Nicola's feet crunched through the debris, she stood beside Sarah. For a moment a deadly silence hung in the air.

'Oh Sarah, this all must have happened in the night, when I came in this morning I found it all like this.'

'I can't believe anyone could do such a thing,' said Sarah. She went through to the back of the shop and was amazed to find her grandmother's wind chime still intact hanging in the window. She climbed onto the chair and removed it from the hook, very carefully she wrapped it in her scarf and tucked it deep into the pocket of her cloak.

'There is nothing I can do here at the moment. I must get the twins home and then I'll arrange for somebody to come and clear up. I don't think I shall bother to open the shop again. I can do my healing from my home, I was going to close down at Christmas as I shall be going away in the spring.'

As she left the shop a few customers who had been waiting outside came to tell her how sorry they were about the shop. At the back of the group stood a few young men that Sarah did not recognise but she instantly felt they were enemies. One started to shout at her.

'Got what she deserved, bloody witch.'

'She made people ill so she could sell them her poisonous cures,' shouted another.

'And she made a lot of money off the backs of sick people. Look at the people in the hovels that she fed her potions to, killed the lot of them.'

Sarah could not understand why these strangers were doing this to her.

'Who's put you up to this?' she asked. 'Everything you say is a lie. Did you wreck my shop?'

The boys scuffed their feet and started to move away when the butcher from down the road and his assistant came to Sarah's rescue. Sarah returned shakily to the coach and told the driver and Janet all that had happened. Sam the driver worked for Charles and had been assigned to look after Sarah and the twins, he decided the safest thing to do at the moment was to get his charges back home as quickly as possible. His master had told him to be extra vigilant, as he feared there could be some sort of repercussion from his father.

Tobias waited patiently for Sarah to notice him, she had been back at the cottage for a few hours. Sam had gone to the house to tell Grace about the incident at the shop, the twins were sitting in their high chairs at the table eating their tea. Tobias had been entertaining them and Janet could not make out why they were having fits of giggles at nothing in particular. The old man enjoyed knowing the children could see him, all infants were naturally aware of second sight, it was always such a shame when they grew up and lost that ability. He truly hoped that the twins would retain their mother's gift and then he would be elected their Guardian Angel.

Sarah waited until Luke and Rosie were tucked up in bed before she spoke to Tobias.

'Can you tell me what all that was about Tobias? I am sure you must know who is responsible for such devastation.'

'I don't know the reason for everything that goes wrong but I would keep your eyes wide open, I think someone has instigated a campaign of hatred against you and I am sure that this is just the beginning.'

'Someone must really dislike me, do you know who it is?'

'If I did I would tell you and then you could be wary of that person, all that I feel is an immense feeling of their anger and their obsession to destroy and discredit you.'

'Could it be Peter?' then she thought for a moment. 'I think I know who would take great pleasure in doing that to me and he would have the power and the money to pay people to carry out his illegal practises. Ralph Trevallian has made it perfectly clear on many occasions that he would do anything to stop me being anywhere near Charles, I think he is at the bottom of all this. But it won't work it just makes me more determined to start a new life far away from here with the man I love and the father of my twins. I've never intentionally done anything to hurt anyone.'

'But indirectly you have upset quite a few people

Sarah,' added Tobias.

'This sort of thing makes me want to stop my healing and trying to help everyone and become selfish like most people and get on with my own life.'

'Oh for goodness sake Sarah, getting to grips with all the hurdles in life makes you stronger and more confident, it gives you the knowledge to cope with the shadows, yours or other peoples. And if you become weak and give up sharing your kindness you know full well;

THAT FOR EVIL TO TRIUMPH IT ONLY NEEDS THE GOOD PEOPLE TO DO NOTHING.

Don't give in, fight it, and get your feet firmly on the ground and stop wallowing in your own self misery.'

Grace Trevallian listened carefully to Sam's story about Sarah's shop. She was quite upset to think that someone had caused so much destruction. She could not possibly think who could have done such a terrible thing. She asked her husband if he knew of anything. It all came as a complete surprise to him and he said that it was bound to happen the girl had made a lot of enemies. Grace was annoyed with his attitude, he had been very difficult recently and had refused to discuss Charles or his son's association with the girl. He had also denied that Peter Pendarvis had visited him a few weeks ago and he insinuated that his wife was very mistaken about overhearing any conversation between the two men about money. She was also wrong that he ever said that he was sick of women and babies about the place and it all had to stop and that the matter must be sorted out once and for all. He told her to stop inventing stories and to mind her own business and to refrain from eavesdropping outside his study door. He also reminded her he was master of the house and she should not question anything he said.

'You are you up to something,' she accused. 'I know when you are lying to me.'

'I think you are suffering from some sort of paranoia my dear wife and I should make an appointment for the doctor to see you.'

That had stopped her from pursuing the matter any further, but it had left her feeling very uncomfortable.

The next day Sarah, Nicola and Sam started to clear the shop of all the mess. Sarah had arranged for a builder to come and reglaze the windows and doors and paint the walls, covering all the obscenities. They worked hard all day, Janet stayed at the cottage with the twins, Sarah said that they would all be back at lunchtime for something to eat. The time just flew by and it was well into the afternoon before Sarah realised the time.

'Look at the time, poor Janet must be wondering where we are, she said she was going to make a meat pie for us and one of her special apple turnovers. I am getting really hungry now.'

'Me too,' said Nicola. 'I hope the invitation is for me as well?'

'Of course it is, come on Sam put that broom down, we are ready for our lunch.'

Sam woke up the horses with a gentle flick of the whip as they lazily ambled through the woodland track to the cottage. When the group entered the kitchen all was quiet, the table was set ready for lunch, Sarah went through the back door to the garden but there was no sign of Janet or the twins.

Suddenly a horrific scream filled the air and Sarah knew instantly that something was terribly wrong. Janet ran into the cottage her eyes were wild with fear. The girl was hysterical. Sarah had to shake her to calm her down so she could understand what she was trying to tell them. The girl's hands trembled violently as she used her fingers to talk.

'They're gone, someone's taken them, I put them both upstairs for their afternoon nap and went into the garden to peg the washing out. When I came back indoors I noticed the front door was open and I couldn't find Rufus anywhere, I went upstairs to make sure he wasn't disturbing the twins and that's when I noticed they had both gone along with the dog and a lot of their clothes and belongings.'

Sarah did not stop to hear anymore but raced through the house searching all the cupboards, she even climbed up into the attic, not a sign of them. Instinctively she knew they were not here, she could not sense their presence but she could feel the bond she shared with them getting further and further away.

'Janet did you see anything at all?' she asked desperately.

'No, nothing, sorry it's all my fault.'

'We must search quickly perhaps they are not too far,' said Sam and left the cottage and headed for the woodland.

Sarah scribbled a note to Grace and told Janet to run as fast as she could to get help to search.

Within the hour a dozen men with dogs joined in the search for Luke and Rosie. Not an inch of the surrounding countryside was left undisturbed. Ralph Trevallian did what was expected of him and alerted the local police and organised a search party. People in the village were questioned as to whether they had seen any strangers with small children. It was as if they had vanished into thin air. The officer then went to Jackdaw cottage to question Sarah and Janet. Sarah mentioned that she thought that Mr Trevallian and her husband Peter Pendarvis might have had something to do with their disappearance and she tried to explain the situation between her and Charles. The Sergeant stopped making notes and raised his eyebrows at the story she told him. He then insisted he would have to talk to Mr Trevallian before he proceeded further with this investigation. He also mentioned that he thought her story was quite untrue, he had known the man for some thirty years and he also doubted what she said about Charles being the twin's father.

Ralph Trevallian had already warned him that she was a strange one and had tried to compromise his son. In the end the boy couldn't stand anymore of her bizarre behaviour and had gone back abroad to escape the mad girl and her accusations.

'Ask Mrs Trevallian if you don't believe me,' she pleaded. 'She knows exactly what has been happening. She will tell you the truth. Why do you think they organised a search party if they are nothing to do with the children and me?'

'They are good kind people and you involved them by cleverly asking them for help.'

'I would like you to come down to the station and make a statement. There are a few things that I would like to go over with you.'

'Please don't waste your time questioning me, you should be out there looking for my children,' she shouted angrily.

'Excuse me,' said the officer standing up to his full height, 'I think you know a lot more about this incident than you are telling me.'

He stepped forward to grasp Sarah's arm but as quick as a flash she stepped away from him and turned and ran out through the kitchen door, she ran like the wind through the garden and into the dense woodland that she was so familiar with. A conversation raged rapidly inside her head.

'Tell me Tobias where are they? Help me to find them.'

'Run,' said the voice, 'run like the wind, follow your instinct like a wild creature.'

She skirted around the back of High Markham and stopped to catch her breath. Her eyes penetrated the side door, she ran up the stairs to the study. Just as she had anticipated Charles's father sat in his leather chair sipping brandy. He jumped to his feet when he saw Sarah.

'What are you doing here? I thought the police were arresting you.'

'Why? You are the person that knows what has happened to my twins, I know you do.'

'Now they are gone,' he said impatiently, 'you must leave my wife and son alone.' And he gulped down more of the fiery liquid.

'Did you pay Peter to take Luke and Rosie? Please I beg of you. I swear on my children's lives, if you just tell me where they are I will move far away from here and from you and your family. Honestly you will never ever see me and the twins again.'

'Oh no, I made that sort of bargain with your so-called husband before and look what he did, he took the money and left you and the brats here. This time I warned him, do the job properly and then he might get paid. So now you can stop all the play acting and see that Pendarvis keeps to his side of the bargain.'

Sarah was absolutely shocked to hear what he was saying. She listened no further and hurriedly left the room. Peter must have them she must find him. The door nearly came off the hinges as Sarah burst into the large kitchen and startled a very frightened Molly. The girl looked at Sarah's strange eyes and backed away from her until her back was right up against the sink. Nellie saw the piercing yellow and black eyes glaring menacingly at Molly and witnessed Sarah's rage as she crept stealthily towards the petrified form that was now cornered, she heard the unearthly roar as Sarah's long nails penetrated the soft flesh of Molly's arm.

'Tell me where my babies are or I will kill you slowly and very painfully, I will shred your face to bits and rip out your evil tongue. I know Peter has taken them, tell me where I can find him. Speak now,' she roared.

The girl twisted with pain, blood spurted from the wounds on her arm as Sarah retracted her long nails and then sunk them deep into her shoulder only stopping when they reached hard bone. Molly felt her knees go weak and her own warm blood soak through her dress. In between sobs Molly blurted out that Peter was living with a girl called Jane, Jane Parminter who owned a farm somewhere near Penzance. Sarah demanded she wrote down the exact address. The girl collapsed into a heap on the floor. Nellie Nap joined her when she saw the bloody gaping wound in the maid's shoulder. Sometime later Hodges found both the women unconscious on the floor. Sarah picked up the piece of paper from the limp hand and wiped away the red smudges. *'Parminters Stud, Lodge lane, Penzance.'*

Sarah did not return to Jackdaw Cottage but let

her mind travel far into the distance to the coast and then beyond to the port of Penzance, where only a short time ago she had said goodbye to Charles. Her inner strength gathered and gave her courage and confidence to set off on her own to find her children. A million worries raced through her mind but not for one moment did she believe that Peter would ever harm Luke and Rosie.

Driven by the pure love of a mother she ran, walked and trotted across the fields, through ditches and streams trying to take the shortest route as a bird flies to Penzance. She did not notice her sore feet and the cuts and scratches to her legs as she stumbled through hedges and over rocks. At one point a cart stopped and the driver offered to give her a ride for the last three miles of her journey, she gratefully accepted. After a slow silent journey she was dropped off just before dawn on a deserted stretch of rough road. She followed the instructions the driver had given her and walked for about a mile along an unmade dirt track. Her mind raced as she planned what she would say to Peter when she next saw him. She was worried for Luke and Rosie as they did not know Peter and would most probably be missing her. At last she came to a driveway with a wooden sign across the closed five bar gate. 'Pendarvis Stud' was written in green flaking paint, directly above it was an auction notice, the words on it faded by the sun and rain. A large padlock prevented entry and Sarah had to hitch up her skirt to climb over the splintered wood. Her heart sank when she approached the buildings and realised they were completely empty, there was not a sign of any life at all. The silence pounded in her ears. She searched through the outbuildings, nothing, no livestock or machinery which you would expect to find on a farm. The stable doors were open and the stalls were empty. She reached for a stone and smashed a pane of glass in a downstairs window and carefully put her hand through to open the window latch. Once inside the house she made a search of the downstairs rooms, all that remained were a few household items scattered around the floor but nothing to give her any clues as to the whereabouts of the occupants of the house. She climbed the stairs and looked into each room, she sensed that one room had belonged to a child but the feelings and fragments of emotion in the room were not familiar to her.

Where could Peter have gone, did he still have the children? So many questions raced through her head.

She sat down on the top stair and tried to calm her mind. Closing her eyes she tried to communicate with her children. Many small voices chattered together and Sarah could hardly make out Rosie and Luke's but they were there amongst all the excited chatter, if only she could find which direction the voices were coming from. She felt a strong arm lift her gently from the stair and guide her downwards and out through the door. Tobias tried to help her as much as he could.

She left the farm and retraced her footsteps back up the dirt track and out onto the roadway, she let her instincts guide her towards the next village. To her left she could see the far horizon, where the dark night sky met the equally midnight blue sea. She knew she would eventually come across the town, the place where she had stood on the quayside and waved a sad farewell to Charles, what a menace this place had become.

After what seemed about two miles she came across a hamlet of about four small houses and a white stone building which was an inn. A light shone from the windows, she peered through, a young girl was clearing the long wooden tables of tankards and plates, a man that looked like he could have been the girl's father sat with his legs outstretched, the soles of his shoes were almost touching the sizzling log fire. A dog on a chain in the backyard began to bark, the man rose from his chair to see what he was barking at. Sarah recognised the yapping and ran around to the rear of the building. A sturdy wooden door set into a high stone wall stopped her from reaching her dog, Rufus.

'Quiet boy, what's the matter with you, feeling lonely are we?'

'Excuse me,' called Sarah over the wall.

Rufus heard her voice and set up an awful howl.

'That's my dog you have there. I beg of you please tell me where you got him from and what happened to the people who were with him.'

The landlord of the inn looked over the wall.

'Where did you come from? You shouldn't be out on your own in these parts.'

And he unlocked the door and let Sarah into the yard. She rushed towards Rufus, he was so pleased to see her, he barked, howled and squealed all at the same time.

'I have come from the village of Hellstone, I was looking for Peter Pendarvis, I was told that he lived at The Parminters Stud. It is most urgent that I find him. Can you help me? I went to the farm and there was a sold notice outside and the place was empty. Do you know what has happened and where they might have moved to?'

'Oh dear you had better come in and bring that noisy dog with you. I can see he is yours, he was left here yesterday afternoon. I don't know who left him but I found him tied to the gatepost.'

Sarah and Rufus followed the man into the warm kitchen of the inn. He fetched her a tankard of ale and filled his own, the young girl smiled at Sarah and carried on washing the crockery that filled the deep sink.

Rufus spread himself out at Sarah feet and dozed with one eye closed in front of the warm fire.

'Well I don't know whether it will be of much help but all I know is that the girl, Parminter, has married again and the farm and the contents were auctioned off about two weeks ago. Rumour has it that the bank foreclosed on her and she sold it to pay off the debts.'

'I know a bit about them,' said Peggy, 'Jane was quite a nice girl it was really sad when her first husband died, he was a lot older than she was. He left her everything but she couldn't manage the farm and the horses on her own, then I heard that she had met a chap who was going to put a lot of money into the farm and bring it up to scratch, she got pregnant and had a little boy. I think she only got married to the father a few weeks before the bank took the farm. I never met the man she married but I heard he gambled a lot when he took over the farm, he also ran the business of the whores who lived with Jane. He managed them, hiring them out to some of the wealthier men of Cornwall.'

'Do you know where they are now, or where they moved to?'

'The girls are back in a house in the town, but I'm not sure exactly where.'

'I'll tell you who would know of the whereabouts of them,' said the landlord,
'Pingale the solicitor, he dealt with all the legal side, I know that, because one of the girls ran up a huge bill here for bottles of gin and I had to apply to him for my money.'
Sarah's head reeled with all the information that she had been given, she tried to take in all that she had been told. Her nerves were on edge and all she could think of was Luke and Rosie and how they must be feeling. She hoped that the man at the farm that they had referred to was Peter. If so the solicitor or the girls in Penzance would know of his whereabouts or perhaps his forwarding address. The man and his daughter were really helpful and Sarah decided to tell them why she was looking for Peter. They were horrified and shocked that Jane could have had anything to do with the kidnap of Sarah's twins.
'Look, you can do nothing tonight, you look absolutely exhausted, stay here and get a good night's sleep and I'll take you to town first thing in the morning.'
'I really can't waste any more time they must have passed through here today because you found Rufus. Could I ask you to do me a great favour? I will make sure you get reimbursed for the trouble, would you keep Rufus for me until I return? I will pick him up on my way back with the twins.'
The landlord readily agreed to help all that he could. He was quite upset when she insisted on leaving, it was now the early hours of the morning and not a nice time for a young women to be out in the countryside on her own. He drew her a crude map of directions and watched her walk off into the darkness.

Sarah and Tobias reached the crossroads on the moors and remembering the directions she chose the left turning which should take her down to the sea and the town.

'Have you found Luke and Rosie yet?' she asked her silent friend.

'I can sense they are in this area of the world, but I cannot tell you their exact location.'

'You are of no use to me Tobias,' she said angrily.

'Where have all your prophecies and preaching got me. If you can't help me now, when I really need you, just stay out of my life. Go away,' she cried at him.

He remained silently beside her.

The road started to drop down steeply. Sarah could hear the rush of the sea and smell the stale odour of drying nets. As she walked along the quayside, the first of the early morning fishermen were hauling their nets aboard their small boat. They glanced at Sarah and presumed she was one of the girls from the whorehouse returning from a late night customer. She approached the men and they laughed at her and shouted, 'No good coming over here love, we can't afford you.'

'Can you tell me where this place is please?' and she showed them the piece of paper with Pingale's address on, they told her how to reach it. Then she thought she would ask them about the girls who used to stay at Parminters.

'I know where they have set up,' he said, 'they used to be at the same house before they moved away.'

'You looking for a job there then,' he enquired jokingly.

'If you work there you can book me in for half an hour,' said the older man.

'You're not far from there, if you continue down here to the bottom of the quay and then turn right, halfway up the street, on the left you'll see the girls' house, you can't mistake it. There's always a light burning brightly in the windows all night long, you could say they're night workers,' he laughed loudly at his own humour.

Sarah thanked the men and continued her journey, a few times she had to stop because she thought she could hear the twins crying out but as soon as she stood still the crying ceased.

Her body felt tired and she had to mentally will herself to walk up the steep hill to the address she had been given. Her clothes were covered in mud and her light shoes were worn through. She had left home yesterday without thinking about the clothes she was wearing or taking any money with her. She did not care what she looked like, all she wanted was to find her twins.

Long before she reached the girls' house she could see it illuminated from the bottom of the street. The cobbles were wet and slippery under her thin shoes. The early morning dew matted her hair and it stuck to her face in black streaks. She raised her hand gripped the knocker and rapped loudly on the door. A window upstairs opened and a large lady clad in the smallest of petticoats thrust her ample bosoms out of the window.

'What do you want lady? There ain't no jobs going here.'

'I'm looking for Peter Pendarvis. I thought you might be able to help me find him,' then she added, 'It's really urgent.'

'Is it a job you want, cause I'm the boss of this house, he's finished with the girls, they work for me now.'

'Do you know where he has gone to? I really need to find him,' she pleaded.

'No I haven't seen him for a long time, can't help you.'

'Please could you ask the girls that used to live at Parminters, if they know anything?'

The fat lady slammed the window shut. Sarah waited and waited. Weak daylight started to creep up the damp street but the sun's early warmth was not enough to dry the damp stones, again Sarah grasped the knocker and rapped hard on the door. A window opened and a voice bellowed, 'No one knows nothing, bugger off.'

As she walked back down the steep street fatigue and disappointment overwhelmed Sarah.

Eventually she arrived at the offices of Pingale's the solicitors just as Mark Pingale junior was unlocking the door.

'Can I help at all?' he enquired when he noticed Sarah waiting behind him.

'I need to talk to somebody about the whereabouts of Mr Peter Pendarvis,' she hesitated then added,

'My husband.' The last statement had the effect that she had intended.

'I am sorry, would you like to repeat what you have just said.'

She repeated it word for word.

'And may I ask your name?' he enquired in a more gentle voice.

'Sarah Pendarvis, I used to be Sarah Miller.'

'I think you had better come in,' and he led Sarah upstairs to the offices. 'You look very tired, please take a seat.' He could not help but notice Sarah's agitation and the state her clothes were in. 'Can I get you a glass of water or anything, my secretary will be here in a while and he'll make us a hot drink.'

'Please, there is no time to lose, if you know where he is please tell me, he has taken my twins and I am afraid for them.' Tears streamed down her face and she slumped wearily into the chair. The young man put his hand on her shoulder. 'I'm totally confused, you will have to bear with me, and I am not sure who you are. I know a Mrs Pendarvis and she was nee Sarah Miller and you are certainly not she. Excuse me for a moment,' and he went into his father's office. Sarah could hear him cussing and cursing as he rummaged through the piles of files scattered about the dark office. At last he returned with a brown file tied with string. He opened it out on his desk and sifted through the papers inside it. At that moment a choking cough sounded from the stairs and Pingale senior just made it to the top before his cough nearly shook him to pieces.

'Father I would like you to get in here right away I think we might have a bit of a problem on our hands.'

Marcus Pingale looked intently at Sarah trying hard to understand what the poor woman was telling him.

'So what you are saying is that the person your husband has recently married is Jane Parminter and yet you are Sarah Miller from Mill Farm, Hellstone, do you have any proof of this?' Sarah thought for a moment. 'No, not with me I left in such a hurry. It's the twins I'm worried about. I am sure Ralph Trevallian has something to do with all this, he could not accept the twins were his son's and I know he is at the bottom of this with Peter.'

The name Trevallian rang an alarm bell inside the young man's head. Only last week his father's deer hunting friend Ralph Trevallian was at the house, he and his father were in the study for hours, he presumed they were reminiscing about old times they had spent together.

'Do excuse us for a while, Sarah. I need to talk to my father in private.' He ushered his father into the old man's office.

'Father what is all this about? I just hope you have acted within the rules of the law if not I can see we will both be in for an awful lot of trouble if it becomes public. I want you to start right from the beginning and whether it is good or bad I want you to be perfectly truthful with me.'

'We've done nothing wrong son, I wouldn't risk bringing our good name in to disrepute, not after all these years.'

'As you know Ralph and I have been good friends since we were children and he came to me to ask me to deal with a very delicate issue, In fact he pleaded for my help with the matter. I was asked to delicately and confidentially handle the adoption of his son's bastard children. It's all perfectly legal, don't look at me like that, I am telling you the truth. Goodness knows who that woman is out there, I know for a fact that she is definitely not Sarah Pendarvis and you should know that too you have met the women in question. It appears that the women we know as Sarah Pendarvis nee Miller had a bit of a servant come master fling with young Charles before she married Peter Pendarvis. And low and behold got herself pregnant, well then as you know son she married this man Pendarvis. Well, twins were born showing an absolute family likeness to the Trevallian trait, they were an absolute embarrassment to the mother and her husband and of course as you can well understand when my dear friend Ralph was approached by the

Pendarvis's to support the bastards it was decided that the best thing all round was for them to be adopted. All I had to do was arrange for the mother to consent to the adoption and then pay compensation to Peter Pendarvis for the inconvenience of it all. The children will be fine, if you remember correctly the aunt has a baby farm, I handle all her legal adoptions and transfers of unwanted children. Look somewhere here I have all the papers concerning the adoption.' He shuffled documents around until he found the relevant papers.

'Charles Trevallian signed his consent for the children and look, so did the mother, exactly the same signature as she gave before. The Pendarvis's got their money and Maisie Banks will find a good home for the kids, what's the problem? The Trevallians are free of the scandal that could have marred their good name.'

'Oh father what have you done? I told you that there was something suspicious about that couple, she was not the real Sarah Miller. The real Sarah is outside in my office bereft with grief over her lost children. And I think you will find Charles Trevallian is abroad and completely unaware of the fate of his children. Give me the address of the baby farm now. Hopefully I can get there before they are sold. Fancy giving them to that awful women and how could you pay that man to steal them from their rightful mother.'

Marcus snatched the file from his father and gathered his coat. He could not comprehend the chain of illegal events that had been executed by his family firm. First they had given the girls inheritance to a complete stranger and now they had legally kidnapped her children. Well he would do all within his power to right the wrongs that had been committed against this innocent girl.

'Come with me,' he said to Sarah as they left the office. 'I think I know where they are.'

'Oh thank god,' said Sarah. He put his coat around Sarah and raced her to the stables at the rear of the offices. In a very short while the coach was weaving in and out of the busy streets and heading for the countryside. On the journey he related all that his father had told him. He mentioned that Charles had signed the adoption papers and had agreed to pay compensation to Peter and Sarah Pendarvis which his father had carried out. Sarah found it hard to understand that this could be true but at the moment she was mistrusting the Trevallians more and more. Perhaps Charles had purposely left England so his father could clear up the mess he had made whilst he was out of the way.

They stopped frequently to let the horses drink water, around midday the temperature rose and the roads became dusty and dry. The cloudless blue sky provided no shelter from the bright sun. Somehow they took a wrong turning and the signposts stopped making any sense, twice this happened and Sarah could feel herself starting to become quite anxious again. Her mind tried to create the place where the twins were being kept, over and over she rehearsed the words she would say to her old nurse and what she would do to her if the twins had already been adopted and how she would make her divulge their destination. Her mind was becoming quite exhausted she had not rested for well over twenty-four hours and had not eaten for longer than that. Mark pulled the horses up beside a stream and let them take another long drink, the heat of the day had really exhausted them, he felt that they would collapse if he pushed them any harder. Sarah said she would go on by foot but Mark assured her it would still be quicker to let the horses get some rest and to travel in the cool of the evening. Sarah sat down with Mark under a tall green oak tree that provided perfect shade, the small stream passed by them busily on its journey, she pulled off her shoes and plunged her feet into the water, instant coolness, she rinsed her face and hands in the cool liquid. Mark asked her many questions and each answer she gave him reassured him that he was right, she really was Sarah Miller. She told him about her marriage to Peter and how the preacher was most probably not ordained, so it was to be annulled which was why Peter had been able to marry the other girl. She told him of the plans that she and Charles had for the twins and how they had both looked forward to living in the Indies.

A welcome grey cloud covered the slowly setting sun and they decided it was cool enough to continue on their journey.

An uneasy feeling like a faint touch of nettles crept over Sarah's body and a voice inside her head alerted her that the twins were in some sort of danger. It was the same dreadful feeling that she had when her grandmother had died all those years ago. A bright flash filled her head and the sound of hysterical screaming.

'Please can you go any faster, I know Luke and Rosie are in some sort of danger.'

Marcus looked at the expression on her face and didn't doubt her, he urged the horses to go faster. The sound of clanging bells made him suddenly slow down and pull the coach over to the side of the road, a fire wagon charged past them, the team of horses responding wildly to the whipping they were receiving. The crying inside her began and would not stop, she could see the twins in her mind but she could also see glimpses of their silver rattles buried in grey smouldering ashes.

In front of them in the far distance the sky was glowing a warm orange colour and Sarah knew that it was all too late. She didn't know how long it took to get to the burning building, all that she remembered was witnessing something that was part of a nightmare. In a daze Sarah saw the bright golden flames light up the night sky, dark figures shouting loudly pouring water onto the hungry flames hoping to douse them, but all that happened was the water turned to steam and spiralled out of the inferno into the night.

At some point Marcus tried to hold Sarah back from rushing into the blackened building. A woman's body was lying on the grass completely unrecognisable as a human being. People from nearby houses had gathered and were caring for some of the children and babies that had been rescued before the fire took hold. Sarah rushed to look at all the sooty smudged faces hoping that they would be her children.

A doctor knelt beside the body of a woman, her clothes had been burnt and her hair was singed off of her head but Sarah still knew exactly who she was even though she looked a little fatter and a little older. The badly burned nurse sobbed into her burnt raw hands. The doctor poured a liquid into her mouth to deaden the awful pain she was in. Sarah knelt down beside her.

'Nursey look at me, its Sarah, remember me, you looked after me and I married Peter your nephew.'

The nurse opened her eyes and cried even more when she saw Sarah's face.

'Nursey, please where are my babies? I know you have them, are they here?'

'Oh please forgive me I didn't mean to harm them they were beautiful children, they would have been safe with me. It's not all my fault that Trevallian family are to blame, you ask Peter and Molly they will tell you.'

'Where are they?' shouted Sarah. 'Please tell me.'

'They are up in the attic rooms, send someone to get them,' she shouted and then she looked down at her burnt clothes and her blackened peeling legs and let out a dreadful scream. 'I'm going to die, I know I am, please God forgive me,' she wailed. 'They have all gone, what have I done?' Moments later she took her last painful breath and departed from this world.

The doctor said he suspected that she had been drinking very heavily and most probably knocked over an oil lamp which had started the fire. A young girl who worked in the orphanage had managed to rescue quite a lot of the children but it seemed a few had died of smoke inhalation and others had perished and were still in the burning building. Marcus led Sarah to a row of little bodies that were covered in sacking and laid out in a line on the wet grass.

'Luke and Rosie were both wearing gold christening bracelets,' sobbed Sarah hardly able to speak and unable to put one heavy foot in front of the other.

Marcus took a deep breath as he looked beneath each piece of sacking, this was the saddest thing he had ever had to do in his life. His anger for his father and everyone concerned with this awful injustice gave him courage to see this through to the end. He pulled back the cover on the little angel who lay on the grass, she appeared as though she was sound asleep and would wake any minute. The sunlight glinted on the small gold band around her wrist. Sarah stumbled towards the little body of Rosie, she sunk down on the grass beside her and cradled her in her arms, the baby was so cold, Sarah held her so tightly to her chest hoping to force some of her life into the small empty body of her beautiful daughter. There was not a mark on her. Sarah rocked back and forwards her grief was silent, inside she died with her child. A priest wandered amongst the dead and gave his prayers to them to make their last journey easier. Sarah did not hear the words of comfort that were spoken, she became deaf with her own sadness. Her heart exploded and shattered into a thousand more pieces when she realised that Luke had most probably perished inside the building.

Men with carts came to take all the bodies to the local mortuary, Sarah refused to let them touch Rosie and insisted to Mark that she take her own baby home to Hellstone where she would be buried in a very special place.

Sarah had never felt so much utter despair and loneliness, she sat all night with Rosie in her arms watching the cruel building devour itself, hoping and praying that in the morning there would be some miracle and Luke would be alive perhaps rescued the night before.

In the half-light of dawn all that remained of the building was just a heap of smouldering ashes and not a sign of any life amongst the total destruction.

Sarah carried her beautiful daughter Rosie to the coach and cradled her small still body to her.

Marcus sat in silence beside her. He found the journey back to Penzance the most harrowing he had ever made. He could not take his eyes from the blonde little girl that appeared to be sleeping in her mother's arms.

In Penzance he stopped at the funeral directors and made all the arrangements for the journey to Hellstone. He decided to accompany Sarah and Rosie, it would give him the opportunity to confront Ralph Trevallian who as far as he was concerned had caused all this heartache.

The undertaker watched sadly as the mother washed the soot and smoke from her daughter's hair and face. She dressed the small pink body in a tiny white shroud and then gently laid Rosie in a small wooden coffin. Placing a small bunch of hedgerow daisies in her cold hands she kissed her daughter and closed the lid of the casket.

The sunshine streamed through the small chapel's stained glass windows. Sarah stared annoyed at the sun's intrusion into her grief and wondered how it could shine so normally on such a sad day.

She thanked Marcus for all his help and said she was now ready to take Rosie on her final journey.

I think that soon I will awake from the nightmare
But I don't, I am locked in it everyday
And I am awake but in a dream state, how can I forget them
Their clothes are folded in a drawer, flat and empty
Waiting to be full again with their pink plump flesh
To be full of their life, full of their laughter and tears
My arms are empty and ache to be holding them again
I can feel and hear them, my eyes strain to see
They are here, their threads of spun gold entangled

in the brush that caressed their locks
I aimlessly wander from room to room searching
Searching for their love, I want to go back and back
Please God erase the now and let me travel back
To a time before I had all that Love

If you never love you cannot grieve. xxx

Grace Trevallian looked on in amazement as a coach and horses slowly came up the drive. The thing that baffled her was the coach had black plumes on the front of it, she summoned Hodges to fetch her husband and then come back and help her down the stairs to see what it was all about.

Hodges opened the door to greet Mark Pingale, Ralph Trevallian pushed his way forward.

'What do you want?' He asked as he looked past the young solicitor and saw Sarah sitting inside the coach beside a small wooden coffin. 'What's all this young man, where is your father?'

'I am afraid the deal you had with my father has gone horribly wrong and has resulted in the death of your son's children.'

'I paid your father well for confidentiality, you better have a good explanation for this intrusion into my private affairs.'

Grace Trevallian heard everything that was said between the angry men. She rushed past them and pulled open the coach door. Sarah sat motionless and looked at Grace with blank empty eyes. The old lady could not take her eyes from the small coffin.

'Oh Sarah I didn't realise what he was up to, honestly, please believe me.'

Sarah looked at the women as if she was a stranger

and wished she had never set eyes on the Trevallian family.

'I curse all of you who had a hand in Luke and Rosie's death, I wish that all you gave out be returned to you threefold and never will another child under the cursed name of Trevallian live on this earth.' She pointed her index finger at Ralph and sent the curse. 'So be it.'

Ralph Trevallian on hearing the whole sad story sank down heavily in a chair.

'Oh my god,' he uttered and put his head in his hands. 'I never intended any harm to come to the children. I just wanted them out of the way. I've paid everyone well. How could my son continue with his life with two illegitimate children and a woman that wasn't right in the head and practised witchcraft? I had so many plans for his future. You're a well-bred man Mark, you know what these girls can be like. The rich are like you and me the poor are just workers like bee's there to serve us. You're father understood the reasons why, he said I was right, agreed with me, helped me.'

'I am afraid my father is an old man and I can assure you he will never practise the law again, He is retiring. And as for you I cannot agree with any of your reasons. I am afraid the authorities have already been informed about the kidnap of the children and I have offered to give them all the assistance I can to bring you to justice. And please just answer me one question, your son was he aware of what you were doing?'

'Of course he was, do you think I would have gone to all this trouble without his consent, he had to get away. Away from her, she's mad, I'm not lying she's a witch possessed by evil.'

CHAPTER TWENTYNINE

The willow tree a symbol of grief and lost love.

Tobias stood closely behind Sarah, his love enveloping her in a cloak of comfort and compassion. With her own hands, Sarah had cleared the fine grass from the fairy ring, the ring of fresh grass that the children loved to play barefoot in, then she dug at the soft earth until her nails were broken and her fingers raw. The only person that she had allowed to help her was Janet, the girl had loved the twins as much as she had. Finally Rosie's resting place was ready to receive her.

For the last five days and nights Sarah had sat with the small lifeless body of her beautiful daughter, silently comforting and communicating with the new spirit that played around the coffin which contained the earthly vehicle for her soul. The small child had discarded it as soon as she breathed her last breath on this earth. Now she had no use for the inanimate shell. The child continued to play in an old familiar pattern unaware that she was now safe in the Summerland of Heaven.

The small coffin was lowered into the newly dug grave beneath the small willow tree, Grace stood behind Sarah and sobbed uncontrollably as young Matthew said a few words to commit Rosie's body to the earth. Gwen, Janet and Daniel stood well back offering their presence as a comfort to Sarah, after all they had brought her up as their own. Gwen thought she would never ever forgive her son for what he had done. Sarah had made a small wreath of roses from her garden, she laid them on the grave. Pulling a blood red stem from the wreath she pushed it into the earth. She knew it would flourish and grow for years but it would only ever bloom once again and that would be a sign that it was time for Sarah to leave this earth and join her family that had all gone before.

Sarah stared at her sore cupped hands they held fresh soil.

'Ashes to ashes, dust to dust,' droned Matthew.

She heard none of the ritual that the boy was reciting. Her eyes were watching the small girl in the rosebud and lace dress walk away from them. Rosie was holding the hand of Sarah's grandmother and giggling and laughing at something the elderly lady was saying to her. Just before they disappeared into the woodland the ghostly couple turned and waved at Sarah. Sarah's hand lifted and waived a final farewell to them.

Sarah and Tobias walked away from the grave together.

'I've really had enough of people Tobias, I don't know who to trust anymore. All I ever wanted to do was to give my love to help everyone and now look what has happened. I have been so stupid.'

From that sad day when Sarah walked away from the grave she changed drastically, her life turned inwards, she became a recluse mistrusting everyone and refusing to talk to people. The only interest she ever showed in making friends was with the wildlife that roamed the woodland. She gathered a steady stream of misfit creatures that she healed and encouraged to share her life. Mark Pingale arranged for the Trevallian family to make provisions for Sarah to remain in Jackdaw Cottage for the rest of her life with a small income to provide for her daily needs. Charles returned to England and mourned the death of his children, Sarah refused to see him and over the years burnt all his letters, unread. He could very well understand why she changed like she did and did not blame her. After he had visited the grave of his daughter his heart was also broken. He had now lost everything that he had ever loved. He returned to the Indies with the only reminders he could find and that was Luke and Rosie's christening photograph and a lock of Sarah's raven black hair.

FINAL CHAPTER

Young Jack George was quite surprised to see Sarah's dog Moses sitting on his doorstep so early in the morning.

'Hello Moses, whatever are you doing here?' He reached down and tussled the fur on the dog's head.

Moses was agitated and could not keep still, he walked to the gate and then stopped and looked back at Jack, he waited just for a moment and then came back to stand in front of the young man. Jack knelt beside the dog, he noticed that his tail hung low between his legs.

'What's the matter boy are you trying to tell me something?'

Moses walked a few steps forward and then stopped again for Jack to catch up with him.

'Do you want me to follow you? Hang on a minute I'll just get my boots and coat on.'

Jack pulled up the collar of his heavy overcoat to shut out the cold frosty air that whipped around his neck. The man and dog walked silently together along the lane that led to Hellstone. Moses left the road and climbed under a stile and again patiently waited for Jack to follow him across the fields.

'I didn't know this was a short cut. Moses. I bet you and your mistress know all the quick paths away from the roads.' They crossed the vast field trying to keep to the edge. Jack found it difficult to walk on the frozen furrows and kept slipping and sliding. He climbed over another stile that was tucked in the corner of the field, this brought them out into the lane that led to Jackdaw Cottage.

It was still only just dawn and quite early in the morning, the lazy sun had only managed to faintly tinge the edges of the heavy grey clouds that shrouded the woodland. A heavy frost during the night had coated the trees and undergrowth with an icing of sparkling white crystals. When the frost thawed the beauty would be lost and the foliage that remained would be black and limp. Jack had intended to visit Jackdaw Cottage today, but much later in the morning, he now had all the materials to make a start on repairing Sarah's thatching before winter. Moses walked at a constant pace ahead of Jack every so often he would glance around to make sure he was there. Jack knew that something must be wrong with Sarah and that she must have sent Moses to fetch him.

As they approached the cottage Jack was surprised that not a sign of wildlife could be heard or seen in the woods. No twigs or bracken crackled with foraging wildlife. The whole of the woodland was shrouded in an eerie silence. A shiver ran down his back, this stillness made him extremely nervous, he hastened his steps towards the cottage. Jack was surprised when Moses slowly plodded past the cottage gate not even glancing at his home, with his head still low and his eyes set firmly on the path the dog tried to lead Jack into the dense undergrowth. Jack stopped at the gate.

'Just wait a minute Moses, I thought I was coming to see Sarah. Just stop for a minute and let me look inside the place.' Jack started to walk up the garden path but tripped on something, gaining his balance he looked down to see the path was completely covered in trailing ivy and brambles, he could not make out the stone cobbles beneath the overgrowth of plants.

'That's strange,' he thought. 'I was only here yesterday and the path was quite clear of any plants.' Then the roof of the cottage caught his eye apart from the lack of smoke spiralling from the chimney, the roof which up until today only had a large untidy hole in it was now entirely dilapidated, exposing broken and rotted wooden rafters. Looking around he could see that the cottage was absolutely derelict. The windows that were shiny and clean yesterday were today vacant of any glass, the frames splintered and decayed. The outside walls had been covered with barbed briars and green mould. Where the old oak front door should be there was nothing but an empty gaping cavity looking black and foreboding.

Jack was absolutely mystified by the whole appearance of the place. He called out for Sarah but of course there was no reply. With the brambles dragging at his trouser legs he fought his way towards the front porch, the doves that lived there had deserted the place along with every other form of wildlife. Great black cobwebs hung down from the porch and wound around his face and caught in his hair. He shuddered as he tried to pull the sticky threads from his skin. Cautiously he stepped inside the cottage. Overnight the place had decayed as if it had been uninhabited for many years. Walking through the dead leaves and dust on the floor he expected to find Sarah in her rocking chair, but the cottage was completely empty. The bunches of dried flowers and herbs that hung from the ceiling were brown and dusty and as he touched the crisp petals and leaves they crumbled noisily in his hands. Jack looked at the small window fully expecting to see the crystal ball and wind chimes, nothing, all that remained were the fragments of a blue piece of fabric that once resembled curtains. He turned around to look about the room, there in the middle of the sitting room floor was Sarah's rusty old chest just where Jack had placed it for her. Nervously he lifted open the metal lid, on the very top of the contents sat a large brown envelope that bore his name. He ripped it open and carefully read the contents. In beautiful flowing writing he read "Sarah's last will and testament."

She gave him instructions for her disposal and thanked him for being her friend and for looking after Moses. She explained in the letter that the contents of the chest were all his now. She also mentioned that on the rocking chair he would find her journal and if he read the last chapter all would be revealed to her whereabouts. He turned to look at the old brown chair fully expecting to see Sarah rocking to and fro in it, sadly she was not there. But the chair unoccupied rocked silently back and forwards. He picked up the dog-eared note book that sat on the seat in place of Sarah.

Opening it he read the first line, *This Journal is to be called*

"THE SPIRIT OF THE WILLOW"

Sitting down in the rocking chair he turned to the last chapter and started to read.

Sometime later he heavily walked out of the cottage and joined Moses who was standing patiently waiting for him. They walked side by side towards the woodland that skirted the grounds of High Markham. Jack was extremely apprehensive as to what he was going to find when they reached the old wooden pagoda. As they neared the area where the fairy ring was situated a very strange thing happened. The sun burst a brilliant blinding beam through the grey clouds, warming him instantly, it was not the weak autumn sun but a penetrating summer sun. The grey clouds rolled back to reveal a powder blue sky. The temperature soared and Jack wiped the sweat from his forehead, he stripped off his heavy coat and scarf. Before his eyes the sun's warmth turned the barren woodland into life. The icy coating on the trees and undergrowth melted away leaving fresh green leaves and buds on the trees and plants. Herbs and wild flowers bloomed sending their fragrance up into his nostrils awakening his senses. Wildlife stirred and emerged from their abode. The sound of bird song heralding the sunshine echoed around the trees. A slight warm breeze brushed past his face and he walked on as if in a dream, his eyes could not take in the instant transformation of the stark frosty scene in the woods.

Even though he knew he had a grim task ahead of him he felt happy and at peace with the world. This is how it must of been when the world first began, he thought. The fire of the sun gave life to the earth and then the rivers and the seas filled with life-giving water and the air filled the lungs of every living creature chosen to live on this earth. Yes it must of been a beautiful day just like today when the world was created.

Seeing everything through new eyes he wandered past the fairy ring. The small willow tree rustled as a warm breeze stirred its green crinoline exposing the single black rose blooming on the small grave beneath it, the whole scene was breathtaking. Straining his ears he thought that on the breeze he could faintly hear the sound of music playing, it came from somewhere in the distance, mesmerised by the heavenly sound of an orchestra playing and angels singing he was drawn towards the pagoda.

He stood outside the pentagonal shaped building that he clearly remembered as being a ramshackled sunroom full of garden tools and broken furniture. At this moment he could see it was far from an unused sunroom now. The domed glass roof swept down on all five sides and curled up at the edges, each section was topped with a gold sphere that he had never noticed before. The marbled outside walls had intricately patterned oriental panels. Each side of the heavy wooden doors stood huge black marble pillars that were embossed with gold vine leaves. The divine music from a heavenly orchestra caressed his sense of hearing, the melody of a waltz rang through the woodland. Still intoxicated by the hypnotic tune, he stumbled up the steps towards the doors and gripped the large brass handles. Without hesitation he pushed the heavy doors open. Nothing could have prepared him for the sight that met his eyes.

The brightness of the room almost blinded him. Gold candle sconces hanging on the pure white walls radiated a mysterious light that reflected in the gilt framed mirrors that adorned the startlingly white walls of the pagoda. A lick of air swirled around the room and moved the crystal chimes that hung from the ceiling, still the music played urging Jack further into the pagoda. His heavy working boots made no sound on the white marble floor as he cautiously walked into the room, his eyes took in the interior. To the far side a gold brocade chaise longue sat against the wall, beside it stood a small gilt table which bore two tall glasses of amber liquid that glittered in the candlelight. As his eyes became accustom to the bright light he saw that he was not alone in the room. His breath caught in his throat and his knees became weak as he witnessed a sight that would remain with him for the rest of his life. He stepped back against the wall for fear of being seen by the radiant couple that glided around the room. Their feet hardly touched the floor as they danced a majestic waltz. Their arms held each other passionately, the young women threw back her head and laughed, the happiness in her voice echoed around the walls vibrating the very essence of the universe. Her raven black hair tumbled in curls around her face as she looked up into the laughing face of her partner. Her happy azure blue eyes matched the sapphires and diamonds that cascaded from her ears and formed a waterfall from her long slender neck. Her blue velvet dress rustled as she was swept around the room by her handsome ghostly partner. She radiated a love and warmth that Jack had never witnessed before. Sarah's tall handsome partner looked down into her eyes and they were both lost in the oblivion of intense love. Charles Trevallian held Sarah in his arms, never again would he have to let her go away from him. He stood tall above Sarah and as he looked down into her eyes his mop of blonde hair masked the tears of love that flowed from his very soul.

Charles Trevallian and Sarah had spent a lifetime of adventures apart but now in death they were united, free at last to be together, to love and travel the realms of Summerland. All the pain and hurt in their lives was erased. Now they would only remember the joy. They had a love so strong that incarcerated them spiritually as soul mates from the moment they had first set eyes on each other and no matter what had occurred between them over the years that golden thread of love could never be broken.

The music faded away into the far distance and Jack rubbed his eyes trying to wake up from the dream that he thought he was experiencing. The light slowly ebbed out of the room as the candles flickered and died. In the darkness the ghostly lovers still held hands and as Jack watched them their bodies started to diminish, and when he could only just make out the faint shadows of the lovers they dissolved into the dim light and vanished for eternity.

An icy gale stormed at the doors sending them crashing open and filling the pagoda with dust and autumn debris. Jack shivered as the temperature returned to normal. His eyes swept around the cold interior of the room. Sitting in the corner of the room was the remains of the chaise longue, the fabric was threadbare and did not resemble the gold brocade of a fleeting moment ago, tufts of horse hair spilled out through the thin material.

He gasped as he recognised one of the elderly figures sitting on the seat. The couple appeared as though they were only asleep, their faces portrayed an expression of complete contentment. Their arms were locked about each other in a last embrace. The lines of years of sunshine and shadows had completely vanished from Sarah's and Charles's faces and replaced by the smiling mask of death. Her grey hair was pinned up high upon her head and secured with rusty grips, it tumbled down over her face. The azure blue dress that she had treasured all these years hung loosely from her small thin frame, it now had become her shroud.

Sarah's precious diamonds and sapphires glinted in the faint autumn light completely unaffected by age, they were of no value to her now, as Tobias had always told Sarah, we are all equally poor in death, there are no pockets in a shroud.

Outside the pagoda the sun had disappeared behind the grey swirling snow clouds. White frozen flakes fell on Jack and Moses as they both trudged silently towards the town to report Jacks findings.

Two smiling figures stood hand in hand as they watched the boy and the dog leave the pagoda.

Extracts from the Western Herald.

It is with great sadness that the family solicitor of High Markham has to announce the death by natural causes of Charles Trevallian on the 31st October. Mr Trevallian had only recently returned to High Markham after years living in the West Indies. He was unmarried and leaves no living relatives. The funeral will be held on 3rd November in the chapel on the estate and his remains will be interred in the family grave.

There was no mention of the circumstances in which he was found.

The following was the only connection that was made to Charles and Sarah.

Death of local character.

Sarah Rose Miller of Jackdaw Cottage was found dead on the 31st October by a workman. The body was discovered in a dilapidated building on the estate of High Markham. She was a well-known character nick-named by local people as Mad Miller on account of her eccentric and sometimes bizarre behaviour. Not a lot of people actually knew the strange lady but the workman who discovered the body said that he had in his possession evidence that would explain her odd way of life. Through documents held by the late Mr Charles Trevallians family solicitor, instructions for her funeral have been arranged for the 3rd November in the chapel on the estate at High Markham followed by interment of her remains into the Trevallian family vault. It is presumed that she had no living relatives.

The two young people laughed as they stood beside the preacher and witnessed the vehicles for their souls returned to the earth. They were bound in a love that could never die.

The end, or is it just the beginning...
xxxx

Made in the USA
Charleston, SC
27 June 2013